Lydia Maria Francis Child

Looking toward Sunset

From Sources Old and New, Original and Selected

Lydia Maria Francis Child

Looking toward Sunset
From Sources Old and New, Original and Selected

ISBN/EAN: 9783744746328

Printed in Europe, USA, Canada, Australia, Japan

Cover: Foto ©Andreas Hilbeck / pixelio.de

More available books at **www.hansebooks.com**

LOOKING TOWARD SUNSET.

From Sources Old and New, Original and Selected.

By L. MARIA CHILD.

"When the Sun is setting, cool fall its gleams upon the earth, and the shadows lengthen; but they all point toward the Morning."
JEAN PAUL RICHTER.

"I am fully convinced that the Soul is indestructible, and that its activity will continue through eternity. It is like the Sun, which, to our eyes, seems to set in night; but it has in reality only gone to diffuse its light elsewhere." — GOETHE.

BOSTON:
TICKNOR AND FIELDS.
1865.

TO

MY DEAR AND HONORED FRIENDS,

Miss LUCY OSGOOD

AND

Miss HENRIETTA SARGENT,

This Volume

IS AFFECTIONATELY INSCRIBED,

IN TOKEN OF GRATITUDE FOR THEIR EXAMPLE,

WHICH CONFERS BEAUTY AND DIGNITY ON DECLINING YEARS,

BY ACTIVE USEFULNESS AND KINDLY SYMPATHY

WITH THE HUMAN RACE.

PREFACE.

 OCCASIONALLY meet people who
say to me, " I had many a pleasant
hour, in my childhood, reading your
Juvenile Miscellany; and now I am enjoying
it over again, with my own little folks."

Such remarks remind me that I have been a
long time in the world; but if a few acknowledge me as the household friend of two generations, it is a pleasant assurance that I have not
lived altogether in vain.

When I was myself near the fairy-land of
childhood, I used my pen for the pleasure of
children; and now that I am travelling down
the hill I was then ascending, I would fain give
some words of consolation and cheer to my
companions on the way. If the rays of my
morning have helped to germinate seeds that
ripened into flowers and fruit, I am grateful to

Him, from whom all light and warmth proceeds. And now I reverently ask His blessing on this attempt to imitate, in my humble way, the setting rays of that great luminary, which throws cheerful gleams into so many lonely old homes, which kindles golden fires on trees whose foliage is falling, and lights up the silvered heads on which it rests with a glory that reminds one of immortal crowns.

L. MARIA CHILD.

CONTENTS.

LOOKING TOWARD SUNSET.

FROM

SOURCES OLD, NEW, ORIGINAL,
AND SELECTED.

THE FRIENDS.

By L. M. CHILD.

" By some especial care
Her temper had been framed, as if to make
A being, who, by adding love to peace,
Might live on earth a life of happiness."

Wordsworth.

N the interior of Maine two girls grew
to womanhood in houses so near that
they could nod and smile to each other
while they were making the beds in
the morning, and chat through the open fence
that separated their gardens when they went to
pick currants for the tea-table. Both were daughters of farmers; but Harriet Brown's father had

money in the bank, while Jane White's father
was struggling hard to pay off a mortgage. Jane
was not a beauty, but her fresh, healthy countenance was pleasant to look upon. Her large blue
eyes had a very innocent expression, and there was
always in them the suggestion of a smile, as if they
sung the first note of a merry song for the lips to
follow. Harriet was the belle of the county; with
rosy cheeks, a well-shaped mouth, and black eyes,
that were very bright, without being luminous from
within. A close observer of physiognomy could
easily determine which of the girls had most of
heart and soul. But they were both favorites in
the village, and the young men thought it was
a pretty sight to see them together. In fact, they
were rarely seen apart. Their leisure moments,
on bright winter days, were spent in snow-balling
each other across the garden-fence; and they kept
up the sport hilariously long after their hands were
numb and red with cold. In the long evenings,
they made wagers which would soonest finish a
pair of socks; and merry were the little crowings
over the vanquished party. In spring, they hunted anemones and violets together. In autumn,
they filled their aprons with brilliant-colored leaves
to decorate the mantel-piece; stopping ever and
anon to twine the prettiest specimens in each
other's hair. They both sat in the singing-seats
at meeting. Harriet's shrill voice was always
heard above Jane's, but it was defective in mod-

ulation, while music flowed through the warb-
ling voice of her companion. They often bought
dresses alike, with the agreement that, when the
sleeves were worn, the two skirts should be used
to make a new dress for the one who first needed
it; and shrewd observers remarked that Harriet
usually had the benefit of such bargains. Jane
waited assiduously upon her mother, while Harriet's mother waited upon her. One seemed to
have come into the world to be ministered unto,
and the other to minister. Harriet was prim in
company, and some called her rather proud; but
Jane was deemed imprudent, because whatever
she said or did bubbled out of her heart. Their
friendship was not founded on any harmonious
accord of character; few friendships are. They
were born next door to each other, and no other
girls of their own age happened to be near neighbors. The youthful heart runs over so perpetu-
ally, that it needs another into which to pour its
ever-flowing stream. Impelled by this necessity,
they often shared each other's sleeping apartments,
and talked late into the night. They could not have
told, the next day, what they had talked about.
Their conversation was a continuous movement
of hilarious nothings, with a running accompani-
ment of laughter. It was like the froth of whip-
syllabub, of which the rustic took a spoonful into
his mouth, and finding it gone without leaving
a taste behind, he searched the carpet for it. The

girls, however, never looked after the silly bubbles
.of their bubbling syllables.   Harriet thought Jane
excessively funny, and such an appreciative audience was stimulus sufficient to keep her friend's
tongue in motion.

" O Hatty, the moon 's up, and it 's as light as
a cork ! " exclaimed Jane, springing out of bed in
the summer's night, and looking out of the window.

" What a droll creature you are ! " replied Hatty ; and they laughed more heartily than they
would have done over one of Dr. Holmes's wit-
tiest sayings.

When merriment subsided into a more serious
mood, each gave her opinion whether Harry Blake,
the young lawyer, or Frank May, the young store-
keeper, had the handsomest eyes.   Jane said,
there was a report that the young lawyer was
engaged to somebody before he came to their village ; but Harriet said she did n't believe it; because he pressed her hand when they came home
from the County Ball, and he whispered something, too; but she did n't know whether it would
be fair to tell of it.   Then came the entreaty, " Do
tell "; and she told.   And with various similar
confidings, they at last fell asleep.

Thus life flowed on, like a sunny, babbling brook,
with these girls of sixteen summers.   Fond as they
were of recreation, they were capable, in the New
England sense of the term, and accomplished a

great deal of work. It was generally agreed that Harriet made the best butter and Jane the best bread that the village produced. Thrifty fathers said to their sons, that whoever obtained one of those girls for a wife would be a lucky fellow. Harriet refused several offers, and the rejected beaux revenged themselves by saying, she was fishing for the lawyer, in hopes of being the wife of a judge, or a member of Congress. There was less gossip about Jane's love affairs. Nobody was surprised when the banns were published between her and Frank May. She had always maintained that his eyes were handsomer than the lawyer's. It was easy enough for anybody to read her heart. Soon after Jane's marriage with the young store-keeper Harriet went to visit an uncle in New York. There she attracted the attention of a prosperous merchant, nearly as old as her father, and came home to busy herself with preparations for a wedding. Jane expressed surprise, in view of certain confidences with regard to the young lawyer; but Harriet replied: "Mr. Gray is a very good sort of man, and really seems to be very much in love with me. And you know, Jenny, it must be a long time before Harry Blake can earn enough to support a wife handsomely."

A few weeks afterward, they had their parting interview. They kissed and shed tears, and exchanged lockets with braids of hair. Jane's voice was choked, as she said: "O Hatty, it seems so

hard that we should be separated! I thought to
be sure we should always be neighbors."

And Harriet wiped her eyes, and tried to answer cheerfully: "You must come and see me,
dear Jenny. It is n't such a great way to New
York, after all."

The next day Jane attended the wedding in her
own simple bridal dress of white muslin; and the
last she saw of Harriet was the waving of her
white handkerchief from a genteel carriage, drawn
by two shining black horses. It was the first link
that had been broken in the chain of her quiet
life; and the separation of these first links startles
the youthful mind with a sort of painful surprise,
such as an infant feels waking from sleep to be
frightened by a strange face bending over its cradle. She said to her husband: "I did n't feel at
all as I always imagined I should feel at Hatty's
wedding. It was so unexpected to have her go
off with that stranger! But I suppose she is the
best judge of what is for her own happiness."

The void left by this separation was soon filled
by new pleasures and duties. A little boy and
girl came. Then her husband was seized with
a disease of the spine, which totally unfitted him
for business. Jane had acquired considerable skill
in mantua-making, which now proved a valuable
assistance in the support of her family. The neighboring farmers said, " Young Mrs. May has a hard
row to hoe." But her life was a mingled cup,

which she had no wish to exchange for any other. Care and fatigue were sweetened by the tenderness and patience of her household mate, and brightened by the gambols of children, who clung to her with confiding love. When people expressed sympathy with her hard lot, she answered, cheerfully : " I am happier than I was when I was a girl. It is a happiness that I feel deeper down in my heart." This feeling was expressed in her face also. The innocent blue eyes became motherly and thoughtful in their tenderness, but still a smile lay sleeping there. Her husband said she was handsomer than when he first loved her ; and so all thought who appreciated beauty of expression above fairness of skin.

During the first year of her residence in New York, Harriet wrote every few weeks ; but the intervals between her letters lengthened, and the apology was the necessity of giving dinner-parties, making calls, and attending to mantua-makers. To Jane, who was constantly working to nurse and support her dear ones, they seemed like letters in a foreign language, of which we can study out the meaning, but in which it is impossible for us to think. She felt herself more really separated from the friend of her girlhood than she could have been by visible mountains. They were not only living in different worlds, but the ways of each world did not interest the other. The correspondence finally ceased altogether, and years passed without any communication.

The circle of Jane's duties enlarged. Her husband's parents became feeble in health; they needed the presence of children, and could also assist their invalid son by receiving him into their house. So Frank May and his wife removed to their home, in a country village of Massachusetts. Her parents, unwilling to relinquish the light of her presence, removed with them. There was, of course, great increase of care, to which was added the necessity for vigilant economy; but the energy of the young matron grew with the demands upon it. Her husband's mother was a little unreasonable at times, but it was obvious that she considered her son very fortunate in his wife; and Jane thankfully accepted her somewhat reluctant affection. If a neighbor alluded to her numerous cares, she replied cheerfully: "Yes, it is true that I have a good deal on my shoulders; but somehow it never seems very heavy. The fact is," she added, smiling, "there's great satisfaction in feeling one's self of so much importance. There are my husband, my two children, my two fathers, and my two mothers, all telling me that they could n't get along without me; and I think that's blessing enough for one poor woman. Nobody can tell, until they try it, what a satisfaction there is in making old folks comfortable. They cling so to those that take good care of them, that, I declare, I find it does me about as much good as it did to tend upon my babies." Blessed woman!

she carried sunshine within her, and so external circumstances could not darken her life.

The external pressure increased as years passed on. Her husband, her parents, her son, departed from her, one after another. Still she smiled through her tears, and said: "God has been very merciful to me. It was *such* a comfort to be able to tend upon them to the last, and to have them die blessing me!" The daughter married and removed to Illinois. The heart of the bereaved mother yearned to follow her; but her husband's parents were very infirm, and she had become necessary to their comfort. When she gave the farewell kiss to her child, she said: "There is no one to take good care of the old folks if I leave them. I will stay and close their eyes, and then, if it be God's will, I will come to you."

Two years afterward, the old father died, but his wife survived him several years. When the estates of both fathers were settled, there remained for the two widowed women a small house, an acre of land, and a thousand dollars in the bank. There they lived alone. The rooms that had been so full of voices were silent now. Only, as Jane moved about, "on household cares intent," she was often heard singing the tune her dear Frank used to sing under the apple-tree by her window, in their old courting days: —

> "The moon was shining silver bright,
> No cloud the eye could view;

Her lover's step, in silent night,·
Well pleased, the damsel knew."

Sometimes the blue eyes moistened as she sang;
but, ere the tears fell, tender memories would
modulate themselves into the tune of "Auld lang
syne." And sometimes the old mother, who sat
knitting in the sunshine, would say: "Sing that
again, Jenny. How my old man used to love to
hear you sing it! Don't you remember he used
to say you sung like a thrush?" Jenny would
smile, and say, "Yes, mother," and sing it over
again. Then, tenderly adapting herself to the old
woman's memories, she would strike into "John
Anderson, my Jo," to which her aged companion
would listen with an expression of serene satisfaction. It was indeed a pleasure to listen; for
Jenny's sweet voice remained unbroken by years;
its tones were as silvery as her hair. Time, the
old crow, had traversed her face and left his foot-
prints there; and the ploughshare of successive
sorrows had cut deep lines into the once smooth
surface; but the beauty of the soul illumined her
faded countenance, as moonlight softens and glori-
fies ruins. When she carefully arranged the pil-
lows of the easy-chair, the aged mother, ere she
settled down for her afternoon's nap, would often
look up gratefully, and say, "Your eyes are just
as good as a baby's." It was a pleasant sound to
the dutiful daughter's ears, and made her forget
the querulous complaints in which her infirm companion sometimes indulged.

The time came when this duty was finished also; and Mrs. Frank May found herself all alone in the house, whither she had carried her sunshine thirty years before. She wrote to her daughter that, as soon as she could sell or let her little homestead, she would start for Illinois. She busied herself to hasten the necessary arrangements; for her lonely heart was longing for her only child, whose face she had not seen for seven years. One afternoon, as she sat by the window adding up accounts, her plans for the journey to meet her daughter gradually melted into loving reminiscences of her childhood, till she seemed to see again the little smiling face that had looked to her the most beautiful in all the world, and to hear again the little pattering feet that once made sweetest music in her ears. As she sat thus in reverie at the open window, the setting sun brightened the broad meadows, crowned the distant hill-tops with glory, and threw a ribbon of gold across the wall of her humble little room. The breath of lilacs floated in, and with it came memories of how her little children used to come in with their arms full of spring-blossoms, filling every mug and pitcher they could find. The current of her thoughts was interrupted by the sound of a wagon. It stopped before her house. A stranger with two little children! Who could it be? She opened the door. The stranger, taking off his hat and bowing respectfully, said, "Are you Mrs. Frank May?"

" Yes, sir," she replied.

" Well, then," rejoined he, " if you please, I 'll walk in, for I 've got some news to tell you. But first I 'll bring in the children, for the little things have been riding all day, and are pretty tired."

" Certainly, sir, bring them in and let them rest, and I will give them a cup of milk," replied the kindly matron.

A little boy and girl were lifted from the wagon and led in. Mrs. May made an exclamation of joyful surprise. The very vision she had had in her mind a few minutes previous stood before her bodily! She took the little girl in her arms and covered her face with kisses. " Why, bless your little soul!" she exclaimed; " how much you look like my daughter Jenny!"

" My name *ith* Jenny," lisped the little one.

" Why, you see, ma'am —" stammered the stranger; he paused, in an embarrassed way, and smoothed the nap of his hat with his sleeve. " You see, ma'am—" he resumed; then, breaking down again, he suddenly seized the boy by the hand, led him up to her, and said, " There, Robin! that 's your good old granny, you 've heard so much about."

With a look of astonishment, Mrs. May said to him : " And where is my daughter, sir? Surely these little children would n't come so far without their mother."

The man again began to say, " You see,

ma'am —" but his heart came up and choked his voice with a great sob. The old mother understood its meaning. She encircled the two children with her arms, and drew them closely to her side. After a brief silence, she asked, in a subdued voice, "When did she die?"

Her calmness reassured the stranger, and with a steady voice he replied: "You see, ma'am, your daughter and her husband have been neighbors of mine ever since they went to Illinois. There's been an epidemic fever raging among us, and they both died of it. The last words your daughter said were, 'Carry the children to my good mother.' I've been wanting to come and see my old father, who lives about three miles from here, so I brought them along with me. It's sorrowful news for you, ma'am, and I meant to have sort of prepared you for it; but somehow I lost my presence of mind, and forgot what I was going to say. But I'm glad to see you so sustained under it, ma'am."

"I thank God that *these* are left," she replied; and she kissed the little faces that were upturned to hers with an expression that seemed to say they thought they should like their grandmother.

"I'm so glad you're helped to take it so," rejoined the stranger. "Your daughter always told me you was a woman that went straight ahead and did your duty, trusting the Lord to bring you through."

. " I am forgetting my duty now," she replied.
" You must be hungry and tired. If you 'll drive
to Neighbor Harrington's barn, he will take good
care of your horse, and I will prepare your supper."

" Thank you kindly, ma'am ; but I must jog on
to my old father's, to take supper with him."

Some boxes containing the clothing of the children and their mother were brought in ; and, having deposited them, the stranger departed amid
thanks and benedictions.

Mrs. Harrington had seen the wagon stop at
Mrs. May's door, and go off without the children.
Being of an inquiring mind, she straightway put
on her cape-bonnet, and went to see about it. She
found her worthy neighbor pinning towels round
the children's necks, preparatory to their supper
of brown bread and molasses, which they were in
a great hurry to eat.

" Why who on earth have you got here ! " exclaimed Neighbor Harrington.

" They are my daughter's children," replied
Mrs. May. " Bless their little souls ! if I 'd have
known they were coming, I 'd have had some
turnovers ready for them."

" I guess you 'll find they 'll *make* turnovers
enough," replied Mrs. Harrington smiling. " That
boy looks to me like a born rogue. But where 's
your daughter ? I did n't see any woman in the
wagon."

" The Lord has taken her to himself," replied Mrs May, in quivering tones.

" You *don't* say so ! " exclaimed Neighbor Harrington, raising both hands. " Bless me ! if I 'd known that, I would n't have come right in upon you so sudden."

They sat down and began to talk over the particulars which the stranger had related. Meanwhile, the children, in hungry haste, were daubing their chins and fingers with molasses. The little four-year-old Jenny was the first to pause. Drawing a long breath, expressive of great satisfaction, she lisped out, " O Bubby ! *larthiz* top on bread ! what *can* be dooder ? "

Robin, who was two years her senior, and felt as if he were as much as ten, gave a great shout of laughter, and called out, " O Granny ! you don't know how funny Sissy talks."

Grandmother went with a wet towel to wipe their hands and faces, and when she heard what the little Tot had said, she could not help smiling, notwithstanding the heaviness of her heart. As for Neighbor Harrington, she laughed outright.

" You see they are just as well satisfied as they would have been with a dozen turnovers," said she. " But this is a sad blow for you, Neighbor May; coming, too, just at the time when you were taking so much comfort in the thoughts of going to see your daughter; and it will be a pretty heavy load for a woman of your years to bring up these orphans."

"O, it's wonderful how the dispensations of Providence are softened for us poor weak mortals," replied Mrs. May. "Only think what a mercy it is that I have these treasures left? Why, she looks so much like her dear mother, that I seem to have my own little Jenny right over again ; and I can't seem to realize that it is n't so. You see, Neighbor Harrington, *that* softens the blow wonderfully. As for bringing up the children, I have faith that the Lord will strengthen those who trust in him."

"That 's just like you," rejoined Neighbor Harrington. "You always talk in that way. You always seem to think that what happens is the best that *could* happen. You 're pretty much like this little one here. If you don't get tarts and turnovers, you smack your lips and say, 'Lasses top on bread ! what *can* be gooder ? '"

The neighbors bade each other a smiling goodnight. When Mrs. Harrington returned home, she told her husband the mournful news, and added, "Mrs. May don't seem to feel it so much as. I should think she would." Yet the good grandmother dropped many tears on the pillow where those little orphans slept ; and kneeling by their bedside, she prayed long and fervently for support and guidance in rearing the precious souls thus committed to her charge.

She had long been unused to children ; and they did, as Neighbor Harrington had predicted, make

plenty of turnovers in the house. Robin had
remarkable gifts in that line. Endless were his
variations of mischief. Sometimes the stillness of
the premises was suddenly disturbed by a tremen-
dous fluttering and cackling, caused by his efforts
to catch the cockerel. The next thing, there was
the cat squalling and hissing, because he was
pulling her backward by the tail. Then he was
seized with a desire to explore the pig's sleeping
apartment, and by that process let him out into
the garden, and had the capital fun of chasing him
over flowers and vegetables. Once when the pig
upset little Sissy in his rounds, he had to lie down
and roll in the mud himself, with loud explosions
of laughter. Quiet little Jenny liked to make
gardens by sticking flowers in the sand, but it
particularly pleased him to send them all flying
into the air, at the point of his boot. When the
leaves were gay with autumn tints, she would
bring her apron full and sit at grandmother's feet
weaving garlands for the mantel-piece ; and it was
Master Robin's delight to pull them to pieces,
and toss them hither and yon. It was wonderful
how patiently the good grandmother put up with
his roguish pranks. " O Robin, dear, don't behave so," she would say. " Be a good boy.
Come ! I want to see how fast you grow. Take
off your boots, and Jenny will take off hers, and
stand even, and then we 'll see which is the
tallest."

"O, I'm *ever* so much taller. I'm almost a man," responded Robin, kicking off his boots.

Honest little Jenny stood squarely and demurely while grandmother compared their heights. But roguish Robin raised himself as much as possible. To hide his mirth, he darted out of doors as soon as it was over, calling Jenny after him. Then he gave her a poke, that toppled her half over, and said, with a chuckle, "Sissy, I cheated grand-mother. I stood tiptoe. But don't you *tell!*"

But wild as Robin was, he dearly loved his grandmother, and she loved him better than any-thing else, excepting little Jenny. When Neigh-bor Harrington said, "I should think that boy would wear your life out," she answered, with a smile: "I don't know what I should do with-out the dear little creatures. I always liked to be called by my Christian name, because it sounds more hearty. There's nobody to call me Jenny now. The little ones call me granny, and the neighbors call me old Mrs. Frank May. But I have a *little* Jenny, and every time I hear her name called, it makes me feel as if I was young again. But what I like best is to hear her tuning up her little songs. The little darling sings like a robin."

"Then she sings like *me*," exclaimed her ubiq-uitous brother, who had climbed up to the open window, holding on by the sill. "I can whistle most any tune; *can't* I?"

" Yes, dear, you whistle like a quail," replied his grandmother.

Satisfied with this share of praise, down he dropped; and the next minute they saw him rushing down the road, in full chase after a passing dog. Mrs. May laughed, as she said : " It seems as if he was in twenty places at once. But he's a good boy. There's nothing the matter with him, only he's so full of fun that it *will* run over all the time. He'll grow steadier, by and by. He brought in a basket of chips today without upsetting them ; and he never made out to do that before. He's as bright as a steel button ; and if I am only enabled to guide him right, he will make such a man as my dear husband would have been proud to own for a grandson. I used to think it was impossible to love anything better than I loved my little ones ; but I declare I think a grandmother takes more comfort in her grandchildren than she did in her own children."

" Well, you do beat all," replied Mrs. Harrington. " You've had about as much affliction as any woman I know ; but you never seem to *think* you've had any trouble. I told my husband I reckoned you *would* admit it was a tough job to bring up that boy, at your age ; but it seems you don't."

" Why the fact is," rejoined Mrs. May, " the troubles of this life come so mixed up with blessings, that we are willing to endure one for the sake of having the other; and then our afflictions do us so much good, that I reckon *they* are blessings, too."

"I suppose they are," replied Mrs. Harrington, "though they don't always seem so. But I came in to tell you that we are going to Mount Nobscot for huckleberries to-morrow; and if you and the children would like to go, there's room enough in our big wagon."

"Thank you heartily," replied Mrs. May. "It will be a charming frolic for the little folks. But pray don't tell them anything about it to-night; if you do, Robin won't sleep a wink, or let anybody else sleep."

The sun rose clear, and the landscape, recently washed by copious showers, looked clean and fresh. The children were in ecstasies at the idea of going to the hill behind which they had so often seen the sun go down. But so confused were their ideas of space, that, while Jenny inquired whether Nobscot was as far off as Illinois, Robin asked, every five minutes, whether they had got there. When they were lifted from the wagon, they eagerly ran forward, and Robin's voice was soon heard shouting, "O Granny! here's lots o' berries!" They went to picking green, red, and black ones with all zeal, while grandmother proceeded to fill her basket. When Mrs. Harrington came, she said,

"O, don't stop to pick here. We shall find them twice as thick farther up the hill."

"I 'll make sure of these," replied Mrs. May. "I 'm of the old woman's mind, who said she always took her comfort in this world as she went along, for fear it would n't be here when she came back."

"You 're a funny old soul," rejoined Neighbor Harrington. "How young you look to-day!"

In fact, the morning air, the pleasant drive, the joyous little ones, and the novelty of going from home, so renovated the old lady, that her spirits rose to the temperature of youth, her color heightened, and her step was more elastic than usual.

When they had filled their baskets, they sat under the trees, and opened the boxes of luncheon. The children did their full share toward making them empty. When Robin could eat no more, he followed Joe Harrington into a neighboring field to examine some cows that were grazing. The women took out their knitting, and little Jenny sat at their feet, making hills of moss, while she sang about

> A kitty with soft white fur,
> Whose only talk was a pleasant purr.

The grandmother hummed the same tune, but in tones too low to drown the voice of her darling. Looking round on the broad panorama of hills, meadows, and cornfields, dotted with farmhouses, her soul was filled with the spirit of summer, and she began to sing, in tones wonderfully clear and strong for her years,

> " Among the trees, when humming-bees
> At buds and flowers were hanging,"

when Robin scrambled up the hill, calling out, " Sing something funny, Granny! Sing that song about *me!*" He made a motion to scatter Jenny's mosses with his foot; but his grandmother said, " If you want me to sing to you, you must keep quiet." He stretched himself full length before her, and ·throwing his feet up, gazed in her face while she sang :

> " Robin was a rovin' boy,
> Rantin' rovin', rantin' rovin';
> Robin was a rovin' boy,
> · Rantin' rovin' Robin.
>
> " He 'll have misfortunes great and sma',
> But ay a heart aboon them a';
> He 'll be a credit till us a';
> We 'll a' be proud o' Robin."

" That means *me!*" he said, with an exultant air ; and, turning a somerset, he rolled down the hill, from the bottom of which they heard him whistling the tune.

Altogether, they had a very pleasant day among the trees and bushes. It brought back very vividly to Mrs. May's mind similar ramblings with Hatty Brown in the fields of Maine. . As they walked slowly toward their wagon, she was looking dreamily down the long vista of her life, at the entrance of which she seemed to see a vision of her handsome friend Hatty pelting her with flowers in girlish glee. The children ran on, while older members of the party lingered to arrange the baskets. Presently Jenny came running back, and said, " Granny, there's a carriage down there ; and a lady asked me my name, and said I was a pretty little girl."

" Pretty *is* that pretty *does*," replied the grandmother. " That means it is pretty to be good." Then, turning to Mrs. Harrington, she asked, " Whose carriage is that ? "

She answered, " It passed us last Sunday, when we were going to meeting, and husband said it belonged to Mr. Jones, that New York gentleman who bought the Simmes estate, you know. I guess that old lady is Mrs. Gray, his wife's mother."

" Mrs. *who ?* " exclaimed her companion, in a very excited tone.

" They say her name is Gray," replied Mrs. Harrington ; " but what *is* the matter with you ? You're all of a tremble."

Without answering, Mrs. May hurried forward with a degree of agility that surprised them all. She paused in front of an old lady very handsomely dressed in silver-gray silk. She looked at the thin, sharp features, the dull black eyes, and the wrinkled forehead. It was *so* unlike the charming vision she had seen throwing flowers in the far-off vista of memory ! She asked herself,

" *Can* it be she ? " Then, with a suppressed, half-embarrassed eagerness, she asked, " Are you the Mrs. Gray who used to be Hatty Brown ? "

" That was formerly my name," replied the lady, with dignified politeness.

She threw her arms round her neck, nothing doubting, and exclaimed : " O Hatty ! dear Hatty ! How glad I am to see you ! I 've been thinking of you a deal to-day."

The old lady received the embrace passively, and, readjusting her tumbled cape, replied, " I think I 've seen your face somewhere, ma'am, but I don't remember where."

" What ! don't you know *me ?* Your old friend, Jenny White, who married Frank May ? "

" O yes, I remember. But you 've changed a good deal since I used to know you. Has your health been good since I saw you, Mrs. May ? "

This response chilled her friend's heart like an east wind upon spring flowers. In a confused way, she stammered out, " I 've been very well, thank you ; and I hope you have enjoyed the same blessing. But I must go and see to the children now. I thought to be sure you 'd know me. Good by."

" Good by, ma'am," responded the old lady in gray.

The carriage was gone when Mrs. Harrington and her party entered the big wagon to return home. Mrs. May, having made a brief explanation of her proceedings, became unusually silent.

It was a lovely afternoon, but she did not comment on the beauty of the landscape, as she had done in the morning. She was kind and pleasant, but her gayety had vanished. The thought revolved through her mind: " Could it be my shabby gown? Hatty always thought a deal of dress." But the suspicion seemed to her mean, and she strove to drive it away.

" Meeting that old acquaintance seems to make you down-hearted," remarked .Mrs. Harrington; " and that's something new for *you.*"

" I *was* disappointed that she did n't know me," replied Mrs. May; " but when I reflect, it seems very natural. I doubt whether I should have known *her*, if you had n't told me her name. I'm. glad it did n't happen in the morning; for it might have clouded my day a little. I've had a beautiful time."

" Whatever comes, you are always thankful it was n't something worse," rejoined Mrs. Harrington. " Little Jenny is going to be just like you. *She*'ll never be pining after other people's pies and cakes. Whatever she has, she'll call it ' Lasses top on bread! What *can* be gooder?' Won't you, Sissy?"

" Bless the dear little soul! she's fast asleep!" said her grandmother. She placed the pretty little head in her lap, and tenderly stroked back the silky curls. The slight cloud soon floated away from her serene soul, and she began to sing,

2

" Away with melancholy," and " Life let us cher-
ish." As the wagon rolled toward home, people
who happened to be at their doors or windows
said : " That is old Mrs. Frank May. What a
clear, sweet voice she has for a woman of her
years ! "

Mrs. May looked in her glass that night longer
than she had done for years. " I *am* changed,"
said she to herself. " No wonder Hatty did n't
know me ! " She took from the till of her trunk
a locket containing a braid of glossy black hair.
She gazed at it awhile, and then took off her spectacles, to wipe from them the moisture of her
tears. " And *this* is my first meeting with Hatty
since we exchanged lockets ! " murmured she.
" If we had foreseen it then, could we have believed it ? "

The question whether or not it was a duty to
call on Mrs. Gray disturbed her mind considerably. Mrs. Harrington settled it for her off-hand.
" She did not ask you to come," said she ; " and
if she 's a mind to set herself up, let her take the
comfort of it. Folks say she 's a dreadful stiff,
prim old body ; rigid Orthodox ; sure that everybody who don't think just as she does will go to
the bad place."

These words were not uttered with evil intention, but their effect was to increase the sense of
separation. On the other hand, influences were
not wanting to prejudice Mrs. Gray against her

former friend, whose sudden appearance and enthusiastic proceedings had disconcerted her precise habits. When the Sewing-Society met at her son-in-law's house, she happened to be seated next to an austere woman, of whom she inquired, " What sort of person is Mrs. Frank May? "

" I don't know her," was the reply. " She goes to the Unitarian meeting, and I have no acquaintance with people of that society. I should judge she was rather light-minded. When I 've passed by her house, I 've often heard her singing songs; and I should think psalms and hymns would be more suitable to her time of life. I rode by there once on Sunday, when I was coming home from a funeral, and she was singing something that sounded too lively for a psalm-tune. Miss Crosby told me she heard her say that heathens were just as likely to be saved as Christians."

" O, I am sorry to hear that," replied Mrs. Gray. " She and I were brought up under the Rev. Mr. Peat's preaching, and he was sound Orthodox."

" I did n't know she was an acquaintance of yours," rejoined the austere lady, " or I would n't have called her light-minded. I never heard anything against her, only what she said about the heathen."

Mrs. May, having revolved the subject in her straightforward mind, came to the conclusion that

Neighbor Harrington's advice was not in conformity with the spirit of kindness. " Since Mrs. Gray is a stranger in town, it is my place to call first," said she. " I will perform my duty, and then she can do as she pleases about returning the visit." So she arrayed herself in the best she had, placed the children in the care of Mrs. Harrington, and went forth on her mission of politeness. The large mirror, the chairs covered with green damask, and the paper touched here and there with gold, that shimmered in the rays of the setting sun, formed a striking contrast to her own humble home. Perhaps this unaccustomed feeling imparted a degree of constraint to her manner when her old friend entered the room, in ample folds of shining gray silk, and a rich lace cap with pearl-colored ribbons. Mrs. Gray remarked to her that she bore her age remarkably well; to which Mrs. May replied that folks told her so, and she supposed it was because she generally had pretty good health. It did not occur to her to return the compliment, for it would not have been true. Jenny was now better-looking than Hatty. Much of this difference might be attributed to her more perfect health, but still more it was owing to the fact that, all their lives long, one had lived to be ministered unto, and the other to minister. The interview was necessarily a formal one. Mrs. Gray inquired about old acquaintances in Maine, but her visitor had been so long absent

from that part of the country that she had little
or nothing to tell, and all she had struggled
through meanwhile would have been difficult for
the New York lady to realize. The remark about
her light-mindedness was constantly present in
Mrs. Gray's mind, and at parting she thus expressed the anxiety it occasioned : " You say you
have a great deal to do, Mrs. May, and indeed
you must have, with all the care of those little
children ; but I hope you find time to think about
the salvation of your soul."

Her visitor replied, with characteristic simplicity : " I don't know whether I do, in the sense I
suppose you mean. I have thought a great deal
about what is right and what is wrong, and I have
prayed for light to see what was my duty, and for
strength to perform it. But the fact is, I have
had so much to do for others, that I have n't had
much time to think about myself, in *any* way."
Then, with some passing remark about the vines
at the door, the old ladies bade each other good-
by.

When Mrs. Harrington was informed of the
conversation, she said, in her blunt way : " It was
a great piece of impertinence in her. She 'd better take care of her own soul than trouble herself
about yours."

" I don't think so," replied Mrs. May. " I believe she meant it kindly. She don't seem to me
to be stern or proud. But we 've been doing and

thinking such very different things, for a great
many years, that she don't know what to say to
me, and I am just as much puzzled how to get at
her. I reckon all these things will come right in
another world."

During the summer she often saw Mr. Jones's
carriage pass her house, and many a time, when
the weather was fine, she placed fresh flowers
on the mantel-piece, in a pretty vase which Hatty
had given her for a bridal present, thinking to
herself that Mrs. Gray would be likely to ride
out, and might give her a call. When autumn
came, she filled the vase with grasses and bright
berries, which she gathered in her ramblings with
the children. Once, the carriage passed her as
she was walking home, with a little one in either
hand, and Mrs. Gray looked out and bowed. At
last a man came with a barrel of apples and a
message. The purport of it was, that she had
gone with her daughter's family to New York for
the winter; that she intended to have called on
Mrs. May, but had been poorly and made no
visits.

Winter passed rapidly. The children attended
school constantly; it was grandmother's business
to help them about their lessons, to knit them
warm socks and mittens, to mend their clothes,
and fill their little dinner-kettle with provisions.
The minister, the deacon, and the neighbors in
general felt interested to help the worthy woman

along in the task she had undertaken. Many
times a week she repeated, " How my path is
strewn with blessings ! "

With the lilacs the New York family came
back to their summer residence. The tidings
soon spread abroad that Mrs. Gray was failing
fast, and was seldom strong enough to ride out.
Mrs. May recalled to mind certain goodies, of
which Hatty used to be particularly fond in their
old girlish times. The next day she started from
home with a basket nicely covered with a white
damask napkin, on the top of which lay a large
bunch of Lilies of the Valley, imbedded in one of
their broad green leaves.· She found Mrs. Gray
bolstered up in her easy-chair, looking quite thin
and pale. " I know you have everything you
want, and better than I can bring," said she ;
" but I remembered you used to like these goodies
when we were girls, and I wanted to bring you
something, so I brought these." She laid the
flowers in the thin hand, and uncovered her
basket.

The invalid looked up in her face with a smile,
and said, " Thank you, Jenny ; this is very kind
of you."

" God bless you for calling me Jenny ! " exclaimed her warm-hearted old friend, with a gush
of tears. " There is nobody left to call me Jenny
now. The children call me Granny, and the
neighbors call me old Mrs. Frank May. O, it
sounds like old times, Hatty."

The ice gave way under the touch of that one sunbeam. Mrs. Gray and Mrs. May vanished from their conversation, and only Hatty and Jenny remained. For several months they met every day, and warmed their old hearts with youthful memories. Once only, a little of the former restraint returned for a few minutes. Mrs. Gray betrayed what was in her mind, by saying: "I suppose, Jenny, you know I haven't any property. My husband failed before he died, and I am dependent on my daughter."

"I never inquired about your property, and I don't care anything about it," replied Mrs. May, rather bruskly, and with a slight flush on her cheeks ; but, immediately subsiding into a gentler tone, she added, "I'm very glad, Hatty, that you have a daughter who is able to make you so comfortable."

Thenceforth the invalid accepted her disinterested services without question or doubt. True to her old habits of being ministered unto, she made large demands on her friend's time and strength, apparently unconscious how much inconvenience it must occasion to an old person charged with the whole care of two orphan children. Mrs. May carefully concealed any impediments in the way, and, by help of Mrs. Harrington, was always ready to attend upon her old friend. She was often called upon to sing "Auld Lang Syne"; and sometimes, when the invalid felt stronger than common, she would join in with her feeble, cracked voice. Jenny sat looking at Hatty's withered face, and dim black eyes, and she often felt a choking in her throat, while they sang together:

> " We twa hae ran about the braes,
> And pu'd the gowans fine."

More frequently they sang the psalm-tunes they used to sing when both sat in the singing-seats with Frank May and Harry Blake. They seldom parted without Jenny's reading a chapter of the New Testament in a soft, serious tone. One day Mrs. Gray said : " I have a confession to make, Jenny. I was a little prejudiced against you, and thought I should n't care to renew our acquaintance. Somebody told me you was light-minded, and that you told Miss Crosby the heathen were just as likely to be saved as Christians. But you seem to put your trust in God, Jenny ; and it is a great comfort to me to hear you read and sing."

" I have a confession to make, too," replied Mrs. May. " They told me you was a very stern and bigoted Orthodox ; and you know, when we were girls, Hatty, I never took much to folks that were too strict to brew a Saturday, for fear the beer would work a Sunday."

" Ah, we were giddy young things in those days," replied her friend, with much solemnity in her manner.

" Well, Hatty dear, I 'm a sort of an old girl now," replied Mrs. May. " I am disposed to

2* c

be merciful toward the short-comings of my fellow-creatures, and I cannot believe our Heavenly Father will be less so. I remember Miss Crosby talked to me about the heathen one day, and I thought she talked hard. I don't recollect what I said to her; but after I arrived at years of reflection I came to some conclusions different from the views we were brought up in. You know my dear Frank was an invalid many years. He was always in the house, and we read to each other, and talked over what we read. In that way, I got the best part of the education I have after I was married. Among other things he read to me some translations from what the Hindoos believe in as their Bible; and some of the writings of Rammohun Roy; and we both came to the conclusion that some who were called heathens might be nearer to God than many professing Christians. You know, Hatty, that Jesus walked and talked with his disciples, and their hearts were stirred, but they did n't know him. Now it seems to me that the spirit of Jesus may walk and talk with good pious Hindoos and Mahometans, and may stir their hearts, though they don't know him." ·

"You may be right," rejoined the invalid. "God's ways are above our ways. It's a pity friends should be set against one another on account of what they believe, or don't believe. Pray for *me*, Jenny, and I will pray for *you*."

It was the latter part of October, when Mrs. May carried a garland of bright autumn leaves to pin up opposite her friend's bed. "It is beautiful," said the invalid; "but the colors are not so brilliant as those you and I used to gather in Maine. O, how the woods glowed there, at this season! I wish I could see them again."

Mrs. May smiled, and answered, "Perhaps you *will*, dear."

Her friend looked in her face, with an earnest, questioning glance; but she only said, "Sing our old favorite tune of St. Martin's, Jenny." She seated herself by the bedside and sang:

> "The Lord my shepherd is,
> I shall be well supplied;
> Since he is mine, and I am his,
> What can I want beside?"

Perceiving that the invalid grew drowsy, she continued to hum in a low, lulling tone. When she was fast asleep, she rose up, and, after gazing tenderly upon her, crept softly out of the room. She never looked in those old dim eyes again. The next morning they told her the spirit had departed from its frail tenement.

Some clothing and a few keepsakes were transmitted to Mrs. May soon after, in compliance with the expressed wish of her departed friend. Among them was the locket containing a braid of her own youthful hair. It was the very color of little Jenny's, only the glossy brown was a

shade darker. She placed the two lockets side
by side, and wiped the moisture from her spectacles as she gazed upon them. Then she wrapped
them together, and wrote on them, with a trembling hand, "The hair of Grandmother and her
old friend Hatty; for my darling little Jenny."

When Neighbor Harrington came in to examine the articles that had been sent, the old
lady said to her: "There is nobody left now to
call me Jenny. But here is my precious *little*
Jenny. *She* 'll never forsake her old granny;
will she, darling?" The child snuggled fondly
to her side, and stood on tiptoe to kiss the wrinkled face, which was to her the dearest face in
the whole world.

She never did desert her good old friend. She
declined marrying during Mrs. May's lifetime, and
waited upon her tenderly to the last. Robin,
who proved a bright scholar, went to the West
to teach school, with the view of earning money
to buy a farm, where grandmother should be
the queen. He wrote her many loving letters,
and sent portions of his earnings to her and
Sissy; but she departed this life before his earthly
paradise was made ready for her. The last tune
she sang was St. Martin's; and the last words
she spoke were: "How many blessings I have
received! Thank the Lord for all his mercies!"

THE GOOD OLD GRANDMOTHER,

WHO DIED AGED EIGHTY.

O SOFTLY wave the silver hair
From off that aged brow!
That crown of glory, worn so long,
A fitting crown is now.

Fold reverently the weary hands,
That toiled so long and well;
And, while your tears of sorrow fall,
Let sweet thanksgivings swell.

That life-work, stretching o'er long years,
A varied web has been;
With silver strands by sorrow wrought,
And sunny gleams between.

These silver hairs stole softly on,
Like flakes of falling snow,
That wrap the green earth lovingly,
When autumn breezes blow.

Each silver hair, each wrinkle there,
Records some good deed done;

Some flower she cast along the way,
   Some spark from love's bright sun.

How bright she always made her home!
   It seemed as if the floor
Was always flecked with spots of sun,
   And barred with brightness o'er.

The very falling of her step
   Made music as she went;
A loving song was on her lip,
   The song of full content.

And now, in later years, her word
   Has been a blessed thing
In many a home, where glad she saw
   Her children's children spring.

Her widowed life has happy been,
   With brightness born of heaven;
So pearl and gold in drapery fold
   The sunset couch at even.

O gently fold the weary hands
   That toiled so long and well;
The spirit rose to angel bands,
   When off earth's mantle fell.

She's safe within her Father's house,
   Where many mansions be;
O pray that thus such rest may come,
   Dear heart, to thee and me!

ANONYMOUS.

THE CONSOLATIONS OF AGE.

TRANSLATED FROM THE GERMAN OF ZSCHOKKE'S
AUTOBIOGRAPHY.

ROM all I have narrated concerning my good and evil days, some may infer that I have been on the whole a favorite of fortune; that I may very well be philosophic, and maintain a rosy good-humor, since, with the exception of a few self-torments of the fancy, I have seldom or never experienced a misfortune. But indeed I *have* met with what men usually style great misfortunes, or evils, though I never so named them. Like every mortal, I have had my share of what is called human misery. The weight of a sudden load has sometimes, for a moment, staggered me and pressed me down, as is the case with others. But, with renewed buoyancy of spirit, I have soon risen again, and borne the burden allotted to me, without discontent. Nay, more than this, though some may shake their heads incredulously, it is a fact that worldly suffering has often not been disagreeable to me.

It has weaned me from placing my trust in transitory things. It has shown me the degree of strength and self-reliance I could retain, even at that period of life when the passions reign. I am fully convinced that there is no evil in the world but sin. Nothing but consciousness of guilt spins a dark thread, which reaches through the web of all our days, even unto the grave. God is not the author of calamity, but only man, by his weakness, his over-estimate of pompous vanities, and the selfish nurture of his appetites. He weeps like a child because he cannot have his own way, and even at seventy years of age is not yet a man. He bewails himself, because God does not mind him. Yet every outward misfortune is in truth as worthy a gift of God as outward success.

In common with others, I have met with ingratitude from many; but it did not disquiet me; because what I had done for them was not done for thanks. Friends have deceived me, but it did not make me angry with them; for I saw that I had only deceived myself with regard to them. I have endured misapprehension and persecution with composure, being aware of the unavoidable diversity of opinions, and of the passions thereby excited. I have borne the crosses of poverty without a murmur; for experience had taught me that outward poverty often brings inward wealth. I have lost a moderate property, which I had acquired by toil, but such losses did not imbitter me

for a single day; they only taught me to work
and spare. I have been the happy father of happy
children. Twelve sons and one daughter I have
counted; and I have had to sit, with a bleeding
heart, at the death-bed of four of those sons. As
they drew their last breath, I felt that divine
sorrow which transforms the inner man. My
spirit rested on the Father of the universe, and
it was well with me. My dead ones were not
parted from me. Those who remained behind
drew the more closely to one another, while eagerly looking toward those who had gone before
them to other mansions of the Great Father. It
was our custom to think of the deceased as still
living in the midst of us. We were wont to talk
about their little adventures, their amusing sallies,
and the noble traits of their characters. Everything noteworthy concerning *them*, as well as
what related to the *living* members of the family,
was recorded by the children in a chronicle they
kept in the form of a newspaper, and was thus
preserved from oblivion. Death is something festal, great, like all the manifestations of God here
below. The death of my children hallowed me;
it lifted me more and more out of the shows of
earth, into the divine. It purified my thoughts
and feelings. I wept, as a child of the dust *must*
do; but in spirit I was calm and cheerful, because
I knew to whom I and mine belonged.

At the beginning of old age, I could indeed

call myself a happy man.   On my seventieth
birthday, I felt as if I were standing on a mountain height, at whose foot the ocean of eternity
was audibly rushing; while behind me, life, with
its deserts and flower-gardens, its sunny days and
its stormy days, spread out green, wild, and beautiful.   Formerly, when I read or heard of the
joylessness of age, I was filled with sadness; but
I now wondered that it presented so much that
was agreeable.   The more the world diminished
and grew dark, the less I felt the loss of it; for
the dawn of the next world grew ever clearer
and clearer.

Thus rejoicing in God, and with him, I advance into the winter of life, beyond which no
spring awaits me on this planet.   The twilight
of my existence on earth is shining round me;
but the world floats therein in a rosy light, more
beautiful than the dawn of life.   Others may
look back with homesickness to the lost paradise
of childhood.   That paradise was never mine.
I wandered about, an orphan, unloved, and for-
saken of all but God.   I thank him for this
allotment; for it taught me to build my paradise
within.   The solemn evening is at hand, and it
is welcome.   I repent not that I have lived.
Others, in their autumn, can survey and count
up their collected harvests.   This I cannot.   I
have scattered seed, but whither the wind has
carried it I know not.   The good-will alone was

mine. God's hand decided concerning the success of my labor. Many an unproductive seed
I have sown ; but I do not, on that account,
complain either of myself or of Heaven. Fortune has lavished on me no golden treasures ; but
contented with what my industry has acquired,
and my economy has preserved, I enjoy that
noble independence at which I have
always aimed ; and out of the little
I possess I have been sometimes able to afford assistance to others who
were less for-
tunate.

As healthy old fellow, that is not a fool, is the
happiest creature living. It is at that time of life
only men enjoy their faculties with pleasure and
satisfaction. It is then we have nothing to *manage*,
as the phrase is ; we speak the downright truth ;
and whether the rest of the world will *give* us the
privilege, or not, we have so little to ask of them,
that we can *take* it. — STEELE.

THE OLD MAN DREAMS.

By OLIVER WENDELL HOLMES.

O FOR one hour of youthful joy!
   Give back my twentieth spring!
I'd rather laugh a bright-haired boy,
   Than reign a gray-beard king!

Off with the wrinkled spoils of age!
   Away with learning's crown!
Tear out life's wisdom-written page,
   And dash its trophies down!

One moment let my life-blood stream
   From boyhood's fount of fame!
Give me one giddy, reeling dream
   Of life all love and flame!

My listening angel heard the prayer,
   And, calmly smiling, said,
"If I but touch thy silvered hair,
   Thy hasty wish hath sped.

"But is there nothing in thy track
   To bid thee fondly stay,

While the swift seasons hurry back
  To find the wished-for day?"

Ah, truest soul of womankind!
  Without *thee*, what were life?
One bliss I cannot leave behind:
  I'll take — my — precious — wife!

The angel took a sapphire pen
  And wrote in rainbow dew,
" The man would be a boy again,
  And be a husband too!"

" And is there nothing yet unsaid,
  Before the change appears?
Remember, all their gifts have fled
  With those dissolving years!"

Why, yes; for memory would recall
  My fond paternal joys;
I could not bear to leave them all:
  I'll take — my — girl — and — boys!

The smiling angel dropped his pen, —
  " Why, this will never do;
The man would be a boy again,
  And be a father too!"

And so I laughed, — my laughter woke
  The household with its noise, —
And wrote my dream, when morning broke,
  To please the gray-haired boys.

A RUSSIAN LADY

OF THE OLD SCHOOL.*

GIVE me your hand, dear reader, and accompany me on a visit to one of my neighbors. The day is fine, the blue sky of the month of May is a beautiful object; the smooth young leaves of the white hazel-trees are as brilliant as if they had been newly washed. The large, smooth fields are covered with that fine young grass which the sheep love so much to crop; on the right and left, on the long slopes of the hills, the rye-grass is waving, and over its smooth swell glide the shadows of the little flying clouds. In the distance, the woods are resplendent with the brilliant light; the ponds glitter, and the villages are bathed in yellow rays. Innumerable larks fly about, singing and beating their wings in unison; making their appearance first in one spot, then in another, they rise lightly from the fields, and again are as quick-

* From Life in the Interior of Russia.

ly lost in them. The rooks station themselves on the highway, looking up fixedly at the sun; they move aside to let you pass, or foolishly fly forward ten paces on the edge of the road. On the slopes beyond a ravine a laborer is at his plough, and a piebald foal, with its miserable little tail, dishevelled mane, and long, frail legs, runs after its mother, and we may just hear its plaintive neigh. We enter a birch wood, and a fresh and strong odor fills the air; we reach the gate of an enclosure; the coachman descends, and, while the horses snort, and the right wheeler plays with his tail, and rubs his jaw against the pole, he opens the creaking gate, and, reseating himself, we roll on.

A village now presents itself, and, after passing five or six farm-yards, we turn to the right, and descending rapidly, are soon driving along an embankment. Beyond a pond of moderate extent, and behind apple-trees and clustering lilacs, an old wooden house is now visible, painted red, and possessing two chimneys. We drive along a paling on the left, and pass through a large open carriage entrance, saluted by the husky barkings of three old worn-out dogs. My groom gallantly salutes an old housekeeper, who is peeping out of the pantry through a foot and a half window. We draw up before the door near the veranda of a gloomy little house. It is the abode of Tatiana Borissovna. But there she is herself, saluting us

from the window. "Good morning, good morning, Madame."

Tatiana Borissovna is a woman of about fifty;
she has large bluish-gray eyes, slightly prominent,
a nose inclined to flatness, cherry cheeks, and a
double chin. Her face beams with sweetness and
goodness. She once had a husband, but so long
ago that no one has any recollection of it. She
scarcely ever leaves her little property, keeps up
but a slight connection with her neighbors, seldom
invites them to her house, and likes none but
young people. Her father was a poor gentleman,
and she consequently received a very imperfect
education; in other words, she does not speak
French, and has never seen even Moscow, not
to speak of St. Petersburg. But, spite of these
little defects, she manages all her affairs in her
country life so simply and wisely; she has so large
a way of thinking, of feeling, and comprehending
things; she is so little accessible to the thousand
weaknesses which are generally found in our good
provincial ladies, — poor things, — that, in truth,
one cannot help admiring her. Only consider
that she lives all the year round within the precincts of her own village and estate, quite isolated,
and that she remains a stranger to all the tittle-
tattle of the locality; does not rail, slander, take
offence, or choke and fret with curiosity; that
envy, jealousy, aversion, and restlessness of body
and mind, are all unknown to her; only consider

this, and grant that she is a marvel. Every day after eleven o'clock she is dressed in a gown of iron-gray taffeta, and a white cap with long pure ribbons; she likes to eat, and make others do the same; but she eats moderately, and lets others follow her example. Preserves, fruits, pickled meats, are all intrusted to the housekeeper. With what, then, does she occupy herself, and how does she fill up her day? She reads, perhaps, you will say. No, she does not read; and, to speak the truth, people must think of others than Tatiana Borissovna when they print a book. In winter, if she is alone, our Tatiana Borissovna sits near a window, and quietly knits a stocking; in summer she goes and comes in her garden, where she plants and waters flowers, picks the caterpillars from her shrubs, puts props under her bushes, and sprinkles sand over the garden paths; then she can amuse herself for hours with the feathered race in her court-yard, with her kittens and pigeons, all of which she feeds herself. She occupies herself very little with housekeeping. If, unexpectedly, any good young neighbor chances to look in, she is then as happy as possible; she establishes herself upon her divan, regales her visitor with tea, hears all he has to say, sometimes gives him little friendly pats on the cheek, laughs heartily at his sallies, and speaks little herself. Are you annoyed, or the victim of some misfortune? She consoles you with the most sympathizing words,

and opens up various means of relief, all full of good sense. How many there are, who, after confiding to her their family secrets and their private griefs, have found themselves so relieved by unburdening their minds, that they have bathed her hands with their tears. In general, she sits right before her guest, her head leaning lightly on her left hand, looking in his face with so much kindly interest, smiling with such friendly good-nature, that one can scarcely keep himself from saying, " Ah ! what an excellent woman you are, Tatiana Borissovna. Come, I will conceal from you nothing that weighs upon my heart. "
In her delightful, nice little rooms, one
is so pleased with himself and everybody, that he is unwilling to
leave them ; in this little
heaven, the weather
is always at
"set fair."

THE happiness of life may be greatly increased by small courtesies in which there is no parade, whose voice is too still to tease, and which manifest themselves by tender and affectionate looks, and little kind acts of attention, giving others the preference in every little enjoyment at the table, in the field, walking, sitting, or standing. — STERNE.

THE OLD MAN'S SONG.

TO HIS WIFE.

OH, don't be sorrowful, darling!
  Now don't be sorrowful, pray!
For, taking the year together, my dear,
  There is n't more night than day.

'T is rainy weather, my darling;
  Time's waves they heavily run;
But, taking the year together, my dear,
  There is n't more cloud than sun.

We are old folks now, my darling;
  Our heads they are growing gray;
But, taking the year all round, my dear,
  You will always find the May.

We 've *had* our May, my darling,
  And our roses, long ago;
And the time of the year is coming, my dear,
  For the long dark nights and the snow.

But God is God, my darling,
  Of night, as well as of day;
And we feel and know that we can go
  Wherever He leads the way.

Ay, God of the night, my darling;
  Of the night of death so grim.
The gate that from life leads out, good wife,
  Is the gate that leads to Him.

ANONYMOUS.

THE TWENTY–SEVENTH OF MARCH.

THE BIRTHDAY OF ———.

Now be the hours that yet remain to thee
Stormy or sunny, sympathy and love,
That inextinguishably·dwell within
Thy heart, shall give a beauty and a light
To the most desolate moments, like the glow
Of a bright fireside in the wildest day;
And kindly words and offices of good
Shall wait upon thy steps, as thou goest on,
Where God shall lead thee, till thou reach the gates
Of a more genial season, and thy path
Be lost to human eye among the bowers
And living fountains of a brighter land.

WM. C. BRYANT.

A CHRISTMAS STORY FOR GRANDFATHER.

By CHARLES DICKENS.

NCE upon a time, a good many years ago, there was a traveller, and he set out upon a journey. It was a magic journey, and was to seem very long when he began it, and very short when he got half-way through.

He travelled along a rather dark path for some little time, without meeting anything, until at last he came to a beautiful child. So he said to the child, " What do you here ? " And the child said, " I am always at play. Come and play with me ! "

So, he played with that child the whole day long, and they were very merry. The sky was so blue, the sun was so bright, the water was so sparkling, the leaves were so green, the flowers were so lovely, and they heard such singing-birds, and saw so many butterflies, that everything was beautiful. This was in fine weather. When it rained, they loved to watch the falling drops and to smell the fresh scents. When it blew, it was delightful to listen to the wind, and fancy what it said, as it came rushing from its home — where was that, they wondered! — whistling and howling, and driving the clouds before it, bending the trees, rumbling in the chimneys, shaking the house, and making the sea roar in fury. But when it snowed, that was the best of all; for they liked nothing so well as to look up at the white flakes falling fast and thick, like down from the breasts of millions of white birds; and to see how smooth and deep the drift was, and to listen to the hush upon the paths and roads.

They had plenty of the finest toys in the world, and the most astonishing picture-books, all about scimitars and slippers and turbans, and dwarfs and giants, and genii and fairies, and blue-beards and bean-stalks, and riches, and caverns and forests, and Valentines and Orsons: and all new and all true.

But one day, of a sudden, the traveller lost the child. He called to him over and over again, but got no answer. So, he went upon his road, and went on for a little while without meeting anything, until at last he came to a handsome boy. So, he said to the boy, "What do you here?" And the boy said, "I am always learning. Come and learn with me."

So he learned with that boy about Jupiter and

Juno, and the Greeks and the Romans, and I don't know what, and learned more than I could tell, — or he either; for he soon forgot a great deal of it. But they were not always learning; they had the merriest games that ever were played. They rowed upon the river in summer, and skated on the ice in winter; they were active afoot, and active on horseback; at cricket, and all games at ball; at prisoners' base, hare and hounds, follow my leader, and more sports than I can think of; nobody could beat them. They had holidays, too, and Twelfth cakes, and parties where they danced all night till midnight, and real theatres, where they saw palaces of real gold and silver rise out of the real earth, and saw all the wonders of the world at once. As to friends, they had such dear friends, and so many of them, that I want the time to reckon them up. They were all young, like the handsome boy, and were never to be strange to one another all their lives through.

Still, one day, in the midst of all these pleasures, the traveller lost the boy, as he had lost the child, and, after calling on him in vain, went on upon his journey. So he went on for a little while without seeing anything, until at last he came to a young man. So, he said to the young man, "What do you here?" And the young man said, "I am always in love. Come and love with me."

So, he went away with that young man, and

presently they came to one of the prettiest girls
that ever was seen, — just like Fanny in the corner
there, — and she had eyes like Fanny, and hair
like Fanny, and dimples like Fanny's, and she
laughed and colored just as Fanny does while I
am talking about her. So, the young man fell in
love directly, — just as Somebody I won't mention,
the first time he came here, did with Fanny.
Well! He was teased sometimes, — just as Somebody used to be by Fanny; and they quarrelled
sometimes, — just as Somebody and Fanny used
to quarrel; and they made it up, and sat in the
dark, and wrote letters every day, and never
were happy asunder, and were always looking
out for one another, and pretending not to, and
were engaged at Christmas time, and sat close to
one another by the fire, and were going to be
married very soon, — all exactly like Somebody I
won't mention and Fanny!

But the traveller lost them one day, as he had
lost the rest of his friends, and, after calling to
them to come back, which they never did, went
on upon his journey. So, he went on for a little
while without seeing anything, until at last he
came to a middle-aged gentleman. So, he said to
the gentleman, "What are you doing here?"
And his answer was, "I am always busy. Come
and be busy with me!"

So, then he began to be very busy with that
gentleman, and they went on through the wood

together. The whole journey was through a wood, only it had been open and green at first, like a wood in spring; and now began to be thick and dark, like a wood in summer; some of the little trees that had come out earliest were even turning brown. The gentleman was not alone, but had a lady of about the same age with him, who was his wife: and they had children, who were with them too. So, they all went on together through the wood, cutting down the trees, and making a path through the branches and the fallen leaves, and carrying burdens, and working hard.

Sometimes they came to a long green avenue that opened into deeper woods. Then they would hear a very little distant voice crying, "Father, father, I am another child! Stop for me!" And presently they would see a very little figure, growing larger as it came along, running to join them. When it came up, they all crowded round it, and kissed and welcomed it; and then they all went on together.

Sometimes they came to several avenues at once; and then they all stood still, and one of the children said, "Father, I am going to sea"; and another said, "Father, I am going to India"; and another, "Father, I am going to seek my fortune where I can"; and another, "Father, I am going to heaven!" So, with many tears at parting, they went, solitary, down those avenues, each

3*

child upon its way; and the child who went to heaven, rose into the golden air and vanished.

Whenever these partings happened, the traveller looked at the gentleman, and saw him glance up at the sky above the trees, where the day was beginning to decline, and the sunset to come on. He saw, too, that his hair was turning gray. But they never could rest long, for they had their journey to perform, and it was necessary for them to be always busy.

At last, there had been so many partings that there were no children left, and only the traveller, the gentleman, and the lady went upon their way in company. And now the wood was yellow; and now brown; and the leaves, even of the forest-trees, began to fall.

So they came to an avenue that was darker than the rest, and were pressing forward on their journey without looking down it, when the lady stopped.

" My husband," said the lady, " I am called."

They listened, and they heard a voice a long way down the avenue say, " Mother, mother!"

It was the voice of the first child who had said, " I am going to heaven!" and the father said, " I pray not yet. The sunset is very near. I pray not yet."

But the voice cried, " Mother, mother!" without minding him, though his hair was now quite white, and tears were on his face.

Then, the mother, who was already drawn into

the shade of the dark avenue, and moving away with her arms still around his neck, kissed him and said, " My dearest, I am summoned, and I go ! " And she was gone. And the traveller and he were left alone together.

And they went on and on together, until they came to very near the end of the wood ; so near, that they could see the sunset shining red before them through the trees.

Yet, once more, while he broke his way among the branches, the traveller lost his friend. He called and called, but there was no reply, and when he passed out of the wood and saw the peaceful sun going down upon a wide purple prospect, he came to an old man sitting upon a fallen tree. So, he said to the old man, " What do you here ? " And the old man said, with a calm smile, " I am always remembering. Come and remember with me."

So, the traveller sat down by the side of the old man, face to face with the serene sunset ; and all his friends came softly back and stood around him. The beautiful child, the handsome boy, the young man in love, the father, mother, and children : every one of them was there, and he had lost nothing. So, he loved them all, and was kind and forbearing with them all, and was always pleased to watch them all, and they all honored and loved . him. And I think the traveller must be yourself, dear grandfather, because it is what you do to us, and what we do to you.

JOHN ANDERSON, MY JO.

By ROBERT BURNS.

JOHN ANDERSON, my jo, John,
　　When we were first acquent,
Your locks were like the raven,
　　Your bonnie brow was brent *;
But now your head 's turned bald, John,
　　Your locks are like the snow;
But blessings on your frosty pow,
　　John Anderson, my jo.

John Anderson, my jo, John,
　　We clamb the hill thegither;
And mony a canty † day, John,
　　We 've had wi' ane anither:
Now we maun totter down, John,
　　But hand in hand we 'll go,
And sleep thegither at the foot,
　　John Anderson, my jo.

When thoughtful people sing these admirable verses, they are apt to long to hear of something *beyond* the foot of the hill. This want has been extremely well supplied by Mr. Charles Gould, of New York, in the following verse: —

* Smooth.　　　　　　† Merry.

John Anderson, my jo, John,
  When we have slept thegither
The sleep that a' maun sleep, John,
  We 'll wake wi' ane anither :
And in that better warld, John,
  Nae sorrow shall we know ;
Nor fear we e'er shall part again,
  John Anderson, my jo.

OLD FOLKS AT HOME.

MORE pleasant seem their own surroundings,
  Though quaint and old,
Than newer homes, with their aboundings
  Of marble, silk, and gold.
For 't is the heart inspires home-feelings,
  In hut or hall,
Where memory, with its fond revealings,
  Sheds a tender light o'er all.

They love the wonted call to meeting,
  By their old bell ;
They love the old familiar greeting
  From friends who know them well.
Their homesick hearts are always yearning,
  When they 're away ;
And ever is their memory turning
  To scenes where they used to stay.

L. M. C.

EVERLASTING YOUTH.

By Rev. EDMUND H. SEARS.*

OLD age, in some of its aspects, is a most interesting and solemn mystery, though to the outward eye it is merely the gradual waning and extinction of existence. All the faculties fold themselves up to a long, last sleep. First, the senses begin to close, and lock in the soul from the outward world. The hearing is generally the first to fail, shutting off the mind from the tones of affection and of melody. The sight fails next; and the pictures of beauty, on the canvas spread round us morning and evening, become blurred. The doors and windows are shut toward the street. The invasion keeps on steadily toward the seat of life. The images of the memory lose their outline, run together, and at last melt away into darkness. Now and then, by a special effort, rents are made in the clouds, and we see a vista opening through

* From Foregleams of Immortality.

the green glades of other years. But the edges of the cloud soon close again. It settles down more densely than ever, and all the past is blotted out. Then the reason fails, and the truths it had elaborated flicker and are extinguished. Only the affections remain. Happy for us, if these also have not become soured or chilled. It is our belief, however, that these *may* be preserved in their primitive freshness and glow; and that in the old age where the work of regeneration is consummating, the affections are always preserved bright and sweet, like roses of Eden, occupying a charmed spot in the midst of snows. In old age, men generally seem to have grown either better or worse. The reason is, that the internal life is then more revealed, and its spontaneous workings are more fully manifested. The intellectual powers are no longer vigilant to control the expression of the internal feelings, and so the heart is generally laid open. What we call the moroseness and peevishness of age is none other than the real disposition, no longer hedged in, and kept in decency, by the intellect, but coming forth without disguise. So again, that beautiful simplicity and infantile meekness, sometimes apparent in old age, beaming forth, like the dawn of the coming heaven, through all the relics of natural decay, are the spontaneous effusions of sanctified affections. There is, therefore, a good and a bad sense, in which we speak of the second childhood. Childhood is the state of spontaneity. In the first childhood, before the intellect is formed, the heart answers truly to all impressions from without; as the Æolian harp answers to every touch of the breeze. In the second childhood, after the intellect is broken down, the same phenomenon comes round again; and in it you read the history of all the intervening years. What those years have done for the regeneration of the soul will appear, now that its inmost state is translucent, no longer concealed by the expediencies learned of intellectual prudence. When the second childhood is true and genial, the work of regeneration approaches its consummation; and the light of heaven is reflected from silver hairs, as if one stood nearer to Paradise, and caught reflections of the resurrection glories.

But alas! is this *all* that is left of us, amid the memorials of natural decay? Senses, memory, reason, all blotted out, in succession, and instinctive affection left *alone* to its spontaneous workings, like a solitary flower breathing its fragrance upon snows? And how do we know but *this*, too, will close up its leaves, and fall before the touch of the invader? Then the last remnant of the man is no more. Or, if otherwise, must so many souls enter upon their immortality denuded of everything but the heart's inmost and ruling love?

How specious and deceptive are natural appearances! What *seemed* to the outward eye the waning of existence, and the loss of faculties, is only locking them up successively, in order to keep them more secure. Old age, rather than death, answers strictly to the analogies of *sleep*. It is the gradual folding in and closing up of all the voluntary powers, after they have become worn and tired, that they may wake again refreshed and renovated for the higher work that awaits them. The psychological evidence is pretty full and decisive, that old age is sleep, but not decay. The reason lives, though its eye is temporarily closed ; and some future day it will give a more perfect and pliant form to the affections. Memory remains, though its functions are suspended for a while. All its chambers may be exhumed hereafter, and their frescoes, like those of the buried temples at Meroë, will be found preserved in unfading colors. The *whole* record of our life is laid up *within* us ; and only the overlayings of the physical man prevent the record from being always visible. The years leave their *débris* successively upon the spiritual nature, till it seems buried and lost beneath the layers. On the old man's memory every period seems to have obliterated a former one ; but the life which he has lived can no more be lost to him, or destroyed, than the rock-strata can be destroyed by being buried under layers of sand. In those hours when the bondage of the senses is less firm, and the life within has freer motion ; or, in those hours of self-revelation, which are sometimes experienced under a clearer and

E

more pervading light from above, — the past withdraws its veil; and we see, rank beyond rank, as along the rows of an expanding amphitheatre, the images of successive years, called out as by some wand of enchantment. There are abundant facts, which go to prove that the decline and forgetfulness of years are nothing more than the hardening of the mere *envelopment* of the man, shutting in the inmost life, which merely waits the hour to break away from its bondage.

De Quincey says: "I am assured that there is no such thing as *forgetting* possible to the mind. A thousand circumstances may and will interpose a veil between our present consciousness and the secret inscriptions of the mind; but alike, whether veiled or unveiled, the inscription remains forever; just as the stars *seem* to withdraw from the common light of day; whereas, we all know that it is the light which is drawn over them, as a veil, and that they are waiting to be revealed, when the obscuring daylight shall have withdrawn."

The resurrection is the exact inverse of natural decay; and the former is preparing ere the latter has ended. The affections, being the inmost life, are the nucleus of the whole man. They are the creative and organific centre, whence are formed the reason and the memory, and thence their embodiment in the more outward form of members and organs. The whole interior mechanism is complete in the chrysalis, ere the wings, spotted with light, are fluttering in the zephyrs of morning. St. Paul, who, in this connection, is speaking specially of the resurrection of the just, presents three distinct points of contrast between the natural body and the spiritual. One is weak, the other is strong. One is corruptible, the other is incorruptible. One is without honor, the other is glorious. By saying that one is natural, and the other spiritual, he certainly implies that one is better adapted than the other to do the functions of spirit, and more perfectly to organize and manifest its powers. How clearly conceivable then is it that when man becomes free of the coverings of mere natural decay, he comes into complete possession of all that he is, and all that he has ever lived ; that leaf after leaf in our whole book of life is opened backward, and all its words and letters come out in more vivid colors !

In the other life, therefore, appears the wonderful paradox that the oldest people are the youngest. To grow in age is to come into everlasting youth. To become old in years is to put on the freshness of perpetual prime. We drop from us the *débris* of the past, we breathe the ether of immortality, and our cheeks mantle with eternal bloom.

LIFE.

Tʜᴇ following lines were by Mrs. Anna Letitia Barbauld, an English writer of great merit, extensively known as the author of excellent Hymns, and Early Lessons for Children. She was born in 1743, and lived to be nearly eighty-two years old. She employed the latter part of her life in editing a series of the best English novels and essays, accompanied with biographical sketches of the authors; and compositions in prose and verse continued to be her favorite occupation to the last.

L IFE! I know not what thou art,
But know that thou and I must part;
And when, or how, or where we met,
I own to me 's a secret yet.

Life! we have been long together,
Through pleasant and through cloudy weather.
'T is hard to part when friends are dear;
Perhaps 't will cost a sigh, a tear.
Then steal away; give little warning;
Choose thine own time;
Say not Good Night; but in some brighter clime
Bid me Good Morning!

THE MYSTERIOUS PILGRIMAGE.

By L. MARIA CHILD.

HERE was a traveller who set out upon a new road, not knowing whither it would lead him, nor whence he came, for he had been conveyed thither blindfold, and the bandage had been removed in his sleep. When he woke up he found himself among all sorts of pretty novelties, and he ran about hither and thither, eagerly asking, "What is this?" "What is that?" His activity was untiring. He tried to catch everything he saw, and hold it fast in his hand. But humming-birds whirred in his ears, and as soon as he tried to grasp them they soared up out of his reach, and left him gazing at their burnished throats glistening in the sunshine. Daintily painted butterflies poised themselves on such lowly flowers, that he thought he had but to stoop and take them; but they also floated away as soon as he approached. He walked through stately groves, where the sunshine was waltzing with leaf-shadows, and he tried to pick up the airy little dancers. "They won't let me catch 'em!" he exclaimed, petulantly. But on he hurried in pursuit of a squirrel, which ran nimbly away from him up into a tree, and there he sat on the high boughs, flourishing his pretty tail in the air. And so the traveller went along the wondrous road, always trying for something he could n't catch, not knowing that the pleasure was in the pursuit.

As he went on, the path widened and grew more attractive. Birds of radiant colors flitted about, and filled the air with charming variations of melody. Trees threw down showers of blossoms as he passed, and beneath his feet was a carpet of emerald-colored velvet, embroidered with a profusion of golden stars. Better than all, troops of handsome young men and lovely maidens joined him, all put blindfolded into the road, and travelling they knew not whither. And now they all set out upon a race after something higher up than squirrels or butterflies could go. "Look there! Look there! See what is before us!" they exclaimed. And lo! they all saw, away beyond, on hills of fleecy cloud, the most beautiful castles! The walls were of pearl, and rainbow pennons waved from the gold-pointed turrets. "We will take possession of those beautiful castles! That is where we are going to live!" they shouted to each other; and on they ran in pursuit of the rainbows. But they often paused in the chase, to frolic together. They laughed, and sang merry songs, and pelted each other with flowers, and danced within a ring of roses. It was a beautiful sight to see their silky ringlets tossed about by the breeze, and shining in the sunlight. But the game they liked best was looking into each other's eyes. They said they could see a blind boy there, with a bow and arrow; and always they were playing bo-peep with that blind boy, who was n't so blind as he seemed; for whenever he aimed his arrow at one of them, he was almost sure to hit. But they said the arrow was wreathed with flowers, and carried honey on its point; and there was nothing they liked quite so well as being shot at by the blind boy.

Sometimes their sport was interrupted by some stern-looking traveller, who said to them, in solemn tones, "Why do you make such fools of yourselves? Do you know whither this road leads?" Then they looked at each other bewildered, and said they did not. "I have been on this road much longer than you have," he replied; "and I think it is my duty to turn back sometimes and warn those who are coming after me. I tell you this road, where you go dancing so carelessly, abounds with pitfalls, generally concealed by flowers; and it ends in an awful, deep, dark hole. You are all running, like crazy fools, after rainbow castles in the air. You will never come up with them. They will vanish and leave nothing but a great black cloud. But what you have most to fear is a cruel giant, who is sure to meet you somewhere on the road. Nobody ever knows where; for he is invisible. Whatever he touches with his dart turns first to marble and then to ashes. You ought to be thinking of *him* and his dreadful arrow, instead of the foolish archer that you call the blind boy. Instead of chattering about roses and rainbows, you ought to be thinking of the awful black pit at the end of the road."

His words chilled the young men and maidens, like wind from a cavern. They looked at each other thoughtfully, and said, " Why does he try to spoil our sport with stories of pitfalls and invisible giants ? We don't know where the pitfalls are ; and if we go poking on the ground for them, how can we see the sunshine and the birds ? " Some of the more merry began to laugh at the solemn traveller, and soon they were all dancing again, or hurrying after the rainbow castles. They threw roses at each other by the way ; and often the little blind archer was in the heart of the roses, and played them mischievous tricks. They laughed merrily, and said to each other, " This is a beautiful road. It is a pity old Howlit don't know how to enjoy it."

But as our traveller passed on his way, he found that the words of the lugubrious prophet were sometimes verified. Now and then some of his companions danced into pitfalls covered with flowers. He himself slipped several times, but recovered his balance, and said it would teach him to walk more carefully. Others were bruised and faint in consequence of falls, and made no effort to rise up. In the kindness of his heart, he would not leave them thus; but always he tried to cheer them, saying, "Up, and try again, my brother! You won't make the same mistake again." Cheerful and courageous as he was, however, he saw the rainbow castles gradually fading from his vision; but they did not leave a great black cloud, as the solemn traveller had foretold; they melted into mild and steady sunlight. The young men and maidens, who had frolicked with him, went off in pairs, some into one bypath, some into another. Hand in hand with our traveller went a gentle companion, named Mary, in whose eyes he had long been playing at bo-peep with the blind boy. When they talked of this, they said they could still see him in each other's eye-mirrors, but now he had put his arrows into the quiver, and was stringing pearls. Mary brought little children to her companion, and they were more charming than all the playthings of their former time. They gazed fondly into the eyes of the little strangers, and said, " We see angels in these azure depths, and they are lovelier than the blind boy ever was." They played no more with roses now, but

4

gathered ripe fruits, glowing like red and purple
jewels, and planted grain which grew golden in
the sunshine.   Companions with whom they had
parted by the way occasionally came into their
path again, as they journeyed on.   Their moods
were various, according to their experiences.
Some still talked joyfully of the ever-varying beauty of the road.   Others sighed deeply, and said
they had found nothing to console them for
withered roses, and rainbows vanished.   Sometimes, when inquiries were made about former
acquaintances, the answer was that the invisible
giant had touched them, and they had changed to
marble.   Then a shadow seemed to darken the
pleasant road, and they spoke to each other in low
tones.   Some of those who sighed over withered
roses, told of frightful things done by this invisible
giant, and of horrid places whither they had heard
he conveyed his victims.   To children who were
chasing butterflies, and to young men and maidens
who were twining rose-wreaths, they said, " You
ought not to be wasting your time with such friv-
olous pastimes ; you ought to be thinking of the
awful invisible one, who is near us when we least
think of it."   They spoke in lugubrious tones, as
the solemn traveller had aforetime spoken to them.
But our traveller, who was cheerful of heart, said :
" It is not kind to throw a shadow across their
sunshine.   Let them enjoy themselves."   And his
Mary asked whether HE who made the beautiful

road had wasted time when HE *made* the roses
and the butterflies? And *why* had HE made
them, if they were not to be enjoyed?

But clouds sometimes came over this sunshine
of their souls. One of the little cherub boys
whom Mary had brought to her companion received the invisible touch, and became as marble.
Then a shadow fell across their path, and went
with them as they walked. They pressed each
other's hands in silence, but the thought was ever
in their hearts, "Whom will he touch next?"
The little cherub was not *in* the marble form; he
was still with them, though they knew it not.
Gradually their pain was softened, and they found
comfort in remembering his winning ways. Mary
said to her companion: "As we have travelled
along this mysterious road, the scenery has been
continually changing, even as we have changed.
But one form of beauty has melted into another,
so gently, so imperceptibly, that we have been
unconscious of the change, until it had passed.
Where all is so full of blessing, dearest, it cannot
be that this invisible touch is an exception." The
traveller sighed, and merely answered, "It is a
great mystery"; but her words fell on his heart
like summer dew on thirsty flowers. They
thought of the cherub boy, who had disappeared
from their vision, and the tears dropped slowly;
but as they fell, a ray of light from heaven kissed
them and illumined them with rainbows. They

clasped each other's hands more closely, and travelled on. Sometimes they smiled at each other, as they looked on their remaining little ones, running hither and thither chasing the bright butterflies. And Mary, who was filled with gentle wisdom, said, " The butterfly was once a crawling worm; but when it became stiff and cold, there emerged from it this wingéd creature, clothed with beauty." He pressed her hand tenderly; for again her soothing words fell upon his heart like dew on thirsty flowers.

Thus lovingly they passed on together, and many a blessing followed them; for whenever a traveller came along who was burdened and weary, they cheered him with hopeful words and helped to carry his load; and ever as they did so a softer light shone upon the landscape and bathed all things with a luminous glory. And still the scene was changing, ever changing. The glowing fruit had disappeared, and the golden grain was gathered. But now the forest-trees were all aglow, and looked like great pyramids of gorgeous flowers. The fallen foliage of the pines formed a soft carpet under their feet, ornamented with the shaded brown of cones and acorns, and sprinkled with gold-tinted leaves from the trees. As they looked on the mellowed beauty of the scenery, Mary said: " The Being who fashioned us, and created this marvellous road for us to travel in, must be wondrously wise and loving. How gradually and gently all things grow, and pass through magical changes. When we had had enough of chasing butterflies, the roses came to bind us together in fragrant wreaths. When the roses withered, the grain-fields waved beautifully in the wind, and purple and yellow grapes hung from the vines, like great clusters of jewels. And now, when fruit and grain are gathered, the forests are gorgeous in the sunlight, like immense beds of tulips. A friendly 'Good morning' to something new, mingles ever with the 'Good night, beloved,' to something that is passing away. Surely, dearest, this road, so full of magical transformations, *must* lead us to something more beautiful than itself." The traveller uncovered his head, raised his eyes reverently toward heaven, and said : " It is a great mystery. O Father, give us faith ! "

Before the glowing tints departed from the trees, Mary's cheek grew pale, and the light of her eyes began to fade. Then the traveller shuddered and shivered ; for a great shadow came between him and the sunshine ; he felt the approach of the invisible. More and more closely he pressed the beloved companion, to warm her with his heart. But her mild eyes closed, and the graceful form became as marble. No more could he look into those serene depths, where he had first seen the blind boy shooting his arrows, afterward stringing pearls, and then as an angel twining amaranthine crowns. In the anguish of his desolation, he

groaned aloud, and exclaimed: " O thou Dread
Destroyer! take me, too! I cannot live alone!
I cannot!" A gentle voice whispered, " Thou
art not alone, dearest. I am still with thee!" but
in the tumult of his grief he heard it not. The
children Mary had given him twined their soft
arms about his neck, and said: "Do not leave us
alone! We cannot find our way, without thee to
guide us." For their sakes, he stifled his groans,
and knelt down and prayed, " O Father, give me
strength and faith!"

Patiently he travelled on, leading the children.
By degrees they joined themselves to companions,
and went off in pairs into new paths, as he and his
Mary had done. The scenery around him grew
more dreary. The black branches of the trees
stood in gloomy relief against a cold gray sky.
The beautiful fields of grain ripening in the sunshine had changed to dry stubble fluttering mourn-
fully in the wind. But Nature, loath to part with
Beauty, still wore a few red berries, as a necklace
among her rags, and trimmed her scanty garments
with evergreen. But the wonderful transformations had not ceased. The fluttering brown rags
suddenly changed to the softest ermine robe, flashing with diamonds, and surmounted by a resplendent silver crown. The magical change reminded
our traveller that his lost companion had said,
" Surely a road so full of beautiful changes must
lead to something more beautiful than itself."
Again he knelt in reverence, and said, " All

things around me are miraculous. O Father, give me faith!"

The road descended into a deep valley, ever more narrow and dark. The nights grew longer. The ground was rugged and frozen, and the rough places hurt the pilgrim's stiff and weary feet. But when he was joined by pilgrims more exhausted than himself, he spoke to them in words of good cheer, and tried to help them over the rough places. The sunshine was no longer warm and golden, but its silvery light was still beautiful, and through the leafless boughs of the trees the moon and the stars looked down serenely on him. The children whom he had guided sometimes came and sang sweetly to him; and sometimes, when he was listening in the stillness, he seemed to hear mysterious echoes within himself, as if from a musical chime of bells on the other side of a river.

The shudderings and shiverings he had felt in presence of the cold shadow became more frequent; and he said to himself, " The Dread Destroyer is approaching more and more near." With trembling hands he uncovered his snow-white head, and looking upward, he said, " It is a fearful mystery. O Father, give me faith!" Praying thus, he sank on the cold ground, and sleepiness came over him. He felt something gently raising him, and slowly opening his eyes, he said, " Who art thou?" The stranger answered, " I am that Dread Destroyer, whose shadow always made thee shudder."

" Thou ! " exclaimed the tired pilgrim, in tones of joyful surprise; " why *thou* art an angel! " " Yes, I am an angel," he replied ; " and none but I can lead thee to thy loved ones. Thy Heavenly Father has sent me to take thee home." Gratefully the weary one sank into the arms of the giant he had so much dreaded. " All things are ordered in love," he said. " Thy touch is friendly, and thy voice like music."

They passed a narrow bridge over a dark river. On the other side was a flowery arch, bearing the motto, " The Gate of Life." Within it stood Mary and her cherub-boy, shining in transfigured light. The child stretched out his hands for an embrace, and Mary's welcoming smile was more beautiful than it had ever been in the happy old time of roses and rainbows. " This is only one more of the magical transformations, my beloved," she said. " It is as I told thee. The beautiful, mysterious road leads to something far more beautiful than itself. Come and see ! " With tender joy he kissed her and the angel child. There was a sound of harps and voices above him, singing, " The shadow has departed ! " And a cheerful response came from well-remembered voices he had left behind him on the road : " We are coming ! We are coming ! " Through all the chambers of his soul went ringing the triumphant chorus, " The shadow has departed ! " with the cheerful response, " We are coming ! We are coming ! "

THE HAPPIEST TIME.

By ELIZA COOK.

AN old man sat in his chimney-seat,
   As the morning sunbeam crept to his feet;
And he watched the Spring light as it came
With wider ray on his window frame.
He looked right on to the Eastern sky,
But his breath grew long in a trembling sigh,
And those who heard it wondered much
What Spirit hand made him feel its touch.

For the old man was not one of the fair
And sensitive plants in earth's parterre;
His heart was among the senseless things,
That rarely are fanned by the honey-bee's wings;
It bore no film of delicate pride,
No dew of emotion gathered inside;
O, that old man's heart was of hardy kind,
That seemeth to heed not the sun or the wind.

He had lived in the world as millions live,
Ever more ready to take than give;

He had worked and wedded, and murmured and blamed,
And just paid to the fraction what honesty claimed;
He had driven his bargains and counted his gold,
Till upwards of threescore years were told;
And his keen blue eye held nothing to show
That feeling had ever been busy below.

The old man sighed again, and hid
His keen blue eye beneath its lid;
And his wrinkled forehead, bending down,
Was knitting itself in a painful frown.
" I 've been looking back," the old man said,
On every spot where my path has laid,
Over every year my brain can trace,
To find the happiest time and place."

" And where and when," cried one by his side,
" Have you found the brightest wave in your tide?
Come tell me freely, and let me learn,
How the spark was struck that yet can burn.
Was it when you stood in stalwart strength,
With the blood of youth, and felt that at length
Your stout right arm could win its bread?"
The old man quietly shook his head.

" Then it must have been when love had come,
With a faithful bride to glad your home;
Or when the first-born cooed and smiled,
And your bosom cradled its own sweet child;
Or was it when that first-born joy,
Grew up to your hope, — a brave, strong boy, —
And promised to fill the world in your stead?"
The old man quietly shook his head.

" Say, was it then when fortune brought
The round sum you had frugally sought?
Was the year the happiest that beheld
The vision of poverty all dispelled?
Or was it when you still had more,
And found you could boast a goodly store
With labor finished and plenty spread?"
The old man quietly shook his head.

" Ah, no! ah, no! it was longer ago,"
The old man muttered, — sadly and low!
" It was when I took my lonely way
To the lonely woods in the month of May.
When the Spring light fell as it falleth now,
With the bloom on the sod and the leaf on the bough;
When I tossed up my cap at the nest in the tree;
O, that was the happiest time for me.

" When I used to leap and laugh and shout,
Though I never knew what my joy was about;
And something seemed to warm my breast,
As I sat on a mossy bank to rest.
That was the time; when I used to roll
On the blue-bells that covered the upland knoll,
And I never could tell why the thought should be,
But I fancied the flowers talked to me.

" Well I remember climbing to reach
A squirrel brood rocked on the top of a beech;
Well I remember the lilies so sweet,
That I toiled with back to the city street;
Yes, *that* was the time, — the happiest time, —
When I went to the woods in their May-day prime."

And the old man breathed with a longer sigh,
And the lid fell closer over his eye.

O, who would have thought this hard old man
Had room in his heart for such rainbow span?
Who would have deemed that wild copse flowers
Were tenderly haunting his latest hours?
But what did the old man's spirit tell,
In confessing it loved the woods so well?
What do we learn from the old man's sigh,
But that *Nature and Poetry cannot die?*

ODE OF ANACREON.

TRANSLATED FROM THE GREEK.

THE women tell me, every day,
That all my bloom has passed away.
"Behold!" the lively lasses cry,
Behold this mirror with a sigh!
Old wintry Time has shed his snows,
And bald and bare your forehead shows."
I will not either think or care
Whether old Time has thinned my hair;
But this I know and this I feel,
As years advancing on me steal,
And ever bring the end more near,
The joys of life become more dear;
And had I but one hour to live,
That hour to cheerfulness I'd give.

CICERO'S ESSAY ON OLD AGE.

THE following extracts are from a discourse "De Senectute," by Cicero, the world-renowned Roman orator, who was born one hundred and six years before Christ. He is one among many pleasant proofs that God never leaves himself without a witness in the hearts of men, in any age or country. Cicero says: "I have represented these reflections as delivered by the venerable Cato; but in delivering *his* sentiments, I desire to be understood as fully declaring *my own.*"

HOSE who have no internal resources of happiness will find themselves uneasy in every stage of human life; but to him who is accustomed to derive happiness from within himself, no state will appear as a real evil into which he is conducted by the common and regular course of Nature; and this is peculiarly the case with respect to old age. I follow Nature, as the surest guide, and resign myself with implicit obedience to her sacred ordinances. After having wisely distributed peculiar and proper enjoyments to all the preceding periods of life, it cannot be supposed that she would neglect the last, and leave it destitute of suitable advantages.   After a certain point of maturity is attained, marks of decay must necessarily appear ; but to this unavoidable condition of his present being every wise and good man will submit with contented and cheerful acquiescence.

Nothing can be more void of foundation than the assertion that old age necessarily disqualifies a man for taking part in the great affairs of the world.   If an old man cannot perform in business a part which requires the bodily strength and energy of more vigorous years, he can act in a nobler and more important character.   Momentous affairs of state are not conducted by corporeal strength and activity ; they require cool deliberation, prudent counsel, and authoritative influence ; qualifications which are strengthened and improved by increase of years.   Few among mankind arrive at old age; and this suggests a reason why the affairs of the world are not better conducted ; for age brings experience, discretion, and judgment, without which no well-formed government could have been established, or can be maintained.   Appius Claudius was not only old but blind, when he remonstrated in the Senate, with so much force and spirit, against concluding a peace with Pyrrhus.   The celebrated General Quintus Maximus led our troops to battle in his old age, with as much spirit as if he had been in the prime and vigor of life.   It was by his advice and eloquence, when he was extremely old, that the Cincian law concerning donatives was enacted. And it was not merely in the conspicuous paths of the world that this excellent man was truly great. He appeared still greater in the private and domestic scenes of life. There was a dignity in his deportment, tempered with singular politeness and affability ; and time wrought no alteration in his amiable qualities. How pleasing and instructive was his conversation ! How profound his knowledge of antiquity and the laws ! His memory was so retentive, that there was no event of any note, connected with our public affairs, with which he was not well acquainted. I eagerly embraced every opportunity to enjoy his society, feeling that after his death I should never again meet with so wise and improving a companion.

But it is not necessary to be a hero or a statesman, in order to lead an easy and agreeable old age. That season of life may prove equally serene and pleasant to him who has passed his days in the retired paths of learning. It is urged that old age impairs the memory. It may have that effect on those in whom memory was originally infirm, or who have not preserved its native vigor by exercising it properly. But the faculties of the mind will preserve their power in old age, unless they are suffered to become languid for want of due cultivation. Caius Gallus employed himself to the very last moments of his long life in measuring the distances of the heavenly orbs, and determining the dimensions of this our earth. How often has the sun risen on his astronomical calculations! How frequently has night overtaken him in the same elevated studies! With what delight did he amuse himself in predicting to us, long before they happened, the several lunar and solar eclipses! Other ingenious applications of the mind there are, though of a lighter nature, which may greatly contribute to enliven and amuse the decline of life. Thus Nœvius, in composing his poem on the Carthaginian war, and Plautus in writing his two last comedies, filled up the leisure of their latter days with wonderful complacency and satisfaction. I can affirm the same of our dramatic poet Livius, whom I remember to have seen in his old age; and let me not forget Marcus Cethegus, justly styled the soul of eloquence, whom I likewise saw in his old age exercising even his oratorical talents with uncommon force and vivacity. All these old men I saw pursuing their respective studies with the utmost ardor and alacrity. Solon, in one of his poems, written when he was advanced in years, glories that he learned something every day he lived. Plato occupied himself with philosophical studies, 'till they were interrupted by death at eighty-one years of age. Isocrates composed his famous discourse when he was ninety-four years old, and he lived five years afterward. Sophocles continued to write tragedies when he

was extremely old. Gray hair proved no obstacle
to the philosophic pursuits of Pythagoras, Zeno,
Cleanthes, or the venerable Diogenes. These
eminent persons persevered in their studies with
undiminished earnestness to the last moment of
their extended lives. Leontinus Gorgias, who
lived to be one hundred and seven years old, pursued his studies with unremitting assiduity to the
last. When asked if he did not wish to rid himself of the burden of such prolonged years, he
replied, " I find no reason to complain of old age."

The statement that age impairs our strength is
not without foundation. But, after all, imbecility
of body is more frequently caused by youthful
irregularities than by the natural and unavoidable
consequences of long life. By temperance and
exercise, a man may secure to his old age no
inconsiderable degree of his former spirit and
activity. The venerable Lucius Metellus preserved such a florid old age to his last moments,
as to have no reason to lament the depredations of
time. If it must be acknowledged that time in-
evitably undermines physical strength, it is equally
true that great bodily vigor is not required in the
decline of life. A moderate degree of force is
sufficient for all rational purposes. ˙I no more
regret the absence of youthful vigor, than when
young I lamented because I was not endowed with
the strength of a bull or an elephant. Old age
has, at least, sufficient strength remaining to train

the rising generation, and instruct them in the
duties to which they may hereafter be called; and
certainly there cannot be a more important or a
more honorable occupation.   There is satisfaction
in communicating every kind of useful knowledge;
and it must render a man happy to employ the
faculties of his mind to so noble and beneficial a
purpose, how much soever time may have impaired
his bodily powers.   Men of good sense, in the
evening of life, are generally fond of associating
with the younger part of the world, and, when
they discover amiable qualities in them, they find
it an alleviation of their infirmities to gain their
affection and esteem; and well-inclined young
men think themselves equally happy to be guided
into the paths of knowledge and virtue by the instructions of experienced elders.   I love to see the
fire of youth somewhat tempered by the sobriety
of age, and it is also pleasant to see the gravity of
age enlivened by the vivacity of youth.   Whoever
combines these two qualities in his character will
never exhibit traces of senility in his mind, though
his body may bear the marks of years.

As for the natural and necessary inconveniences
attendant upon length of years, we ought to counteract their progress by constant and resolute
opposition.   The infirmities of age should be resisted like the approaches of disease.   To this end
we should use regular and moderate exercise, and
merely eat and drink as much as is necessary to

repair our strength, without oppressing the organs of digestion. And the intellectual faculties, as well as the physical, should be carefully assisted. Mind and body thrive equally by suitable exercise of their powers ; with this difference, however, that bodily exertion ends in fatigue, whereas the mind is never wearied by its activity.

Another charge against old age is that it deprives us of sensual gratifications. Happy effect, indeed, to be delivered from those snares which allure youth into some of the worst vices ! "Reason," said Archytas, "is the noblest gift which God or Nature has bestowed on men. Now nothing is so great an enemy to that divine endowment as the pleasures of sense ; for neither temperance, nor any of the more exalted virtues, can find a place in that breast which is under the dominion of voluptuous passions. Imagine to yourself a man in the actual enjoyment of the highest gratifications mere animal nature is capable of receiving ; there can be no doubt that during his continuance in that state it would be utterly impossible for him to exert any one power of his rational faculties." The inference I draw from this is, that if the principles of reason and virtue have not proved sufficient to inspire us with proper contempt for mere sensual pleasures, we have cause to feel grateful to old age for at least weaning us from appetites it would ill become us to gratify ; for voluptuous passions are utter enemies to all the nobler faculties of the soul; they hold no communion with the manly virtues; and they cast a mist before the eye of reason. The little relish which old age leaves us for enjoyments merely sensual, instead of being a disparagement to that period of life, considerably enhances its value. If age renders us incapable of taking an equal share in the flowing cups and luxurious dishes of wealthy tables, it thereby secures us from painful indigestion, restless nights, and disordered reason.

But though his years will guard an old man from excess, they by no means exclude him from enjoying convivial gratifications in a moderate degree. I always took singular satisfaction in the anniversaries of those little societies called Confraternities. But the gratification I received from their entertainments arose much less from the pleasures of the palate than from the opportunities they afforded for enjoying the company and conversation of friends. I derive so much pleasure from hours devoted to cheerful discourse, that I love to prolong my meals, not only when the company is composed of men of my own years, few of whom indeed are now remaining, but also when it chiefly consists of young persons. And I acknowledge my obligations to old age for having increased my passion for the pleasures of conversation, while it has abated it for those which depend solely on the palate; though I do not find myself disqualified for that species of gratification, also.

The advantages of age are inestimable, if we consider it as delivering us from the tyranny of lust and ambition, from angry and contentious passions, from inordinate and irrational desires ; in a word, as teaching us to retire within ourselves, and look for happiness in our own souls. If to these moral benefits, which naturally result from length of days, be added the sweet food of the mind, gathered in the fields of science, I know of no season of life that is passed more agreeably than the learned leisure of a virtuous old age. Can the luxuries of the table, or the amusements of the theatre, supply their votaries with enjoyments worthy to be compared with the calm delights of intellectual employments ? And, in minds rightly formed and properly cultivated, these exalted delights never fail to improve and gather strength with years.

From the pleasures which attend a studious old age, let us turn to those derived from rural occupations, of which I am a warm admirer. Pleasures of this class are perfectly consistent with every degree of advanced years, as they approach more nearly than any others to those of a purely philosophical kind. They are derived from observing the nature and properties of our earth, which yields ready obedience to the cultivator's industry, and returns, with interest, whatever he places in her charge. But the profit arising from this fertility is by no means the most desirable circumstance of the farmer's labors. I am principally delighted with observing the powers of Nature, and tracing her processes in vegetable productions. How wonderful it is that each species is endowed with power to continue itself; and that minute seeds should develop so amazingly into large trunks and branches! The orchard, the vegetable garden, and the parterre diversify the pleasures of farming ; not to mention the feeding of cattle and the rearing of bees. Among my friends and neighbors in the country are several men far advanced in life, who employ themselves with so much activity and industry in agricultural business, that nothing important is carried on without their supervision. And these rural veterans do not confine their energies to those sorts of crops which are sown and reaped in one year. They occupy themselves in branches of husbandry from which they know they cannot live to derive any advantage. If asked why they thus expend their labor, they might well reply : " We do it in obedience to the immortal gods. By their bountiful providence we received these fields from our ancestors, and it is their will that we should transmit them to posterity with improvements." In my opinion there is no happier occupation than agriculture ; not only on account of its great utility to mankind, but also as the source of peculiar pleasures. I might expatiate on the beauties of verdant groves, and meadows, on the charming landscape of olive-trees and vineyards; but to say all in one word, there cannot be a more pleasing, or a more profitable scene than that of a well-cultivated farm. And where else can a man in the last stages of life more easily find warm sunshine, or a good fire in winter, or the pleasure of cooling shades and refreshing streams in summer?

It is often argued that old age must necessarily be a state of much anxiety and disquietude, on account of the near approach of death. That the hour of dissolution cannot be far distant from an aged man is undoubtedly true. But every event that is agreeable to the course of nature ought to be regarded as a real good; and surely nothing can be more natural than for the old to die. It is true that youth also is exposed to dissolution; but it is a dissolution obviously contrary to Nature's intentions, and in opposition to her strongest efforts. Fruit, before it is ripe, cannot be separated from the stalk without some degree of force; but when it is perfectly mature, it drops of itself: so the disunion of the soul and body is effected in the young by violence, but in the old it takes place by mere fulness and completion of years. This ripeness for death I perceive in myself with much satisfaction; and I look forward to my dissolution as to a secure haven, where I shall at length find a happy repose from the fatigues of a long voyage.

With regard to the consequences of our final
dissolution, I will venture to say that the nearer
death approaches the more clearly do I seem to
discern its real nature.   When I consider the
faculties with which the human mind is endowed,
its amazing celerity, its wonderful power in recol-
lecting past events, and its sagacity in discerning
the future, together with its numberless discoveries in arts and sciences, I feel a conscious conviction that this active, comprehensive principle cannot possibly be of a mortal nature.   And as this
unceasing activity of the soul derives its energy
from its own intrinsic and essential powers, without receiving it from any foreign or external impulse, it necessarily follows that its activity must
continue forever.   I am induced to embrace this
opinion, not only as agreeable to the best deduc-
tions of reason, but also in deference to the
authority of the noblest and most distinguished
philosophers.

I am well convinced that my dear departed
friends are so far from having ceased to live, that
the state they now enjoy can alone with propriety
be called life.   I feel myself transported with im-
patience to rejoin those whose characters I have
greatly respected and whose persons I have loved.
Nor is this earnest desire confined alone to those
excellent persons with whom I have been connected.   I ardently wish also to visit those celebrated
worthies of whom I have heard or read much.   To

this glorious *assembly I am speedily advancing;
and I would not be turned back on my journey,
even on the assured condition that my youth
should be again restored.   The sincere truth is,
if some divinity would confer on me a new grant
of life, I would reject the offer without the least
hesitation.   I have wellnigh finished the race,
and have no disposition to return to the starting-
point.   I do not mean to imitate those philosophers who represent the condition of human
nature as a subject of just lamentation.   The
satisfactions of this life are many ; but there
comes a time when we have had a sufficient
measure of its enjoyments, and may well depart
contented with our share of the feast.   I am far
from regretting that this life was bestowed on
me ; and I have the satisfaction of thinking that
I have employed it in such a manner as not to
have lived in vain.   In short, I consider this
world as a place which Nature never intended for my permanent abode ;
and I look on my departure
from it, not as being driven
from my habitation,
but simply as
leaving an
inn.

THE FOUNTAIN.

By WILLIAM WORDSWORTH.

WE talked with open heart, and tongue
　　Affectionate and true,
A pair of friends, though I was young,
　And Matthew seventy-two.

A village schoolmaster was he,
　With hair of glittering gray;
As blithe a man as you could see
　On a spring holiday.

And on that morning, through the grass
　And by the steaming rills,
We travelled merrily, to pass
　A day among the hills.

We lay beneath a spreading oak,
　Beside a mossy seat;
And from the turf a fountain broke,
　And gurgled at our feet.

" Now, Matthew," said I, "let us match
   This water's pleasant tune
With some old Border-Song, or Catch,
   That suits a summer's noon.

" Or of the church-clock and the chimes
   Sing here beneath the shade,
That half-mad thing of witty rhymes
   Which you last April made."

In silence Matthew lay, and eyed
   The spring beneath the tree ;
And thus the dear old man replied,
   The gray-haired man of glee :

" Down to the vale this water steers ;
   How merrily it goes !
'T will murmur on a thousand years,
   And flow as now it flows.

" And here, on this delightful day,
   I cannot choose but think
How oft, a vigorous man, I lay
   Beside this fountain's brink.

" My eyes are dim with childish tears,
   My heart is idly stirred,
For the same sound is in my ears
   Which in those days I heard.

" Thus fares it still in our decay ;
   And yet the wiser mind
Mourns less for what age takes away,
   Than what it leaves behind.

" The blackbird in the summer trees,
   The lark upon the hill,
Let loose their carols when they please,
   Are quiet when they will.

" With Nature never do *they* wage
   A foolish strife ; they see
A happy youth, and their old age
   Is beautiful and free.

" But *we* are pressed by heavy laws ;
   And often, glad no more,
We wear a face of joy, because
   We have been glad of yore.

" If there is one who need bemoan
   His kindred laid in earth,
The household hearts that were his own,
   It is the man of mirth.

" My days, my friend, are almost gone ;
   My life has been approved,
And many love me ; but by none
   Am I *enough* beloved."

" Now both himself and me he wrongs,
   The man who thus complains !
I live and sing my idle songs
   Upon these happy plains ;

" And, Matthew, for thy children dead,
   I 'll be a son to thee ! "
At this, he grasped my hand, and said,
   " Alas ! that cannot be ! "

We rose up from the fountain-side ;
　And down the smooth descent
Of the green sheep-track did we glide,
　And through the wood we went.

And ere we came to Leonard's Rock,
　He sang those witty rhymes
About the crazy old church-clock,
　And the bewildered chimes.

A POET'S BLESSING.

FROM THE GERMAN OF UHLAND.

As I wandered the fields along,
Listening to the lark's sweet song,
I saw an old man working there,
A laborer with hoary hair.

" Blessings upon this field ! " I said ;
" Fruitful by faithful labor made.
And blessings on thy wrinkled hand,
Thus scattering seed along the land ! "

He answered me, with earnest face,
"A poet's blessing 's out of place ;
Likely enough that Heaven, in scorn,
Will send us flowers instead of corn."

" Nay, friend," said I, " my tuneful powers
Wake not to life too many flowers ;
Only enough to grace the land,
And fill thy little grandson's hand."

BERNARD PALISSY.*

> " Call him not old, whose visionary brain
> Holds o'er the past its undivided reign.
> For him in vain the envious seasons roll,
> Who bears eternal summer in his *soul*.
> If yet the minstrel's song, the poet's lay,
> Spring with her birds, or children with their play,
> Or maiden's smile, or heavenly dream of Art,
> Stir the few life-drops creeping round his heart, —
> Turn to the record where his years are told, —
> Count his gray hairs, — *they* cannot make him old ! "

BERNARD PALISSY was born in one of the southwestern districts of France, in 1509 ; more than three hundred and fifty years ago, and more than a century before our forefathers landed on Plymouth Rock. The art of making colored glass, and of painting on glass, had been for centuries in great requisition, for the windows of castles and cathedrals. It was considered an occupation so honorable, that poor nobles sometimes resorted to it with-

* These facts are gleaned from Morley's Life of Palissy the Potter.

out losing caste ; though the prejudices concerning
rank were at that time very strong. The manufacture was generally carried on in the depths of
forests, partly for the convenience of gathering fuel
for the furnaces, and partly to avoid the danger
of fire in towns. Around these manufactories the
workmen erected their cabins, and night and day
the red flames of the furnaces lighted up trees and
shrubbery with a lurid glow. It is supposed that
Bernard was born and reared in one of these ham-
lets, secluded from the world. The immense forests furnished a vast amount of chestnuts, which
constituted the principal food of the peasantry.
Constant labor in the open air, combined with this
extreme simplicity of diet, formed healthy, vigorous men, free-hearted, simple, and brave. Whether
Bernard's father, who is supposed to have been a
modeller of glass, was a decayed gentleman, or
simply a peasant, is not known. Bernard, by some
means, learned to read and write, which was not
an ordinary accomplishment at that period. He
also had a great talent for drawing, which he
improved, either by practice or instruction. In
other respects his education was simply that of the
peasantry around him. In his own account of
his early days he says, " I had no other books than
heaven and earth, which are open to all." These
volumes, however, he studied with lively interest
and the closest observation. He took notice of
the growth of plants and the habits of animals.

He soon began to paint on paper the likenesses of
birds, lizards, and trees. As his skill increased, he
made portraits of his mother and the neighbors,
and landscapes containing the houses they lived
in. The preparation of colors for glass early
awakened an interest in chemical combinations;
but there were then no books on the subject, and
he could only increase his stock of knowledge by
repeated experiments. His skill in drawing enabled him to produce a variety of new patterns
for glass-work, and this, combined with his knowledge of colors, rendered his services much more
important than those of a common workman. But
the once profitable business was now in its decline.
People began to find out that the exclusion of
sunshine was unwholesome, and that the obstruc-
tion of light rendered their dwellings gloomy.
Moreover, windows in those days, being opened
on hinges, were much more exposed to be shat-
tered by storms. To repair stained or painted glass
was an expensive process; and in order to avoid
the frequent necessity of it, people fastened their
windows into the wall, so that they could not be
opened. This excluded air, as well as light and
sun-warmth; and gradually colored windows fell
into disuse.

Bernard's father was poor, and the profits of his
business were too scanty to yield a comfortable
support for his family. Therefore, the young
man, when he was eighteen years old, strapped

a scantily filled wallet upon his shoulders, and marched forth into the world to seek his fortune. Francis I. and Charles V. were then devastating half Europe by their wars, and the highways were filled with military adventurers and crippled soldiers. From these the young traveller obtained his first glimpses of the violence and intrigues going on in the world beyond· his native forests.

He was also overtaken by a travelling cloth-merchant, who told him of many new things. In order to dignify his own calling, he enumerated many great men who had been employed in trade. Among others, he mentioned a renowned Athenian, called " the divine Plato," by reason of the excellence of his wisdom, who had sold olive-oil in Egypt, to defray the expenses of travelling there. " I never heard of Plato," said Bernard. " O, you are a wild bird from the forest," replied the trader ; " you can only pipe as you have been taught by nature. But I advise you to make acquaintance with books. Our King Francis is now doing so much to encourage the arts and sciences, that every artisan can become wise, if he makes good use of his leisure. Our shops may now be our schools." " Then I should wish the whole world to be my shop," rejoined Bernard. " I feel that earth and air are full of mysteries and wonders ; full of the sublime wisdom of God."

So he wandered on, reading, as he had done

5 *

from childhood, in " the book of earth and heaven, which is open to all."

> " For Nature, the old nurse, took
>   The child upon her knee,
>   Saying, ' Here is a story-book
>   Thy Father has written for thee.'

> " ' Come, wander with me,' she said,
> .   ' Into regions yet untrod ;
>   And read what is still unread
>   In the manuscripts of God.'

> " And he wandered away and away,
>   With Nature, the dear old nurse,
>   Who sang to him night and day
>   The rhymes of the universe."

If lizards were basking in the sunshine, he stopped to admire their gliding motions, and prismatic changes of color. If he found a half-covered snail among the wet mosses, he lingered till he ascertained that it was gradually making a new shell from its own saliva. If a stone was curious in form or shape, he picked it up and put it in his wallet ; and oftentimes he would crack them, to discover their interior structure. Every new flower and seed attracted his attention, and excited wonder at the marvellous varieties of Nature. These things are hinted at all through his writings. He says : " In walking under the fruit-trees, I received a great contentment and many joyous pleasures ; for I saw the squirrels gathering the fruits, and leaping from branch to branch, with

many pretty looks and gestures. I saw nuts gathered by the rooks, who rejoiced in taking their
repast, dining on the said nuts. Under the apple-
trees, I found hedgehogs, that rolled themselves
into a round form, and, thrusting out their sharp
quills, they rolled over the apples, which stuck on
the points, and so they went burdened. These
things have made me such a lover of the fields,
that it seems to me there are no treasures in the
world so precious as the little branches of trees and
plants. I hold them in more esteem than mines
of gold and silver." This loving communion with
Nature was not mere idle dreaming. Always he
was drawing inferences from what he saw, and
curiously inquiring into the causes of things.

He supported himself by painting glass, and
sketching portraits. He says, in his modest way,
" They thought me a better painter than I was."
If he arrived in a town where a cathedral or an
abbey was being built, he sometimes tarried long to
make a variety of rich patterns for the windows.
In other places, he would find only a few repairs
required in the windows of castles or churches, and
so would quickly pass on. To arrange mosaic patterns of different-colored glass required constant
use of rule and compass, and this suggested the
study of geometry, which he pursued with characteristic eagerness. The knowledge thus acquired
made him a skilful surveyor, and he was much
employed in mapping out boundaries, and making

plans for houses and gardens, a business which he found more profitable than glass-work or portraits. These various occupations brought him occasionally into contact with men who were learned in the arts and sciences, according to the standard of learning at that time, and his active mind never failed to glean something from such interviews. A French translation of the Scriptures had been published in 1498. He seems to have had a copy with him during his travels, and to have studied it with reverential attention. Thus constantly observing and acquiring, the young man traversed France, from Spain to the Netherlands, and roamed through a portion of Germany. Ten years were spent in this way, during which he obtained the best portion of that education which he afterward turned to good account.

He is supposed to·have been about twenty-nine years old, when he married, and settled in the town of Saintes, in the western part of France. He supported his family by glass-work, portraits, and surveying. A few years after his marriage, some one showed him an enamelled cup, brought from Italy. It seemed a slight incident ; but it woke the artistic spirit slumbering in his soul, and was destined to effect a complete revolution in his life. He says : " It was an earthen cup, turned and enamelled with so much beauty, that from that time I entered into controversy with my own thoughts. I began to think that if I should discover how to måke enamels, I could make earthen vessels very prettily ; because God had gifted me with some knowledge of drawing. So, regardless of the fact that I had no knowledge of clays, I began to seek for the enamel, as a man gropes in the dark."

In order to begin to comprehend the difficulties he had to encounter, we must know that only the rudest kind of common pottery had then been made in France, and even with the manufacture of that he was entirely unacquainted. If he had been unmarried, he might have travelled among the potters of Europe, as he had among the glass-makers, and have obtained useful hints from them ; but his family increased fast, and needed his protection and support. Tea was not introduced into Europe till a hundred years later ; and there were no specimens of porcelain from China, except here and there a costly article imported by the rich. He was obliged to test the qualities of various kinds of clays ; what chemical agents would produce enamel ; what other agents would produce colors ; and the action of heat on all of them. He bought quantities of earthen jars, broke them into fragments, applied to each piece some particular chemical substance, and tried them all in a furnace. He says : " I pounded all the substances I could suppose likely to make anything. Having blundered several times, at great expense, and through much labor, I was every day pounding and grinding new materials, and constructing new furnaces, which cost much money and consumed my wood and my time." While these expenses were going on, his former occupations were necessarily suspended; thus " the candle was burning out at both ends." His wife began to complain. Still he went on, trying new compounds, as he says, " always with great cost, loss of time, confusion and sorrow." The privations of his family and the anxiety of his wife gave him so much pain, that he relinquished his experiments for a while. He says : " Seeing I could not in this way come at my intention, I occupied myself in my art of painting and glass-working, and comported myself as if I were not zealous to dive any more into the secret of enamels." The king ordered extensive surveys, and he found that employment so profitable, that his family were soon at ease again. But that Italian cup was always in his mind. He says : " When I found myself with a little money, I resumed my affection for pursuing in the track of the enamels." For two years he kept up a series of experiments, under all manner of difficulties, and always without success. His wife scolded, and even his own courage began to fail. At last he applied more than three hundred kinds of mixtures to more than three hundred fragments, and put them all in the furnace ; resolved that if this experiment proved a failure, he would try no more. He tells us : " *One* of the pieces came out white and polished, in a way that caused me such joy, as made me think I was become a new creature." He was then thirty-seven years old.

He was merely at the beginning of what he aimed to accomplish. He had discovered how to make the enamel, but he still knew nothing of pottery, or of the effect which various degrees of heat would produce on colors. A new furnace was necessary, and he proceeded to build it, with prodigious labor. Being too poor to hire help, he brought bricks on his own back from a distant kiln ; he made his own mortar, and drew the water with which it was tempered. He fashioned vessels of clay, to which his enamel could be applied. For more than a month he kept up an incessant fire night and day, and was continually grinding materials in a hand-mill, which it usually required two men to turn. He believed himself to be very near complete success, and everything depended upon not letting the heat of the furnaces go down. In the desperation of his poverty and the excitement of his sanguine hopes, he burned the garden-fence, and even some of the tables, doors, and floors of his house. His wife became frantic, and gave him no peace. She was to be pitied, poor woman! Not being acquainted with chemical experiments, she did not know, as *he* did, that he was really on the point of making a great and lucrative discovery. She had heard it so long that she did n't believe it. They had a large family of children, and while their father was trying expensive experiments, several of them were dying of a disease prevalent at that time.   It was a gloomy and trying period for all of them.   He says : " I suffered an anguish that I cannot speak. I was quite exhausted and dried up by the heat of the furnace.   It was more than a month since my shirt had been dry upon me.   I was the object of mockery.   Even those from whom solace was due ran crying through the town that I was burning my floors.   In this way I came to be regarded as a madman.   I was in debt in several places.   I had two children at nurse, and was unable to pay the nurses.   Men jested at me as I passed through the streets, and said it was right for me to die of hunger, since I had left following my trade.   Some hope still remained to sustain me, for my last experiments had turned out tolerably well, and I thought I knew enough to get my living ; but I found I was far enough from that yet.

The want of means to build sheds to cover his clay vessels was another great difficulty.   After working all day, and late into the night, sometimes a heavy rain would spoil all his work, just as he had it ready to bake.   He describes himself, on such occasions, as utterly weak and exhausted, so that walking home he " reeled like a man drunk with wine."   He says : " Filled with a great sorrow, inasmuch as having labored long I saw my labor wasted, I would retire soiled and drenched,

to find in my chamber a second persecution worse
than the first; which now causes me to marvel
that I was not consumed by suffering."

In the midst of all this tribulation, the struggling artist had one source of consolation. Jean
Cauvin, better known to us as John Calvin, had
been preaching Protestant doctrines in France, and
had given rise to the sect called Huguenots. The
extravagance and licentiousness of society at that
period, and the abuses practised by a powerful and.
wealthy priesthood, naturally inclined this pure
and simple-minded man to the doctrines of the
Reformers. He became acquainted with an artisan
of the same turn of mind, whom he describes as
"simple, unlearned, and marvellously poor." His
delight was to hear Palissy read the Scriptures.
Gradually his listeners increased to ten, and they
formed a little society, which took turns in exhortation and prayer. One of them is supposed to
have been an innkeeper, who, from religious sympathy, allowed poor Palissy to take meals at his
house on credit.

He still continued his experiments, and met
with successive disappointments of one kind or
another. At last, he thought he had learned
how to adjust everything just right; and confident of success, he one day put into the oven a
batch of vessels, beautifully formed and painted.
But a new misfortune awaited him. The materials of his furnace contained flints. These ex-

H

panded and burst with the great heat, and struck
into the vessels while they were soft, injuring the
enamel, and covering the surface with irregular
sharp points. This blow almost prostrated him;
for he had expected this beautiful batch would
bring a considerable sum of money for the support
of his family, and put to silence those that jeered
at him. But he was a man of wonderful endur-
ance. He says: " Having remained some time .
upon the bed, I reflected that if a man should fall
into a pit, it would be his duty to try to get out
again." So the brave soul roused himself, and set
to work diligently to earn money, by his old trades
of painting and surveying.

Having supplied the necessities of his family, he
again returned to his pottery; fully believing that
his losses and hazards were over, and that he could
now make articles that would bring good prices.
But new disappointments awaited him. The green
with which he painted his lizards burnt before the
brown of the serpents melted; a strong current of
air in the furnace blew ashes all over his beautiful
vessels and spoiled the enamel. He says: " Before I could render my different enamels fusible
at the same degree of heat, I thought I should be
at the door of my sepulchre. I was so wasted in
my person that there was no form nor prominence
in the muscles of my arms or legs; also the said
legs were throughout of one size; so that when I
walked, garters and stockings were at once down

upon my heels. I often roamed about the fields, considering my miseries and weariness, and above all things, that in my own house I could have no peace, nor do anything that was considered good. I was despised and mocked by all. Nevertheless, I had a hope, which caused me to work so like a man, that I often did my best to laugh and amuse people who came to see me, though within me all was very sad."

At the end of ten years from the commencement of his experiments, he succeeded in making a kind of ware, of mixed enamels, resembling jasper. It was not what he had been aiming to accomplish, but it was considered pretty, and sold well enough to support his family comfortably. While he was making continual improvements in his pottery, the Huguenots were increasing to a degree that provoked persecution. A schoolmaster in a neighboring town, who " preached on Sundays, and was much beloved by the people," was brought to Saintes and publicly burnt. But Palissy and his little band were not intimidated. They continued to meet for exhortation and prayer. At first it was done mostly at midnight; but the pure and pious lives of these men and women formed such a contrast to the licentiousness and blasphemy prevailing round them, that they gradually gained respect; insomuch that they influenced the magistrates of the town to pass laws restraining gambling and dissipation. So

great a change was produced, that, when Palissy
was fifty-one years old, he says: "On Sundays
you might see tradesmen rambling through the
fields, groves, and other places, in bands, singing
psalms, canticles, and spiritual songs, or reading
and instructing each other. You might see young
women seated in gardens and other places, who
in like way delighted themselves with singing all
holy things. The very children were so well instructed that they had no longer a puerility of
manner, but a look of manly fortitude. These
things had so well prospered that people had
changed their old manners, even to their very
countenances."

After six years more of successive improvements, making sixteen years in the whole, this
persevering man at last accomplished the object
for which he had toiled and suffered so much.
He produced a very beautiful kind of china, which
became celebrated under the name of Palissy
Ware. These articles were elaborately adorned
with vines, flowers, butterflies, lizards, serpents,
and other animals. He had always been such a
loving observer of nature that we cannot wonder
at being told " he copied these, in form and color,
with the minute exactness of a naturalist, so that
the species of each could be determined accu-
rately." These beautiful articles sold at high
prices. Orders flowed in from kings and nobles.
The Constable Montmorenci, a nobleman of im-

mense wealth, employed Palissy to decorate his magnificent Chateau d'Ecouen, about twelve miles from Paris. There he made richly painted windows, covered with Scripture scenes, some of his own designing, others copied from Raphael and Albert Durer. Vases and statuettes of his beautiful china were deposited in various places ; and the floors of chapel and galleries were inlaid with china tiles of his painting. Among the groves he formed a very curious grotto of china. He modelled rugged rocks, " sloping, tortuous, and lumpy," which he painted with imitations of such herbs and mosses as grow in moist places. Brilliant lizards appeared to glide over its surface, " in many pleasant gestures and agreeable contortions." In the trenches of water were some living frogs and fishes, and other china ones, which so closely resembled them as not to be easily distinguished. At the foot of the rocks, branches of coral, of his manufacture, appeared to grow in the water. A poet of that period, praising this work, says: " The real lizard on the moss has not more lustre than the lizards in that house made famous by your new work. The plants look not sweeter in the fields, and green meadows are not more preciously enamelled, than those which grow under your hand." The Constable Montmorenci built a convenient shop for him, where he worked with two of his sons. A large china dog at the door was so natural, that the dogs often barked at it and challenged it to fight.

Meanwhile, a terrible storm was gathering over
the heads of the Huguenots. Civil war broke out
between the Catholics and Protestants. Old men
were burnt for quoting Scripture, and young girls
stabbed for singing psalms. But worldly prosperity and the flattery of the great could not tempt
Palissy to renounce or conceal his faith. He pursued his artistic labors, though he says, " For two
months I was greatly terrified, hearing nothing
every day but reports of horrible murders." He
would have fallen among the first victims, had it
not been for written protections from powerful
nobles, who wanted ornamental work done which
no other man could do. The horrible massacre
of St. Bartholomew occurred when he was sixty-
three years old, but he escaped by aid of his
powerful patrons. The officers appointed to hunt
out Huguenots longed to arrest him, but did not
dare to do it in the daytime. At last they came
tramping about his house at midnight, and carried
him off to a prison in Bordeaux. The judges
would gladly have put him to death, but their
proceedings were stopped by orders from the
Queen Mother, Catherine de Medicis. Montmorenci, Montpensier, and other influential Catholic
nobles, who had works uncompleted, and who
doubtless felt kindly toward the old artist, inter-
ceded with her, and she protected him ; not because he was a good man, but because the art he
practised was unique and valuable. The enam-

elled Italian cup, which had troubled so many
years of his life, proved the cause of its being
saved.

The last ten years of Palissy's mortal existence
were spent in Paris. He had an establishment in
the grounds of the Tuileries, where he manufactured vases, cups, plates, and curious garden-basins
and baskets, ornamented with figures in relief.
His high reputation drew toward him many men
of taste and learning, who, knowing his interest in
all the productions of Nature, presented him with
·many curious specimens of shells, minerals, fos-
sils, &c. He formed these into a Museum, where
scholars met to discuss the laws and operations of
Nature. This is said to have been the first society
established in Paris for the pure advancement of
science. When he was sixty-six years old, he began a course of public lectures, which he continued
to deliver annually for ten years. These were the
first lectures on Natural History ever delivered in
Paris. The best men of the Capital went there to
discuss with him, and to hear him state, in his simple, earnest fashion, the variety of curious things
he had observed in travels by mountain and sea-
shore, through field and forest, and in his experiments on glass and china. Some pedants were
disposed to undervalue his teachings, because he
had never learned Greek or Latin. Undisturbed
by this, he cordially invited them to come and dis-
prove his statements if they could, saying : "I want

to ascertain whether the Latins know more upon these subjects than I do. I am indeed a simple artisan, poorly enough trained in letters; but the things themselves have not less value than if they were uttered by a man more eloquent. I had rather speak truth in my rustic tongue, than lie in rhetoric."

He published several books on Agriculture, Volcanoes, the Formation of Rocks, the Laws of Water, &c. His last book was written when he was seventy-one years old. Scientific knowledge was then in its infancy, but adequate judges consider his ideas far in advance of his time. A modern French scholar calls him, " So great a naturalist as only Nature could produce." There is a refreshing simplicity about his style of writing, and his communications with the world were obviously not the result of vanity, but of general benevolence and religious reverence. He felt that all he had was from God, and that it was a duty to impart it freely. He says : " I had employed much time in the study of earths, stones, waters, and metals; and old age pressed me to multiply the talents God had given me. For that reason, I thought it would be good to bring to the light those excellent secrets, in order to bequeath them to posterity."

He continued vigorous in mind and body, and was remarked for acuteness and ready wit. He abstained from theological discussions in his teach-

ings, but made no secret of the fact that his opinions remained unchanged. Amid the frivolity,
dissipation, and horrid scenes of violence that were
going on in Paris, he quietly busied himself making artistic designs, and imparting his knowledge
of natural history ; recreating himself frequently
with the old pleasure of rambling in field and
forest, taking loving observation of all God's little
creatures.

He was seventy-six years old, when the king,
Henry III., issued a decree forbidding Protestants to exercise their worship, on pain of death,
and banishing all who had previously practised it.
Angry bigots clamored for the death of the brave
old potter. The powerful patrons of his art
again prevented his execution ; but the tide was
so strong against the Reformers, that he was sent
to the Bastile. Two Huguenot girls were in prison
with him, and they mutually sustained each other
with prayer and psalms. The king, in his fashionable frills and curls, occasionally visited the prisons,
and he naturally felt a great desire that the distinguished old Bernard Palissy should make a
recantation of his faith. One day he said to him :
" My good man, you have been forty-five years in
the service of the queen, my mother, or in mine ;
and in the midst of all the executions and mas-
sacres, we have allowed you to live in your religion.
But now I am so hardly pressed by the Guise party,
and by my people, that I am compelled, in spite of

6

myself, to order the execution of these two poor young women, and of yourself also, unless you recant." " Sire," replied the old man, " that is not spoken like a king. You have often said you pitied *me ;* but now I pity *you ;* because you have said, ' I am *compelled.*' These girls and I, who have our part in the kingdom of Heaven, will teach you to talk more royally. Neither the Guises, nor all your people, nor yourself, can compel the old potter to bow down to your images of clay. I can die."

The two girls were burnt a few months afterward. Palissy remained in prison four years, and there he died at eighty years of age. The secrets of the Bastile were well kept, and we have no record of those years. We only know that, like John Bunyan, he wrote a good deal in prison. The thick, dark walls must have been dismal to one who so loved the free air, and who valued trees and shrubs " beyond silver and gold." But the martyr was not alone. He had with him the God whom he trusted, and the memories of an honest, useful, and religious life.

OLD AGE COMING.

By Elizabeth Hamilton, a Scotch writer, author of "The Cottagers of Glenburnie," and several other sensible and interesting works. She died, unmarried, about fifty years ago, nearly sixty years old. These lines were written in such very broad Scotch, that I have taken the liberty to render them in English, making no changes, except a few slight variations, which the necessities of rhyme required.

IS that Old Age, who's knocking at the gate?
I trow it is. He sha'n't be asked to wait.
You're kindly welcome, friend! Nay, do not fear
To show yourself! You'll cause no trouble here.
I know there're some who tremble at your name,
As though you brought with you reproach or shame;
And who of thousand lies would bear the sin,
Rather than own you for their kith and kin.
But far from shirking you as a disgrace,
Thankful I am to live to see your face.
Nor will I e'er disown you, or take pride
To think how long I might your visit hide.
I'll do my best to make you well respected,
And fear not for your sake to be neglected.

Now you have come, and, through all kinds of weather,
We're doomed from this time forth to jog together,
I'd fain make compact with you, firm and strong,
On terms of give and take, to hold out long.
If you'll be civil, I will liberal be ;
Witness the list of what I'll give to thee.
First then, I here make o'er, for good and aye,
All youthful fancies, whether bright or gay.
Beauties and graces, too, might be resigned,
But much I fear they would be hard to find ;
For 'gainst your daddy Time they could not stand,
Nor bear the grip of his relentless hand.
But there's my skin, which you may further crinkle,
And write your name, at length, on ev'ry wrinkle.
On my brown locks your powder you may throw,
And bleach them to your fancy, white as snow.
But look not, Age, so wistful at my mouth,
As if you longed to pull out ev'ry tooth !
Let them, I do beseech you, keep their places !
Though, if you like, you're free to paint their faces.
My limbs I yield you ; and if you see meet
To clap your icy shackles on my feet,
I'll not refuse ; but if you drive out gout,
Will bless you for 't, and offer thanks devout.
So much I give to you with free good-will ;
But, O, I fear that more you look for still.
I know, by your stern look and meaning leers,
You want to clap your fingers on my ears.
Right willing, too, you are, as I surmise,
To cast your misty powder in my eyes.
But, O, in mercy spare my little twinklers !
And I will always wear your crystal blinkers.

Then 'bout my ears I 'd fain a bargain strike,
And give my hand upon it, if you like.
Well then — would you consent their use to *share?*
'T would serve us both, and be a bargain rare.
I 'd have it thus, — When babbling fools intrude,
Gabbling their noisy nonsense for no good ;
Or when ill-nature, well brushed up with wit,
With sneer sarcastic, takes its aim to hit ;
Or when detraction, meanest sort of pride,
Spies out small faults, and seeks great worth to hide ;
Then make me deaf as ever deaf can be !
At all *such* times, my ears I lend to thee.
But when, in social hours, you see combined
Genius and wisdom, fruits of heart and mind,
Good sense, good nature, wit in playful mood,
And candor, e'en from ill extracting good ;
O, then, old friend, I *must* have back my hearing !
To want it then would be an ill past bearing.
I 'd rather sit alone, in wakeful dreaming,
Than catch the sound of words without their meaning.
You will not promise ?   O, you 're very glum !
Right hard to manage, you 're so cold and dumb !
No matter. — Whole and sound I 'll keep my *heart.*
Not from one crumb on 't will I ever part.
Its kindly warmth shall ne'er be chilled by all
The coldest breath that from your lips can fall.
You need n't vex yourself, old churl, nor fret !
My kindly feelings you shall never get.
And though to take my hearing you rejoice,
In spite of you, I 'll still hear friendship's voice.
And though you take the rest, it shall not grieve me ;
For gleams of cheerful spirits you *must* leave me.

But let me whisper in your ear, Old Age,
I 'm bound to travel with you but one stage.
Be 't long or short, you cannot keep me back ;
And when we reach the *end* on 't, you must pack !
Be 't soon or late, we part forever there !
Other companionship I then shall share.
This blessed change to me you 're bound to bring.
You need not think I shall be loath to spring
From your poor feeble side, you churl uncouth !
Into the arms of Everlasting Youth.
All that your thieving hands have stolen away
He will, with interest, to me repay.
Fresh gifts and graces freely he 'll bestow,
More than the heart has wished, or mind can know.
You need not wonder then, nor swell with pride,
That I so kindly welcomed you as guide
To one who 's far your better.   Now all 's told.
Let us set out upon our journey cold.
With no vain boasts, no vain regrets tormented,
We 'll quietly jog on our way, contented.

———————

" On he moves to meet his latter end,
    Angels around befriending virtue's friend ;
    Sinks to the grave with unperceived decay,
    While resignation gently slopes the way ;
    And, all his prospects brightening to the last,
    His heaven commences ere the world is past."

GOLDSMITH.

UNMARRIED WOMEN.

By L. MARIA CHILD.

OCIETY moves slowly toward civilization, but when we compare epochs half
a century, or even a quarter of a century apart, we perceive many signs that
progress *is* made. Among these pleasant indications is the fact that the phrase " old maid " has
gone wellnigh out of fashion; that jests on the
subject are no longer considered witty, and are
never uttered by gentlemen. In my youth, I not
unfrequently heard women of thirty addressed
something in this style: " What, not married yet?
If you don't take care, you will outstand your
market." Such words could never be otherwise
than disagreeable, nay, positively offensive, to any
woman of sensibility and natural refinement; and
that not merely on account of wounded vanity, or
disappointed affection, or youthful visions receding
in the distance, but because the idea of being in

the *market*, of being a *commodity*, rather than an individual, is odious to every human being.

I believe a large proportion of unmarried women are so simply because they have too much conscience and delicacy of feeling to form marriages of interest or convenience, without the concurrence of their affections and their taste. A woman who is determined to be married, and who "plays her cards well," as the phrase is, usually succeeds. But how much more estimable and honorable is she who regards a life-union as too important and sacred to be entered into from motives of vanity or selfishness.

To rear families is the ordination of Nature, and where it is done conscientiously it is doubtless the best education that men or women can receive. But I doubt the truth of the common remark that the discharge of these duties makes married people less selfish than unmarried ones. The selfishness of single women doubtless shows itself in more petty forms; such as being disturbed by crumbs on the carpet, and a litter of toys about the house. But fathers and mothers are often selfish on a large scale, for the sake of advancing the worldly prosperity or social condition of their children. Not only is spiritual growth frequently sacrificed in pursuit of these objects, but principles are trampled on, which involve the welfare of the whole human race. Within the sphere of my own observation, I must confess that there is a larger proportion of unmarried than of married women whose sympathies are active and extensive.

I have before my mind two learned sisters, familiar with Greek, Latin, and French, and who, late in life, acquired a knowledge of German also. They spent more than sixty years together, quietly digging out gold, silver, or iron from the rich mines of ancient and modern literature, and freely imparting their treasures wherever they were called for. No married couple could have been more careful of each other in illness, or more accommodating toward each other's peculiarities; yet they were decided individuals; and their talk never wanted

> " An animated No,
> To brush its surface, and to make it flow."

Cultivated people enjoyed their conversation, which was both wise and racy; a steady light of good sense and large information, with an occasional flashing rocket of not ill-natured satire. Yet their intellectual acquisitions produced no contempt for the customary occupations of women. All their friends received tasteful keepsakes of their knitting, netting, or crocheting, and all the poor of the town had garments of their handiwork. Neither their sympathies nor their views were narrowed by celibacy. Early education had taught them to reverence everything that was established; but with this reverence they mingled

6 * I

a lively interest in all the great progressive questions of the day.   Their ears were open to the
recital of everybody's troubles and everybody's
joys.   On New Year's day, children thronged
round them for books and toys, and every poor
person's face lighted up as they approached; for
they were sure of kindly inquiries and sympathizing words from them, and their cloaks usually
opened to distribute comfortable slippers, or warm
stockings of their own manufacture.   When this
sisterly bond, rendered so beautiful by usefulness
and culture, was dissolved by death, the survivor
said of her who had departed: " During all her
illness she leaned upon me as a child upon its
mother; and O, how blessed is now the consciousness that I never disappointed her! "   This
great bereavement was borne with calmness, for
loneliness was cheered by hope of reunion.   On the
anniversary of her lōss the survivor wrote to me:
" I find a growing sense of familiarity with the
unseen world.   It is as if the door were invitingly
left ajar, and the distance were hourly diminishing.
I never think of *her* as alone.   The unusual number of departed friends for whom we had recently
mourned seem now but an increase to her happiness."

I had two other unmarried friends, as devoted,
to each other, and as tender of each other's peculiarities as any wedded couple I ever knew.
Without being learned, they had a love of general

reading, which, with active charities, made their days pass profitably and pleasantly. They had the orderly, systematic habits common to single ladies, but their sympathies and their views were larger and more liberal than those of their married sisters. Their fingers were busy for the poor, whom they were always ready to aid and comfort, irrespective of nation or color. Their family affections were remarkably strong, yet they had the moral courage to espouse the unpopular cause of the slave, in quiet opposition to the prejudices of beloved relatives. Death sundered this tie when both were advanced in years. The departed one, though not distinguished for beauty during her mortal life, had, after her decease, a wonderful loveliness, like that of an angelic child. It was the outward impress of her interior life.

Few marriages are more beautiful or more happy than these sisterly unions; and the same may be said of a brother and sister, whose lives are bound together. All lovers of English literature know how charmingly united in mind and heart were Charles Lamb and his gifted sister; and our own poet, Whittier, so dear to the people's heart, has a home made lovely by the same fraternal relation of mutual love and dependence.

A dear friend of mine, whom it was some good man's loss not to have for a life-mate, adopted the orphan sons of her brother, and reared them with more than parental wisdom and tenderness, caring for all their physical wants, guiding them in precept and example by the most elevated moral standard, bestowing on them the highest intellectual culture, and studying all branches with them, that she might in all things be their companion.

Nor is it merely in such connections, which somewhat resemble wedded life, that single women make themselves useful and respected. Many remember the store kept for so long a time in Boston by Miss Ann Bent.

Her parents being poor, she early began to support herself by teaching. A relative subsequently furnished her with goods to sell on commission; and in this new employment she manifested such good judgment, integrity, and general business capacity, that merchants were willing to trust her to any extent. She acquired a handsome property, which she used liberally to assist a large family of sisters and nieces, some of whom she established in business similar to her own. No mother or grandmother was ever more useful or beloved. One of her nieces said: "I know the beauty and purity of my aunt's character, for I lived with her forty years, and I never knew her to say or do anything which might not have been said or done before the whole world."

I am ignorant of the particulars of Miss Bent's private history; but doubtless a woman of her comely looks, agreeable manners, and excellent character, might have found opportunities to marry, if that had been a paramount object with her. She lived to be more than eighty-eight years old, universally respected and beloved; and the numerous relatives, toward whom she had performed a mother's part, cheered her old age with grateful affection.

There have also been many instances of single women who have enlivened and illustrated their lives by devotion to the beautiful arts. Of these none are perhaps more celebrated than the Italian Sofonisba Angusciola and her two accomplished sisters. These three " virtuous gentlewomen," as Vasari calls them, spent their lives together in most charming union. All of them had uncommon talent for painting, but Sofonisba was the most gifted. One of her most beautiful pictures represents her two sisters playing at chess, attended by the faithful old duenna, who accompanied them everywhere. This admirable artist lived to be old and blind; and the celebrated Vandyke said of her, in her later years: " I have learned more from one blind old woman in Italy, than from all the masters of the art."

Many single women have also employed their lives usefully and agreeably as authors. There is the charming Miss Mitford, whose writings cheer the soul like a meadow of cowslips in the spring-time. There is Frederica Bremer, whose writings have blessed so many souls. There is Joanna Baillie, Maria Edgeworth, Elizabeth Hamilton, and our own honored Catherine M. Sedgwick, whose books have made the world wiser and better than they found it.

I am glad to be sustained in my opinions on this subject by a friend whose own character invests single life with peculiar dignity. In a letter to me, she says: " I object to having single women called a *class*. They are *individuals*, differing in the qualities of their characters, like other human beings. Their isolation, as a general thing, is the result of unavoidable circumstances. The Author of Nature doubtless intended that men and women should live together. But, in the present state of the world's progress, society has, in many respects, become artificial in proportion to its civilization ; and consequently the number of single women must constantly increase. If humanity were in a 'state of natural, healthy development, this would not be so; for young people would then be willing to begin married life with simplicity and frugality, and real happiness would increase in proportion to the diminution of artificial wants. This prospect, however, lies in the future, and many generations of single women must come and go before it will be realized.

" But the achievement of *character* is the highest end that can be proposed to any human being, and there is nothing in single life to prevent a woman from attaining this great object; on the contrary, it is in many respects peculiarly favorable to it.

The measure of strength in character is the power to conquer circumstances when they refuse to co-operate with us. The temptations peculiarly incident to single life are petty selfishness, despondency under the suspicion of neglect, and *ennui* from the want of interesting occupation. If an ordinary, feeble-minded woman is exposed to these temptations, she will be very likely to yield to them. But she would not be greatly different in character, if protected by a husband and flanked with children; her feebleness would remain the same, and would only manifest itself under new forms.

"Marriage, under favorable circumstances, is unquestionably a promoter of human happiness. But mistakes are so frequently made by entering thoughtlessly into this indissoluble connection, and so much wretchedness ensues from want of sufficient mental discipline to make the best of what cannot be remedied, that most people can discover among their acquaintance as large a proportion of happy single women as they can of happy wives. Moreover, the happiness of unmarried women is as independent of mere gifts of fortune, as that of other individuals. Indeed, all solid happiness must spring from inward sources. Some of the most truly contented and respectable women I have ever known have been domestics, who grew old in one family, and were carefully looked after, in their declining days, by the children of those whom they faithfully served in youth.

"Most single women might have married, had they seized upon the first opportunity that offered; but some unrevealed attachment, too high an ideal, or an innate fastidiousness, have left them solitary; therefore, it is fair to assume that many of them have more sensibility and true tenderness than some of their married sisters. Those who remain single in consequence of too much worldly ambition, or from the gratification of coquettish vanity, naturally swell the ranks of those peevish, discontented ones, who bring discredit on single life in the abstract. But when a delicate gentlewoman deliberately prefers passing through life alone, to linking her fate with that of a man toward whom she feels no attraction, why should she ever repent of so high an exercise of her reason? This class of women are often the brightest ornaments of society. Men find in them calm, thoughtful friends, and safe confidants, on whose sympathy they can rely without danger. In the nursery, their labors, being voluntary, are less exhausting than a parent's. When the weary, fretted mother turns a deaf ear to the twenty-times-repeated question, the baffled urchins retreat to the indulgent aunt, or dear old familiar friend, sure of obtaining a patient hearing and a kind response. Almost everybody can remember some samples of such *Penates*, whose hearts seem to be too large to be confined to any one set of children.

"Some of my fairest patterns of feminine excellence have been of the single sisterhood. Of those unfortunate˙ ones who are beacons, rather than models, I cannot recall an individual whose character I think would have been materially improved by marriage. The faults which make a single woman disagreeable would probably exist to the same degree if she were a wife ; and the virtues which adorn her in a state of celibacy would make her equally beloved and honored if she were married. The human soul is placed here for development and progress ; and it is capable of converting all circumstances into means of growth and advancement.

" Among my early recollections is that of a lady of stately presence, who died while I was still young, but not till she had done much to remove from my mind the idea that the name of 'old maid' was a term of reproach. She was the daughter of Judge Russell, and aunt to the late Reverend and beloved Dr. Lowell. She had been one of a numerous family of brothers and sisters, but in my childhood was sole possessor of the old family mansion, where she received her friends and practised those virtues which gained for her the respect of the whole community. Sixty years ago, it was customary to speak of single women with far less deference than it now is ; and I remember being puzzled by the extremely respectful manner in which she was always mentioned. If there were difficulties in the parish, or if any doubtful matters were under discussion, the usual question was ' What is Miss Russell's opinion ? '   I used to think to myself, ' She is an old maid, after all, yet people always speak of her as if she were some great person.'

" Miss Burleigh was another person of whom I used to hear much through the medium of mutual friends. She resided with a married sister in Salem, and was the ' dear Aunt Susan,' not only of the large circle of her own nephews and nieces, but of all their friends and favorites. Having ample means, she surrounded herself with choice books and pictures, and such objects of Art or .Nature as would entertain and instruct young minds. Her stores of knowledge were prodigious, and she had such a happy way of imparting it, that lively boys were glad to leave their play, to spend an hour with Aunt Susan. She read to her young friends at stated times, and made herself perfectly familiar with them ; and as they grew older she became their chosen confidant. She was, in fact, such a centre of light and warmth, that no one could approach her sphere without being conscious of its vivifying influence.

" ' Aunt Sarah Stetson,' another single lady, was a dear and honored friend of my own. She was of masculine size and stature, gaunt and ungainly in the extreme. But before she had uttered three sentences, her hearers said to themselves, ' Here is a wise woman ! ' She was the oldest of thirteen

children, early deprived of their father, and she
bore the brunt of life from youth upward. She
received only such education as was afforded by
the public school of an obscure town seventy years
ago. To add to their scanty means of subsistence,
she learned the tailor's trade. In process of time,
the other children swarmed off from the parental
hive, the little farm was sold, and she lived alone
with her mother. She built a small cottage out of
her own earnings, and had the sacred pleasure of
taking her aged parent to her own home, and ministering with her own hands to all her wants. For
sixteen years, she never spent a night from home,
but assiduously devoted herself to the discharge of
this filial duty, and to the pursuance of her trade.
Yet in the midst of this busy life, she managed to
become respectably familiar with English literature,
especially with history. Whatever she read, she
derived from it healthful aliment for the growth of
her mental powers. She was full of wise maxims
and rules of life; not doled out with see-saw prosi-
ness, but with strong common sense, rich and racy,
and frequently flavored with the keenest satire.
She had a flashing wit, and wonderful power of
detecting shams of all sorts. Her religious opinions were orthodox, and she was an embodiment .
of the Puritan character. She was kindly in her
feelings, and alive to every demonstration of affection, but she had a granite firmness of principle,
which rendered her awful toward deceivers and

transgressors. All the intellectual people of the
town sought her company with avidity. The Unitarian minister and his family, a wealthy man, who
happened to be also the chief scholar in the place,
and the young people generally, took pleasure in
resorting to Aunt Sarah's humble home, to minister to her simple wants, and gather up her words of
wisdom. Her spirit was bright and cheerful to the
last. One of her sisters, who had been laboring
sixteen years as a missionary among the southwestern Indians, came to New England to visit
the scattered members of her family. After seeing them in their respective homes, she declared:
'Sarah is the most light-hearted of them all; and
it is only by *her* fireside that I have been able to
forget past hardships in merry peals of laughter.'

"During my last interview with Aunt Sarah,
when she was past seventy years of age, she said,
'I have lived very agreeably single; but if I become infirm, I suppose I shall feel the want of life's
nearest ties.' In her case, however, the need was
of short duration, and an affectionate niece supplied the place of a daughter.

"Undoubtedly, the arms of children and grandchildren form the most natural and beautiful cradle
for old age. But loneliness is often the widow's
portion, as well as that of the single woman; and
parents are often left solitary by the death or emi-
gration of their children.

"I am tempted to speak also of a living friend,

now past her sixtieth year. She is different from
the others, but this difference only confirms my
theory that the mind can subdue all things to itself.
This lady is strictly feminine in all her habits and
pursuits, and regards the needle as the chief im-
plement of woman's usefulness. If the Dorcas
labors performed by her one pair of hands could
be collected into a mass, out of the wear and waste
of half a century, they would form an amazing
pile. In former years, when her health allowed
her to circulate among numerous family connections, her visits were always welcomed as a jubilee ;
for every dilapidated wardrobe was sure to be
renovated by Aunt Mary's nimble fingers. She
had also a magic power of drawing the little ones
to herself. Next to their fathers and mothers, she
was the best beloved. The influence which her
loving heart gained over them in childhood increased with advancing years. She is now the best
and dearest friend of twenty or thirty nephews and
nieces, some of whom have families of their own.

" A large amount of what is termed mother-wit, a
readiness at repartee, and quickness in seizing unexpected associations of words or ideas, rendered
her generally popular in company ; but the deep
cravings of her heart could never be satisfied with
what is termed success in society. The intimate
love of a few valued friends was what she always
coveted, and never failed to win. For several years
she has been compelled by ill health to live entirely

at home. There she now is, fulfilling the most important mission of her whole beneficent life, training to virtue and usefulness five motherless children of her brother. Feeble and emaciated, she lives in her chamber surrounded by these orphans, who now constitute her chief hold on life. She shares all their pleasures, is the depositary of their little griefs, and unites in herself the relations of aunt, mother, and grandmother. She has faith to believe that her frail thread of existence will be prolonged for the sake of these little ones. The world still comes to her, in her seclusion, through a swarm of humble friends and dependants, who find themselves comforted and ennobled by the benignant patience with which she listens to their various experiences, and gives them kindly, sympathizing counsel, more valuable to them than mere pecuniary aid. Her spirit of self-abnegation is carried almost to asceticism; but she reserves her severity wholly for herself; toward others she is prodigal of indulgence. This goodly temple of a human soul was reared in these fair proportions upon a foundation of struggles, disappointments, and bereavements. A friend described her serene exterior as a ' placid, ocean-deep manner '; under it lies a silent history of trouble and trial, converted into spiritual blessings.

" The conclusion of the matter in my mind is, that a woman may make a respectable appearance as a wife, with a character far less noble than

is necessary to enable her to lead a single life with usefulness and dignity. She is sheltered and concealed behind her husband; but the unmarried woman must rely upon herself; and she lives in a glass house, open to the gaze of every passer-by. To the feeble-minded, marriage is almost a necessity, and if wisely formed it doubtless renders the life of any woman more happy. But happiness is not the sole end and aim of this life. We are sent here to build up a character; and sensible women may easily reconcile themselves to a single life, since even its disadvantages may be converted into means of develop-
ment of all the faculties
with which God
has endowed
them."

You are " getting into years." Yes, but the years are getting into you; the ripe, mellow years. One by one, the crudities of your youth are falling off from you; the vanity, the egotism, the bewil-derment, the uncertainty. Every wrong road into which you have wandered has brought you, by the knowledge of that mistake, nearer to the truth. Nearer and nearer you are approaching your-self. — GAIL HAMILTON.

THE OLD-MAID'S PRAYER TO DIANA.

By Mrs. Tighe, an Irish author, who wrote more than fifty years ago, when single women had not attained to the honorable position which they now occupy.

SINCE thou and the stars, my dear goddess, decree
That, old maid as I am, an old maid I must be,
O, hear the petition I offer to thee!
For to bear it must be my endeavor:
From the grief of my friendships all drooping around,
Till not one whom I loved in my youth can be found;
From the legacy-hunters, that near us abound,
Diana, thy servant deliver!

From the scorn of the young, and the flaunts of the gay,
From all the trite ridicule rattled away
By the pert ones, who know nothing wiser to say, —
Or a spirit to laugh at them, give her!
From repining at fancied neglected desert;
Or, vain of a civil speech, bridling alert;
From finical niceness, or slatternly dirt;
Diana, thy servant deliver!

From over solicitous guarding of pelf;
From humor unchecked, that most obstinate elf;
From every unsocial attention to self,
Or ridiculous whim whatsoever;
From the vaporish freaks, or methodical airs,
Apt to sprout in a brain that's exempted from cares;
From impertinent meddling in others' affairs;
Diana, thy servant deliver!

From the erring attachments of desolate souls;
From the love of spadille, and of matadore voles; *
Or of lap-dogs, and parrots, and monkeys, and owls,
Be they ne'er so uncommon and clever;
But chief from the love, with all loveliness flown,
Which makes the dim eye condescend to look down
On some ape of a fop, or some owl of a clown;
Diana, thy servant deliver!

From spleen at beholding the young more caressed;
From pettish asperity, tartly expressed;
From scandal, detraction, and every such pest;
From all, thy true servant deliver!
Nor let satisfaction depart from her cot;
Let her sing, if at ease, and be patient if not;
Be pleased when regarded, content when forgot,
Till the Fates her slight thread shall dissever.

* Terms used in Ombre, a game at cards.

GRANDFATHER'S REVERIE.

By THEODORE PARKER.

RANDFATHER is old. His back is bent. In the street he sees crowds of men looking dreadfully young, and walking fearfully swift. He wonders where all the *old* folks are. Once, when a boy, he could not find people young enough for him, and sidled up to any young stranger he met on Sundays, wondering why God made the world so old. Now he goes to Commençement to see his grandson take his degree, and is astonished at the youth of the audience. " This is new," he says ; " it did not use to be so fifty years ago." At meeting, the minister seems surprisingly young, and the audience young. He looks round, and is astonished that there are so few venerable heads. The audience seem not decorous. They come in late, and hurry off early, clapping the doors after them with irreverent bang. But grandfather is decorous, well mannered, early in his seat ; if jostled, he jostles not again; elbowed, he returns it not; crowded, he thinks no evil. He is gentlemanly to the rude, obliging to the insolent and vulgar; for grandfather is a gentleman; not puffed up with mere money, but edified with well-grown manliness. Time has dignified his good manners.

It is night. The family are all abed. Grandfather sits by his old-fashioned fire. He draws his old-fashioned chair nearer to the hearth. On the stand which his mother gave him are the candlesticks, also of old time. The candles are three quarters burnt down; the fire on the hearth also is low. He has been thoughtful all day, talking half to himself, chanting a bit of verse, humming a snatch of an old tune. He kissed his pet granddaughter more tenderly than common, before she went to bed. He takes out of his bosom a little locket; nobody ever sees it. Therein are two little twists of hair. As Grandfather looks at them, the outer twist of hair becomes a whole head of ambrosial curls. He remembers stolen interviews, meetings by moonlight. He remembers how sweet the evening star looked, and how he laid his hand on another's shoulder, and said, " *You* are my evening star."

The church-clock strikes the midnight hour. He looks in his locket again. The other twist is the hair of his first-born son. At this same hour of midnight, once, many years ago, he knelt and prayed, when the long agony was over, — " My

God, I thank thee that, though I am a father, I am still a husband, too! What am I, that unto me a life should be given and another spared!"
Now he has children, and children's children, the joy of his old age. But for many a year his wife has looked to him from beyond the evening star. She is still the evening star herself, yet more beautiful; a star that never sets; not mortal wife now, but angel.

The last stick on his andirons snaps asunder, and
falls outward. Two faintly smoking brands
stand there. Grandfather lays them together, and they flame up; the
two smokes are united in one
flame. "Even so let it
be in heaven," says
Grandfather.

Useless, do you say you are? You are of *great* use. You really are. How are you useful? By being a man that is old. Your old age is a public good. It is indeed. No child ever listens to your talk without having a good done it that no schooling could do. When you are walking, no one ever opens a gate for you to pass through, and no one ever honors you with any kind of help, without being himself the better for what he does; for fellow-feeling with you ripens his soul for him. — Mountford.

THE OLD COUPLE.

IT stands in a sunny meadow,
  The house so mossy and brown,
With its cumbrous old stone chimneys,
  And the gray roof sloping down.

The trees fold their green arms round it,
  The trees a century old,
And the winds go chanting through them,
  And the sunbeams drop their gold.

The cowslips spring in the marshes,
  And the roses bloom on the hill,
And beside the brook in the pastures
  The herds go feeding at will.

The children have gone and left them;
  They sit in the sun alone;
And the old wife's tears are falling,
  As she harks to the well-known tone

That won her heart in girlhood,
  That has soothed her in many a care,
And praises her now for the brightness
  Her old face used to wear.

She thinks again of her bridal, —
  How, dressed in her robe of white,
She stood by her gay young lover
  In the morning's rosy light.

O, the morning is rosy as ever,
  But the rose from her cheek is fled;
And the sunshine still is golden,
  But it falls on a silvery head.

And the spring-like dreams, once vanished,
  Come back in her winter-time,
Till her feeble pulses tremble
  With the thrill of girlhood's prime.

And, looking forth from the window,
  She thinks how the trees have grown,
Since, clad in her bridal whiteness,
  She crossed the old door-stone.

Though dimmed her eyes' bright azure,
  And dimmed her hair's young gold,
The love in her girlhood plighted
  Has never grown dim nor old.

They sat in peace in the sunshine,
  Till the day was almost done;
And then at its close an angel
  Stole over the threshold stone

He folded their hands together;
  He touched their eyes with balm;
And their last breath floated upward,
  Like the close of a solemn psalm.

Like a bridal pair they traversed
    The unseen mystical road,
That leads to the beautiful city,
    " Whose Builder and Maker is God."

Perhaps, in that miracle country,
    They will give her lost youth back,
And the flowers of a vanished spring-time
    Will bloom in the spirit's track.

One draught of the living waters
    Shall call back his manhood's prime,
And eternal years shall measure
    The love that outlived time.

But the forms that they left behind them,
    The wrinkles and silver hair,
Made holy to us by the kisses
    The angel had printed there,

We will hide away 'neath the willows
    When the day is low in the west,
Where the sunshine gleams upon them,
    And no winds disturb their rest.

And we 'll suffer no telltale tombstone,
    With its age and date, to rise
O'er the two who are old no longer,
    In their Father's house in the skies.

                                        HOME JOURNAL.

A STORY OF ST. MARK'S EVE.

By THOMAS HOOD.

St. Mark's Day is a festival which has been observed on the 25th of April, in Catholic countries, from time immemorial. The superstition alluded to in the following story was formerly very generally believed, and vigils in the church-porch at midnight were common.

 HOPE it 'll choke thee ! " said Master Giles, the yeoman ; and, as he said it, he banged his big red fist on the old oak table. " I do say I hope it 'll choke thee ! "

The dame made no reply. She was choking with passion and a fowl's liver, which was the cause of the dispute. Much has been said and sung concerning the advantage of congenial tastes amongst married people ; but the quarrels of this Kentish couple arose from too great coincidence in their tastes. They were both fond of the little delicacy in question, but the dame had managed to secure the morsel to herself. This was sufficient to cause a storm of high words, which, properly understood, signifies very low language. Their

meal times seldom passed over without some con-
tention of this sort. As sure as the knives and
forks clashed, so did they; being in fact equally
greedy and disagreedy; and when they did pick a
quarrel, they picked it to the bone.

It was reported that, on some occasions, they
had not even contented themselves with hard
speeches, but had come to scuffling; he taking to
boxing and she to pinching, though in a far less
amicable manner than is practised by the taker of
snuff. On the present difference, however, they
were satisfied with " wishing each other dead with
all their hearts "; and there seemed little doubt of
the sincerity of the aspiration, on looking at their
malignant faces; for they made a horrible picture
in this frame of mind.

Now it happened that this quarrel took place on
the morning of St. Mark; a saint who was supposed on that festival to favor his votaries with a
peep into the book of fate. For it was the popular belief in those days, that, if a person should
keep watch at midnight beside the church, the ap-
paritions of all those of the parish who were to be
taken by death before the next anniversary would
be seen entering the porch. The yeoman, like his
neighbors, believed most devoutly in this superstition; and in the very moment that he breathed
the unseemly aspiration aforesaid, it occurred to
him that the eve was at hand, when, by observing
the rite of St. Mark, he might know to a certainty

7 *

whether this unchristian wish was to be one of
those that bear fruit. Accordingly, a little before
midnight, he stole quietly out of the house, and
set forth on his way to the church.

In the mean time, the dame called to mind the
same ceremonial ; and, having the like motive for
curiosity with her husband, she also put on her
cloak and calash, and set out, though by a different
path, on the same errand.

The night of the Saint was as dark and chill as
the mysteries he was supposed to reveal ; the moon
throwing but a short occasional glance, as sluggish
masses of cloud were driven slowly from her face.
Thus it fell out that our two adventurers were
quite unconscious of being in company, till a sudden glimpse of moonlight showed them to each
other, only a few yards apart. Both, through a
natural panic, became pale as ghosts ; and both
made eagerly toward the church porch. Much
as they had wished for this vision, they could not
help quaking and stopping on the spot, as if turned
to stones ; and in this position the dark again threw
a sudden curtain over them, and they disappeared
from each other.

The two came to one conclusion ; each conceiv-
ing that St. Mark had marked the other to himself.
With this comfortable knowledge, the widow and
widower elect hied home again by the roads they
came ; and as their custom was to sit apart after a
quarrel, they repaired to separate chambers, each
ignorant of the other's excursion.

By and by, being called to supper, instead of sulking as aforetime, they came down together, each being secretly in the best humor, though mutually suspected of the worst. Amongst other things on the table, there was a calf's sweetbread, being one of those very dainties that had often set them together by the ears. The dame looked and longed, but she refrained from its appropriation, thinking within herself that she could give up sweetbreads *for one year ;* and the farmer made a similar reflection. After pushing the dish to and fro several times, by a common impulse they divided the treat; and then, having supped, they retired amicably to rest, whereas until then they had seldom gone to bed without falling out. The truth was, each looked upon the other as being already in the churchyard.

On the morrow, which happened to be the dame's birthday, the farmer was the first to wake ; and *knowing what he knew,* and having, besides, but just roused himself out of a dream strictly confirmatory of the late vigil, he did not scruple to salute his wife, and wish her many happy returns of the day. The wife, *who knew as much as he,* very readily wished him the same ; having, in truth, but just rubbed out of her eyes the pattern of a widow's bonnet that had been submitted to her in her sleep. She took care, however, at dinner to give the fowl's liver to the doomed man ; considering that when he was dead and gone she

could have them, if she pleased, seven days in the
week; and the farmer, on his part, took care to
help her to many tidbits.   Their feeling toward
each other was that of an impatient host with regard to an unwelcome guest, showing scarcely a
bare civility while in expectation of his stay, but
overloading him with hospitality when made certain of his departure.

In this manner they went on for some six months,
without any addition of love between them, and as
much selfishness as ever, yet living in a subservi-
ence to the comforts and inclinations of each other,
sometimes not to be found even amongst couples
of sincerer affections.   There were as many causes
for quarrel as ever, but every day it became less
worth while to quarrel; so letting bygones be bygones, they were indifferent to the present, and
thought only of the future, considering each other
(to adopt a common phrase) " as *good* as dead."

Ten months wore away, and the farmer's birthday arrived in its turn.   The dame, who had passed
an uncomfortable night, having dreamed, in truth,
that she did not much like herself in mourning,
saluted him as soon as the day dawned, and, with a
sigh, wished him many years to come.   The farmer
repaid her in kind, the sigh included; his own
visions having been of the painful sort; for he
dreamed of having a headache from wearing a
black hat-band, and the malady still clung to him
when awake.   The whole morning was spent in

silent meditation and melancholy, on both sides ;
and when dinner came, although the most favorite
dishes were upon the table, they could not eat. The
farmer, resting his elbows upon the board, with his
face between his hands, gazed wistfully on his wife.
The dame, leaning back in her high arm-chair,
regarded the yeoman quite as ruefully. Their
minds, travelling in the same direction, and at an
equal rate, arrived together at the same reflection;
but the farmer was the first to give it utterancê :

" Thee'd be *missed*, dame, if thee were to die ! "

The dame started. Although she had nothing
but death at that moment before her eyes, she was
far from dreaming of her own exit. Recovering,
however, from the shock, her thoughts flowed into
their old channel, and she rejoined in the same
spirit :

" I wish, master, thee may live so long as I ! "

The farmer, in his own mind, wished to live
rather longer ; for, at the utmost, he considered that
his wife's bill of mortality had but two months
to run ; the calculation made him sorrowful.; during the last few months she had consulted his
appetite, bent to his humor, and conformed her
own inclinations to his, in a manner that could
never be supplied.

His wife, from being at first useful to him, had
become agreeable, and at last dear ; and as he
contemplated her approaching fate, he could not
help thinking out audibly, " that he should be a

lonesome man when she was gone." The dame,
this time, heard the survivorship foreboded without starting; but she marvelled much at what she
thought the infatuation of a doomed man. So
perfect was her faith in the infallibility of St.
Mark, that she had even seen the symptoms of
mortal disease, as palpable as plague-spots, on the
devoted yeoman. Giving his body up, therefore,
for lost, a strong sense of duty persuaded her that
it was imperative on her, as a Christian, to warn
the unsuspecting farmer of his dissolution. Accordingly, with a solemnity adapted to the subject,
a tenderness of recent growth, and a *memento mori*
face, she broached the matter in the following
question :

" Master, how bee'st thee ? "

" As hearty as a buck, dame ; and I wish thee
the like."

A dead silence ensued ; the farmer was as un-
prepared as ever. There is a great fancy for
breaking the truth by dropping it gently ; an experiment which has never answered, any more
than with iron-stone china. The dame felt this ;
and, thinking it better to throw the news at her
husband at once, she told him, in as many words,
that he was a dead man.

It was now the yeoman's turn to be staggered.
By a parallel course of reasoning, he had just
wrought himself up to a similar disclosure, and
the dame's death-warrant was just ready upon his

tongue, when he met with his own despatch, signed, sealed, and delivered. Conscience instantly pointed out the oracle from which she had derived the omen.

"Thee hast watched, dame, at the church porch, then?"

"Ay, master."

"And thee didst see me spirituously?"

"In the brown wrap, with the boot hose. Thee were coming to the church, by Fairthorn Gap; in the while I were coming by the Holly Hedge."

For a minute the farmer paused; but the next he burst into a fit of uncontrollable laughter; peal after peal, each higher than the last. The poor woman had but one explanation for this phenomenon. She thought it a delirium; a lightening before death; and was beginning to wring her hands, and lament, when she was checked by the merry yeoman:

"Dame, thee bee'st a fool. It was I myself thee seed at the church porch. I seed thee, too; with a notice to quit upon thy face; but, thanks to God, thee bee'st a living; and that is more than I cared to say of thee this day ten-month!"

The dame made no answer. Her heart was too full to speak; but, throwing her arms round her husband, she showed that she shared in his sentiment. And from that hour, by practising a careful abstinence from offence, or a temperate sufferance of its appearance, they became the most united couple in the county. But it must be said, that their comfort was not complete till they had seen each other, in safety, over the perilous anniversary of St. Mark's Eve.

―――――

The moral this story conveys is one which might prove a useful monitor to us all, if we could keep it in daily remembrance. Few, indeed, are so coarse in their manifestations of ill-temper as this Kentish couple are described; but we all indulge, more or less, in unreasonable fretfulness, and petty acts of selfishness, in the relations of husband and wife, parents and children, brothers and sisters, — in fact, in all the relations of life. It would help us greatly to be kind, forbearing, and self-sacrificing toward neighbors, friends, and relatives, if it were always present to our minds that death may speedily close our intercourse with them in this world. — L. M. C.

WHAT THE OLD WOMAN SAID.

ONE summer eve, I chanced to pass, where, by the
    cottage gate,
An aged woman in the town sat crooning to her mate.
The frost of age was on her brow, its dimness in her
    eye,
And her bent figure to and fro rocked all unconsciously.
The frost of age was on her brow, yet garrulous her
    tongue,
As she compared the "*doings now*," with those when
    she was young.
" When *I* was young, young gals were meek, and looked
    round kind of shy ;
And when they were compelled to speak, they did so
    modestly.
They stayed at home, and did the work; made Indian
    bread and wheaten ;
And only went to singing-school, and *sometimes* to night
    meetin'.
And *children* were obedient *then ;* they had no saucy
    airs ;
And minded what their mothers said, and learned their
    hymns and prayers.

But *now-a-days* they know enough, before they know
their letters ;
And young ones that can hardly walk will contradict
their betters.
Young women *now* go kiting round, and looking out for
beaux ;
And scarcely one in ten is found, who makes or mends
her clothes !
But then, I tell my daughter,
Folks don't do as they'd ought'-ter.

When *I* was young, if a man had failed, he shut up
house and hall,
And never ventured out till night, if he ventured out at
all ;
And his wife sold all her china plates ; and his sons
came home from college ;
And his gals left school, and learned to wash and bake,
and such like knowledge ;
They gave up cake and pumpkin-pies, and had the
plainest eatin' ;
And never asked folks home to tea, and scarcely went
to meetin'.
The man that was a Bankrupt called, was kind'er
shunned by men,
And hardly dared to show his head amongst his town
folks *then*.
But *now-a-days*, when a merchant fails, they say he
makes a penny ;
The wife don't have a gown the less, and his daughters
just as many ;
His sons they smoke their choice cigars, and drink their
costly wine ;

And *she* goes to the opera, and *he* has folks to dine!
He walks the streets, he drives his gig; men show him
     all civilities;
And what in *my* day we called *debts*, are now his *lie-
     abilities*!
They call the man unfortunate who ruins half the city, —
In my day 't was his *creditors* to whom we gave our pity.
    But then, I'll tell my daughter,
    Folks don't do as they'd ough'-ter.
FROM THE OLIVE BRANCH.

THE SPRING JOURNEY.

O, GREEN was the corn as I rode on my way,
And bright were the dews on the blossoms of May,
And dark was the sycamore's shade to behold,
And the oak's tender leaf was of emerald and gold.

The thrush from his holly, the lark from his cloud,
Their chorus of rapture sung jovial and loud;
From the soft vernal sky to the soft grassy ground,
There was beauty above me, beneath, and around.

The mild southern breeze brought a shower from the hill,
And yet, though it left me all dripping and chill,
I felt a new pleasure, as onward I sped,
To gaze where the rainbow gleamed broad overhead.

O such be *life's* journey! and such be our skill
To lose in its blessings the sense of its ill;
Through sunshine and shower may our progress be even,
And our tears add a charm to the prospect of heaven.
BISHOP HEBER.

MORAL HINTS.

By L. MARIA CHILD.

PROBABLY there are no two things that tend so much to make human beings unhappy in themselves and unpleasant to others, as habits of fretfulness and despondency; two faults peculiarly apt to grow upon people after they have passed their youth. Both these ought to be resisted with constant vigilance, as we would resist a disease. This we should do for our own sakes, and as a duty we owe to others. Life is made utterly disagreeable when we are daily obliged to listen to a complaining house-mate. How annoying and disheartening are such remarks as these : "I was not invited to the party last night. I suppose I am getting to be of no consequence to anybody now." "Yes, that is a beautiful present you have had sent you. Nobody sends *me* presents." "I am a useless encumbrance now. I can see that people want me out of their way." Yet such observations are not unfrequently heard from persons surrounded by external comforts, and who are consequently envied by others of similar disposition in less favorable circumstances.

No virtue has been so much recommended to the old as cheerfulness. Colton says: " Cheerfulness ought to be the viaticum of their life to the old. Age without cheerfulness is a Lapland winter without a sun."

Montaigne says: " The most manifest sign of wisdom is continued cheerfulness."

Dr. Johnson says: " The habit of looking on the best side of every event is worth more than a thousand pounds a year."

Tucker says: " The point of aim for our vigilance to hold in view is to dwell upon the brightest parts in every prospect; to call off the thoughts when running upon disagreeable objects, and strive to be pleased with the present circumstances surrounding us."

Southey says, in one of his letters: " I have told you of the Spaniard, who always put on his spectacles when about to eat cherries, that they might look bigger and more tempting. In like manner, I make the most of my enjoyments; and though I do not cast my eyes away from my troubles, I pack them in as little compass as I can for myself, and never let them annoy others."

Perhaps you will say: " All this is very fine talk for people who are naturally cheerful. But I am low-spirited by temperament; and how is that to be helped?" In the first place, it would be well to ascertain whether what you call being naturally low-spirited does not arise from the infringement of some physical law; something wrong in what you eat or drink, or something unhealthy in other personal habits. But if you inherit a tendency to look on the dark side of things, resolutely call in the aid of your reason to counteract it. Leigh Hunt says: "If you are melancholy for the first time, you will find, upon a little inquiry, that others have been melancholy many times, and yet are cheerful now. If you have been melancholy many times, recollect that you have got over all those times; and try if you cannot find means of getting over them better."

If reason will not afford sufficient help, call in the aid of conscience. In this world of sorrow and disappointment, every human being has trouble enough of his own. It is unkind to add the weight of your despondency to the burdens of another, who, if you knew all his secrets, you might find had a heavier load than yours to carry. You find yourself refreshed by the presence of cheerful people. Why not make earnest efforts to confer that pleasure on others? You will find half the battle is gained, if you never allow yourself to *say* anything gloomy. If you habitually try to pack your troubles away out of other people's sight, you will be in a fair way to forget them yourself; first, because evils become exaggerated to the imagination by repetition ; and, secondly, because an effort made for the happiness of others lifts us above ourselves.

Those who are conscious of a tendency to dejection should also increase as much as possible the circle of simple and healthy enjoyments. They should cultivate music and flowers, take walks to look at beautiful sunsets, read entertaining books, and avail themselves of any agreeable social intercourse within their reach. They should also endeavor to surround themselves with pleasant external objects.

Our states of feeling, and even our characters, are influenced by the things we habitually look upon or listen to. A sweet singer in a household, or a musical instrument played with feeling, do more than afford us mere sensuous pleasure ; they help us morally, by their tendency to harmonize discordant moods. Pictures of pleasant scenes, or innocent objects, are, for similar reasons, desirable in the rooms we inhabit. Even the paper on the walls may help somewhat to drive away " blue devils," if ornamented with graceful patterns, that light up cheerfully. The paper on the parlor of Linnæus represented beautiful flowering plants from the East and West Indies ; and on the walls of his bedroom were delineated a great variety of butterflies, dragon-flies, and other brilliant insects. Doubtless it contributed not a little to the happi-

ness of the great naturalist thus to live in the
midst of his pictured thoughts.   To cultivate flowers, to arrange them in pretty vases, to observe
their beauties of form and color, has a healthy
effect, both on mind and body.   Some temper-
aments are more susceptible than others to these
fine influences, but they are not entirely without
effect on any human soul ; and forms of beauty
can now be obtained with so little expenditure
of money, that few need to be entirely destitute of
them.

Perhaps you will say, " If I feel low-spirited,
even if I do not speak of it, I cannot help showing
it."   The best way to avoid the intrusion of sad
feelings is to immerse yourself in some occupation.
Adam Clarke said : " I have lived to know that
the secret of happiness is never to allow your
energies to stagnate."   If you are so unfortunate
as to have nothing to do at home, then, the moment you begin to feel a tendency to depression,
start forth for the homes of others.   Tidy up the
room of some helpless person, who has nobody to
wait upon her ; carry flowers to some invalid, or
read to some lonely old body.   If you are a man,
saw and split wood for some poor widow, or lone
woman, in the neighborhood.   If you are a woman,
knit stockings for poor children, or mend caps for
those whose eyesight is failing ; and when you
have done them, don't send them home, but take
them yourself.   Merely to have every hour of life

fully occupied is a great blessing; but the full benefit of constant employment cannot be experienced unless we are occupied in a way that promotes the good of others, while it exercises our own bodies and employs our own minds. Plato went so far as to call exercise a cure for a wounded conscience; and, provided usefulness is combined with it, there is certainly a good deal of truth in the assertion; inasmuch as constant helpful activity leaves the mind no leisure to brood over useless regrets, and by thus covering the wound from the corrosion of thought, helps it to become a scar.

Against that listless indifference, which the French call *ennui,* industry is even a better preservative than it is against vain regrets. Therefore, it seems to me unwise for people in the decline of life to quit entirely their customary occupations and pursuits. The happiest specimens of old age are those men and women who have been busy to the last; and there can be no doubt that the decay of our powers, both bodily and mental, is much hindered by their constant exercise, provided it be not excessive.

It is recorded of Michael Angelo, that "after he was sixty years old, though not very robust, he would cut away as many scales from a block of very hard marble, in a quarter of an hour, as three young sculptors would have effected in three or four hours. Such was the impetuosity and fire with which he pursued his labors, that with a single

8

stroke he brought down fragments three or four
fingers thick, and so close upon his mark, that had
he passed it, even in the slightest degree, there
would have been danger of ruining the whole."
From the time he was seventy-one years old till he
was seventy-five, he was employed in painting the
Pauline Chapel. It was done in fresco, which is
exceedingly laborious, and he confessed that it
fatigued him greatly. He was seventy-three years
old when he was appointed architect of the wonderful church of St. Peter's, at Rome; upon which
he expended the vast powers of his mind during
seventeen years. He persisted in refusing compensation, and labored solely for the honor of his
country and his church. In his eighty-seventh
year, some envious detractors raised a report that
he had fallen into dotage; but he triumphantly
refuted the charge, by producing a very beautiful
model of St. Peter's, planned by his own mind,
and in a great measure executed by his own hand.
He was eighty-three, when his faithful old servant
Urbino, who had lived with him twenty-six years,
sickened and died. Michael Angelo, notwithstanding his great age, and the arduous labors of
superintending the mighty structure of St. Peter's,
and planning new fortifications for Rome, under-
took the charge of nursing him. He even watched
over him through the night; sleeping by his side,
without undressing. This remarkable man lived
ninety years, lacking a fortnight. He wrote many

beautiful sonnets during his last years, and continued to make drawings, plans, and models, to the
day of his death, though infirmities increased upon
him, and his memory failed.

Handel lived to be seventy-five years old, and
though afflicted with blindness in his last years, he
continued to produce oratorios and anthems. He
superintended music in the orchestra only a week
before he died. Haydn was sixty-five years old,
when he composed his oratorio of The Creation,
the music of which is as bright as the morning
sunshine. When he was seventy-seven years old,
he went to a great concert to hear it performed.
It affected him deeply to have his old inspirations
thus recalled to mind. When they came to the
passage, " It was light ! " he was so overpowered
by the harmonies, that he burst into tears, and,
pointing upwards, exclaimed : " Not from *me !* Not
from *me !* but *thence* did all this come ! "

Linnæus was past sixty-two years old when he
built a museum at his country-seat, where he clas-
sified and arranged a great number of plants,
zoöphytes, shells, insects, and minerals. Besides
this, he superintended the Royal Gardens, zeal-
ously pursued his scientific researches, corre-
sponded by letter with many learned men, taught
pupils, and lectured constantly in the Academic
Gardens. His pupils travelled to all parts of the
world, and sent him new plants and minerals to
examine and classify. In the midst of this con-

stant occupation, he wrote: "I tell the truth when I say that I am happier than the King of Persia. My pupils send me treasures from the East and the West; treasures more precious to me than Babylonish garments or Chinese vases. Here in the Academic Gardens is my Elysium. Here I learn and teach; here I admire, and point out to others, the wisdom of the Great Artificer, manifested in the structure of His wondrous works." It is said that even when he was quite ill, the arrival of an unknown plant would infuse new life into him. He continued to labor with unremitting diligence till he was sixty-seven years old, when a fit of apoplexy attacked him in the midst of a public lecture, and so far impaired his memory that he became unable to teach.

The celebrated Alexander von Humboldt lived ninety years, and continued to pursue his scientific researches and to publish learned books up to the very year of his departure from this world.

The Rev. John Wesley continued to preach and write till his body was fairly worn out. Southey, his biographer, says: "When you met him in the street of a crowded city, he attracted notice, not only by his band and cassock, and his long hair, white and bright as silver, but by his pace and manner, both indicating that all his minutes were numbered, and that not one was to be lost." Wesley himself wrote: "Though I am always in haste, I am never in a hurry; because I never undertake more work than I can go through with perfect calmness of spirit." Upon completing his eighty-second year, he wrote : " It is now eleven years since I have felt any such thing as weariness. Many times I speak till my voice fails me, and I can speak no longer. Frequently I walk till my strength fails, and I can walk no farther. Yet even then I feel no sensation of weariness, but am perfectly easy from head to foot. I dare not impute this to natural causes. It is the will of God." A year later, he wrote : " I am a wonder to myself. Such is the goodness of God, that I am never tired, either with writing, preaching, or travelling."

Isaac T. Hopper, who lived to be past eighty, was actively employed in helping fugitive slaves, and travelling about to exercise a kindly and beneficent influence in prisons, until a very short time before his death. When he was compelled to take to his bed, he said to me : " I am ready and willing to go, only there is so much that I want to do."

Some will say it is not in their power to do such things as these men did. That may be. But there is something that everybody can do. Those whose early habits render it difficult, or impossible, to learn a new science, or a new language, in the afternoon of life, can at least oil the hinges of memory by learning hymns, chapters, ballads, and stories, wherewith to console and amuse themselves

and others.   A stock of nursery rhymes to amuse
little children is far from being a foolish or worth-
less acquisition, since it enables one to impart
delight to the little souls,

> " With their wonder so intense,
> And their small experience."

Women undoubtedly have the advantage of men,
in those in-door occupations best suited to the infirm ; for there is no end to the shoes that may be
knit for the babies of relatives, the tidies that may
be crocheted for the parlors of friends, and the
socks that may be knit for the poor.   But men also
can find employment for tedious hours, when the
period of youthful activity has passed.   In summer, gardening is a never-failing resource both to
men and women ; and genial qualities of character
are developed by imparting to others the flowers,
fruit, and vegetables we have had the pleasure of
raising.   The Rev. Dr. Prince of Salem was always busy, in his old age, making telescopes,
kaleidoscopes, and a variety of toys for scientific
illustrations, with which he instructed and enter-
tained the young people who visited him.   My old
father amused himself, and benefited others, by
making bird-houses for children, and clothes-horses
and towel-stands for all the girls of his acquaintance who were going to housekeeping.   I knew
an old blind man, who passed his winter evenings
pleasantly weaving mats from corn-husks, while

another old man read to him. A lathe is a valuable resource for elderly people ; and this employment for mind and hands may also exercise the moral qualities, as it admits of· affording pleasure to family and friends by innumerable neatly-turned little articles. The value of occupation is threefold to elderly people, if usefulness is combined with exercise ; for in that way the machinery of body, mind, and heart may all be kept from rusting.

A sister of the celebrated John Wilkes, a wise and kindly old lady, who resided in Boston a very long time ago, was accustomed to say, " The true secret of happiness is always to have a little less time than one wants, and a little more money than one needs." There is much wisdom in the saying, but I think it might be improved by adding, that the money should be of one's own earning.

After life has passed its maturity, great care should be taken not to become indifferent to the affairs of the world. It is salutary, both for mind and heart, to take an interest in some of the great questions of the age ; whether it be slavery or war, or intemperance, or the elevation of women, or righting the wrongs of the Indians, or the progress of education, or the regulation of prisons, or improvements in architecture, or investigation into the natural sciences, from which proceed results so important to the daily comfort and occupations of mankind. It is for each one to choose his object of

especial interest; but it should be remembered that
no person has a right to be entirely indifferent concerning questions involving great moral principles.
Care should be taken that the daily social influence
which every man and woman exerts, more or less,
should be employed in the right direction. A con-
scientious man feels himself in some degree respon-
sible for the evil he does not seek to prevent. In
the Rev. John Wesley's journal for self-examina-
tion this suggestive question occurs: " Have I
embraced every probable opportunity of doing
good, and of preventing, removing, or lessening
evil?" Such habits of mind tend greatly to the
improvement of our own characters, while at the
same time they may help to improve the character
and condition of others. Nothing is more healthy
for the soul than to go out of ourselves, and stay
out of ourselves. We thus avoid brooding over
our own bodily pains, our mental deficiencies, or
past moral shortcomings; we forget to notice
whether others neglect us, or not; whether they
duly appreciate us, or not; whether their advantages are superior to ours, or not. He who leads
a true, active, and useful life has no time for
such corrosive thoughts. All self-consciousness
indicates disease. We never think about our
stomachs till we have dyspepsia. The moral diseases which induce self-consciousness are worse
than the physical, both in their origin and their
results. To indulge in repinings over our own

deficiencies, compared with others, while it indicates the baneful presence of envy, prevents our
making the best use of such endowments as we
have.   If we are conscious of our merits, bodily or
mental, it takes away half their value.   There is
selfishness even in anxiety whether we shall go to
heaven or not, or whether our souls are immortal
or not.   A continual *preparation* for eternal progress is the wisest and the happiest way to live *here*.
If we daily strive to make ourselves fit companions
for angels, we shall be in constant readiness for a
better world, while we make sure of enjoying some
degree of heaven upon this earth ; and, what is still
better, of helping to make it a paradise for others.

   Perhaps there is no error of human nature productive of so much unhappiness as the indulgence
of temper.   Often everything in a household is
made to go wrong through the entire day, because
one member of the family rises in a fretful mood.
An outburst of anger brings a cloud of gloom over
the domestic atmosphere, which is not easily dissipated.   Strenuous efforts should be made to guard
against this, especially by the old ; who, as they
lose external attractions, should strive all the more
earnestly to attain that internal beauty which is of
infinitely more value.   And here, again, the question may be asked, " What am I to do, if I have
naturally a hasty or fretful temper, and if those
around me act in a manner to provoke it ? "   In
the first place, strong self-constraint may be made

to become a habit ; and this, though very difficult
in many cases, is possible to all. People of the
most ungoverned tempers will often become suddenly calm and courteous when a stranger enters ;
and they can control their habitual outbreaks, when
they are before people whose good opinion they are
particularly desirous to obtain or preserve. Constraint may be made more easy by leaving the
presence of those with whom you are tempted to
jangle. Go out into the open air ; feed animals ;
gather flowers or fruit for the very person you
were tempted to annoy. By thus opening a door
for devils to walk out of your soul, angels will be
sure to walk in. If circumstances prevent your
doing anything of this kind, you can retire to your
own chamber for a while, and there wrestle for victory over your evil mood. If necessary avocations
render this impossible, time can at least be snatched
for a brief and earnest prayer for help in overcom-
ing your besetting sin ; and prayer is a golden
gate, through which angels are wont to enter.

> " And the lady prayed in heaviness,
>   That looked not for relief ;
> But slowly did her succor come,
>   And a patience to her grief.

> " O, there is never sorrow of heart
>   That shall lack a timely end,
> If but to God we turn and ask
>   Of Him to be our friend."

There is a reason for governing our tempers which

is still more important than our own happiness, or
even the happiness of others. I allude to its influence on the characters of those around us ; an
influence which may mar their whole destiny here,
and perhaps hinder their progress hereafter. None
of us are sufficiently careful to keep pure and
wholesome the spiritual atmosphere which sur-
rounds every human being, and which must be
more or less inhaled by the spiritual lungs of all
those with whom he enters into the various relations of life.   Jean Paul said : " Newton, who
uncovered his head whenever the name of God
was pronounced, thus became, without words, a
teacher of religion to children."   Many a girl has
formed an injudicious marriage, in consequence of
hearing sneering remarks, or vulgar jokes, about
" old maids."   Poisonous prejudices against na-
tions, races, sects, and classes are often instilled
by thoughtless incidental expressions.   There is
education for evil in the very words " Nigger,"
" Paddy," " old Jew," " old maid," &c.   It is recorded of the Rabbi Sera, that when he was asked
how he had attained to such a serene and lovable
old age, he replied : " I have never rejoiced at any
evil which happened to my neighbor ; and I never
called any man by a nickname given to him in
derision or sport."

False ideas with regard to the importance of
wealth and rank are very generally, though often
unconsciously. inculcated by modes of speech, or

habits of action.   To treat *mere* wealth with
more respect than honest poverty ; to speak more
deferentially of a man whose *only* claim is a distinguished ancestry, than you do of the faithful
laborer who ditches your meadows, is a slow but
sure process of education, which sermons and cate-
chisms will never be able entirely to undo.   It is
important to realize fully that all merely conventional distinctions are false and illusory ; that only
worth and usefulness can really ennoble man or
woman.   If we look at the subject from a rational
point of view, the artificial classifications of society
appear even in a ludicrous light.   It would be
considered a shocking violation of etiquette for
the baronet's lady to call upon the queen.   The
wife of the wealthy banker, or merchant, cannot
be admitted to the baronet's social circle.   The
intelligent mechanic and prosperous farmer is excluded from the merchant's parlor.   The farmer
and mechanic would think they let themselves
down by inviting a worthy day-laborer to their
parties.   And the day-laborer, though he were an
ignoramus and a drunkard, would feel authorized
to treat with contempt any intelligent and excellent man whose complexion happened to be black
or brown.   I once knew a grocer's wife, who, with
infinite condescension of manner, said to the wife
of her neighbor the cobbler, " Why don't you
come in to see me sometimes ?   You need n't
keep away because my house is carpeted all over."

Hannah More tells us that the Duchess of Glouces-
ter, wishing to circulate some tracts and verses,
requested one of her ladies in waiting to stop a
woman who was wheeling a barrow of oranges
past the window, and ask her if she would take
some ballads to sell. " No indeed ! " replied the
orange-woman, with an air of offended dignity.
" I don't do anything so mean as that. I don't
even sell apples." The Duchess was much amused
by her ideas of rank ; but they were in fact no
more absurd than her own. It is the same mean,
selfish spirit which manifests itself through all
these gradations. External rank belongs to the
" phantom dynasties "; and if we wish our children to enjoy sound moral health, we should be
careful not to teach any deference for it, either in
our words or our habits. Mrs. Gaskell, in her
sketch of a very conservative and prejudiced English gentlewoman, " one of the olden time," gives
a lovely touch to the picture, indicating that true
natural refinement was not stifled by the prejudices
of rank. Lady Ludlow had, with patronizing
kindness, invited several of her social inferiors to
tea. Among them was the wife of a rich baker,
who, being unaccustomed to the etiquette of such
company, spread a silk handkerchief in her lap,
when she took a piece of cake ; whereupon some
of the curate's wives began to titter, in order to
show that they knew polite manners better than
she did. Lady Ludlow, perceiving this, imme-

diately spread her own handkerchief in her lap;
and when the baker's wife went to the fireplace
to shake out her crumbs, my lady did the same.
This silent rebuke was sufficient to prevent any
further rudeness to the unsophisticated wife of the
baker.   No elaborate rules are necessary to teach
us true natural politeness.   We need only remember two short texts of Scripture: " Do unto others
as ye would that they should do unto you."
" God is your Father, and all ye are brethren."

Elderly people are apt to think that their years
exempt them from paying so much attention to
good manners as the young are required to do.
On the contrary, they ought to be more careful in
their deportment and conversation, because their
influence is greater.   Impure words or stories
repeated by parents or grandparents may make
indelible stains on the minds of their descendants,
and perhaps give a sensual direction to their characters through life.   No story, however funny,
should ever be told, if it will leave in the memory
unclean associations, either physically or morally.

A love of gossiping about other people's affairs
is apt to grow upon those who have retired from
the active pursuits of life; and this is one among
many reasons why it is best to keep constantly
occupied.   A great deal of trouble is made in
neighborhoods, from no malicious motives, but
from the mere excitement of telling news, and the
temporary importance derived therefrom.   Most

village gossip, when sifted down, amounts to the little school-girl's definition. Being asked what it was to bear false witness against thy neighbor, she replied : " It 's when nobody don't do nothing, and somebody goes and tells of it." One of the best and most genial of the Boston merchants, when he heard people discussing themes of scandal, was accustomed to interrupt them, by saying : " Don't talk any more about it ! Perhaps they did n't do it ; and may be they could n't help it." For myself, I deem it the greatest unkindness to be told of anything said against me. I may, prevent its exciting resentment in my mind ; but the consciousness of not being liked unavoidably disturbs my relations with the person implicated. There is no better safeguard against the injurious habit of gossiping, than the being interested in *principles* and *occupations ;* if you have these to employ your mind, you will have no inclination to talk about matters merely personal.

When we reflect that life is so full of neglected little opportunities to improve ourselves and others, we shall feel that there is no need of aspiring after great occasions to do good.

> " The *trivial* round, the *common* task,
> Would furnish all we need to ask ;
> Room to deny ourselves, — a road
> To bring us daily nearer God."

THE BOYS.

WRITTEN FOR A MEETING OF COLLEGE CLASSMATES.

By OLIVER W. HOLMES. ·

HAS there any *old* fellow got mixed with the boys?
  If there has, take him out, without making a
    noise!
Hang the Almanac's cheat, and the Catalogue's spite!
Old Time is a liar! We 're twenty to-night.

We 're twenty! We 're twenty! Who says we are
    more?
He 's tipsy, young jackanapes! Show him the door!
"Gray temples at twenty?" Yes! *white*, if we please;
Where the snow-flakes fall thickest, there 's nothing
    can freeze.

Was it snowing I spoke of? Excuse the mistake!
Look close, — you will see not a sign of a flake;
We want some new garlands for those we have shed, —
And these are white roses in place of the red.

We 've a trick, we young fellows, you may have been
    told,
Of talking (in public) as if we were old; —
That boy we call "Doctor," and this we call "Judge"; —
It 's a neat little fiction, — of course, it 's all fudge.

That fellow's "the Speaker," — the one on the right;
"Mr. Mayor," my young one, how are you to-night?
That's our "Member of Congress," we say when we
    chaff;
There's the "Reverend" What's his name? Don't
    make me laugh!

.   .   .   .   .

Yes, we're boys, — always playing with tongue or with
    pen, —
And I sometimes have asked, Shall we ever be men?
Shall we always be youthful, and laughing and gay,
Till the last dear companion drops smiling away?

Then here's to our boyhood, its gold and its gray!
The stars of its Winter, the dews of its May!
And when we have done with our life-lasting toys,
Dear Father, take care of thy children, the Boys!

ODE OF ANACREON.

TRANSLATED FROM THE GREEK.

I LOVE a mellow, cheerful sage,
Whose feelings are unchilled by age;
I love a youth who dances well
To music of the sounding shell;
But when a man of years, like me,
Joins with the dancers playfully,
Though age in silvery hair appears,
His heart is young, despite of years.

MYSTERIOUSNESS OF LIFE.

FROM MOUNTFORD'S EUTHANASY.

ABOUT the world to come, it ought not to be as though we did not know *surely*, because we do not know *much*. From the nearest star, our earth, if it is seen, looks hardly anything at all. It shines, or rather it twinkles, and that is all. To them afar off, this earth is only a shining point. But to us who live in it, it is wide and various. It is sea and land; it is Europe, Asia, Africa, and America; it is the lair of the lion, and the pasture of the ox, and the pathway of the worm, and the support of the robin; it is what has day and night in it; it is what customs and languages obtain in; it is many countries; it is the habitation of a thousand million men; and it is our home. All this the world is to *us;* though, looked at from one of the stars, it is only a something that twinkles in the distance. It is seen only as a few intermittent rays of light; though, to us who live in it, it is hill and valley, and land and water, and many thousands of miles wide. So that if the future world is a star of guidance for us, it is enough ; because it is not for us to *know*, but to *believe*, that it will prove our dear home.

. . . . . .

We live mortal lives for immortal good. And really this world is so mysterious, that there is not one of its commonest ways but is perhaps sublimer to walk on than we at all think. At night, when we walk about and see at all, it is by the light of *other* worlds ; though we do not often think of this. It is the same in life. There is many a matter concerning us that is little thought of, but which is ours, as it were, from out of the infinite. Yes, our lives are to be felt as being very great, even in their nothingness. Even our mortal lives are as wonderful as immortality. Is the next life a mystery ? So it is. But then how mysterious even *now* life is. Food is not all that a man lives by. There is some way by which food has to turn to strength in him ; and that way is something else than his own will. I am hungry, I sit down to a meal, and I enjoy it. And the next day, from what I ate and drank for my pleasure, there is blood in my veins, and moisture on my skin, and new flesh making in all my limbs. And this is not my doing or willing ; for I do not even know how my nails grow from under the skin of my fingers. I can well believe in my being to live hereafter. *How*, indeed, I am to live, I do not know ; but, then, neither do I know how I do live *now*. When I am asleep, my lungs keep breathing, my heart keeps beating, my stomach keeps digesting, and my whole body keeps making anew. And in the morning, when I look in the glass, it is as though I see myself a new creature ; and really, for the wonder of it, it is all the same as though another body had grown about me in my sleep. This living from day to day is astonishing, when it is thought of ; and we are let feel the miracle of it, so, perhaps, that our being to live again may not be too wonderful for our be- lief.

THOUGH there be storm and turbulence on this earth, one would rise but little way, through the blackened air, before he would come to a region of calm and peace, where the stars shine unobstructed, and where there is no storm. And a little above our cloud, a little higher than our darkness, a little beyond our storm, is God's upper region of tranquil peace and calm. And when we have had the discipline of winter here, it will be possible for us to have eternal summer there.

HENRY WARD BEECHER.

EXTRACTS FROM

THE GRANDMOTHER'S APOLOGY.

By ALFRED TENNYSON.

AND Willy, my eldest born, is gone you say, little
  Ann?
Ruddy and white and strong on his legs, he looks like a
  man.
" Here 's a leg for a babe of a week ! " says doctor; and
  he would be bound
There was not his like that year in twenty parishes
  round.

Strong of his hands, and strong on his legs, but still of
  his tongue !
I ought to have gone before him; I wonder he went so
  young.
I cannot cry for him, Annie; I have not long to stay;
Perhaps I shall see him the sooner, for he lived far
  away.

Why do you look at me, Annie? you think I am hard
  and cold;
But all my children have gone before me, I am so old:

I cannot weep for Willy, nor can I weep for the rest;
Only at your age, Annie, I could have wept with the
best.

The first child that ever I bore was dead before he was
born:
Shadow and shine is life, little Annie, flower and thorn.
I had not wept, little Annie, not since I had been a
wife;
But I wept like a child, that day; for the babe had
fought for his life.

His dear little face was troubled, as if with anger or
pain;
I looked at the still little body, — his trouble had all
been in vain.
For Willy I cannot weep; I shall see him another
morn;
But I wept like a child for the child that was dead before he was born.

But he cheered me, my good man, for he seldom said
me nay:
Kind, like a man, was he; like a man, too, would have
his way;
Never jealous, — not he: we had many a happy year:
And he died, and I could not weep, — my own time
seemed so near.

But I wished it had been God's will that I, too, then
could have died:
I began to be tired a little, and fain had slept at his
side;

And that was ten years back, or more, if I don't forget:
But as for the children, Annie, they are all about me
yet.

Pattering over the boards, my Annie, who left me at
two;
Patter she goes, my own little Annie, — an Annie like
you.
Pattering over the boards, she comes and goes at her
will,
While Harry is in the five-acre and Charlie ploughing
the hill.

And Harry and Charlie, I hear them, too, — they sing
to their team;
Often they come to the door in a pleasant kind of
dream.
They come and sit by my chair, they hover about my
bed:
I am not always certain if they be alive or dead.

And yet I know for a truth, there's none of them left
alive;
For Harry went at sixty, your father at sixty-five;
And Willy, my eldest born, at nigh threescore and
ten;
I knew them all as babies, and now they are elderly
men.

For mine is a time of peace; it is not often I grieve;
I am oftener sitting at home in my father's farm at
eve;

And the neighbors come and laugh and gossip, and so
 do I;
I find myself often laughing at things that have long
 gone by.

To be sure the preacher says our sins should make us
 sad;
But mine is a time of peace, and there is grace to be
 had;
And God, not man, is the Judge of us all when life shall
 cease;
And in this Book, little Annie, the message is one of
 peace.

And age is a time of peace, so it be free from pain;
And happy has been my life, but I would not live it
 again.
I seem to be tired a little, that's all, and long for rest;
Only at your age, Annie, I could have wept with the
 best.

So Willy has gone, — my beauty, my eldest born, my
 flower;
But how can I weep for Willy? he has but gone for an
 hour, —
Gone for a minute, my son, from this room into the
 next;
I too shall go in a minute. What time have I to be
 vext?

THE ANCI·ENT MAN.

TRANSLATED BY L. O. FROM THE GERMAN OF JEAN PAUL RICH-
TER'S MEMOIR OF FIBEL, AUTHOR OF THE BIENENRODA SPELL-
ING-BOOK.

> " He is insensibly subdued
> To settled quiet.   He is one by whom
> All effort seems forgotten ; one to whom
> Long patience hath such mild composure given,
> That patience now doth seem a thing of which
> He hath no need.   He is by Nature led
> To peace so perfect, that the young behold
> With envy what the old man hardly feels."
>
> Wordsworth.

THE stream of Fibel's history having vanished under ground, like a second river Rhone, I was obliged to explore where story or stream again burst forth, and for this purpose I questioned every one. I was told that no one could better inform me than an exceedingly aged man, more than a hundred and twenty-five years old, who lived a few miles from the village of Bienenroda, and who, having been young at the same time with Fibel, must

know all about him.   The prospect of shaking
hands with the very oldest man living on the face
of the earth enraptured me.   I said to myself that
a most novel and peculiar sensation must be excited
by having a whole past century before you, bodily
present, compact and alive, in the century now
passing; by holding, hand to hand, a man of the
age of the antediluvians, over whose head so many
entire generations of young mornings and old evenings have fled, and before whom one stands, in fact,
as neither young nor old; to listen to a human
spirit, outlandish, behind the time, almost mysteri-
ously awful; sole survivor of the thousand gray,
cold sleepers, coevals of his own remote, hoary
age; standing as sentinel before the ancient dead,
looking coldly and strangely on life's silly novelties; finding in the present no cooling for his in-
born spirit-thirst, no more enchanting yesterdays
or to-morrows, but only the day-before-yesterday
of youth, and the day-after-to-morrow of death.
It may consequently be imagined that so very old
a man would speak only of his *farthest* past, of
his early day-dawn, which, of course, in the long
evening of his protracted day, must now be blending with his midnight.   On the other hand, that
one like myself would not feel particularly younger
before such a millionnaire of hours, as the Bienenroda Patriarch must be; and that his presence
must make one feel more conscious of death than
of immortality.   A very aged man is a more pow-

erful memento than a grave ; for the older a grave is, the farther we look back to the succession of young persons who have mouldered in it ; sometimes a maiden is concealed in an ancient grave ; but an ancient dwindled body hides only an imprisoned spirit.

An opportunity for visiting the Patriarch was presented by a return coach-and-six, belonging to a count, on which I was admitted to a seat with the coachman. Just before arriving at Bienenroda, he pointed with his whip toward an orchard, tuneful with song, and said, " There sits the old man with his little animals around him." I sprang from the noble equipage and went toward him. I ventured to expect that the Count's six horses would give me, before the old man, the appearance of a person of rank, apart from the simplicity of my dress, whereby princes and heroes are wont to distinguish themselves from their tinselled lackeys. I was, therefore, a little surprised that the old man kept on playing with his pet hare, not even checking the barking of his poodle, as if counts were his daily bread, until, at last, he lifted his oil-cloth hat from his head. A buttoned overcoat, which gave room to see his vest, a long pair of knit over-alls, which were, in fact, enormous stockings, and a neckerchief, which hung down to his bosom, made his dress look modern enough. His time-worn frame was far more peculiar. The inner part of the eye, which is black in childhood,

was quite white ; his tallness, more than his years,
seemed .to bow him over into an arch ; the out-
turned point of his chin gave to his speech the
appearance of mumbling ; yet the expression of
his countenance was lively, his eyes bright, his
jaws full of white teeth, and his head covered with
light hair.

I began by saying: " I came here solely on your
account to see a man for whom there can assuredly
be little new under the sun, though he himself is
something very new under it. You are now strictly in your five and twenties ; a man in your best
years ; since after a century a *new* reckoning com-
mences. For myself, I confess that after once
clambering over the century terminus, or church-
wall of a hundred years, I should neither know
how old I was, nor whether I was myself. I
should begin fresh and free, just as the world's
history has often done, counting again from the
year one, in the middle of a thousand years. Yet
why can not a man live to be as old as is many a
giant tree of India still standing? It is well to
question very old people concerning the methods
by 'which they have prolonged their lives. How
do you account for it, dear old sir ? "

I was beginning to be vexed at the good man's
silence, when he softly replied : " Some suppose it
is because I have always been cheerful ; because I
have adopted the maxim, ' Never sad, ever glad';
but I ascribe it wholly to our dear Lord God ; since

the animals, which here surround us, though never
sad, but happy for the most part, by no means so
frequently exceed the usual boundary of their life,
as does man. He exhibits an image of the eternal
God, even in the length of his duration."

Such words concerning God, uttered by a tongue
one hundred and twenty-five years old, had great
weight and consolation ; and I at once felt their
beautiful attraction. On mentioning animals, the
old man turned again to his own ; and, as though
indifferent to him who had come in a coach-and-
six, he began again to play with his menagerie, the
hare, the spaniel, the silky poodle, the starling, and
a couple of turtle-doves on his bosom ; a pleasant
bee-colony in the orchard also gave heed to him ;
with one whistle he sent the bees away, and with
another summoned them into the ring of creatures, which surrounded him like a court-circle.

At last, he said : " No one need be surprised
that a very old man, who has forgotten everything,
and whom no one but the dear God knows or cares
for, should give himself wholly to the dear animals. To whom can such an old man be of much
use ? I wander about in the villages, as in cities,
wholly strange. If I see children, they come before me like my own remote childhood. If I meet
old men, they seem like my past hoary years. I
do not quite know where I now belong. I hang
between heaven and earth. Yet God ever looks
upon me bright and lovingly, with his two eyes,

the sun and the moon. Moreover, animals lead
into no sin, but rather to devotion. When my
turtle-doves brood over their young and feed them,
it seems to me just as if I saw God himself doing
a great deal; for they derive their love and instinct toward their young, as a gift from him.''

The old man became silent, and looked pen-
sively before him, as was his wont. A ringing of
christening bells sounded from Bienenroda among
the trees in the garden. He wept a little. I
know not how I could have been so simple, after
the beautiful words he had uttered, as to have mis-
taken his tears for a sign of weakness in his eyes.
" I do not hear well, on account of my great age,"
said he ; " and it seems to me as if the baptismal
bell from the distant sanctuary sounded up here
very faintly. The old years of my childhood,
more than a hundred years ago, ascend from the
ancient depths of time, and gaze on me in wonder,
while I and they know not whether we ought to
weep or laugh." Then, addressing his silky
poodle, he called out, " Ho! ho! come here old
fellow ! "

'The allusion to his childhood brought me to the
purpose of my visit. " Excellent sir," said I, " I
am preparing the biography of the deceased Master
Gotthelf Fibel, author of the famous Spelling-
Book ; and all I now need to complete it is the
account of his death." The old man smiled, and
made a low bow. I continued, " No one is more

likely to know the particulars of his decease than
yourself; and you are the only person who can
enrich me with the rare traits of his childhood;
because every incident inscribed on a child's brain
grows deeper with years, like names cut into a
gourd, while later inscriptions disappear. Tell
me, I pray you, all that you know concerning the
departed man; for I am to publish his Life at the
Michaelmas Fair."

He murmured, "Excellent genius; scholar;
man of letters; author most famous; these and
other fine titles I learned by heart and applied to
myself, while I was that vain, blinded Fibel, who
wrote and published the ordinary Spelling-Book in
question."

So then, this old man was the blessed Fibel
himself! A hundred and twenty-five notes of
admiration, ay, eighteen hundred and eleven
notes in a row, would but feebly express my astonishment.

[Here follows a long conversation concerning
Fibel, after which the narrative continues as follows:—]

The old man went into his little garden-house,
and I followed him. He whistled, and instantly
his black squirrel came down from a tree, whither
it had gone more for pleasure than for food.
Nightingales, thrushes, starlings, and other birds,
flew back into the open window from the tops of
the trees. A bulfinch, whose color had been

changed by age from red to black, strutted about the room, uttering droll sounds, which it could not make distinct. The hare pattered about in the twilight, sometimes on his hind feet, sometimes on all fours. Every dog in the house bounded forward in glad, loving, human glee. But the most joyful of all was the poodle ; for he knew he was to have a box with compartments fastened to his neck, containing a list of the articles wanted for supper, which it was his business to bring from the inn in Bienenroda. He was Fibel's victualler, or provision-wagon. Children, who ran back and forth, were the only other ones who ministered to his wants.

In allusion to his pets, he said : "We ought to assist the circumscribed faculties of animals, by educating them, as far as we can, since we stand toward them, in a certain degree, as their Lord God ; and we ought to train them to good morals, too ; for very possibly they may continue to live after death. God and the animals are always good ; but not so with man."

Aged men impart spiritual things, as they give material things, with a shaking hand, which drops half. In the effort to gather up his recollections, he permitted me to quicken his memory with my own ; and thus I obtained a connected account of some particulars in his experience. He said he might have been about a hundred years old, when he cut a new set of teeth, the pain of which disturbed him with wild dreams. One night he seemed to be holding in his hands a large sieve, and it was his task to pull the meshes apart, one by one. The close net-work, and the fastening to the wooden rim, gave him indescribable trouble. But as his dream went on, he seemed to hold in his hand the great bright sun, which flamed up into his face. He woke with a new-born feeling, and slumbered again, as if on waving tulips. He dreamed again that he was a hundred years old, and that he died as an innocent yearling child, without any of the sin or woe of earth ; that he found his parents on high, who brought before him a long procession of his children, who had remained invisible to him while he was in this world, because they were transparent, like the angels. He rose from his bed with new teeth and new ideas. The old Fibel was consumed, and a true Phœnix stood in his place, sunning its colored wings. He had risen glorified out of no other grave than his own body. The world retreated ; heaven came down.

When he had related these things, he at once bade me good night. Without waiting for the return of his ministering poodle, and with hands folded for prayer, he showed me the road. I withdrew, but I rambled a long time round the orchard, which had sprung entirely from seed of his own planting. Indeed he seldom ate a cherry without smuggling the stone and burying it in the ground

9 *

for a resurrection. This habit often annoyed the neighboring peasants, who did not want high things growing on their boundaries. " But," said he, " I cannot destroy a fruit-stone. If the peasants pull up the tree it produces, it will still have lived a little while, and die as a child dies."

While loitering in the orchard, I heard an evening hymn played and sung. I returned near Fibel's window, and saw him slowly turning a hand-organ, and accompanying the tune by softly singing an evening hymn. This organ, aided by his fragment of a voice, sufficed, in its monotonous uniformity, for his domestic devotion. I went away repeating the song.

Beautiful was the orchard when I returned the next morning. And the hoar-frost of age seemed thawed and fluid, and to glisten only as morning dew on Fibel's after-blossom. The affection of his animals toward him rendered the morning still more beautiful, in an orchard every tree of which had for its mother the stone of some fruit that he had enjoyed. His animals were an inheritance from his parents ; though, of course they were the great, great, great grandchildren of those which had belonged to them. The trees were full of brooding birds, and by a slight whistle he could lure down to his shoulders this tame posterity of his father's singing-school. It was refreshing to the heart to see how quickly the tender flutterers surrounded him.

With the infantine satisfaction of a gray-headed child, he was accustomed to hang up on sticks, or in the trees, wherever the rays of the sun could best shine upon them, little balls of colored glass ; and he took indescribable delight in this accordion of silver, gold, and jewel hues. These parti-colored sun-balls, varying the green with many flaming tints, were like crystal tulip-beds. Some of the red ones seemed like ripe apples among the branches. But what charmed the old man most were reflections of the landscape from these little world-spheres. They resembled the moving pros-pects shadowed forth in a diminishing mirror. " Ah," said he, " when I contemplate the colors produced by the sunshine, which God gives to this dark world, it seems to me as if I had departed, and were already with God. And yet, since HE is *in* us, we are always with God."

I asked him how it happened that, at his age, he spoke German almost purer than that used even by our best writers. Counting his birth from the end of his century [the new birth described in his dream], he replied : " I was somewhere about two years old, when I happened to hear a holy, spir-itual minister, who spoke German with such an angel tongue, that he would not have needed a better in heaven. I heard him every Sabbath during several years." He could not tell me the preacher's name, but he vividly described his man-ner in the pulpit. He told how he spoke with no superfluity of words, airs, or gestures; how he uttered, in mild tones, things the most beautiful and forcible; how, like the Apostle John, with his resting-place close to heaven, this man spoke to the world, laying his hands calmly on the pulpit-desk, as an arm-case; how his every tone was a heart, and his every look a blessing; how the energy of this disciple of Christ was embedded in love, as the firm diamond is encased in ductile gold; how the pulpit was to him a Mount Tabor, whereon he transfigured both himself and his hearers; and how, of all clergymen, he best per-formed that which is the most difficult, — the *praying* worthily.

My feelings grew constantly warmer toward this time-worn man, while I did not require a full return of affection from him any more than I should from a little child. But I remembered that I ought not to disturb the evening of his days with things of the world, and that I ought to depart. I would have him preserve undisturbed that sub-lime position of old age, where man lives, as it were, at the pole; where no star rises or sets; where the whole firmament is motionless and clear, while the Pole-Star of another world shines fixedly overhead. I therefore said to him, that I would return in the evening, and take my leave. To my surprise, he replied, that perhaps he should himself take leave of the whole world at evening, and that he wished not to be disturbed when dying. He

- said that he should that evening read to the end
of the Revelation of St. John, and perhaps it
might be the end with *him* also. I ought to have
mentioned previously that he read continually, and
read nothing but the Bible, regularly through from
the beginning to the end ; and he had a fixed impression that he should depart on concluding the
twentieth and twenty-first verses of the twenty-
second chapter of the Revelation of John : " He
which testifieth of these things saith, Surely I come
quickly : Amen. Even so, come, Lord Jesus.
The grace of our Lord Jesus Christ be with you
all. Amen." In consequence of this belief, he
was in the habit of reading the last books of the
Bible faster.

Little as I believed in so sudden a withering of
his protracted after-blossom, I obeyed his latest-
formed wish. Whenever a right wish is expressed
by any man, we should do well to remember that
it may be his *last.* I took my leave, requesting
him to intrust me with his testamentary commissions for the village. He said they had been taken
charge of long ago, and the children knew them.
He cut a twig from a Christmas-tree, coeval with
his childhood, and presented me with it as a keep-
sake.

In the beautiful summer evening, I could not refrain from stealthily approaching the house, through
the orchard, to ascertain whether the good old man
had ended his Bible and his life together. On the

way, I found the torn envelope of a letter sealed
with a black seal, and over me the white storks
were speeding their way to a warmer country.   I
was not much encouraged when I heard all the
birds singing in his orchard ; for their ancestors
had done the same when his father died.   A tow-
ering cloud, full of the latest twilight, spread itself
before my short-sighted vision, like a far-off, blooming, foreign landscape ; and I could not comprehend how it was that I had never before noticed
this strange-looking, reddish land ; so much the
more easily did it occur to me that this might be
his Orient, whither God was leading the weary
one.   I had become so confused, as actually to
mistake red bean-blossoms for a bit of fallen sunset.
Presently, I heard a man singing to the accompa-
niment of an organ.   It was the aged man singing
his evening hymn :

> "Lord of my life, another day
> Once more hath sped away."

The birds in the room, and those on the distant
branches also, chimed in with his song.   The bees,
too, joined in with their humming, as in the warm
summer evening they dived into the cups of the
linden-blossoms.   My joy kindled into a flame.
He was alive !   But I would not disturb his holy
evening.   I would let him remain with Him who
had surrounded him with gifts and with years, and
not call upon him to think of any man here below.
I listened to the last verse of his hymn, that I

might be still more certain of the actual continuance of his life, and then tardily I slipped away.
To my joy, I still found, in the eternal youth of
Nature, beautiful references to his lengthened age;
from the everlasting rippling of the brook in the
meadow, to a late swarm of bees, which had settled
themselves on a linden-tree, probably in the forenoon, before two o'clock, as if, by taking their
lodging with him, he was to be their bee-father,
and continue to live. Every star twinkled to me
a hope.

I went to the orchard very early in the morning, wishing to look upon the aged man in sleep;
death's ancient prelude, the warm dream of cold
death. But he was reading, and had read, in his
large-printed Bible, far beyond the Deluge, as I
could see by the engravings. I held it to be a duty
not to interrupt his solitude long. I told him I
was going away, and gave him a little farewell
billet, instead of farewell words. I was much
moved, though silent. It was not the kind of
emotion with which we take leave of a friend, or a
youth, or an old man; it was like parting from a
remote stranger-being, who scarcely glances at us
from the high, cold clouds which hold him between
the earth and the sun. There is a stillness of soul
which resembles the stillness of bodies on a frozen
sea, or on high mountains; every loud tone is an
interruption too prosaically harsh, as in the softest
adagio. Even those words, " for the last time,"

the old man had long since left behind him. Yet he hastily presented to me my favorite flower, a blue Spanish vetch, in an earthen pot. This butterfly-flower is the sweeter, inasmuch as it so easily exhales its perfume and dies. He said he had not yet sung the usual morning-hymn, which followed the survival of his death-evening; and he begged me not to take it amiss that he did not accompany me, or even once look after me, especially as he could not see very well. He then added, almost with emotion, "O friend, may you live virtuously! We shall meet again, where my departed relatives will be present, and also that great preacher, whose name I have forgotten. We meet again."

He turned immediately, quite tranquilly, to his organ. I parted from him, as from a life. He played on his organ beneath the trees, and his face was turned toward me; but to his dim eyes I knew that I should soon become as a motionless cloud. So I remained until he began his morning hymn, from old Neander:

"The Lord still leaves me living,
  I hasten Him to praise;
My joyful spirit giving,
  He hears my early lays."

While he was singing, the birds flew round him; the dogs accustomed to the music, were silent; and it even wafted the swarm of bees into their hive. Bowed down as he was by age, his figure

was so tall, that from the distance where I stood
he looked sufficiently erect. I remained until the
old man had sung the twelfth and last verse of his
morning hymn :

> " Ready my course to finish,
>   And come, O God, to Thee ;
> A conscience pure I cherish,
>   Till death shall summon me."

Nothing of God's making can a man love
rightly, without being the surer of God's loving
himself; neither the moon, nor the stars, nor a
rock, nor a tree, nor a flower, nor a bird. Not
the least grateful of my thanksgivings have been
hymns that have come to my lips while I have been
listening to the birds of an evening. Only let us
love what God loves, and then His love of ourselves will feel certain, and the sight of his face
we shall be sure of; and immortality, and heaven,
and the freedom of the universe, will be as easy for
us to believe in, as a father's giving good gifts to
his children. —Mountford.

MILTON ON HIS LOSS OF SIGHT.

I AM old and blind !
  Men point at me as smitten by God's frown ;
Afflicted, and deserted of my kind,
      Yet I am not cast down.

        I am weak, yet strong ;
I murmur not, that I no longer see ;
Poor, old, and helpless, I the more belong,
      Father supreme ! to thee.

        O merciful One !
When men are farthest, then thou art most near ;
When friends pass by, my weaknesses to shun,
      Thy chariot I hear.

        Thy glorious face
Is leaning towards me, and its holy light
Shines in upon my lonely dwelling-place ;
      And there is no more night.

        On my bended knees,
I recognize thy purpose, clearly shown ;
My vision thou hast dimmed, that I may see
      Thyself, thyself alone.

I have naught to fear ;
This darkness is the shadow of thy wing ;
Beneath it I am almost sacred ; here
    Can come no evil thing.

    O, I seem to stand
Trembling, where foot of mortal ne'er hath been ;
Wrapped in the radiance from the sinless land,
    Which eye hath never seen.

    Visions come and go ;
Shapes of resplendent beauty round me throng ;
From angel lips I seem to hear the flow
    Of soft and holy song.

    It is nothing now, —
When heaven is opening on my sightless eyes,
When airs from paradise refresh my brow, —
    That earth in darkness lies.

    In a purer clime,
My being fills with rapture ! waves of thought
Roll in upon my spirit ! strains sublime
    Break over me unsought.

    Give me now my lyre !
I feel the stirrings of a gift divine ;
Within my bosom glows unearthly fire,
    Lit by no skill of mine.

LETTER FROM AN OLD WOMAN,
ON HER BIRTHDAY.

By L. MARIA CHILD.

YOU ask me, dear friend, whether it does not make me sad to grow old. I tell you frankly it did make me sad for a while; but that time has long since past. The *name* of being old I never dreaded. I am not aware that there ever was a time when I should have made the slightest objection to having my age proclaimed by the town-crier, if people had had any curiosity to know it. But I suppose every human being sympathizes with the sentiment expressed by Wordsworth :

> " Life's Autumn past, I stand on Winter's verge,
> And daily lose what I desire to keep."

The first white streaks in my hair, and the spectre of a small black spider floating before my eyes, foreboding diminished clearness of vision, certainly did induce melancholy reflections. At

that period, it made me nervous to think about the
approaches of old age ; and when young people
thoughtlessly reminded me of it, they cast a shadow
over the remainder of the day.   It was mournful
as the monotonous rasping of crickets, which tells
that " the year is wearing from its prime."   I
dreaded age in the same way that I always dread
the coming of winter ; because I want to keep the
light, the warmth, the flowers, and the growth of
summer.   But, after all, when winter comes, I
soon get used to him, and am obliged to acknowledge that he is a handsome old fellow, and by no
means destitute of pleasant qualities.   And just
so it has proved with old age.   Now that it has
come upon me, I find it full of friendly compensations for all that it takes away.

The period of sadness and nervous dread on
this subject, which I suppose to be a very general
experience, is of longer or shorter duration, according to habits previously formed.   From observation, I judge that those whose happiness
has mainly depended on balls, parties, fashionable
intercourse, and attentions flattering to vanity,
usually experience a prolonged and querulous sadness, as years advance upon them ; because, in the
nature of things, such enjoyments pass out of
the reach of the old, when it is too late to form a
taste for less transient pleasures.   The temporary
depression to which I have alluded soon passed
from my spirit, and I attribute it largely to the

fact that I have always been pleased with very simple and accessible things. I always shudder a little at the approach of winter; yet, when it comes, the trees, dressed in feathery snow, or prismatic icicles, give me far more enjoyment, than I could find in a ball-room full of duchesses, decorated with marabout-feathers, opals, and diamonds. No costly bridal-veil sold in Broadway would interest me so much as the fairy lace-work which frost leaves upon the windows, in an unceasing variety of patterns. The air, filled with minute snow-stars, falling softly, ever falling, to beautify the earth, is to me a far lovelier sight, than would have been Prince Esterhazy, who dropped seed-pearls from his embroidered coat, as he moved in the measured mazes of the dance.

Speaking of the beautiful phenomenon of snow, reminds me how often the question has been asked what snow *is*, and what *makes* it. I have never seen a satisfactory answer; but I happen to know what snow is, because I once saw the process of its formation. I was at the house of a Quaker, whose neat wife washed in an unfinished back-room all winter, that the kitchen might be kept in good order. I passed through the wash-room on the 16th of December, 1835, a day still remembered by many for its remarkable intensity of cold. Clouds of steam, rising from the tubs and boiling kettle, ascended to the ceiling, and fell from thence in the form of a miniature snow-storm. Here was an answer to the question, What *is* snow ? This plainly proved it to be frozen *vapor*, as ice is frozen *water*. The particles of water, expanded by heat, and floatihg in the air, were arrested in their separated state, and congealed in particles. It does not snow when the weather is intensely cold ; for the lower part of the atmosphere must have some degree of warmth, if vapor is floating in it. When this vapor ascends, and meets a colder stratum of air, it is congealed, and falls downward in the form of snow.

" The snow ! The snow ! The beautiful snow ! " How handsome do meadows and fields look in their pure, sparkling robe ! I do not deny that the winter of the year and the winter of life both have intervals of dreariness. The *miserere* howled by stormy winds is not pleasing to the ear, nor are the cold gray river and the dark brown hills refreshing to the eye. But the reading of Whittier's Psalm drowns the howling of the winds, as " the clear tones of a bell are heard above the carts and drays of a city." Even simple voices of mutual affection, by the fireside, have such musical and pervasive power, that the outside storm often passes by unheard. The absence of colors in the landscape is rather dismal, especially in the latter part of the winter. Shall I tell you what I do when I feel a longing for bright hues ? I suspend glass prisms in the windows, and they make the light blossom into rainbows all over the room.

Childish! you will say. I grant it. But is child-
ishness the greatest folly? I told you I was
satisfied with very simple pleasures ; and whether
it be wise or not, I consider it great good fortune.
It is more fortunate certainly to have home-made
rainbows *within*, especially when one is old ; but
even outward home-made rainbows are not to be
despised, when flowers have hidden themselves,
and the sun cannot manifest his prismatic glories,
for want of mediums appropriate for their trans-
mission.

But Nature does not leave us long to pine for
variety. Before the snow-lustre quite passes away,
March comes, sombre in dress, but with a cheerful
voice of promise :

> " The beechen buds begin to swell,
> And woods the blue-bird's warble know."

Here and there a Lady's Delight peeps forth, smiling at me " right peert;" as Westerners say ; and
the first sight of the bright little thing gladdens my
heart, like the crowing of a babe. The phenomena
of spring have never yet failed to replenish the
fountains of my inward life :

> " Spring still makes spring in the *mind*,
>   When sixty years are told ;
> Love wakes anew this throbbing heart,
>   And we are never old."

As the season of Nature's renovation advances, it
multiplies within me spiritual photographs, never
to be destroyed. Last year I saw a striped squirrel

hopping along with a green apple in his paws, hugged up to his pretty little white breast. My mind daguerrotyped him instantaneously. It is there now ; and I expect to find a more vivid copy when my soul opens its portfolio of pictures in the other world.

The wonders which summer brings are more and more suggestive of thought as I grow older. What mysterious vitality, what provident care. what lavishness of ornament, does Nature manifest, even in her most common productions! Look at a dry bean-pod, and observe what a delicate little strip of silver tissue is tenderly placed above and below the seed ! Examine the clusters of Sweet-Williams, and you will find an endless variety of minute embroidery-patterns, prettily dotted into the petals with diverse shades of colors. The shining black seed they produce look all alike ; but scatter' them in the ground, and there will spring forth new combinations of form and color, exceeding the multiform changes of a kaleidoscope. I never can be sufficiently thankful that I early formed the habit of working in the garden with loving good-will. It has contributed more than anything else to promote healthiness of mind and body.

Before one has time to observe a thousandth part of the miracles of summer, winter appears again, in ermine and diamonds, lavishly scattering his pearls. My birthday comes at this season,

10

and so I accept his jewels as a princely largess
peculiarly bestowed upon myself. The day is kept
as a festival. That is such a high-sounding expression, that it may perhaps suggest to you recep-
tion-parties, complimentary verses, and quantities
of presents. Very far from it. Not more than
half a dozen people in the world know when the
day occurs, and they do not all remember it. As
I arrive at the new milestone on my pilgrimage, I
generally find that a few friends have placed garlands upon it. My last anniversary was distinguished by a beautiful novelty. An offering came
from people who never knew me personally, but
who were gracious enough to say they took an
interest in me on account of my writings. That
was a kindness that carried me over into my new
year on fairy wings! I always know that the
flowers in such garlands are genuine; for those
who deal in artificial roses are not in the habit of
presenting them to secluded old people, without
wealth or power. I have heard of a Parisian lady,
who preferred Nattier's manufactured roses to those
produced by Nature, because they were, as she
said, " more like what a rose *ought* to be." But I
never prefer artificial things to natural, even if
they *are* more like what they *ought* to be. So I
rejoice over the genuineness of the offerings which
I find on the milestone, and often give preference
to the simplest of them all. I thankfully add them
to my decorations for the annual festival, which is

kept in the private apartments of my own soul,
where six angel-guests present themselves unbid-
den, — Use and Beauty, Love and Memory, Humility and Gratitude. The first suggests to me to
consecrate the advent of a new year in my life
by some acts of kindness toward the sad, the oppressed, or the needy. Another tells me to collect
all the books, engravings, vases, &c., bestowed by
friendly hands on the preceding birthdays of my
life. Their beauties of thought, of form, and of
color, excite my imagination, and fill me with con-
templations of the scenes they represent, or the
genius that produced them. Other angels bring
back the looks and tones of the givers, and pleasant incidents, and happy meetings, in bygone years.
Sometimes, Memory looks into my eyes too sadly,
and I answer the look with tears. But I say to
her, Nay, my friend, do not fix upon me that
melancholy gaze! Give me some of thy flowers!
Then, with a tender, moonlight smile, she brings
me a handful of fragrant roses, pale, but beautiful.
The other angels bid me remember who bestowed
the innumerable blessings of Nature and Art, of
friendship, and capacity for culture, and how unworthy I am of all His goodness. They move my
heart to earnest prayer that former faults may be
forgiven, and that I may be enabled to live more
worthily during the year on which I am entering.
But I do not try to recall the faults of the past,
lest such meditations should tend to make me weak

for the future. I have learned that self-consciousness is not a healthy state of mind, on whatever theme it employs itself. Therefore, I pray the all-loving Father to enable me to forget *myself;* not to occupy my thoughts with my own merits, or my own defects, my successes, or my disappointments ; but to devote my energies to the benefit of others, as a humble instrument of his goodness, in whatever way He may see fit to point out.

On this particular birthday, I have been thinking more than ever of the many compensations which age brings for its undeniable losses. I count it something to know, that, though the flowers offered me are *few*, they are undoubtedly *genuine.* I never conformed much to the world's ways, but, now that I am an old woman, I feel more free to ignore its conventional forms, and neglect its fleeting fashions. That also is a privilege. Another compensation of years is, that, having outlived expectations, I am free from disappointments. I deem it a great blessing, also, that the desire for knowledge grows more active, as the time for acquiring it diminishes, and as, I realize more fully how much there is to be learned. It is true that in this pursuit one is always coming up against walls of limitation. All sorts of flying and creeping things excite questions in my mind to which I obtain no answers. I want to know what every bird and insect is doing, and what it is done for ;

but I do not understand their language, and no in-
terpreter between us is to be found. They go on,
busily managing their own little affairs, far more
skilfully than we humans could teach them, with
all our boasted superiority of intellect. I peep and
pry into their operations with more and more interest, the older I grow ; but they keep their own
secrets so well, that I discover very little. What
I do find out, however, confirms my belief, that
" the hand which made them is divine "; and that
is better than any acquisitions of science. Looking
upon the world as a mere spectacle of beauty, I
find its attractions increasing. I notice more than
I ever did the gorgeous phantasmagoria of sunsets,
the magical changes of clouds, the endless varieties
of form and color in the flowers of garden and field,
and the shell-flowers of the sea. Something of
tenderness mingles with the admiration excited by
all this fair array of earth, like the lingering, farewell gaze we bestow on scenes from which we are
soon to part.

But the most valuable compensations of age are
those of a spiritual character. I have committed
so many faults myself, that I have become more
tolerant of the faults of others than I was when I
was young. My own strength has so often failed
me when I trusted to it, that I have learned to
look more humbly for aid from on high. I have
formerly been too apt to murmur that I was not
endowed with gifts and opportunities, which it ap-

peared to me would have been highly advantageous.
But I now see the wisdom and goodness of our
Heavenly Father, even more in what He has denied, than in what He has bestowed. The rugged
paths through which I have passed, the sharp regrets I have experienced, seem smoother and softer
in the distance behind me. Even my wrong-doings
and short-comings have often been mercifully trans-
muted into blessings. They have helped me to
descend into the Valley of Humility, through which
it is necessary to pass on our way to the Beautiful
City. My restless aspirations are quieted. They
are now all concentrated in this one prayer:

" Help me, this and every day,
 To live more nearly as I pray."

Having arrived at this state of peacefulness and
submission, I find the last few years the happiest
of my life.

To you, my dear friend, who are so much
younger, I would say, Travel cheerfully toward
the sunset! It will pass gently into a twilight,
which has its own peculiar beauties, though
differing from the morning; and you
will find that the night also
is cheered by friendly
glances of the
stars.

BRIGHT DAYS IN WINTER.

By J. G. WHITTIER.

BLAND as the morning's breath of June,
  The southwest breezes play,
And through its haze, the winter noon
  Seems warm as summer's day.

The snow-plumed Angel of the North
  Has dropped his icy spear;
Again the mossy earth looks forth,
  Again the streams gush clear.

The fox his hillside den forsakes;
  The muskrat leaves his nook;
The blue-bird, in the meadow-brakes,
  Is singing with the brook.

"Bear up, O Mother Nature!" cry
  Bird, breeze, and streamlet free;
"Our winter voices prophesy
  Of summer days to thee."

So in these winters of the *soul*,
  By wintry blasts and drear

O'erswept from Memory's frozen pole,
  Will summer days appear.

Reviving hope and faith, they show
  The soul its living powers,
And how, beneath the winter's snow,
  Lie germs of summer flowers.

The Night is mother of the Day;
  The Winter of the Spring;
And ever upon old decay
  The greenest mosses cling.

Behind the cloud the starlight lurks;
  Through showers the sunbeams fall;
For God, who loveth all his works,
  Has left his Hope with all.

THE CANARY BIRD.

YELLOW, small Canary bird,
  Sweetly singing all day long,
Still in winter you are heard,
  Carolling a summer song.

Thus when days are drear and dim,
  And the *heart* is caged, as you,
May it still, with hopeful hymn,
  Sing of joy and find it true.

JOHN STERLING.

OLD BACHELORS.

By L. MARIA CHILD.

THE use of the term old bachelor might be objected to, with as much reason as that of old maid, were it not for the fact that it has been regarded less contemptuously. Until within the last half-century, books have been written almost entirely by men. Looking at the subject from *their* point of view, they have generally represented that, if a woman remained single, it was because she could not avoid it; and that her unfortunate condition was the consequence of her being repulsive in person or manners. The dramas and general literature of all countries abound with jokes on this subject. Women are described as jumping with ridiculous haste at the first chance to marry, and as being greatly annoyed if no chance presents itself. To speak of women as in the market, and of men as purchasers, has so long been a general habit, that it is done unconsciously; and the habit

10*   o

doubtless embodies a truth, though few people reflect why it is so. Nearly all the trades, professions, and offices are engrossed by men ; hence marriage is almost the only honorable means of support for women, and almost the only avenue open to those who are ambitious of position in society. This state of things gives an unhealthy stimulus to match-making, and does much to degrade the true dignity and purity of marriage. But I allude to it here merely as explanatory why old maid is considered a more reproachful term than old bachelor ; one being supposed to be incurred voluntarily, and the other by compulsion.

There is a germ of vanity, more or less expanded in human nature, under all circumstances. Slaves are often very vain of bringing an unusually high price in the market ; because it implies that they are handsome, vigorous, or intelligent. It is the same feeling, manifested under a different aspect, that makes many women vain of the number of offers they have received, and mortified if they have had none. Men, on the contrary, being masters of the field, are troubled with no sense of shame, if they continue in an isolated position through life, though they may experience regret. The kind of jokes to which *they* are subjected generally imply that they have been less magnanimous than they should have been, in not taking to themselves somebody to protect and support. Such a " railing accusation " is rather gratifying to the pride of human nature. Instead of hanging their heads, they sometimes smile, and say, with an air of gracious condescension : " Perhaps I *may* some day. I have not decided yet. I want to examine the market further." Now it is ten chances to one, that the individual thus speaking *has* been examining the market, as he calls it, for a long time ; that he has been to the Fair, and tried to appropriate various pretty articles, but has been told that they were reserved for a previous purchaser. He may have been disappointed on such occasions ; and if they occurred when youth was passing away, he may have been prompted to look in the mirror, to pull out gray hairs, and ascertain whether crows have been walking over his face. But if he perceives traces of their feet, he says to himself, " Pshaw ! What consequence is it, so long as I have a full purse and a handsome house to offer ? I shall have better luck next time. There are as good fish in the sea as ever were caught. One only needs to have bait on the hook." And so when a married acquaintance reminds him that he ought to take a wife, he answers, complacently, " Perhaps I *shall.* I want to examine the market." He is the one to confer support ; he need not wait to be asked. There is a dignified independence in such a position. Hence the term old bachelor is not so opprobrious as old maid, and no apology is necessary for using it.

It is true, the single brotherhood are not without their annoyances. A meddlesome woman will sometimes remark to a bachelor friend, in a significant sort of way, that the back of his coat has a one-eyed look, by reason of the deficiency of a button ; and she will add, in a compassionate tone, " But what else can be expected, when a man has no wife to look after him ? " Another, still more mischievous, who happens to know of his attending the Fair, and trying to buy various articles otherwise appropriated, will sometimes offer impertinent consolation ; saying, " Don't be discouraged. Try again. Perhaps you 'll have better luck next time. You know the proverb says, There never was so silly a Jack but there 's *as* silly a Gill." Then again, the French phrase for old bachelor, *Vieux Garçon*, translates itself into right impudent English. Why on earth should a man be called the Old Boy, merely because he has not seen fit to marry ? when it is either because he don't like the market, or wants to look further, in order to make sure of getting his money's worth in the article.

I have spoken facetiously, but it may well be excused. Women have for so many generations been the subject of pitiless jokes, rung through all manner of changes, and not always in the best taste, that it is pardonable to throw back a few jests, provided it be done in sport, rather than in malice. The simple fact is, however, that what I

have said of unmarried women is also true of unmarried men ; their being single is often the result
of superior delicacy and refinement of feeling.
Those who are determined to marry, will usually
accomplish their object, sooner or later, while
those who shrink from making wedlock a mere
convenience, unsanctified by affection, will prefer
isolation, though they sometimes find it sad. I
am now thinking of one, who, for many reasons
would probably be accepted by ninety-nine women
out of a hundred. I once said to him, " How is
it, that a man of your domestic tastes and affectionate disposition has never married ? "   He
hesitated a moment, then drew from under his
vest the miniature of a very lovely woman, and
placed it in my hand. I looked up with an
inquiring glance, to which he replied : " Yes,
perhaps it might have been ; perhaps it *ought* to
have been. But I had duties to perform toward
my widowed mother, which made me doubt
whether it were justifiable to declare my feelings
to the young lady. Meanwhile, another offered
himself. She married him, and is, I believe,
happy. I have never seen another woman who
awakened in me the same feelings, and so I have
remained unmarried."

I knew twin brothers, who became attached to
the same lady. One was silent, for his brother's
sake ; but he never married ; and through life he
loved and assisted his brother's children, as if they

had been his own.   There are many such facts to
prove that self-sacrifice and constancy are far from
being exclusively feminine virtues.

But my impression is, that there is a larger proportion of unmarried women than of unmarried
men, who lead unselfish, useful lives.   I, at least,
have happened to know of more " Aunt Kindlys,"
than Uncle Kindlys.   Women, by the nature of
their in-door habits and occupations, can nestle
themselves into the inmost of other people's families, much more readily than men.   The household inmate, who cuts paper-dolls to amuse fretful
children, or soothes them with lullabies when they
are tired, — who sews on buttons for the father,
when he is in a hurry, or makes goodies for the invalid mother, — becomes part and parcel of the
household ; whereas a bachelor is apt to be a sort
of appendage ; beloved and agreeable, perhaps, but
still something on the outside.   He is like moss on
the tree, very pretty and ornamental, especially
when lighted up by sunshine ; but no inherent
part of the tree, essential to its growth.   Sometimes, indeed, one meets with a genial old bachelor,
who cannot enter the house of a married friend, or
relative, without having the children climb into his
lap, pull out his watch, and search his pocket for
sugar-plums.   But generally, it must be confessed
that a *Vieux Garçon* acts like an Old Boy when
he attempts to make himself useful in the house.
His efforts to quiet crying babies are laughable,

and invariably result in making the babies cry
more emphatically. A dignified, scholastic bachelor, who had been spending the night with a married friend, was leaving his house after breakfast,
when a lovely little girl of four or five summers
peeped from the shrubbery, and called out, " Good
morning! " " Good morning, child! " replied he,
with the greatest solemnity of manner, and passed
on. A single *woman* would have said, " Good
morning, dear! " or " Good morning, little one! "
But the bachelor was as dignified as if he had
been making an apostrophe to the stars. Yet he
had a great, kind heart, and was a bachelor because that heart was too refined to easily forget a
first impression.

Bachelors do not become an outside appendage,
if they are fortunate enough to have an unmarried
sister, with whom they can form one household.
There is such a couple in my neighborhood, as
cozy and comfortable as any wedded pair, and
quite as unlikely to separate, as if the law bound
them together. The sister is a notable body, who
does well whatever her hands find to do ; and the
brother adopts wise precautions against tedious
hours. He was a teacher in his youth, but is a
miller now. An old mill is always a picturesque
object, standing as it must in the midst of running
water, whose drops sparkle and gleam in sunlight
and moonlight. And our bachelor's mill is hidden
in a wood, where birds love to build their nests, and

innumerable insects are busy among ferns and mosses. The miller is busy, too, with a lathe to fill up the moments unoccupied by the work of the mill. He has made a powerful telescope for himself, and returns to his home in the evening to watch the changing phases of the planets, or to entertain his neighbors with a vision of Saturn sailing through boundless fields of ether in his beautiful luminous ring. He can also discourse sweet music to his sister, by means of a parlor seraphine.

I know another bachelor, who finds time to be a benefactor to his neighborhood, though his life is full of labors and cares. In addition to the perpetual work of a farm, he devotes himself with filial tenderness to a widowed mother and invalid aunts, and yet he is always ready wherever help or sympathy is needed. If a poor widow needs wood cut, he promptly supplies the want, and few men with a carriage and four are so ready to furnish a horse for any kindly service. The children all know his sleigh, and call after him for a ride. None of his animals have the forlorn, melancholy look which indicates a hard master. The expression of his countenance would never suggest to any one the condition of an old bachelor; on the contrary, you would suppose he had long been accustomed to look into the eyes of little ones clambering upon his knees for a kiss. This is because he adopts all little humans into his heart.

I presume it will generally be admitted that

bachelors are more apt to be epicures, than are un-married women. In the first place, they have fewer details of employment to occupy their thoughts per-petually ; and secondly, they generally have greater pecuniary means for self-indulgence. The gour-mand, who makes himself unhappy, and disturbs everybody around him, if his venison is cooked the fortieth part of a minute too long, is less agreeable, and not less ridiculous than the old fop, who wears false whiskers, and cripples his feet with tight boots.

There is a remedy for this, and for all other self-ishness and vanity; it is to go out of ourselves, and be busy with helping others. Petty annoy-ances slip away and are forgotten when the mind is thus occupied. The wealthy merchant would find it an agreeable variation to the routine of business to interest himself in the welfare and im-provement of the sailors he employs. The pros-perous farmer would find mind and heart enlarged by helping to bring into general use new and im-proved varieties of fruits and vegetables ; not for mere money-making, but for the common good. And all would be happier for taking an active interest in the welfare of their country, and the progress of the world.

Nothing can be more charming than Dickens's description of the Cheeryble Brothers, " whose goodness was so constantly a diffusing of itself over everywhere."

" 'Brother Ned,' said Mr. Cheeryble, tapping with his knuckles, and stooping to listen, ' are you busy, my dear brother ? or can you spare time for a word or two with me ? '

" ' Brother Charles, my dear fellow,' replied a voice from within, ' don't ask me such a question, but come in directly.' Its tones were so exactly like that which had just spoken, that Nicholas started, and almost thought it was the same.

" They went in without further parley. What was the amazement of Nicholas, when his conductor advanced and exchanged a warm greeting with another old gentleman, the very type and model of himself; the same face, the same figure, the same coat, waistcoat, and neckcloth, the same breeches and gaiters ; nay, there was the very same white hat hanging against the wall. Nobody could have doubted their being twin brothers. As they shook each other by the hand, the face of each lighted up with beaming looks of affection, which would have been most delightful to behold in infants, and which in men so old was inexpressibly touching.

" ' Brother Ned,' said Charles, ' here is a young friend that we must assist. We must make proper inquiries into his statements, and if they are confirmed, as they will be, we must assist him.'

" ' It is enough, my dear brother, that you say we should. When you say that, no further inquiries are needed. He *shall* be assisted.'

" ' I 've a plan, my dear brother, I 've a plan,' said Charles. ' Tim Linkinwater is getting old ; and Tim has been a faithful servant, brother Ned ; and I don't think pensioning Tim's mother and sister, and buying a little tomb for the family when his poor brother died, was a sufficient recompense for his faithful services.'

" ' No, no,' replied the other, ' not half enough ; not half.'

" ' If we could lighten Tim's duties,' said the old gentleman, ' and prevail upon him to go into the country now and then, and sleep in the fresh air two or three times a week, Tim Linkinwater would grow young again in time ; and he 's three good years our senior now. Old Tim Linkinwater young again ! Eh, brother Ned, eh ? Why, I recollect old Tim Linkinwater quite a little boy ; don't you ? Ha, ha, ha ! Poor Tim ! Poor Tim ! ' and the fine old fellows laughed pleasantly together ; each with a tear of regard for old Tim Linkinwater standing in his eye.

" ' But you must hear this young gentleman's story,' said Charles ; ' you 'll be very much affected, brother Ned, remembering the time when *we* were two friendless lads, and earned our first shilling in this great city.'

" The twins pressed each other's hands in silence, and, in his own homely manner, Charles related the particulars he had just heard from Nicholas. It is no disparagement to the young man to say, that, at every fresh expression of their kindness and sympathy, he could only wave his hand and sob like a child.

" ' But we are keeping our young friend too long, my dear brother,' said Charles. ' His poor mother and sister will be anxious for his return. So good by for the present. Good by. No, not a word now. Good by.' And the brothers hurried him out, shaking hands with him all the way, and affecting, very unsuccessfully (for they were poor hands at deception), to be wholly unconscious of the feelings that mastered him.

" The next day, he was appointed to the vacant stool in the counting-house of Cheeryble Brothers, with a salary of one hundred and twenty pounds a year. ' And I think, my dear brother,' said Charles, ' that if we were to let them that little cottage at Bow, something under the usual rent — Eh, brother Ned ? '

" ' For nothing at all,' said his brother, ' We are rich, and should be ashamed to touch the rent under such circumstances as these. For nothing at all, my dear brother.'

" ' Perhaps it would be better to say something,' suggested the other, mildly. ' We might say fifteen or twenty pound ; and if it was punctually paid, make it up to them in some other way. It would help to preserve habits of frugality, you know, and remove any painful sense of overwhelming obligation.' And I might secretly ad-

vance a small loan toward a little furniture ; and
you might secretly advance another small loan,
brother Ned.   And if we find them doing well we
can change the loans into gifts ; carefully, and by
degrees, without pressing upon them too much.
What do you say now, brother ? '

" Brother Ned gave his hand upon it, and not
only said it should be done, but had it done.   And
in one short week, Nicholas took possession of his
stool, and his mother and sister took possession of
the house ; and all was hope, bustle, and light-
heartedness."

There are Cheeryble old bachelors in real life ;
genial souls, and genuine benefactors to mankind.
When they are so, I think they deserve
more credit than married men of similar
characters ; for the genial virtues
are fostered by kindly domes-
tic influences, as fruit is
matured and sweet-
ened by the
sunshine.

THE dog in the kennel growls at his fleas ; the
dog that is busy hunting does not feel them.

CHINESE PROVERB.

TAKING IT EASY.

By GEORGE H. CLARK.

ADMIT that I am slightly bald, —
  Pray, who's to blame for that?
And who is wiser for the fact,
  Until I lift my hat?
Beneath the brim my barbered locks
  Fall in a careless way,
Wherein my watchful wife can spy
  No lurking threads of gray.

What though, to read compactest print,
  I'm forced to hold my book
A little farther off than when
  Life's first degree I took?
A yoke of slightly convex lens
  The needful aid bestows,
And you should see how wise I look
  With it astride my nose.

Don't talk of the infernal pangs
  That rheumatism brings!

I'm getting used to pains and aches,
   And all those sort of things.
And when the imp Sciatica
   Makes his malicious call,
I do not need an almanac
   To tell me it is fall.

Besides, it gives one quite an air
   To travel with a cane,
And makes folk think you " well to do,"
   Although you are in pain.
A fashionable hat may crown
   Genteelest coat and vest,
But ah! the sturdy stick redeems
   And sobers all the rest.

A man deprived of natural sleep
   Becomes a stupid elf,
And only steals from Father Time
   To stultify himself.
So, if you'd be a jovial soul,
   And laugh at life's decline,
Take my advice, — turn off the gas,
   And go to bed at nine!

An easy-cushioned rocking-chair
   Suits me uncommon well;
And so do liberal shoes, — like these, —
   With room for corns to swell;
I cotton to the soft lamb's-wool
   That lines my gloves of kid,
And love elastic home-made socks, —
   Indeed, I always did.

But what disturbs me more than all
  Is, that sarcastic boys
Prefer to have me somewhere else,
  When they are at their noise ;
That while I try to look and act
  As like them as I can,
They will persist in *mister*-ing me,
  And calling me a man !

TRUE — Time will seam and blanch my brow.
  Well, I shall sit with aged men,
And my good glass will tell me how
  A grisly beard becomes me then.

And should no foul dishonor lie
  Upon my head, when I am gray,
Love yet shall watch my fading eye,
  And smooth the path of my decay.

Then haste thee, Time, — 't is kindness all
  That speeds thy winged feet so fast ;
Thy pleasures stay not till they pall,
  And all thy pains are quickly past.

Thou fliest and bear'st away our woes,
  And, as thy shadowy train depart,
The memory of sorrow grows
  A lighter burden on the heart.

                W. C. BRYANT.

OLD AUNTY.

THE following is a true story. I well remember the worthy old woman, who sat in Washington Park, behind a table covered with apples and nuts. I also know the family of the little Joanna, who used to carry her a cup of hot tea and warm rolls from one of the big houses in the adjoining Square, and who got up a petition to the Mayor in her behalf. It is a humble picture; but a soft, warm light falls on it from poor Old Aunty's self-sacrificing devotion to her orphans, and from the mutual love between her and the children of the neighborhood.

L. M. C.

ALL the children knew Old Aunty. Every day, in rain or shine, she sat there in the Park, with her little store of candies, cakes, and cigars, spread on a wooden box. Her cheerful smile and hearty "God bless you!" were always ready for the children, whether they bought of her or not. If they stopped to purchase, she gave right generous measure, heaping the nuts till they rolled off the top of the pint, and often throwing in a cake or stick of candy; so generous was her heart.

P

Like all unselfish people, Aunty was happy as the days are long. Had you followed her home at night, you would have seen her travel down a poor old street, narrow and musty, and climb the broken stairs of a poor old house that was full of other lodgers, some of them noisy, disorderly, and intemperate. When she opened the creaking door of her one small room, you would have seen the boards loose in the floor, little furniture, very little that looked like rest or comfort, like *home* for a tired body that had toiled full seventy years, and had once known the pleasure of a cheerful fireside and a full house.

But presently you would hear the patter of little feet, and the music of children's voices, and little hands at work with the rusty door-latch, till open it flew. You would have heard two merry little creatures shouting, "Granny 's come home! Dear Granny 's come home!" You would have seen them dancing about her, clapping their hands, and saying, " O we 're so glad, so glad you 've come back!" These are the orphan grandchildren, to feed and clothe whom Old Aunty is willing to walk so far, and sit so long in the cold, and earn penny by penny, as the days go by.

She kindles no fire, for it is not winter yet, and the poor can eat their supper cold ; but the children's love and a well-spent day kindle a warmth and a light in the good dame's heart, such as I fear seldom beams in some of those great stately houses in the Square.

With such a home, it is not strange that Aunty liked to sit under the pleasant trees of the Parade Ground (for so the Park was called), breathe the fresh air, and watch the orderly people going to and fro. Many stopped to exchange a word with her; even the police officers, in their uniforms, liked a chat with the sociable old lady; and the children, on their way to school, were never too hurried for a " Good morning, Aunty ! ". that would leave a smile on her wrinkled face, long after they had bounded out of sight.

It was nearly as good as if Aunty had a farm of her own ; for it is always country up in the sky, you know ; in the beautiful blue, among the soft clouds, and along the tops of the trees. Even in that dismal, musty street, where she lived, she could see the sunshine, and the wonderful stars at evening. Then all about the Parade Ground stood the fine great houses of Washington Square ; and leading from it, that Fifth Avenue, which is said to be the most splendid street in the world, — whole miles of palaces.

" Don't I enjoy them all, without having the care of them ? " Aunty used to say.

When we asked if she did n't grow tired of sitting there all day, she would answer, " Sure, and who is n't tired sometimes, rich or poor ? "

" But is not the ground damp, Aunty ? "

" I expect it is, especially after a rain ; but what then ? It only gives me the rheumatism ; and that is *all* the trouble I have. God be praised ! "

" But it is so cold now, Aunty ; so late in November ; and you are so old ; it is n't safe."

" O, but it 's safer than to have my children starve or turn beggars, I guess. I have my old umbrella when it rains or snows, and them 's my harvest-days, you see ; for there 's a deal of pity in the world. And besides, the children in that house yonder, often bring me out a hot cup of tea at luncheon-time, or cakes of good warm bread in the morning. Let me alone for being happy ! "

But earthly happiness hangs on a slight thread. There came a change in the city government ; Aunty's good friends among the police were removed ; the new officers proved their zeal by making every change they could think of. " New brooms sweep clean," and they swept off from the Parade Ground, poor Aunty, and all her stock in trade.

But in one of the houses opposite Aunty's corner of the Park, lived a family of children who took especial interest in her ; Charlie, Willie, Vincent, and Joanna, and I can't tell how many more. It was they who christened her " Aunty," till all the neighbors, old and young, took up the name ; it was they who, on wintry days, had offered her the hot cup of tea, and the warm bread. They almost felt as if she were an own relative, or a grown-up child given them to protect and comfort.

One morning, Joanna looked up from the breakfast-table, and exclaimed, " There ! Aunty is not in the Park ; they have sent her away ! "

The children had feared this change. You may
guess how eagerly they ran to the window, and
with what mournful faces they exclaimed again and
again, "It is too bad!" They would eat no more
breakfast; they could think and talk of nothing
but Aunty's wrongs.

It was a bleak December day, and there the
poor old woman sat outside the iron railing, no
pleasant trees above her, but dust and dead leaves
blowing wildly about. Charlie said, with tears in
his eyes, "It's enough to blind poor Old Aunty."

"It's enough to ruin her candy," said Joanna,
who was a practical little body. She had a look
in her eyes that was better than tears; a look that
seemed to say, "Her candy shall *not* be ruined.
Aunty shall go back to her rightful place."

We did not know about Aunty's having any
right to her old seat; but we all agreed that it was
far better for her to sit near the path that ran slant-
wise through the Park, and was trodden by hun-
dreds and thousands of feet every day; clerks
going to Sixth Avenue, and merchants to Broadway; newsmen, porters, school-children, teachers,
preachers, invalids; there was no end to the people.
Many a cake or apple they had taken from Aunty's
board, and in their haste, or kindness, never waited
for change to the bit of silver they tossed her.

In New York every one is in such a hurry that
unless you are almost under their feet they cannot
see you. For this reason, on the day of Aunty's

absence, she had the grief of watching many old friends and customers go past, give a surprised look at her old seat, and hurry on, never observing her, though she sat so near.

A few, who espied Aunty, stopped in their haste to hear her story and condole with her. The children found her out, you may be sure, and gathered about her, telling her how much too bad it was ; and how they should like to set the police-men, Mayor and all, out there on a bench in the dust, for one half-hour ; but what could children do ? So they passed on. Some of the fashionable ladies in the Square stopped to tell Aunty how they pitied her, begged her not to feel unhappy, and passed on. Only Trouble stood still and frowned at her ; all the rest passed on.

No, not all ; not our little Joanna. She came home with a thoughtful face, and asked, very ener-getically, " What do you mean to do about Aunty ? It is a shame that all these rich, strong, grown-up people on the Square, cannot stand up for the rights of one poor old woman."

We told her the city was richer than the rich-est, stronger than the strongest.

" O," persisted Joanna, " if we, or any of them, wanted a new lamp-post, or a hydrant mended, we should muster strength fast enough. And now, what's to become of Aunty and her poor children? that is all I ask."

We smiled at Joey's enthusiasm, and thought it

would soon pass away. When she came home
from school that afternoon, with a whole troop of
little girls, we thought it had already passed away.
As they ran down the area-steps, we wondered what
amusement they were planning now. Presently,
Joanna came up-stairs, her eyes looking very
bright, and said, " Please give me the inkstand."

We asked, " What now, child ? "

" O, do just give me the inkstand ! " said she,
impatiently. " We are not in any mischief; we
are attending to *business* "; and off she ran.

Before very long she appeared again with a
paper, her black eyes burning like stars. " There,
mother, — and all of you, — you must sign this
letter, as quick as ever you can. I have made a
statement of Aunty's case ; all the children have
signed their names ; and now we are going to
every house in the Square, till we have a good
long list."

" And what then ? "

" I shall ask father to take it to the Mayor. He
wont be so unreasonable as to refuse us ; no one
could."

Joanna had written out Aunty's story, in her
own simple, direct way. She told how this nice,
neat, pleasant old person had been turned out of
the Park ; how the children all had liked her, and
found it convenient to buy at her table ; and how
she never scolded if they dropped papers and nut-
shells about, but took her own little pan and brush

and swept them away; she was so orderly.   She
ended her letter with a petition that the Mayor
would be so good to the children, and this excellent old grandmother, as to let her go back to her
old seat.

If the Mayor could refuse, we could not; so
our names went down on the paper; and before
the ink was dry, off ran Joanna.   The hall-door
slammed, and we saw her with all her friends run
up the steps of the neighboring houses, full of
excitement and hope.

Nearly all the families that lived in the great
houses of Washington Square were rich; and some
of them proud and selfish, perhaps; for money
sometimes does sad mischief to the hearts of people.   We asked ourselves, " What will they care
for old Aunty?"

Whatever their tempers might be, however,
when the lady or gentleman came and saw the
bright, eager faces, and the young eyes glistening
with sympathy, and the little hands pointing out
there at the aged woman on the sidewalk, — while
they were in their gilded and cushioned houses, —
they could not refuse a name, and the list swelled
fast.

At one house lived three Jewesses, who were so
pleased with the children's scheme, that they not
only gave their own names, but obtained many
more.   " They are Jews, ma'am, but they 're
Christians!" said Aunty afterwards; by which

she meant, it is not *names*, but *actions*, that prove us followers of the loving, compassionate Christ.

So large was the Square, so many houses to visit, that the ladies' help was very welcome. They could state Aunty's case with propriety; and what with their words and the children's eloquent faces, all went well.

So the paper was filled with signatures, and Joanna's father took it to the Mayor. He smiled, and signed his name, in big letters, to an order that Aunty should return at once to her old seat, and have all the privileges she had ever enjoyed in the Park; and the next morning there she was, in her own old corner!

As soon as she came, the children ran out to welcome her. As she shook hands with them, and looked up in their pleased faces, we saw her again and again wipe the tears from her old eyes.

Everybody that spoke to Aunty that day, congratulated her; and when the schools in the neighborhood were dismissed, the scholars and teachers went together, in procession, and bought everything Aunty had to sell; till the poor old woman could only cover her face and cry, to think that she had so many friends. If ever you go to the Parade Ground, in New York, you may talk with old Aunty, and ask her if this story is not true.

B.

RICHARD AND KATE.

A SUFFOLK BALLAD.

The following verses were written by Robert Bloomfield, an
English shoemaker, more than sixty years ago, when the work-
ing-classes of England had far more limited opportunities for
obtaining education than they now have. Criticism could easily
point out imperfections in the style of this simple story, but the
consolations of age among the poor are presented in such a
touching manner that it is worthy of preservation.

"COME, Goody! stop your humdrum wheel!
    Sweep up your orts, and get your hat!
Old joys revived once more I feel,
    'T is Fair-day! Ay, and *more* than that!

"Have you forgot, Kate, prithee say,
    How many seasons here we 've tarried?
'T is forty years, this very day,
    Since you and I, old girl, were *married.*

"Look out! The sun shines warm and bright;
    The stiles are low, the paths all dry:
I know you cut your corns last night;
    Come! be as free from care as I.

" For I 'm resolved once more to see
    That place where we so often met ;
Though few have had more cares than we,
    We 've none just now to make us fret."

Kate scorned to damp the generous flame,
    That warmed her aged partner's breast ;
Yet, ere determination came,
    She thus some trifling doubts expressed : —

" Night will come on, when seated snug,
    And you 've perhaps begun some tale ;
Can you then leave your dear stone mug ?
    Leave all the folks, and all the ale ? "

" Ay, Kate, I wool ; because I know,
    Though time *has* been we both could run,
Such days are gone and over now.
    I only mean to see the fun."

His mattock he behind the door,
    And hedging gloves, again replaced ;
And looked across the yellow moor,
    And urged his tottering spouse to haste.

The day was up, the air serene,
    The firmament without a cloud ;
The bees hummed o'er the level green,
    Where knots of trembling cowslips bowed.

And Richard thus, with heart elate,
    As past things rushed across his mind,
Over his shoulder talked to Kate,
    Who, snug tucked up, walked slow behind :

" When once a giggling mauther * you,
　And I a red-faced, chubby boy,
Sly tricks you played me, not a few ;
　For mischief was your greatest joy.

"Once, passing by this very tree,
　A gotch † of milk I 'd been to fill ;
You shouldered me ; then laughed to see
　Me and my gotch spin down the hill."

" 'T is true," she said ; " but here behold,
　And marvel at the course of time !
Though you and I are both grown old,
　This tree is only in its prime."

" Well, Goody, don't stand preaching now !
　Folks don't preach sermons at a Fair.
We 've reared ten boys and girls, you know ;
　And I 'll be bound they 'll all be there."

Now friendly nods and smiles had they,
　From many a kind Fair-going face ;
And many a pinch Kate gave away,
　While Richard kept his usual pace.

At length, arrived amid the throng,
　Grandchildren, bawling, hemmed them round,
And dragged them by the skirts along,
　Where gingerbread bestrewed the ground.

And soon the aged couple spied ,
　Their lusty sons, and daughters dear ;
When Richard thus exulting cried :
　" Did n't I *tell* you they 'd be here ? "

* A giddy young girl. 　　　　　　　† A pitcher.

The cordial greetings of the soul
   Were visible in every face;
Affection, void of all control,
   Governed with a resistless grace.

'T was good to see the honest strife.
   Who should contribute most to please;
And hear the long-recounted life,
   Of infant tricks and happy days.

But now, as at some nobler places,
   Among the leaders 't was decreed
Time to begin the Dicky-Races,
   More famed for laughter than for speed.

Richard looked on with wondrous glee,
   And praised the lad who chanced to win.
" Kate, wa'n't I such a one as he?
   As like him, ay, as pin to pin?

" Full fifty years have passed away,
   Since I rode this same ground about;
Lord! I was lively as the day!
   I won the High-lows, out and out.

"I'm surely growing young again,
   I feel myself so kedge and plump!
From head to feet I've not one pain.
   Nay, hang me, if I could n't jump!"

Thus spake the ale in Richard's pate;
   A very little made him mellow;
But still he loved his faithful Kate,
   Who whispered thus: "My good old fellow,

" Remember what you promised me !
  And, see, the sun is getting low !
The children want an hour, ye see,
  To talk a bit before we go."

Like youthful lover, most complying,
  He turned and chucked her by the chin ;
Then all across the green grass hicing ;
  Right merry faces, all akin.

Their farewell quart beneath a tree,
  That drooped its branches from above,
Awaked the pure felicity,
  That waits upon parental love.

Kate viewed her blooming daughters round,
  And sons who shook her withered hand ;.
Her features spoke what joy she found,
  But utterance had made a stand.

The children toppled on the green,
  And bowled their fairings down the hill ;
Richard with pride beheld the scene,
  Nor could he, for his life, sit still.

A father's unchecked feelings gave
  A tenderness to all he said :
" My boys, how proud am I to have
  My name thus round the country spread !

" Through all my days I've labored hard,
  And could of pains and crosses tell ;
But this is labor's great reward,
  To meet ye thus, and see ye well.

" My good old partner, when at home,
  Sometimes with wishes mingles tears ;
Goody, says I, let what wool come,
  We 've nothing for them but our prayers.

" May you be all as old as I,
  And see your sons to manhood grow ;
And many a time, before you die,
  Be just as pleased as I am now."

Then (raising still his mug and voice),
  " An old man's weakness don't despise !
I love you well, my girls and boys.
  God bless you all !"   So said his eyes ;

For, as he spoke, a big round drop
  · Fell bounding on his ample sleeve ;
A witness which he could not stop ;
  A witness which all hearts believe.

Thou, filial piety, wert there ;
  And round the ring. benignly bright,
Dwelt in the luscious half-shed tear,
  And in the parting words, " Good Night !"

With thankful hearts and strengthened love
  The poor old pair, supremely blest,
Saw the sun sink behind the grove,
  And gained once more their lowly rest.

LUDOVICO CORNARO.

DERIVED FROM THE WRITINGS OF CORNARO.

"I do not woo
The means of weakness and debility;
Therefore, my age is as a lusty winter,
Frosty, but kindly."

Varied from SHAKESPEARE.

UDOVICO CORNARO, descended from a noble family in Venice, was born in 1462, thirty years before America was discovered. He removed to Padua, where he married, and late in life had an only child, a daughter, who married one of the Cornaro family.

As an illustration of the physical laws of our being, the outlines of his history are worthy of preservation. He was wealthy, and indulged in the habits common to young men of his class. He was fond of sensual indulgences, and especially drank wine intemperately. The consequence was, that from twenty-five years of age to forty, he was afflicted with dyspepsia, gout, and frequent slow fevers. Medicines failed to do any permanent good, and physicians told him that nothing could restore him but simplicity and regularity of living. This advice was very contrary to his taste, and he continued to indulge in the luxuries of the table, paying the penalty of suffering for it afterwards. At last his health was so nearly ruined, that the doctors predicted he could not live many months. At this crisis, being about forty years old, he resolved to become temperate and abstemious ; but it required so much effort to change his dissipated habits, that he frequently resorted to prayer for aid in keeping the virtuous resolution. His perseverance was more speedily rewarded than might have been expected ; for in less than a year he was freed from the diseases which had so long tormented him. In order to preserve the health thus restored to him, he observed the peculiarities of his constitution, and carefully conformed to them in his habits and modes of living. He says : " It is a favorite maxim with epicures that whatever pleases the palate must agree with the stomach and nourish the body ; but this I found to be false ; for pork, pastry, salads, rough wines,. &c., were very agreeable to my palate, yet they disagreed with me." There seems to have been nothing peculiar in the kinds of food which constituted his nourishment; moderation as to quantity, and simplicity in modes of cooking, were the principal things he deemed of importance. He speaks of

Q

mutton, fish, poultry, birds, eggs, light soups and broths, and new wine in moderate quantities, as among his customary articles of diet. He is particularly earnest in his praises of bread. He says: " Bread, above all things, is man's proper food, and always relishes well when seasoned by a good appetite ; and this natural sauce is never wanting to those who eat but little ; for when the stomach is not burdened, there is no need to wait long for an appetite. I speak from experience ; for I find such sweetness in bread, that I should be afraid of sinning against temperance in eating it, were it not for my being convinced of the absolute necessity for nourishment, and that we cannot make use of a more natural kind of food."

He does not lay down specific rules for others, but very wisely advises each one to govern himself according to the laws of his own constitution. He says every man ought carefully to observe what kinds of food and drink agree or disagree with him, and indulge or refrain accordingly ; but whatever he eats or drinks, it should be in quantities so moderate as to be easily digested. He grows eloquent in his warnings against the fashionable luxury, by which he had himself suffered so severely. He exclaims: " O, unhappy Italy ! Do you not see that intemperance causes more deaths than plague, or fire, or many battles ? These profuse feasts, now so much in fashion, where the tables are not large enough to hold the variety of dishes, I tell

you these cause more murders than so many battles. I beseech you to put a stop to these abuses.
Banish luxury, as you would the plague. I am
certain there is no vice more abominable in the eyes
of the Divine Majesty. It brings on the body a
long and lasting train of disagreeable sensations
and diseases, and at length it destroys the soul also.
I have seen men of fine understanding and amiable disposition carried off by this plague, in the
flower of their youth, who, if they had lived ab-
stemiously, might now be among us, to benefit and
adorn society."

His dissertations on health may be condensed
into the following concise general rules, which are
worthy of all acceptance : —

Let every man study his own constitution, and
regulate food, drink, and other habits in conformity thereto.

Never indulge in anything which has the effect
to render the body uncomfortable or lethargic, or
the mind restless and irritable.

Even healthy food should be cooked with
simplicity, and eaten with moderation. Never
eat or drink to repletion, but make it a rule to
rise from the table with inclination for a little
more.

Be regular in the hours for meals and sleep.

Be in the open air frequently ; riding, walking,
or using other moderate exercise.

Avoid extremes of heat or cold, excessive fatigue,

and places where the air is unwholesome, for want of ventilation.

Restrain anger and fretfulness, and keep all malignant or sensual passions in constant check. Banish melancholy, and do everything to promote cheerfulness. All these things have great influence over bodily health.

Interest yourself constantly in employments of some kind.

He gives it as his opinion that anger, peevishness, and despondency are not likely to trouble those who are temperate and regúlar in their habits, and diligent in their occupations. He says : " I was born with a very choleric disposition, insomuch that there was no living with me. But I reflected that a person under the sway of passion was for the time being no better than a lunatic. I therefore resolved to make my temper give way to reason. I have so far succeeded, that anger never entirely overcomes me, though I 'do not guard myself so well as not to be sometimes hurried away by it. I have, however, learned by experience that hurtful passions of any kind have but little power over those who lead a sober and useful life. Neither despondency nor any other affection of the mind will harm bodies governed by temperance and regularity."

In answer to the objection that he lived too sparingly to make the change which is sometimes necessary in case of sickness, he replies: " Nature is so desirous to preserve men in good health, that she herself teaches them how to ward off illness. When it is not good for them to eat, appetite usually diminishes. Whether a man has been abstemious or not, when he is ill it is necessary to take only such nourishment as is suited to his disorder, and even that in smaller quantities than he was accustomed to in health. But the best answer to this objection is, that those who live very temperately are not liable to be sick. By removing the *cause* of diseases, they prevent the *effects.*"

He also maintains that external injuries are very easily cured, when the blood has been kept in a pure state by abstemious living and regular habits. In proof of it, he tells his own experience when, at seventy years of age, he was overturned in a coach, and dragged a considerable distance by the frightened horses. He was severely bruised, and a leg and arm were broken; but his recovery was so rapid and complete, that physicians were astonished.

Much of his health and cheerfulness he attributes to constant occupation. He says: "The greatest source of my happiness is the power to render some service to my dear country. O, what a glorious amusement! I delight to show Venice how her important harbor can be improved, and how large tracts of lands, marshes and barren sands, can be rendered productive; how her fortifications can be strengthened; how her air, though excel-

lent, can be made still purer; and how, beautiful
as she is, the beauty of her buildings can,still be
increased. For two months together, during the
heat of summer, I have been with those who were
appointed to drain the public marshes; and though
I was seventy-five years old, yet, such is the effi-
cacy of an orderly life, that I found myself none
the worse for the fatigue and inconveniences I suffered. It is also a source of satisfaction to me that,
having lost a considerable portion of my income, I
was enabled to repair it for my grandchildren, by
that most commendable of arts, agriculture. I did
this by infallible methods, worked out by dint of
thought, without any fatigue of body, and very
little of mind. I owned an extensive marshy dis-
trict, where the air was so unwholesome that it
was more fit for snakes than men. I drained off
the stagnant waters, and the air became pure.
People resorted thither so fast, that a village soon
grew up, laid out in regular streets, all terminating
in a large square, in the middle of which stands
the church. The village is divided by a wide and
rapid branch of the river Brenta, on both sides of
which is a considerable extent of well-cultivated
fertile fields. I may say with truth, that in this
place I have erected an altar to God, and brought
thither souls to adore him. When I visit these
people, the sight of these things affords me infinite
satisfaction and enjoyment. In my gardens, too, I
always find something to do that amuses me. It

is also a great satisfaction to me, that I can write treatises with my own hand, for the service of others; and that, old as I am, I can study important, sublime, and difficult subjects, without fatigue."

His writings consisted of short treatises on health, agriculture, architecture, etc. In an essay, entitled, " A Guide to Health," written when he was eighty-three years old, he says : " My faculties are all perfect ; particularly my palate, which now relishes better the simple fare I eat than it formerly did the most luxurious dishes, when I led an irregular life. Change of beds gives me no uneasiness. I sleep everywhere soundly and quietly, and my dreams are always pleasant. I climb hills from bottom to top, afoot, with the greatest ease and unconcern. I am cheerful and good-humored, being free from perturbations and disagreeable thoughts. Joy and peace have so firmly fixed their residence in my bosom, that they never depart from it."

In another essay, called " A Compendium of a Sober Life," he says : " I now find myself sound and hearty, at the age of eighty-six. My senses continue perfect ; even my teeth, my voice, my memory, and my strength. What is more, the powers of my mind do not diminish, as I advance in years ; because, as I grow older, I lessen the quantity of my solid food. I greatly enjoy the beautiful expanse of this visible world, which is really beautiful to those who know how to view it with a philosophic eye. O, thrice-holy Sobriety, thou hast conferred such favors on thine old man, that he better relishes his dry bread, than he did the most dainty dishes in the days of his youth! My spirits, not oppressed by too much food, are always brisk, especially after eating; so that I am accustomed then to sing a song, and afterward to write. I do not find myself the worse for writing immediately after meals; I am not apt to be drowsy, and my understanding is always clearer, the food I take being too small in quantity to send up any fumes into my brain. O, how advantageous it is to an old man to eat but little!"

In a letter to a friend, written when he was ninety-one, the old man rejoices over his vigor and friskiness, as a boy does over his exploits on the ice. He says: "The more I advance in years, the sounder and heartier I grow, to the amazement of the world. My memory, spirits, and understanding, and even my voice and my teeth, remain unimpaired. I employ eight hours a day in writing treatises with my own hand; and when I tell you that I write to be useful to mankind, you may easily conceive what pleasure I enjoy. I spend many hours daily in walking and singing. And O, how melodious my voice has grown! Were you to hear me chant my prayers to my lyre, after the example of David, I am certain it would give you great pleasure, my voice is so musical."

In an essay, entitled, " An Earnest Exhortation," he says : " Arrived at my ninety-fifth year,
I still find myself sound and hearty, content and
cheerful. I· eat with good appetite, and sleep
soundly. My understanding is clear, and my
memory tenacious. I write seven or eight hours
a day, walk, converse, and occasionally attend
concerts. My voice, which is apt to be the first
thing to fail, grows so· strong and sonorous, that I
cannot help chanting my prayers aloud, morning
and evening, instead of murmuring them to myself,
as was formerly my custom. Apprehensions of
death do not disturb my mind, for I have no sens-
uality to nourish such thoughts. I have reason to
think that my soul, having so agreeable a dwelling
in my body, as not to meet with anything in it but
peace, love, and harmony, not only between its
humors, but between my reason and my senses, is
exceedingly contented and pleased with her present
situation, and that, of course, it will require many
years to dislodge her. Whence I conclude that I
have still a series of years to live in health and
spirits, and enjoy this beautiful world, which is indeed beautiful to those who know how to make it
so by virtue and divine regularity of life. If men
would betake themselves to a sober, regular, and
abstemious course of life, they would not grow infirm in their old age, but would continue strong
and hearty as I am, and might attain to a hundred
years and upwards, as I expect will be my case.

12

God has ordained that whoever reaches his natural term should end his days without sickness or pain, by mere dissolution. This is the natural way of quitting mortal life to enter upon immortality, as will be my case."

Once only, in the course of his long life, did Cornaro depart from the strict rules he had laid down for himself. When he was seventy-eight years old, his physician and family united in urging him to take more nutrition; saying, that he required it to keep up his strength, now that he was growing so old. He argued that habit had become with him a second nature, and that it was unsafe to change; moreover, that as the stomach grew more feeble, it was reasonable to suppose that it ought to have less work to do, rather than more. But as they continued to remonstrate, he finally consented to add a little to his daily portion of food and wine. He says: "In eight days, this had such an effect upon me, that from being cheerful and brisk, I began to be peevish and melancholy, so that nothing could please me. I was so strangely disposed, that I neither knew what to say to others, nor what to do with myself." The result was a terrible fever, which lasted thirty-five days, and reduced him almost to a skeleton. He attributes his recovery to the abstinence he had practised for so many years. "During all which time," says he, "I never knew what sickness was; unless it might be some slight indisposition, that continued merely for a day or two." He gives it, as the result of his long experience, that it is well for people, as they become aged, to diminish the quantity of solid food. He also advises that such nourishment as they take should be less at any one time, and taken more frequently.

Never had longevity such a zealous panegyrist as this venerable Italian. He says: "Some sensual, inconsiderate persons affirm that long life is not a blessing; that the state of a man who has passed his seventy-fifth year does not deserve to be called life, but is rather a lingering death. This is a great mistake. And I, who have experienced the salutary effects of temperate, regular habits, am bound to prove that a man may enjoy a terrestrial paradise after he is eighty years old. My own existence, so far from being a lingering death, is a perpetual round of pleasures; and it is my sincere wish that all men would endeavor to attain my age, in order that they also may enjoy that period of life which of all others is the most desirable. For that reason I will give an account of my recreations, and of the relish I find in life at its present advanced stage. I can climb my horse without any assistance, or advantage of situation, and now and then I make one of a hunting party suitable to my age and taste. I have frequent opportunities to converse with intelligent, worthy gentlemen, well acquainted with literature. When I have not such conversation to enjoy, I betake myself to reading some good book. When I have read as much as I like, I write, endeavoring in this, as in everything else, to be of service to others. This I do in my own commodious house, in the most beautiful quarter of this noble and learned city of Padua, and around it are gardens supplied with running waters, where I always find something to do that amuses me. Every spring and autumn I go to a handsome hunting-lodge, belonging to me, in the Euganean mountains, which is also adorned with fountains and gardens. Then I visit my village in the plain, the soil of which I redeemed from the marshes. I visit neighboring cities, to meet old friends, and to converse with architects, painters, sculptors, musicians, and husbandmen, from all of whom I learn something that gives me satisfaction. I visit their new works, and I revisit their old ones. I see churches, palaces, gardens, fortifications, and antiquities, leaving nothing unobserved from which either entertainment or instruction can be derived. But what delights me most is the scenery I pass through, in my journeys backwards and forwards. When I was young, and debauched by an irregular life, I did not observe the beauties of nature; so that I never knew, till I grew old, that the world was beautiful. That no comfort may be wanting to the fulness of my years, I enjoy a kind of immortality in a succession of descendants. When I return home from my journeys, I am greeted by eleven· grandchildren, the oldest eighteen, the youngest two years old; all the offspring of one father and mother. They all have good parts and morals, are blessed with the best of health, and fond of learning. I play with the youngest, and make companions of the older ones. Nature has bestowed on · them fine voices. I delight in hearing them sing and play on various instruments, and I myself sing with them, for I have a clearer and louder pipe now than at any other period of life. Such gayety of spirits has been imparted by my temperate life, that at my present age of eighty-three I have been able to write a very entertaining comedy, abounding with innocent mirth and pleasant jests. I declare I would not not exchange my gray hairs, or my mode of living, with any young men, even of the best constitutions, who seek pleasure through the indulgence of their appetites. I take an interest in seeing the draining of marshes and the improvement of the harbor going on, and it is a great comfort to me that my treatises on a temperate life have proved useful to others, as many have assured me, both by word of mouth, and by letter. I may further add, that I enjoy two lives at once. I enjoy this terrestrial life, in consequence of sobriety and temperance; and, by the grace of God, I enjoy the celestial life, which he makes me anticipate by thought, — a thought so lively, that I affirm the enjoyment to be of the utmost certainty. To die in the manner that I expect to die is not really death, but merely a passage of the soul from this earthly life to an infinitely perfect existence. The prospect of terminating the high gratifications I have enjoyed here gives me no uneasiness; it rather affords me pleasure, as it will be only to make room for another glorious and immortal life. How beautiful the life I lead! How happy my exit!"

His prophecy proved true. He lived to be one hundred and four years old, and passed away without pain, sitting in his elbow-chair. His wife, who was nearly as old as himself, survived him but a short time, and died easily. They were buried in St. Anthony's Church, at Padua, in a very unostentatious manner, according to their testamentary directions.

WHEN Dr. Priestley was young, he preached that old age was the happiest period of life; and when he was himself eighty, he wrote, "I have found it so."

ROBIN AND JEANNIE.

By DORA GREENWELL.

" DO you think of the days that are gone, Jeannie,
   As you sit by the fire at night ?
Do you wish that the morn would bring back the time,
   When your heart and your step were so light ? "

" I think of the days that are gone, Robin,
   And of all that I joyed in then ;
But the brightest that ever arose on me,
   I have never wished back again."

" Do you think of the hopes that are gone, Jeannie,
   As you sit by the fire at night ?
Do you gather them up, as they faded fast,
   Like buds with an early blight ? "

" I think of the hopes that are gone, Robin,
   And I mourn not their stay was fleet,
For they fell as the leaves of the roses fall,
   And were even in falling sweet."

" Do you think of the friends that are gone, Jeannie,
 As you sit by the fire at night?
Do you wish they were round you again once more,
 By the hearth that they made so bright?"

" I think of the friends that are gone, Robin;
 They are dear to my heart as then;
But the best and the dearest among them all
 I have never wished back again."

" WE have lived and loved together,
 Through many changing years;
 We have shared each other's gladness,
 We have wept each other's tears.

" I have never known a sorrow
 That was long unsoothed by thee;
For thy smile can make a summer,
 Where darkness else would be.

" And let us hope the future
 As the past has been, will be;
I will share with thee thy sorrows,
 And thou thy smiles with me."

      ANONYMOUS.

A GOOD OLD AGE.

FROM MOUNTFORD'S EUTHANASY.

GOOD old age is a beautiful sight, and there is nothing earthly that is as noble, — in my eyes, at least. And so I have often thought. A ship is a fine object, when it comes up into a port, with all its sails set, and quite safely, from a long voyage. Many a thousand miles it has come, with the sun for guidance, and the sea for its path, and the winds for its speed. What might have been its grave, a thousand fathoms deep, has yielded it a ready way; and winds that might have been its wreck have been its service. It has come from another meridian than ours; it has come through day and night; it has come by reefs and banks that have been avoided, and past rocks that have been watched for. Not a plank has started, nor one timber in it proved rotten. And now it comes like an answer to the prayers of many hearts; a delight to the owner, a joy to many a sailor's family, and a pleasure to all ashore, that see it.

12*   R

It has been steered over the ocean, and been pilot-
ed through dangers, and now it is safe.

But still more interesting than this is a good life,
as it approaches its threescore years and ten.   It
began in the century before the present ; it has
lasted on through storms and sunshine ; and it has
been guarded against many a rock, on which ship-
wreck of a good conscience might have been made.
On the course it has taken, there has been the
influence of Providence ; and it has been guided
by Christ, that day-star from on high.   Yes, old
age is even a nobler sight than a ship completing a
long, long voyage.

On a summer's evening, the setting sun is grand
to look at.   In his morning beams, the birds awoke
and sang, men rose for their work, and the world
grew light.   In his mid-day heat, wheat-fields grew
yellower, and fruits were ripened, and a thousand
natural purposes were answered, which we mortals
do not know of.   And at his setting, all things
seem to grow harmonious and solemn in his light.

But what is all this to the sight of a good life,
in those years that go down into the grave ?   In
the early days of it, old events had their happen-
ing ; with the light of it many a house has been
brightened ; and under the good influence of it,
souls have grown better, some of whom are now
on high.   And then the closing period of such a
life, — how almost awful is the beauty of it !   From
his setting, the sun will rise again to-morrow ; and
he will shine on men and their work, and on chil-

dren's children and their labors. But when once
finished, even a good life has no renewal in this
world. It will begin again; but it will be in
a new earth, and under new heavens.
Yes, nobler than a ship safely
ending a long voyage, and
sublimer than the setting
sun, is the old age of
a just, a kind,
and useful
life.

A GOOD old man is the best antiquity; one
whom time hath been thus long a working, and,
like winter fruit, ripened when others are shaken
down. He looks over his former life as a danger
well past, and would not hazard himself to begin
again. The next door of death saps him not, but
he expects it calmly, as his turn in nature. All
men look on him as a common father, and on old
age, for his sake, as a reverent thing. He prac-
tises his experience on youth, without harshness
or reproof, and in his council is good company.
You must pardon him if he likes his own times
better than these, because those things are follies
to him now, that were wisdom then; yet he makes
us of that opinion, too, when we see him, and conjecture those times by so good a relic. — BISHOP
EARLE.

MY PSALM.

By JOHN G. WHITTIER.

I MOURN no more my vanished years:
  Beneath a tender rain, —
An April rain of smiles and tears, —
  My heart is young again.

The west winds blow, and, singing low,
  I hear the glad streams run;
The windows of my soul I throw
  Wide open to the sun.

No longer forward nor behind
  I look in hope or fear;
But, grateful, take the good I find,
  The best of now and here.

I plough no more a desert land,
  To harvest weed and tare;
The manna dropping from God's hand
  Rebukes my painful care.

I break my pilgrim staff, I lay
  Aside the toiling oar;
The angel sought so far away,
  I welcome at my door.

The airs of Spring may never play
  Among the ripening corn,
Nor freshness of the flowers of May
  Blow through the Autumn morn ; —

Yet shall the blue-eyed Gentian look
  Through fringèd lids to Heaven,
And the pale Aster in the brook
  Shall see its image given ; —

The woods shall wear their robes of praise,
  The south-wind softly sigh ;
And sweet, calm days, in golden haze,
  Melt down the amber sky.

Not less shall manly deed and word
  Rebuke an age of wrong ;
The graven flowers that wreathe the sword
  Make not the blade less strong.

But smiting hands shall learn to heal,
  To build, as to destroy ;
Nor less my heart for others feel,
  That I the more enjoy.

All as God wills, who wisely heeds
  To give or to withhold,
And knoweth more of all my needs
  Than all my prayers have told.

Enough that blessings undeserved
  Have marked my erring track, —
That, wheresoe'er my feet have swerved,
  His chastening turned me back, —

That more and more a Providence
  Of love is understood,
Making the springs of time and sense
  Sweet with eternal good, —

That death seems but a covered way
  Which opens into light,
Wherein no blinded child can stray
  Beyond the Father's sight, —

That care and trial seem at last,
  Through Memory's sunset air,
Like mountain-ranges, overpast,
  In purple distance fair, —

That all the jarring notes of life
  Seem blending in a psalm,
And all the angles of its strife
  Slow rounding into calm.

And so the shadows fall apart,
  And so the west winds play;
And all the windows of my heart
  I open to the day.

————————————

OVER the winter glaciers,
  I see the summer glow,
And, through the wild piled snow-drift,
  The warm rosebuds below.

                         R. W. EMERSON.

JOHN HENRY VON DANNECKER.

DERIVED FROM MRS. JAMESON'S SKETCHES, LONGFELLOW'S HYPERION, AND FROM VARIOUS EUROPEAN LETTERS.

HIS celebrated German sculptor was born in 1758, at Stuttgard. His father, who was one of the grooms of the Duke of Würtemberg, was a stupid, harsh man. He thought it sufficient for his son to know how to work in the stable; and how the gifted boy contrived to pick up the rudiments of reading and writing, he could not remember in after life. He had an extraordinary passion for drawing, and being too poor to buy paper and pencils, he used to scrawl figures with charcoal on the slabs of á neighboring stone-cutter. When his father discovered this, he beat him for his idleness; but his mother interfered to protect him. After he arrived at manhood, he was accustomed to speak of her with the utmost tenderness and reverence; saying that her promptings were the first softening and elevating influences he ever knew. His bright countenance and alert ways sometimes attracted the notice of the Duke, who saw him running about the precincts of the palace, ragged and barefoot; but he was far enough from foreseeing the wonderful genius that would be developed in this child of one of his meanest servants.

When John Henry was about thirteen years old, the Duke established a military school, into which poor boys, who manifested sufficient intelligence, might be admitted. As soon as he heard of this opportunity, he eagerly announced the intention of presenting himself as a candidate. His surly father became very angry at this, and told him he should stay at home and work. When the lad persisted in saying he wanted to get a chance to learn something, he beat him and locked him up. The persevering boy jumped out of the window, collected several of his comrades together, and proposed to them to go to the Duke and ask to be admitted into his school. The whole court happened to be assembled at the palace when the little troop marched up. Being asked by one of the attendants what they wanted, Dannecker replied, " Tell his Highness the Duke that we want to be admitted to the Charles School." The Duke, who was amused by this specimen of juvenile earnestness, went out to inspect the boys. He led aside one after another, till only Dannecker and two others remained. He used to say afterward that he supposed himself rejected, and suffered such an agony of shame, that he was on the point of running away and hiding himself, when he discovered that those who had been led aside were the rejected ones. The Duke ordered the successful candidates to go next morning to the school, and dismissed them. The father did not dare to resist such high authority, but he was so enraged with his son, that he turned him out of the house and forbade him ever to enter it again. But his good mother packed up a little bundle of necessaries for him, accompanied him some distance on the road, and parted with him with tears and blessings.

He did not find himself well situated in this school. The teachers were accustomed to employ the poorer boys as servants, and he was kept so constantly at work, that what little he learned was mostly accomplished by stealth. But he met with one piece of great good fortune. Schiller, who afterward became world-renowned as a writer, was at this school. The two boys recognized kindred genius in each other, and formed a friendship which lasted through life. When he was fifteen years old, his remarkable talent for drawing caused him to be removed to the School of Art in Stuttgard, where he received instruction from Grubel, the sculptor. The next year, he obtained the highest prize for a statue of Milo, modelled in clay. The Duke, who had forgotten the bright, ragged boy that formerly attracted his attention, was astonished to hear he had carried off the highest honors of the School of Art. He employed him to carve cornices and ornaments for two new palaces he was building.   Ten years were thus spent, during which he acquired a great deal of mere mechanical skill and dexterity.   But he longed to improve himself by the sight of noble models ; and at last he obtained leave to travel.   The allowance granted him by his ducal patron was only one hundred and twenty dollars a year.   With this he set off for Paris, where he studied in the galleries of the Louvre, often going the whole day without food, and in a dress too shabby to be considered respectable.   Those who saw him thus perseveringly employed, passed by without recognizing the divine soul that dwelt within the forlorn exterior.   He afterward went to Rome, where for some months, he wandered about among monuments and ruins, friendless and homesick.   But luckily his illustrious countrymen, Herder and Goethe were there.   He was introduced to them, and their conversation imbued him with higher ideas of Art than he had ever before received.   The celebrated Italian sculptor, Canova, also became acquainted with him, and often visited him in his studio.   There was but a year's difference in their ages, and their friendship became intimate.   He remained five years in Rome, and distinguished himself by the production of several fine statues.   He then returned to his native country, where he married.   At fifty years of age he was considered the greatest sculptor in Germany.   The Grand Duke ennobled nim, as the phrase is; though it seems absurd enough that wearing a ribbon in his button-hole, and being allowed to put *von* before the name his genius had rendered illustrious, could add any nobility to a man like Dannecker.

His two most celebrated works are Ariadne riding on a panther, and his statue of Christ. The circumstances under which the latter was produced are very peculiar. Dannecker was a devout Lutheran, and he often meditated upon a statue of the Mediator between God and man as the highest problem of Art. He sought to embody it, but felt that something was wanting. A child, who was accustomed to run about his studio, came in while he was at his work. " Who do you think that is ? " said the artist, pointing to his model. The child looked, and replied : " I don't know; I guess it is some great king." Ah, thought Dannecker, I have made the expression of power to predominate over love. The search after a perfect ideal of the Divine and human combined took complete possession of his mind. Filled with such thoughts, he fell asleep and dreamed of a face and form transcending anything he had conceived. He hastened to model it in clay, while the vision was still fresh in his mind. When it was shown to the child, he at once exclaimed, " That is the Redeemer. Mother reads to me about him, where he says, ' Suffer little children to come unto me.' " This confirmed

Dannecker in the belief that he had been directly inspired from above.   Others regarded it as a dream produced by the intense activity of his thoughts concentrated upon one subject; but he always viewed it as an immediate revelation.   He was fifty-eight years old when this sublime vision was presented to him in his sleep, and for eight years he devoted to it all the energies of mind and heart.   He studied the Scriptures intently, and prayed for Divine assistance.   His enthusiasm was a compound of Religion and Art.   Under this combined influence, he said he felt as if he were pursued by some irresistible power, which visited him in his sleep, and often compelled him to rise in the night and embody the ideas which had been presented to him.   When he was sixty-six years old, the glorious statue was completed.   It is clothed in a simple robe reaching to the feet.   The hair is parted on the forehead, and falls in ringlets over the shoulders.   The head is purely moral and intellectual in its outline.   One hand is pressed upon the bosom, the other extended, and the lips are partially unclosed, as if in the act of speaking. The expression is said to be a remarkable combination of majesty and tenderness, exciting involuntary reverence in all who look upon it.

Mrs. Jameson visited Dannecker in 1830.   The statue was still standing in his studio.   She says: " He told me that the figure had visited him in a dream three several times, and that he firmly believed he had been predestined to the work, and divinely inspired. I shall not easily forget the countenance of the good and gifted old man, as he leaned on the pedestal, with his cap in his hand, and his long gray hair waving round his face, looking up at his work with a mixture of reverence and exultation."

This remarkable statue was purchased by the Emperor Alexander, and is now in Russia. A year after its completion, he made a colossal statue of the Evangelist John, for the royal chapel at Rothenberg. He had for many years been Professor of the Fine Arts at the Academy in Stuttgard, and the instructions he was obliged to give there, combined with the labors of his studio, kept him very constantly occupied. Mrs. Jameson again visited him in 1833, when he was seventy-five years old. She says : " A change had come over him. His trembling hand could no longer grasp the mallet or guide the chisel. His fine benevolent countenance wore a childish smile, and was only now and then crossed by a gleam. of awakened memory or thought. Yet he seemed perfectly happy. He walked backward and forward from his statue of Christ to his bust of Schiller, with an unwearied self-complacency, in which there was something mournful, yet delightful. While I was looking at the magnificent head of Schiller, he took my hand, and trembling with emotion, said, ' We were friends from boyhood.

I worked upon it with love and grief; and one can do no more.' I took leave of Dannecker with emotion. I shall never see him again. But he is one of those who cannot die. Canova, after he was a melancholy invalid, visited his studio, and was so much struck by his childlike simplicity, his pure, unworldly nature, his genuine goodness, and lively, happy temperament, that he gave him the surname of *Il Beato*, The Blessed. And surely if that epithet can with propriety be bestowed upon any mortal, it is on him whose long life has been one of labor and of love; who has left behind him lasting memorials of his genius; who has never profaned to any unworthy purpose the talents which God has given him, but, in the midst of all the beautiful and exciting influences of Poetry and Art, has kept, from youth to age, a soul serene, a conscience and a life pure in the sight of God and man."

Longfellow, in his prose-poem called "Hyperion," thus introduces the renowned German artist, on a calm Sabbath forenoon: — "Flemming stole out into the deserted street, and went to visit the veteran sculptor Dannecker. He found him in his parlor, sitting alone, with his psalm-book and the reminiscences of his long life. As Flemming entered, he arose from the sofa and tottered toward him; a venerable old man, of low stature, and dressed in a loose white jacket, with a face like Franklin's, his white hair flowing over his shoulders, and a pale blue eye.

"' So you are from America,' said he. 'I have never been in America. I shall never go there. I am now too old. I have been in Paris and in Rome. But that was long ago. I am now seventy-eight years old.'

" He took Flemming by the hand, and made him sit by his side on the sofa. And Flemming felt a mysterious awe creep over him, on touching the hand of the good old man, who sat so serenely amid the gathering shade of years, and listened to life's curfew-bell, telling, with eight and seventy solemn strokes, that the hour had come, when the fires of all earthly passion must be quenched within, and man must prepare to lie down and rest till morning.

" ' You see,' he continued, ' my hands are cold. They were warmer once. I am now an old man.'

" ' Yet these are the hands that sculptured the beautiful Ariadne and the Panther,' replied Flemming. ' The soul never grows old.'

" ' Nor does Nature,' said the old man, pleased with this allusion to his great work, and pointing to the green trees before his window. ' This pleasure I have left to me. My sight is still good. I can even distinguish objects on the side of yonder mountain. My hearing is also unimpaired. For all which I thank God.'

" Directing Flemming's attention to a fine engraving which hung on the opposite wall of the room, he continued : ' That is an engraving of Canova's

Religion.   I love to sit here and look at it, for
hours together.   It is beautiful.   He made the
statue for his native town, where they had no
church, until he built them one.   He placed the
statue in it.   He sent me this engraving as a present.   Ah, he was a dear, good man!   The name
of his native town I have forgotten.   My memory
fails me.   I cannot remember names.'

"Fearful that he had disturbed the old man in
his morning devotions, Flemming did not remain
long; but he took his leave with regret.   There
was something impressive in the scene he had
witnessed; — this beautiful old age of the artist;
sitting by the open window, in the bright summer
morning; the labor of life accomplished; the horizon reached, where heaven and earth meet; thinking it was angel's music when he heard the church
bells ring; himself too old to go.   As he walked
back to his chamber, he thought within himself
whether he likewise might not accomplish something which should live after him; — might not
bring something permanent out of this fast-fleeting
life of man, and then sit down, like the artist, in
serene old age, and fold his hands in silence.   He
wondered how a man felt when he grew so old,
that he could no longer go to church, but must sit
at home, and read the Bible in large print.   His
heart was full of indefinite longings, mingled with
regrets; longings to accomplish something worthy
of life; regret that as yet he had accomplished

nothing, but had felt and dreamed only. Thus the warm days in spring bring forth passion-flowers and forget-me-nots. It is only after mid-summer, when the days grow shorter and hotter, that fruit begins to appear. Then the heat of the day brings forward the harvest; and after the harvest, the leaves fall, and there is a gray frost."

Dannecker lived eighty-five years. His last drawing, done when he was extremely old, represented an angel guiding an aged man
.from the grave, and pointing to him
the opening heaven. It was
a beautiful occupation to
console the last days of
this truly Chris-
tian artist's
life.

WHEN a good man dies, — one that hath lived innocently, — then the joys break forth through the clouds of sickness, and the conscience stands upright, and confesses the glories of God, and owns so much integrity that it can hope for par-don and obtain it too. Then the sorrows of sick-ness do but untie the soul from its chain, and let it go forth, first into liberty and then into glory.

JEREMY TAYLOR.

THE KITTEN AND THE FALLING LEAVES.

By WILLIAM WORDSWORTH.

THAT way look, my infant, lo !
   What a pretty baby-show !
See the kitten on the wall,
Sporting with the leaves that fall !
Withered leaves — one, two, and three —
From the lofty Elder-tree !
— See the kitten ! how she starts,
Crouches, stretches, paws, and darts,
First at one, and then its fellow,
Just as light and just as yellow !
Such a light of gladness breaks,
Pretty kitten, from thy freaks,
Spreads, with such a living grace,
O'er my little Laura's face !
Yes, the sight so stirs and charms
Thee, baby, laughing in my arms,
That almost I could repine
That your transports are not mine ;
That I do not wholly fare
Even as ye do, thoughtless pair !

And I will have my careless season,
Spite of melancholy reason ;
Will walk through life in such a way,
That, when time brings on decay,
Now and then I may possess
Hours of perfect gladsomeness.
— Pleased by any random toy ;
By a kitten's busy joy,
Or an infant's laughing eye,
Sharing in the ecstasy.
I would fare like that, or this ;
Find my wisdom in my bliss ;
Keep the sprightly soul awake ;
And have faculties to take,
Even from things by sorrow wrought,
Matter for a jocund thought ;
Spite of care and spite of grief,
To gambol with Life's falling leaf.

His sixty summers — what are they in truth ?
By Providence peculiarly blest,
With him the strong hilarity of youth
Abides, despite gray hairs, a constant guest.
His sun has veered a point toward the west,
But light as dawn his heart is glowing yet, —
That heart the simplest, gentlest, kindliest, best,
Where truth and manly tenderness are met
With faith and heavenward hope, the suns that never set.

HENRY TAYLOR.

DR. DODDRIDGE'S DREAM.

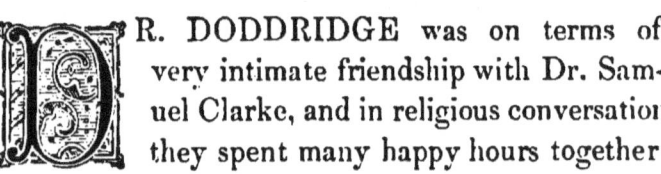R. DODDRIDGE was on terms of very intimate friendship with Dr. Samuel Clarke, and in religious conversation they spent many happy hours together. Among other matters, a very favorite topic was the intermediate state of the soul, and the probability that at the instant of dissolution it was not introduced into the presence of all the heavenly hosts, and the splendors around the throne of God. One evening, after a conversation of this nature, Dr. Doddridge retired to rest with his mind full of the subject discussed, and, in the 'visions of the night,' his ideas were shaped into the following beautiful form. He dreamed that he was at the house of a friend, when he was suddenly taken dangerously ill. By degrees he seemed to grow worse, and at last to expire. In an instant he was sensible that he exchanged the prison-house and sufferings of mortality for a state of liberty and happiness. Embodied in a splendid aerial form, he seemed to float in a region of pure

light. Beneath. him lay the earth; but not a glittering city or village, the forest or the sea, was visible. There was naught to be seen below save the melancholy group of friends, weeping around his lifeless remains.

Himself thrilled with delight, he was surprised at their tears, and attempted to inform them of his change; but, by some mysterious power, utterance was denied; and, as he anxiously leaned over the mourning circle, gazing fondly upon them, and struggling to speak, he rose silently upon the air; their forms became more and more distant, and gradually melted away from his sight. Reposing upon golden clouds, he found himself swiftly mounting the skies, with a venerable figure at his side guiding his mysterious movement, in whose countenance he remarked the lineaments of youth and age were blended together with an intimate harmony and majestic sweetness. They travelled through a vast region of empty space, until at length the battlements of a glorious edifice shone in the distance; and as its form rose brilliant and distinct among the far-off shadows that flitted across their path, the guide informed him, that the palace he beheld was for the present to be his mansion of rest. Gazing upon its splendor, he replied, that while on earth he had heard that eye had not seen, nor had the ear heard, nor could it enter into the heart of man to conceive, the things which God had prepared for those who love him;

but, notwithstanding the building to which they were then rapidly approaching was superior to anything he had ever before seen, yet its grandeur did not exceed the conceptions he had formed.

They were already at the door, and the guide, without reply, introduced him into a spacious apartment, at the extremity of which stood a table covered with a snow-white cloth, a golden cup, and a cluster of grapes, and there he said he must remain, for he would receive in a short time a visit from the Lord of the mansion, and that, during the interval before his arrival, the apartment would furnish him with sufficient entertainment and instruction. The guide vanished, and he was left alone. He began to examine the decorations of the room, and observed that the walls were adorned with a number of pictures. Upon nearer inspection, he found, to his astonishment, that they formed a complete biography of his own life. Here he saw, upon the canvas, that angels, though unseen, had ever been his familiar attendants ; that, sent by God, they had sometimes preserved him from immediate peril. He beheld himself first as an infant just expiring, when his life was prolonged by an angel gently breathing into his nostrils. Most of the occurrences here delineated were perfectly familiar to his recollection, and unfolded many things which he had never before understood, and which had perplexed him with many doubts and much uneasiness.

Among others, he was particularly struck with a picture in which he was represented as falling from his horse, when death would have been inevitable, had not an angel received him in his arms, and broken the force of his descent. These merciful interpositions of God filled him with joy and gratitude ; and his heart overflowed with love as he surveyed in them all an exhibition of goodness and mercy far beyond all that he had imagined.

Suddenly his attention was arrested by a rap at the door. The Lord of the mansion had arrived. The door opened and he entered. So powerful and so overwhelming, and withal of such singular beauty, was his appearance, that he sank down at his feet, completely overcome by his majestic presence. His Lord gently raised him from the ground, and taking his hands led him forward to the table. He pressed with his fingers the juice of the grapes into the cup, and after having drank himself, presented it to him, saying, " This is the new wine in my Father's kingdom." No sooner had he partaken, than all uneasy sensations vanished. Perfect love had cast out fear, and he conversed with his Saviour as an intimate friend. Like the silver rippling of the summer sea, he heard fall from his lips the grateful approbation : " Thy labors are over ; thy work is approved ; rich and glorious is thy reward." Thrilled with an unspeakable bliss, that glided into the very

depth of his soul, he suddenly saw glories upon
glories bursting upon his view.   The Doctor
awoke.   Tears of rapture from this joyful interview were rolling down his cheeks.   Long
did the lively impressions of this charin-
ing dream remain upon his mind,
and never could he speak
of it without emotions
of joy and ten-
derness.

DEATH can only take away the sorrowful from
our affections.   The flower expands; the colorless
film that enveloped it falls off and perishes.   We
may well believe this; and, believing it, let us
cease to be disquieted for their absence, who have
but retired into another chamber.   We are like
those who have overslept the hour: when we
rejoin our friends, there is only the more joyance
and congratulation.   Would we break a precious
vase because it is as capable of containing the
bitter as the sweet?   No: the very things which
touch us the most sensibly are those which we
should be the most reluctant to forget.   The noble mansion is most distinguished by the beautiful
images it retains of beings passed away; and so is
the noble mind.

WALTER SAVAGE LANDOR.

THE OLD PSALM-TUNE.

By HARRIET BEECHER STOWE.

YOU asked, dear friend, the other day,
　　Why still my charméd ear
Rejoiceth in uncultured tone
　　That old psalm-tune to hear.

I 've heard full oft, in foreign lands,
　　The grand orchestral strain,
Where music's ancient masters live,
　　Revealed on earth again :

Where breathing, solemn instruments,
　　In swaying clouds of sound,
Bore up the yearning, trancéd soul,
　　Like silver wings around ; —

I 've heard in old St. Peter's dome,
　　When clouds of incense rise,
Most ravishing the choral swell
　　Mount upward to the skies.

And well I feel the magic power,
　　When skilled and cultured art
Its cunning webs of sweetness weaves
　　Around the captured heart.

13 *

But yet, dear friend, though rudely sung,
  That old psalm-tune hath still
A pulse of power beyond them all
  My inmost soul to thrill.

Those tones, that halting sound to you,
  Are not the tones I hear;
But voices of the loved and lost
  Then meet my longing ear.

I hear my angel mother's voice, —
  Those were the words she sung;
I hear my brother's ringing tones,
  As once on earth they rung;

And friends that walk in white above
  Come round me like a cloud,
And far above those earthly notes
  Their singing sounds aloud.

There may be discord, as you say;
  Those voices poorly ring;
But there's no discord in the strain
  Those upper spirits sing.

For they who sing are of the blest,
  The calm and glorified,
Whose hours are one eternal rest
  On heaven's sweet floating tide.

Their life is music and accord;
  Their souls and hearts keep time
In one sweet concert with the Lord, —
  One concert vast, sublime.

And through the hymns they sang on earth
   Sometimes a sweetness falls,
On those they loved and left below,
   And softly homeward calls.

Bells from our own dear fatherland,
   Borne trembling o'er the sea —
The narrow sea that they have crossed,
   The shores where we shall be.

O sing, sing on! beloved souls;
   Sing cares and griefs to rest;
Sing, till entranced we arise
   To join you 'mid the blest.

O, THUS forever sing to me!
   O, thus forever!
The green bright grass of childhood bring to me,
   Flowing like an emerald river,
   And the bright blue skies above!
O, sing them back as fresh as ever,
   Into the bosom of my love, —
The sunshine and the merriment,
The unsought, evergreen content,
   Of that never cold time,
The joy, that, like a clear breeze, went
   Through and through the old time!
                  J. R. LOWELL.

THE LOST BOOKS OF LIVY.

[It is well known that all the books of the Middle Ages were written by monks, and preserved in manuscript; printing being then an unknown art. These patient scribes had plenty of leisure, and not unfrequently an eye for artistic beauty, especially in the gorgeous style. Hence many monastic manuscripts were richly illuminated, as the phrase is, with Initial Letters of silver or gold, often surrounded with quaint devices, painted in glowing tints of blue, crimson, and purple. Paper was not then invented, and parchment was scarce. Monks generally held Greeks and Romans in contempt, as heathen, and therefore did not scruple to supply themselves with writing material by erasing the productions of classic authors. Early in the nineteenth century it was announced that Signor Maio, an Italian librarian, had discovered valuable Greek and Latin fragments concealed under monkish manuscripts, and that, by chemical processes, he could remove the later writing and bring the ancient to the surface. In this way, "The Republic," of Cicero, deemed one of his finest works, was brought out from under a Commentary of St. Augustine on the Psalms of David. Such parchments are called *Palimpsests*; from two Greek words, which signify erased and re-written. The discovery was very exciting to the scholastic world, and many learned men entered into it with absorbing interest. Several of the books of Livy's lively and picturesque History of Rome are lost; and it was a cherished hope among scholars that they might be discovered by this new process. This explanation is necessary to help some readers to a right understanding of the following story, which is abridged and slightly varied from an English book, entitled, " Stories by an Archæologist."]

 Y dear friend, Dubois d'Erville, whose talents might have rendered him remarkable in any walk of literature, allowed the whole of his faculties to be absorbed in days, nights, years of research, upon one special point of literary interest.   At school, he had become imbued with a love for classic authors, which, with regard to his favorite Livy, kindled into a passion.   He sought eagerly for accounts of discoveries of lost works in *palimpsest* manuscripts.   Finally, he relinquished all other objects of pursuit, and spent many years traversing Europe and Asia, visiting the public libraries and old monasteries, in search of ancient manuscripts.   After a long time, when he was forgotten by family, friends, and acquaintances, he returned to Paris.   Little was known of his wanderings ; but there was a rumor that he formed a romantic marriage, and that his devoted wife had travelled with him among the monasteries of Asia Minor, encountering many hardships and dangers. No one but himself knew where she died.

When he returned to Paris, he brought with him an only child, a girl of nineteen.   She had memorable beauty, and great intelligence ; but these were less noticed than her simple manners, and tender devotion to her father, whom she almost

adored. He took a suite of apartments in the
third story of a house, which, before the Revolution, had been the hotel of a nobleman, and surrounded by extensive gardens. It was in the old
and solitary Rue Cassette. The gardens had been
let out to cow-keepers ; but within the enclosure
of the house remained some noble trees and flowering shrubs. These apartments had been selected
by his daughter Marcelline, on account of the graceful branches of the old lime-trees, which reached
close to the windows, and furnished a pleasant
shade in summer, when birds chirped gayly among
the green foliage. Even in winter, a robin would
sometimes sing snatches of song, among the naked
branches, as if in return for the crumbs which his
pretty patroness never failed to place on the win-
dow-sill.

Beyond Marcelline's chamber was a little sitting-
room, and then came a rather large apartment,
where Dubois pursued his studies, surrounded
with piles of old vellum, and dusty and worm-
eaten manuscripts of all descriptions. The floor
was thus littered in all directions, except in a small
semicircle near one of the windows, where an open
space was preserved for a few chairs and a table.

They had but one servant, an old woman, who
had been cook in Dubois's family in the days of his
boyhood, and whom he accidentally met when he
returned to Paris. Old Madeleine formed a pleasant link between the present and the past. Often,

when she passed through his study, he would remind her of some prank he had played in early days, and ask her if she remembered it, with such a frank, good-natured smile, that the old servant would smile too ; though there was always a tinge of melancholy in her recollections of his boyish roguery. Often, when she left the room, she would shake her head, and mutter to herself, " Ah, young Monsieur Armand was so good, so kind, so gentle ! Only to think that he should leave all his family and friends, and pass his life nobody knows where ! Ah ! it is very mysterious. And the bright, curly hair, that I used to pat with such fondness, to think that I should never see him again, till all that is left of it is a few silver locks about his temples ! " She tried to gain from Marcelline some particulars about her mother ; but the young girl had only a vague recollection of a form that used to press her to her heart, during journeys through strange countries, and who had long disappeared. She remembered something of a time when her father's tall, upright figure suddenly bent under the weight of some great sorrow, from which it never rose erect again. Then, when she grew older, they lived for years in Italian cities, where there were great libraries ; whence they came to Paris.

Nothing could be more delightful than the affectionate congeniality between father and daughter. Their favorite pursuits, though different, had a kind of affinity which rendered their quiet ex-

istence very pleasant. Marcelline had a taste for
painting; and her father's mania for old manuscripts furnished her with many opportunities for
examining the exquisite miniatures and ornamental
illuminations, with which monkish manuscripts
were frequently enriched. When new manuscripts arrived, which they did almost daily, her
first impulse was to examine whether they contained any illuminations worthy of note; and if
so, to copy them with the utmost care and accu-
racy. She had thus formed a very beautiful collection, in which she felt an interest almost as
enthusiastic as that of her father in his long pursuit of a treasure, which, like the horizon, seemed
always in sight, but was never reached.

In the midst of the charming, harmonious routine of this little household, slight contentions
would sometimes arise; but they were sure to
end, like the quarrels of lovers, in a renewal of
love. Sometimes a manuscript arrived which contained exquisite illuminations; but Dubois, thinking it might be a *palimpsest*, regarded the ornaments as so many abominations, concealing some
treasure of classic literature. So the mediæval
romance, with its matchless miniatures, and intricate borderings, glowing with gilding, purple, and
crimson, would soon disappear beneath the sponge,
soap, and acids of the indefatigable seeker after
The Lost Books of Livy. These occasions were
sad trials for Marcelline. She would beg for a

week's delay, just to copy the most beautiful of the illuminations. But if Dubois thought he could perceive traces of erasure under the gorgeous ornaments, he was as impatient as a miner who fancies he sees indications of a vein of gold. When Marcelline saw the sponge trembling in his hand, so eager to commence the work of obliteration, she would turn away with a painful sense of what seemed to her a cruel desecration. She felt that the sacrifice was due to the cause in which her father had enlisted all the energies of his life; but the ruthless destruction of all those quaint and delicately beautiful works of art caused her a pang she could not quite conceal. In spite of herself, a tear would glisten in her eye; and the moment her father perceived it, his resolution melted. He would place the manuscript in her hand, and say, " There, there, my child! a whole week if you want it; and then bring it to me, if you have quite done with it." Then she would reply, " No, no, dear father. Your object is too important to be hindered by the whims of a foolish girl." He would press it upon her, and she would refuse it; and as the combat of love went on, the old man's eyes would fill with tears. Then Marcelline would give way, and take the proffered manuscript; and Dubois, with all the attentive politeness of a young lover, would arrange her desk, and her pieces of new vellum, and place the volume in a good light. Not till he had seen her fairly at work at her

charming task, could he tear himself away; and then
not without pressing her hand, and nodding to her,
as though they were going to part for some long
period.   She would nod too; and then they both
nodded together, smiling at their own affectionate
folly, with tears glistening in their eyes.   Then
Dubois would go to his study, and among his
heaps of manuscripts, bound and unbound, rolled
or folded, he would soon be immersed in the in-
tricacies of his old pursuit.

After a while, the even current of their happy
life became varied by the visits of a third person.
When old Madeleine came to live with them, Dubois often questioned her concerning the relatives
and friends he had known in his boyhood.   Her
answer was, invariably, " Dead."   It seemed as if
all the old he inquired for were dead, and all the
young either dead or scattered.   During one of
these conversations, he said, " What has become
of Uncle Debaye, who used to prophesy that I
should be a member of the Academy, and one of
the illustrious men of France?   Ah, he was a
pleasant specimen of the old bachelor and the *bon
vivant!*   Where is he?"   " He is dead, too,"
replied Madeleine; " but he did not remain an old
bachelor and a *bon vivant.*   He married, some two
and twenty years ago, and gave up his old luxurious habits for the sake of supporting his pretty
young wife.   He even left off cigars and snuff, to
supply her with little luxuries.   She is dead, too.

But they had a very pretty child, little Hyppolite, who is a young man now." " Then it seems that I have one relative remaining," said Dubois ; " but I suppose he has gone off to America, or Australia, or somewhere." " No, Monsieur," rejoined Madeleine, " he is in Paris. He got a situation out by the Barrière du Trone, where he has two thousand francs a year, and apartments in the factory to live in besides. I often meet him on a Sunday, in the gardens of the Luxembourg, and many a forty sous has he given me."

Dubois was pleased to find that he had one relative left, and Madeleine was commissioned to tell him that his father's brother-in-law, his uncle by marriage, had returned to Paris, and would be glad to see him. The young man came soon after, and father and daughter were both pleased with their new-found kinsman. He was not very intellectual or learned ; but he was lively, good-natured, and good-looking. He brought the living, moving world of the present into those secluded apartments, so entirely consecrated to the works and thoughts of ages long past. His free-and-easy conversation, without a single phrase smacking of libraries, or art-galleries, or any kind of learning, seemed a bright sparkling stream of young careless life. His uncle listened willingly to his gossiping anecdotes, told with a certain appreciation of the comic, in a clear, ringing voice, and with good-natured laughter. Hyppolite became a very welcome visitor ; and, after a while, if he did not appear on the days when he was regularly expected, a shadow of disappointment was cast over the little household in the Rue Cassette.

Thus things went on for some time. Marcelline daily added to her collection of exquisite fac-similes, and her father labored diligently in the cause to which he had devoted his life. He did not obtain the result he so ardently desired ; but his perseverance was not without reward. On two occasions he discovered works of great importance, in a literary point of view, covered over with a mass of old law transactions ; and the sums he obtained for them enabled him greatly to increase his stock of manuscripts. He soon became so well known to all who dealt in such articles, that every new importation was offered to him, before it was shown elsewhere.

Meanwhile Marcelline received increasing pleasure from the visits of Hyppolite. She began to suspect that the trivial chat uttered in that fresh young voice, with occasional peals of ringing laughter, possessed for her a greater charm than the noble words of her father, always teeming with knowledge and interest of various kinds. She shrunk from admitting this to herself. She would not believe it, but she had an uneasy suspicion of it. As for Hyppolite, his walk of two or three miles, to visit his new-found relatives, became his greatest pleasure. He found innumerable oppor-

tunities of making the Rue Cassette the shortest
cut to one or other of the distant quarters of
Paris, where the business of his employers carried
him, though in fact it was often miles out of his
way. To gratify Marcelline's peculiar taste, he
frequently brought her ornaments cut from the
pages of old illuminated manuscripts. When asked
where he obtained them, he would merely laugh,
and say he would bring some more soon. Dubois
began to remonstrate against the barbarism of mu-
tilating manuscripts in that way ; but Hyppolite
would point to the piles of manuscripts from which
he had washed both ornaments and writing, and
would put on such a comic look, and laugh so
merrily, that his uncle could not help laughing,
too.

One calm summer evening, Dubois had gone to
the busy part of Paris, and Marcelline sat at the
window, busily employed in copying a noble group
of illuminated letters from a gorgeous manuscript
of the twelfth century, which stood on the desk
before her. The window was open, and the air
gently moved the leaves of crisp vellum, with their
antique writing and their curious enrichments. The
massive silver clasps of the great folio hung back
and glistened in the evening light. As the young
artist looked up at her model, she felt tempted to
make a drawing of the whole superb volume, instead of the especial group of letters she was copying. The foliage of the lime-trees moved gently

in the warm evening breeze, and a linnet, hidden in its recesses, was singing his vesper hymn. Marcelline felt very happy. The balmy hour, the congenial employment, and the bright halo of her twenty. young years, threw around her an atmosphere of soft, pure, gentle pleasure. Thoughts of more homely things mingled with her poetic mood. She thought of the choice little supper Madeleine was preparing for her father, and she tried to conjecture when he would arrive.

The current of her ideas was interrupted by the ringing of the bell on the landing, and Madeleine announced the arrival of Monsieur Hyppolite. An uncontrollable thrill lifted her heart with one great bound. For a moment the illuminated volume, the sweet summer breeze, the tuneful linnet, and the little supper for her father, were all forgotten. By a strong effort she recovered, herself, however, and received Hyppolite as usual; perhaps a little more coolly, for she was inwardly shocked to find that his presence had power, even for a moment, to obliterate the pleasures and affections she had always deemed so sacred. He brought two beautifully illuminated letters, that had evidently formed part of a very fine Italian manuscript. Being in an unusual style of art, they attracted her attention, and diverted her thoughts from the channel they had taken. She reseated herself at her work ; and while he watched her skilful pencil tracing the intricate interlacings of various and many-colored lines and branches, he sought to entertain her with his usual light chat. But Marcelline did not respond so gayly as she was accustomed to do, and he grew unwontedly silent; so silent, that the song of the linnet was heard again, and no other sound disturbed the stillness. At last, Hyppolite, with a great effort, and as if something choked his usual clear utterance, said, " Marcelline, you must have long perceived that I — " she rose hastily, exclaiming, " O don't say that word ! *Don't* say it !, To break the holy spell of filial affection which has always bound my heart, would be sacrilege." But Hyppolite knelt at her feet, and poured forth the fervid language that comes to all when the heart is kindled by a first love. Marcelline turned away her head and wept. The bitter tears, not without sweetness, relieved the deep trouble of her heart. She resumed her seat, and told her cousin decidedly, but kindly, that he must never speak to her of love while her dear father lived ; that she could never allow any earthly affection to come between her and him. The young man, in the midst of his disappointment, could not but wish that his uncle might live long ; for he truly loved his genial nature, and regarded his great learning with almost superstitious veneration. He held out his hand, saying, " My cousin, it is the hand of friendship." She pressed it kindly, and gently admonished him that his visits must be less frequent. After a brief struggle he resigned himself to her guidance, and recovered his equanimity, if not his usual gayety. All was peaceful and pleasant when Dubois returned, and Hyppolite was urged to stay and partake of the choice little supper.

The household continued to go on in the old quiet way, varied occasionally by visits from antiquarians and learned men. On such occasions, it was charming to hear Dubois descant on his favorite topics with the enthusiasm and beautiful flow of language which they always excited. Marcelline was often appealed to in these discussions ; for her intimate knowledge of the beauties of illumination enabled her to judge the age of a manuscript, by delicate peculiarities in its ornaments, more readily than learned men could do by the character of the writing or the nature of the subject. Hyppolite, who was sometimes present by special invitation, would sit apart, drinking in every delicate epithet and daintly selected word uttered by his cousin, as though they were heaven-distilled drops of nectar.

. One morning, Dubois rushed into his daughter's apartment, eagerly exclaiming, " Eureka ! Eureka ! I have found it ! I have found it ! My name will go down to posterity joined with that of Livy ! At last I have found The Lost Books ! " Joyfully, he drew his daughter into his study, and there, spread upon the floor, were several sheets of vellum still wet from the action of his sponge. The more recent writing had been removed, and traces of a nearly erased manuscript, apparently of the tenth century, was gradually becoming more distinct under the influence of a preparation he had applied. The old man drew himself up as he pointed to it, and looking proudly at his daughter, said, " The labor of my life has been well expended. It will be *my* great privilege to be the first among moderns to read the whole of the noble history of Livy ; for I believe the *whole* is there." He insisted that Hyppolite should be sent for to hear the glad tidings. The good-natured youth hastened to the Rue Cassette, and congratulated his uncle upon his great discovery. He' did not, indeed, understand the importance of the recovered annals, for he thought we had a tolerably complete history of Rome without these famous Lost Books, but he cordially sympathized with the joy of his uncle and cousin. It was a day marked with "a white stone " in the annals of the quiet little family. In honor of the occasion, a bottle of the choice wine called Chateaux Margaux, was placed on the generally frugal little dinner-table, and the sun traced upon it bright lights and shadows through the branches of the lime-trees, as if to aid in the celebration.

Day by day, more pages of the *palimpsest* were prepared, and the ancient text developed itself so well, that the exulting Dubois resolved to invite

14

his most learned friends to a grand evening reunion, in honor of his discovery. A lithographed
circular was accordingly prepared, and sent round
in due form. It brought together a select party
of the knowing ones in such matters. Dubois was
all smiles and urbanity. In the fluent language, of
which he had extraordinary command, he related
the successive details of his discovery. He deemed
himself the most fortunate of men. His heart was
running over with enthusiasm. His hearers were
charmed with the copious flood of eloquence that
he poured forth without stint, full of the deepest
erudition, yet warmed and embellished by a pervading gleam of amiable exhilaration, and innocent exultation over the triumphant result of his
life-long labors. The sheets of the recovered
manuscript were placed in a good light, and eagerly examined through many pairs of glittering spectacles and powerful microscopes. It obviously
related to that portion of Roman history lost from
the books of Livy, but many doubts were expressed
whether it were written by that great historian.
Peculiarities of orthography and style were ad-
duced to prove that the writer must have been
a monk. But Dubois ingeniously converted every
objection into an additional proof that they had
before them the identical Lost Books of Livy.

The animated discussion was interrupted by the
entrance of Madeleine, who said that two men were
at the door, with old manuscripts to sell. Dubois

could never resist the temptation to examine musty vellum, and he ordered them to be shown in. The manuscripts did not prove to be of any value ; and Madeleine was very glad to close the door upon the intruders, for she did not like their looks. A similar impression seemed to have been made on the company ; for several of them remarked that it was hazardous to introduce men of that stamp into a room filled with books clasped with silver, and with many other ancient articles of curious workmanship, some of them in the precious metals. But Dubois laughed at the idea that anybody would think of robbing a poor book-antiquarian of his musty treasures, though some of them were clasped with silver.

The dimensions of the table were enlarged by piles of huge folios, and Madeleine spread it with choice viands, in the discussion of which the style and orthography of Livy were for a while forgotten. The lively sallies of Hyppolite, his funny anecdotes, and descriptions of practical jokes, began to entertain the guests more than their own conversation. His merry, thrilling laugh became infectious. First, his pretty cousin joined in with her silvery treble ; then Dubois ; then all of them. No one, listening to this hilarious chorus, would have supposed the company consisted of the most profound scholars that ever enlightened the halls of the Institute or the Academy.

Dubois went to sleep that happy night dreaming

of new discoveries among the as yet unrestored leaves of his precious *palimpsest.* He was wakened very early in the morning by a loud knock at his door, and heard the voice of old Madeleine crying out, " Monsieur Dubois! Monsieur Dubois! Get up! Pray get up immediately!" He hurried on his dressing-gown, and found Madeleine in the middle of his study, her eyes streaming with tears. The room where he had heaped up so many treasures, where he had spent so many hours of calm happiness, where he had the last evening enjoyed so much, was empty. The pile of folios, the rows of richly-bound manuscripts, with the velvet covers and silver clasps, his precious *palimpsest,* and even the bundles of musty vellum, had all disappeared. The window was open, and the little curtain torn; plainly indicating how the robbers had obtained entrance into his sanctuary. The linnet was singing a morning song in the lime-trees, and the early sun checkered the empty floor with bright light and quivering shadows of the foliage. It seemed as if the sweet sounds and the brilliant rays were rejoicing over a scene of gladness, instead of such utter desolation and wretchedness.

No words can describe the pangs which wrung the heart of poor Dubois, thus suddenly and strangely deprived of the treasure which he had spent all the energies of his life in discovering. For a moment, his eyes glared with rage, like those of a tiger deprived of her young. Then he clasped

his trembling hands, and fell heavily, nearly fainting, into his chair. Alarmed by the sound of his
fall, Marcelline came running in. It was long before she and old Madeleine could rouse him from
his lethargy. At last, his stupefied senses were
awakened and concentrated by his daughter's repeated assurances that the lost treasure would be
recovered if an immediate pursuit were instituted.
" It is not likely," said she, " that we shall recover
the richly-illuminated manuscripts, in their valuable bindings ; or the carved ivories ; or those co-
dices written in gold upon grounds of purple ; but
the sheets of that old *palimpsest,* with its half-
obliterated characters, and the old volume containing the rest of the work, cannot possibly be of use
to anybody but yourself. Those can surely be
recovered."

A flood of passionate tears came to her father's
relief. His usual calmness was restored ; and
after drinking a cup of coffee, urged upon him by
the kind old Madeleine, he hurried forth to give
information to the police, and to make all possible
efforts to recover his treasures.

Some fragments of parchment were found under
the lime-trees, but no further traces were discovered, till late in the forenoon it was ascertained
that one of the richly-bound manuscripts had been
offered to a dealer for sale. In the afternoon, another clew was obtained from a waste-paper dealer,
who described a quantity of parchment brought to

him that morning, which he had not, however, purchased.   From the description, it appeared that the precious *palimpsest* was among these bundles. Dubois's hopes were kindled by this information. He was recommended to go to the establishments of various dealers in such articles in remote quarters of the city, and, accompanied by the police, he made diligent search.   Only one more remained, and that was close to the Barrière du Trone.

Arrived at this establishment, Dubois was surprised to see his nephew mounted aloft at a desk in the inner warehouse; for he had never inquired concerning the nature of the factory in which he was employed.   As soon as Hyppolite perceived his uncle, he hurried forward to welcome him, and told him he had intended to call at the Rue Cassette that day, for he had just obtained possession of two illuminated letters that he wished to present to Mademoiselle Marcelline.   He took two slips of vellum from his desk ; " See," said he, " these are very much in the style of that old Roman History you were exhibiting to the company last night."

" Very much in the style !" exclaimed Dubois, his eyes glistening with delight.   " They are identical !   Where did you get them ? "

" Our foreman sent them down to me," rejoined Hyppolite.   " We purchase enormous quantities of old parchment, and frequently a few painted letters are found in the mass.   Our man-

ager, in compliance with my request, cuts them
out and reserves them for me."

" Then the vellum from which they were cut
is here ? "

" Yes, it is, uncle ; but why are you so agitated ? "

" Dubois briefly related the circumstances of
the robbery; and wiping the cold perspiration
from his brow, he added : "But all is safe now!
I would not walk twenty paces to recover all the
silver-clasped volumes, if I can only hold once
more the musty *palimpsest* which contains that
priceless treasure, — The Lost Books of Livy !"

The flush faded from Hyppolite's ruddy cheek.
" There is not a moment to be lost!" exclaimed
he. " Follow me, dear uncle."

Away he ran across court-yards, through long
warehouses filled with merchandise, and up flights
of stairs, two steps at a bound. Dubois, highly
excited, followed with the activity of youth.
They reached a small room adjoining an enormous
mass of lofty chimneys, from which heavy col-
umns of smoke rolled away before the wind.

" Where is the lot of old vellum that came
this morning ? " gasped Hyppolite, all out of
breath.

A man who was busy checking off accounts,
asked, " Do you mean the lot from which you
cut those two letters ? "

" Yes, yes," replied Hyppolite. . " Where is it ?
Where is it ? It is very important !"

" Let me see," said the man. " It was lot number fourteen, purchased at eight o'clock this morning. We happened to be very short of vellum, and I gave out that new lot directly." He opened a creaking door, and called out, " Pierre ! Pierre ! what was the number of the lot you put in last ? "

" Number fourteen," replied a deep voice within ; and the door closed again, with dinning rattle of rope and weight.

" It is too late," said the foreman, turning to Hyppolite. " It went in at eleven o'clock."

" Went *in?* Went in *where?* " exclaimed Dubois, turning first to Hyppolite, and then to the foreman, with a look of haggard anxiety.

" Into the boiler," replied Hyppolite, taking his uncle's hand. " This is a gelatine manufactory. We boil down tons of old parchment every year."

.   .   .   .   .

It was long before Dubois recovered from the shock he had received ; but he did finally recover. He began to accumulate fresh bibliographical treasures around him, and many pleasant evenings were spent in those old apartments. But his former enthusiasm never returned. Any new discovery in the field of his research no longer excited a rapid flow of ardent words, but was merely indicated by a faint smile. He was always kindly and genial, and was only roused to an occasional word or look of bitterness when some circumstance happened to remind him of the treasure he had lost. " To think that what I had been hunting for all my life should be found only to be lost in a pot of gelatine!" he would exclaim, indignantly. Then he would fall into a silence which no one ventured to disturb. But, with a slight sigh, and a quiver of his gray locks, he would soon dismiss the subject from his mind, and change the conversation.

If he ever felt regret at having expended all the energies of his life among the dim shadows of the past, no one ever heard him express the feeling. And this was wise ; for his habits were too firmly fixed to be changed. He lived with his dear old volumes as with friends. The monotony of his life was soothed by a daughter's love, and cheered by the kind attentions of his gay young nephew. His uncommon talents and learning left no traces behind them, and his name passed away as do the pleasant clouds of twilight. Hyppolite's constant love was rewarded by the heart and hand of Marcelline ; and the two who most reverenced the old man's learning, and most tenderly cherished the memory of his genial character, lived to talk of them often to each other, and to teach - them to their descendants.

TO ONE WHO WISHED ME SIX-TEEN YEARS OLD.

By ALICE CARY.

SUPPOSE your hand with power supplied,
  Say, would you slip it 'neath my hair,
And turn it to the golden side
  Of sixteen years? Suppose you dare,

And I stood here with smiling mouth,
  Red cheeks, and hands all softly white,
Exceeding beautiful with youth,
  And that some tiptoe-treading sprite

Brought dreams as bright as they could be,
  To keep the shadows from my brow,
And plucked down hearts to pleasure me,
  As you would roses from a bough.

What could I do then? Idly wear,
  While all my mates went on before,
The bashful looks and golden hair
  Of sixteen years! and nothing more?

Nay, done with youth are my desires,
　　Life has no pain I fear to meet ;
Experience, with its dreadful fires,
　　Melts knowledge to a welding heat.

And all its fires of heart and brain,
　　Where purpose into power was wrought,
I 'd bear, and gladly bear again,
　　Rather than be put back a thought.

So, sigh no more, my gentle friend,
　　That I am at the time of day
When white hair comes, and heart-beats send
　　No blushes through the cheeks astray.

For could you mould my destiny,
　　As clay, within your loving hand,
I 'd leave my youth's sweet company,
　　And suffer back to where I stand.

THE SILVERY HEAD.

Though youth may boast the curls that flow,
In sunny waves of auburn glow,
　　As graceful, on thy hoary head,
　　Has time the robe of honor spread,
　　And there, O, softly, softly shed
　　　　His wreath of snow.

　　　　　　　　　　　FELICIA HEMANS.

GROWING OLD.*

ADDRESSED TO UNMARRIED WOMEN.

T is a trying crisis in life to feel that you have had your fair half at least of the ordinary term of years allotted to mortals; that you have no right to expect to be any handsomer, or stronger, or happier than you are now; that you have climbed to the summit of life, whence the next step must necessarily be decadence. The air may be as fresh, the view as grand, still you know that, slower or faster, you are going down hill. It is not a pleasant descent at the beginning. It is rather trying when, from long habit, you unwittingly speak of yourself as a "girl," to detect a covert smile on the face of your interlocutor; or, when led by some chance excitement to deport yourself in an ultra-youthful manner, some instinct warns you that you are making yourself ridiculous; or, catching in some strange looking-glass the face you are

* From Miss Muloch's "Thoughts about Women."

too familiar with to notice much, ordinarily, you suddenly become aware that it is not a young face, and will never be a young face again. With most people, the passing from maturity to middle age is so gradual as to be almost imperceptible to the individual concerned. There is no denying this fact, and it ought to silence many an ill-natured remark upon those unlucky ones who insist upon remaining "young ladies of a certain age." It is very difficult for a woman to recognize that she is growing old ; and to all, this recognition cannot but be fraught with considerable pain. Even the most sensible woman cannot fairly put aside her youth, with all it has·enjoyed, or lost, or missed, and regard it as henceforth to be considered a thing gone by, without a momentary spasm of the heart.

To " grow old gracefully " is a good and beautiful thing ; to grow old worthily is a better. And the first effort to that end is to become reconciled to the fact of youth's departure ; to have faith in the wisdom of that which we call change, but which is in truth progression ; to follow openly and fearlessly, in ourselves and our daily life, the same law which makes spring pass into summer, summer into autumn, and autumn into winter, preserving an especial beauty and fitness in each of the four.

If women could only believe it, there is a wonderful beauty even in growing old. The charm of expression, arising from softened temper or ripened intellect, often atones amply for the loss of form and coloring; consequently, to those who could never boast of either of these latter, years give much more than they take away. A sensitive person often requires half a lifetime to get thoroughly used to this corporeal machine; to attain a wholesome indifference both to its defects and perfections; and to learn at last what nobody would acquire from any teacher but experience, that it is the *mind* alone which is of any consequence. With good temper, sincerity, and a moderate stock of brains, or even with the two former only, any sort of a body can in time be made a useful, respectable, and agreeable travelling-dress for the soul. Many a one who was absolutely plain in youth, thus grows pleasant and well-looking in declining years. You will seldom find anybody, not ugly in mind, who is repulsively ugly in person after middle life.

So it is with character. However we may talk about people being "not a whit altered," "just the same as ever"; the fact is, not one of us is, or can be, for long together, exactly the same. The body we carry with us is not the identical body we were born with, or the one we supposed ours seven years ago; and our spiritual self, which inhabits it, also goes through perpetual change and renewal. In moral and mental, as well as in physical growth, it is impossible to remain stationary. If we do not advance, we retrograde. Talk of being " too late to improve," " too old to learn "! A human being should be improving with every day of a lifetime ; and will probably have to go on learning throughout all the ages of immortality.

One of the pleasures of growing old is, to know, to acquire, to find out, to be able to appreciate the causes of things ; this gradually becomes a necessity and an exquisite delight. We are able to pass out of our own small daily sphere, and to take interest in the marvellous government of the universe ; to see the grand workings of cause and effect ; the educing of good out of apparent evil ; the clearing away of the knots in tangled destinies, general or individual ; the wonderful agency of time, change, and progress in ourselves, in those surrounding us, and in the world at large. In small minds, this feeling expends itself in meddling, gossiping, scandal-mongering ; but such are merely abortive developments of a right noble quality, which, properly guided, results in benefits incalculable to the individual and to society. Undoubtedly the after-half of life is the best working-time. Beautiful is youth's enthusiasm, and grand are its achievements ; but the most solid and permanent good is done by the persistent strength and wide experience of middle age. Contentment rarely comes till then ; not mere resignation, a passive acquiescence in what cannot be

removed, but active contentment.   This is a blessing cheaply bought by a personal share in that
daily account of joy and pain, which the longer
one lives the more one sees is pretty equally bal-
anced in all lives.   Young people enjoy " the top
of life " ecstatically, either in prospect or fruition ;
but they are very seldom contented.   It is not
possible.   Not till the cloudy maze is half travelled
through, and we begin to see the object and purpose of it, can we be really content.

The doubtful question, to marry or, not to marry,
is by this time generally settled.   A woman's relations with the other sex imperceptibly change
their character, or slowly decline.   There are
exceptions ; old lovers who have become friends,
or friends whom no new love could make swerve
from the fealty of years ; still it usually happens
so.   The society of honorable, well-informed gentlemen, who meet a lady on the easy neutral
ground of mutual esteem, is undoubtedly pleasant,
but the time has passed when any one of them is
the one necessary to her happiness.   If she wishes
to retain influence over mankind, she must do it
by means different from those employed in youth.
Even then, be her wit ever so sparkling, her influence ever so pure and true, she will often find
her listener preferring bright eyes to intellectual
conversation, and the satisfaction of his heart to
the improvement of his mind.   And who can
blame him ?   The only way for a woman to pre-

serve the unfeigned respect of men, is to let them
see that she can do without either their attention
or their admiration. The waning coquette, the
ancient beauty, as well as the ordinary woman,
who has had her fair share of both love and liking,
must show by her demeanor that she has learned
this.

It is reckoned among the compensations of time
that we suffer less as we grow older ; that pain,
like joy, becomes dulled by repetition, or by the
callousness that comes with years. In one sense
this is true. If there is no joy like the joy of
youth, the rapture of a first love, the thrill of a
first ambition, God's great mercy has also granted
that there is no anguish like youth's pain ; so total,
so hopeless, blotting out earth and heaven, falling
down upon the whole being like a stone. This
never comes in after life ; because the sufferer, if
he or she have lived to any purpose at all, has
learned that God never meant any human being to
be crushed under any calamity, like a blind worm
under a stone.

For lesser evils, the fact that our interests gradually take a wider range, allows more scope for
the healing power of compensation. Also our
loves, hates, sympathies, and prejudices, having
assumed a more rational and softened shape, do
not present so many angles for the rough attrition
of the world. Likewise, with the eye of faith we
have come to view life in its entireness, instead of

puzzling over its disjointed parts, which were never meant to be made wholly clear to mortal eye. And that calm twilight, which, by nature's kindly law, so soon begins to creep over the past, throws over all things a softened coloring, which transcends and forbids regret.

Another reason why woman has greater capacity for usefulness in middle life than in any previous portion of her existence, is her greater independence. She will have learned to understand herself, mentally and bodily; to be mistress over herself. Nor is this a small advantage; for it often takes years to comprehend, and to act upon when comprehended, the physical peculiarities of one's own constitution. Much valetudinarianism among women arises from ignorance or neglect of the commonest sanitary laws; and from indifference to that grand preservative of a healthy body, *a well-controlled and healthy mind.* Both of these are more attainable in middle age than in youth; and therefore the sort of happiness they bring, a solid, useful, available happiness, is more in her power then than at any earlier period. And why? Because she has ceased to think principally of herself and her own pleasures; because happiness has itself become to her an accidental thing, which the good God may give or withhold, as He sees most fit for her, and most adapted to the work for which he means to use her in her generation. This conviction of being at once an active and a

passive agent is surely consecration enough to
form the peace, nay, the happiness, of any good
woman's life ; enough, be it ever so solitary, to
sustain it until the end.   In what manner such a
conviction should be carried out, no one individual
can venture to advise.   In this age, woman's work
is almost unlimited, when the woman herself so
chooses.   She alone can be a law unto herself ;
deciding and acting according to the circumstances
in which her lot is placed.   And have we not
many who do so act ?   There are women of property, whose names are a proverb for generous and
wide charities ; whose riches, carefully guided,
flow into innumerable channels, freshening the
whole land.   There are women of rank and influence, who use both, or lay aside both, in the
simplest humility, for labors of love, which level
all classes, or rather raise them all, to one common
sphere of womanhood.

Many others, of whom the world knows nothing,
have taken the wisest course that any unmarried
woman can take ; they have made themselves a
home and a position ; some, as the Ladies Bountiful of a country neighborhood ; some, as elder sisters, on whom has fallen the bringing up of whole
families, and to whom has been tacitly accorded
the headship of the same, by the love and respect
of more than one generation thereof.   There are
some who, as writers, painters, and professional
women generally, make the most of whatever spe-

cial gift is allotted to them ; believing that, whether it be great or small, it is not theirs, either to lose or to waste, but that they must one day render up to the Master his own, with usury.

I will not deny that the approach of old age has its sad aspect to a woman who has never married ; and who, when her own generation dies out, nor longer retains, or can expect to retain, any flesh-and-blood claim upon a single human being. When all the downward ties, which give to the decline of life a rightful comfort, and the interest in the new generation which brightens it with a perpetual hope, are to her either unknown, or indulged in chiefly on one side. Of course there are exceptions, where an aunt has been almost like a mother, and where a loving and lovable great-aunt is as important a personage as any grandmother. But, generally speaking, a single woman must make up her mind that the close of her days will be more or less solitary.

Yet there is a solitude which old age feels to be as natural and satisfying as that rest which seems such an irksomeness to youth, but which gradually grows into the best blessing of our lives ; and there is another solitude, so full of peace and hope, that it is like Jacob's sleep in the wilderness, at the foot of the ladder of angels.

The extreme loneliness, which afar off appears sad, may prove to be but as the quiet, dreamy hour, " between the lights," when the day's work is done, and we lean back, closing our eyes, to think it all over before we finally go to rest, or to look forward, with faith and hope, unto the coming Morning.

A life in which the best has been made of all the materials granted to it, and through which the hand of the Great Designer can be plainly traced, whether its web be dark or bright, whether its pattern be clear or clouded, is not a life to be pitied ; for it is a completed life. It has fulfilled its appointed course, and returns to the Giver of all breath, pure as he gave it. Nor will he forget it when he counteth up his jewels.

" TIME wears slippers of list, and his tread is noiseless. The days come softly dawning, one after another ; they creep in at the windows ; their fresh morning air is grateful to the lips as they pant for it ; their music is sweet to the ears that listen to it ; until, before we know it, a whole life of days has possession of the citadel, and time has taken us for its own."

EQUINOCTIAL.

By MRS. A. D. T. WHITNEY.

THE Sun of Life has crossed the line;
   The summer-shine of lengthened light
Faded and failed, — till, where I stand,
   'T is equal Day and equal Night.

One after one, as dwindling hours,
   Youth's glowing hopes have dropped away,
And soon may barely leave the gleam
   That coldly scores a winter's day.

I am not young, I am not old;
   The flush of morn, the sunset calm,
Paling, and deepening, each to each,
   Meet midway with a solemn charm.

One side I see the summer fields,
   Not yet disrobed of all their green;
While westerly, along the hills,
   Flame the first tints of frosty sheen.

Ah, middle-point, where cloud and storm
  Make battle-ground of this my life!
Where, even-matched, the Night and Day
  Wage round me their September strife!

I bow me to the threatening gale:
  I know when that is overpast,
Among the peaceful harvest-days,
  An Indian-summer comes at last.

EPITAPH ON THE UNMATED.

No chosen spot of ground she called her own.
In pilgrim guise o'er earth she wandered on;
Yet always in her path some flowers were strown.
No dear ones were her own peculiar care,
So was her bounty free as heaven's air;
For every claim she had enough to spare.
And, loving more her heart to *give* than lend,
Though oft deceived in many a trusted friend,
She hoped, believed, and trusted to the end.
She had her joys; — 't was joy to her to love,
To labor in the world with God above,
And tender hearts that ever near did move.
She had her griefs; — but they left peace behind,
And healing came on every stormy wind,
And still with silver every cloud was lined.
And every loss sublimed some low desire,
And every sorrow taught her to aspire,
Till waiting angels bade her " Go up higher."

                            E. S.

A BEAUTIFUL THOUGHT.*

BLESSING and blessed, this excellent man passed on to old age; and how beautiful that old age was, none, who had the privilege of knowing it, can ever forget. It was the old age of the Christian scholar and the beloved man. His evening of life could not but be bright and serene, full of hope, and free from sadness. He had a kindly freshness of spirit, which made the society of the young pleasant to him; and they, on their part, were always happy to be with him, enjoying the good-natured wisdom and the modest richness of his conversation. His faculties remained clear, active, and healthy to the last. Advancing years never for a moment closed the capacity, or abated the willingness, to receive new ideas. Though a lover of the past and the established, his opinions never hardened into prejudices. His intellectual vigor

* From the Rev. Dr. Francis's Memoir of the Hon. John Davis.

was not seen to moulder under the quiet which an old man claims as his right. Of him might be said what Solon said of himself in advanced years, that " he learned something every day he lived "; and to no one could be better applied the remark of Cicero concerning the venerable Appius : " He kept his mind bent like a bow, nor was it ever relaxed by old age."

But it was peculiarly his fine moral qualities — his benevolence, his artlessness, his genial kindness — which shed a mellow and beautiful light on his old age. No thought of self ever mingled its alloy with the virtues that adorned Judge Davis's character. His reliance on the truths and promises of Christian faith seemed more confident and vital as he drew nearer to the great realities of the future. For him, life had always a holy meaning. A Grecian philosopher, at the age of eighty-five, is said to have expressed painful discontent at the shortness of life, and complained of nature's hard allotment, which snatches man away just as he is about to reach some perfection of science. Not so our Christian sage ; he found occasion, not for complaint, but rather for thankfulness, because, as the end approached, he saw more distinctly revealed the better light beyond.

He once expressed, in a manner touchingly beautiful, his own estimation of old age. On the occasion of a dinner-party, at which Judge Story and others eminent in the legal profession were

15   v

present, the conversation turned upon the comparative advantages of the different periods of life. Some preferred, for enjoyment, youth and manhood ; others ascribed more solid satisfactions to old age. When the opinion of Judge Davis was asked, he said, with his usual calm simplicity of manner : " In the warm season of the year it is my delight to be in the country ; and every pleasant evening while I am there, I love to sit at the window and look at some beautiful trees which grow near my house. The murmuring of the wind through the branches, the gentle play of the leaves, and the flickering of light upon them when the moon is up, fill me with an indescribable pleasure. As the autumn comes on, I feel very sad to see these leaves falling one by one ; but when they are all gone, I find that they were only a screen before my eyes ; for I experience a new and higher satisfaction as I gaze through the naked branches at the glorious stars of heaven beyond."

AT ANCHOR.*

A H, many a year ago, dear wife,
  We floated down this river,
Where the hoar willows on its brink
 Alternate wave and shiver;
With careless glance we viewed askance
 The kingfisher at quest,
And scarce would heed the reed-wren near,
 Who sang beside her nest;
Nor dreamed that e'er our boat would be
 Thus anchored and at rest,
   Dear love,
 Thus anchored, and at rest!

O, many a time the wren has built
 Where those green shadows quiver,
And many a time the hawthorn shed
 Its blossoms on the river,
Since that sweet noon of sultry June,
 When I my love confessed,
While with the tide our boat did glide
 Adown the stream's smooth breast,

* Author unknown.

Whereon our little shallop lies
  Now anchored, and at rest,
      Dear love,
  Now anchored, and at rest!

The waters still to ocean run,
  Their tribute to deliver,
And still the hawthorns bud and bloom
  Above the dusky river.
Still sings the wren, — the water-hen
  Still skims the ripple's crest;
The sun — as bright as on that night —
  Sinks slowly down the west;
But now our tiny craft is moored,
  Safe anchored and at rest,
      Dear love,
  Safe anchored, and at rest!

For this sweet calm of after-days
  We thank the bounteous Giver,
Who bids our life flow smoothly on
  As this delicious river.
A world — our own — has round us grown,
  Wherein we twain are blest;
Our child's first words than songs of birds
  More music have expressed;
And all our centred happiness
  Is anchored, and at rest,
      Dear love,
  Is anchored, and at rest!

NOVEMBER.

By REV. HENRY WARD BEECHER.

E often hear people say, " O, the dreary days of November ! " The days of November are never dreary, though *men* sometimes are. There are things in November that make us sad. There are suggestions in it that lead us to serious thoughts. At that season of the year, we are apt to feel that life is passing away. After the days in summer begin to grow short, I cannot help sighing often ; and, as they still grow shorter and shorter, I look upon things, not with pain, but with a melancholy eye. And when autumn comes, and the leaves of the trees drop down through the air and find their resting-places, I cannot help thinking, that life is short, that our work is almost ended. It makes me sad ; but there is a sadness that is wholesome, and even pleasurable. There are sorrows that are not painful, but are of the nature of some acids, and give piquancy and flavor to life.

Such is the sorrow which November brings. That month, which sees the year disrobed, is not a dreary month. I like to see the trees go to bed, as much as I like to see little children go to their sleep ; and I think there is nothing prettier in this world than to see a mother disrobe her child and prepare its couch, and sing and talk to it, and finally lay it to rest. I like to see the birds get ready for their repose at night. Did you ever sit at twilight and hear the birds talk of their domestic matters, — apparently going over with each other the troubles and joys of the day? There is an immense deal to be learned from birds, if a person has an ear to hear. Even so I like to see the year prepare for its sleep. I like to see the trees with their clothes taken off. I like to see the lines of a tree; to see its anatomy. I like to see the preparation God makes for winter. How everything is snugged and packed! How all nature gets ready for the cold season! How the leaves heap themselves upon the roots to protect them from the frosts! How all things tender are taken out of the way, and only things tough are left to stand the buffetings of winter! And how do hardy vines and roots bravely sport their bannered leaves, which the frost cannot kill, holding them up clear into the coldest days! November is a dreary month to some, but to me it is only sad ; and it is a sweet sadness that it brings to my mind.

MEDITATIONS ON A BIRTHDAY EVE.

By REV. JOHN PIERPONT.

DAY, with its labors, has withdrawn.
  The stars look down from heaven,
And whisper, "Of thy life are gone
  Full seventy years and seven!"

While those bright worlds, by angels trod,
  · Thus whispering round me roll,
Let me commune with thee, my God!
  Commune with thee, my soul!

Thou, Father, canst not change thy place,
  Nor change thy time to be.
What are the boundless fields of space,
  Or what are years to Thee?

But unto me, revolving years
  Bring change, bring feebler breath;
Bring age, — and, though they bring no fears,
  Bring slower steps, pain, death.

This earthly house thy wisdom plann'd,
  And leased me for a term,
The house I live in, *seems* to stand
  On its foundation firm.

I hardly see that it is old;
  But younger eyes find proof
Of its long standing, who behold
  The gray moss on its roof.

Spirit! thou knowest this house, erelong,
  To kindred dust must fall.
Hast thou, while in it, grown more strong,
  More ready for the call

To meet thy Judge, amid " the cloud
  Of witnesses," who 've run
Their heavenward race, and joined the crowd,
  Who wreaths and crowns have won?

Hast thou, in search of Truth, been true?
  True to thyself and her?
And been, with many or with few,
  Her *honest* worshipper?

E'en truths, wherein the Past hath stood,
  Wouldst thou inherit blind?
They 're good; but there 's a *better* good, —
  The power *more* truths to find.

And hast thou occupied that power,
  And made one talent five?
If so, then peaceful be this hour!
  Thou 'st saved thy soul alive.

Hast thou e'er given the world a page,
    A line that thou wouldst blot,
As adverse to an upward age?
    God knoweth thou hast not!

Giver of life and all my powers,
    To thee my soul I lift!
And in these lone and thoughtful hours,
    I thank thee for the gift.

Day, with its toil and care withdrawn,
    Night's shadows o'er me thrown,
Another of my years is gone,
    And here I sit alone.

No, not alone! for with me sit
    My judges, — God and I;
And the large record we have writ,
    Is lying open by.

And as I hope, erelong, to swell
    The song of seraphim,
And as that song the truth will tell,
    My judgment is with Him.

Spirit! thy race is nearly run.
    Say, hast thou run it well?
Thy work on earth is almost done;
    How done, no *man* can tell.

Spirit, toil on! thy house, that stands
    Seventy years old and seven,
Will fall; but one, "not made with hands,"
    Awaiteth thee in heaven.

15 *

THE GRANDMOTHER OF SLAVES.

BY HER GRANDDAUGHTER.

 HAD a great treasure in my maternal grandmother, who was a remarkable woman in many respects. She was the daughter of a planter in South Carolina, who, at his death, left her and her mother free, with money to go to St. Augustine, where they had relatives. It was during the Revolutionary War, and they were captured on their passage, carried back, and sold to different purchasers. Such was the story my grandmother used to tell me. She was sold to the keeper of a large hotel, and I have often heard her tell how hard she fared during childhood. But as she grew older, she evinced so much intelligence, and was so faithful, that her master and mistress could not help seeing it was for their interest to take care of such a valuable piece of property. She became an indispensable person in the household, officiating in all capacities, from cook and wet-nurse to seamstress.

She was much praised for her cooking; and her nice crackers became so famous in the neighborhood that many people were desirous of obtaining them. In consequence of numerous requests of this kind, she asked permission of her mistress to bake crackers at night, after all the household work was done; and she obtained leave to do it, provided she would clothe herself and the children from the profits. Upon these terms, after working hard all day for her mistress, she began her midnight bakings, assisted by her two oldest children. The business proved profitable; and each year she laid by a little, to create a fund for the purchase of her children. Her master died, and his property was divided among the heirs. My grandmother remained in the service of his widow, as a slave. Her children were divided among her master's children; but, as she had five, Benjamin, the youngest, was sold, in order that the heirs might have an equal portion of dollars and cents. There was so little difference in our ages, that he always seemed to me more like a brother than an uncle. He was a bright, handsome lad, nearly white; for he inherited the complexion my grandmother had derived from Anglo-Saxon ancestors. His sale was a terrible blow to his mother; but she was naturally hopeful, and she went to work with redoubled energy, trusting in time to be able to purchase her children. One day, her mistress begged the loan of three hundred dollars from the little fund she had laid up from the proceeds of her baking. She promised to pay her soon ; but as no promise, or writing, given to a slave is legally binding, she was obliged to trust solely to her honor.

In my master's house very little attention was paid to the slaves' meals. If they could catch a bit of food while it was going, well and good. But I gave myself no trouble on that score ; for on my various errands I passed my grandmother's house, and she always had something to spare for me. I was frequently threatened with punishment if I stopped there ; and my grandmother, to avoid detaining me, often stood at the gate with something for my breakfast or dinner. I was indebted to her for all my comforts, spiritual or temporal. It was *her* labor that supplied my scanty wardrobe. I have a vivid recollection of the linsey-woolsey dress given me every winter by Mrs. Flint. How I hated it ! It was one of the badges of slavery. While my grandmother was thus helping to support me from her hard earnings, the three hundred dollars she lent her mistress was never repaid. When her mistress died, my master, who was her son-in-law, was appointed executor. When grandmother applied to him for payment, he said the estate was insolvent, and the law prohibited payment. It did not, however, prohibit him from retaining the silver candelabra, which had been purchased with that money. I presume they will be handed down in the family, from generation to generation.

My grandmother's mistress had always promised that, at her death, she should be free ; and it was said that in her will she made good the promise. But when the estate was settled, Dr. Flint told the faithful old servant that, under existing circumstances, it was necessary she should be sold.

On the appointed day, the customary advertisement was posted up, proclaiming that there would be " a public sale of negroes, horses, &c." Dr. Flint called to tell my grandmother that he was unwilling to wound her feelings by putting her up at auction, and that he would prefer to dispose of her at private sale. She saw through his hypocrisy, and understood very well that he was ashamed of the job. She was a very spirited woman, and if he was base enough to sell her, after her mistress had made her free by her will, she was determined the public should know it. She had, for a long time, supplied many families with crackers and preserves ; consequently " Aunt Marthy," as she was called, was generally known ; and all who knew her respected her intelligence and good character. It was also well known that her mistress had intended to leave her free, as a reward for her long and faithful services. When the day of sale came, she took her place among the chattels, and at the first call she sprang upon the auction-block. She was then fifty years old. Many

voices called out, " Shame ! Shame ! Who 's going
to sell *you*, Aunt Marthy ?   Don't stand there !
That 's no place for *you !* "   She made no answer,
but quietly awaited her fate.   No one bid for her.
At last, a feeble voice said, " Fifty dollars."   It
came from a maiden lady, seventy years old, the
sister of my grandmother's deceased mistress.   She
had lived forty years under the same roof with my
grandmother ; she knew how faithfully she had
served her owners, and how cruelly she had been
defrauded of her rights, and she resolved to protect her.   The auctioneer waited for a higher bid ;
but her wishes were respected ; no one bid above
her.   The old lady could neither read nor write ;
and when the bill of sale was made out, she signed
it with a cross.   But of what consequence was that,
when she had a big heart overflowing with human
kindness ?   She gave the faithful old servant her
freedom.

My grandmother had always been a mother to
her orphan grandchildren, as far as that was possible in a condition of slavery.   Her perseverance
and unwearied industry continued unabated after
her time was her own, and she soon became mistress of a snug little home, and surrounded herself
with the necessaries of life.   She would have been
happy, if her family could have shared them with
her.   There remained to her but three children and
two grandchildren ; and they were all slaves.   Most
earnestly did she strive to make us feel that it was

the will of God; that He had seen fit to place us
under such circumstances; and, though it seemed
hard, we ought to pray for contentment. It was
a beautiful faith, coming from a mother who could
not call her children her own. But I, and Benjamin, her youngest boy, condemned it. It appeared
to us that it was much more according to the will
of God that we should be free, and able to make a
home for ourselves, as she had done. There we
always found balsam for our troubles. She was so
loving, so sympathizing! She always met us with
a smile, and listened with patience to all our sorrows. She spoke so hopefully, that unconsciously
the clouds gave place to sunshine. There was a
grand big oven there, too, that baked bread and
nice things for the town; and we knew there was
always a choice bit in store for us. But even the
charms of that old oven failed to reconcile us to
our hard lot. Benjamin was now a tall, handsome
lad, strongly and gracefully made, and with a spirit
too bold and daring for a slave.

One day, his master attempted to flog him for
not obeying his summons quickly enough. Benjamin resisted, and in the struggle threw his master
down. To raise his hand against a white man was
a great crime according to the laws of the State,
and to avoid a cruel public whipping, Benjamin
hid himself and made his escape. My grandmother was absent visiting an old friend in the
country, when this happened. When she returned,

and found her youngest child had fled, great was her sorrow. But, with characteristic piety, she said, " God's will be done." Every morning she inquired whether any news had been heard from her boy. Alas, news did come ; sad news. The master received a letter, and was rejoicing over the capture of his human chattel.

That day seems to me but as yesterday, so well do I remember it. I saw him led through the streets in chains to jail. His face was ghastly pale, but full of determination. He had sent some one to his mother's house, to ask her not to come to meet him. He said the sight of her distress would take from him all self-control. Her heart yearned to see him, and she went; but she screened herself in the crowd, that it might be as her child had said.

We were not allowed to visit him. But we had known the jailer for years, and he was a kind-hearted man. At midnight he opened the door for my grandmother and myself to enter, in disguise. When we entered the cell, not a sound broke the stillness. " Benjamin," whispered my grandmother. No answer. " Benjamin ! " said she, again, in a faltering tone. There was a jingling of chains. The moon had just risen, and cast an uncertain light through the bars. We knelt down and took Benjamin's cold hands in ours. Sobs alone were heard, while she wept upon his neck. At last Benjamin's lips were unsealed.

Mother and son talked together. He asked her pardon for the suffering he had caused her. She told him she had nothing to forgive; that she could not blame him for wanting to be free. He told her that he broke away from his captors, and was about to throw himself into the river, but thoughts of her came over him and arrested the movement. She asked him if he did not also think of God. He replied, "No, mother, I did not. When a man is hunted like a wild beast, he forgets that there *is* a God."

The pious mother shuddered, as she said, "Don't talk so, Benjamin. Try to be humble, and put your trust in God."

"I wish I had some of your goodness," he replied. "You bear everything patiently, just as though you thought it was all right. I wish I could."

She told him it had not always been so with her; that once she was like him; but when sore troubles came upon her, and she had no arm to lean upon, she learned to call on God, and he lightened her burdens. She besought him to do so likewise.

The jailer came to tell us we had overstayed our time, and we were obliged to hurry away. Grandmother went to the master and tried to intercede for her son. But he was inexorable. He said Benjamin should be made an example of. That he should be kept in jail till he was sold. For

w

three months he remained within the walls of the prison, during which time grandmother secretly conveyed him changes of clothes, and as often as possible carried him something warm for supper, accompanied with some little luxury for her friend the jailer. He was finally sold to a slave-trader from New Orleans. When they fastened irons upon his wrists to drive him off with the coffle, it was heart-rending to hear the groans of that poor mother, as she clung to the Benjamin of her family, — her youngest, her pet. He was pale and thin now from hardships and long confinement, but still his good looks were so observable, that the slave-trader remarked he would give any price for the handsome lad, if he were a girl. We, who knew so well what slavery was, were thankful that he was not.

Grandmother stifled her grief, and with strong arms and unwavering faith set to work to purchase freedom for Benjamin. She knew the slave-trader would charge three times as much as he gave for him; but she was not discouraged. She employed a lawyer to write to New Orleans, and try to negotiate the business for her. But word came that Benjamin was missing; he had run away again.

Philip, my grandmother's only remaining son, inherited his mother's intelligence. His mistress sometimes trusted him to go with a cargo to New York. One of these occasions occurred not

long after Benjamin's second escape. Through
God's good providence the brothers met in the
streets of New York. It was a happy meeting,
though Benjamin was very pale and thin ; for, on
his way from bondage, he had been taken violently
ill, and brought nigh unto death. Eagerly he
embraced his brother, exclaiming, " O Phil! here
I am at last! I came nigh dying when I was
almost in sight of freedom ; and O how I prayed
that I might live just to get one breath of free
air! And here I am. In the old jail I used to
wish I was dead. But life is worth something
now, and it would be hard to die." He begged
his brother not to go back to the South, but to
stay and work with him till they earned enough
to buy their relatives.

Philip replied : " It would kill mother if I deserted her. She has pledged her house, and is
working harder than ever to buy you. Will you
be bought ? "

"Never!" replied Benjamin, in his resolute
tone. " When I have got so far out of their
clutches, do you suppose, Phil, that I would
ever let them be paid one red cent? Do you
think I would consent to have mother turned out
of her hard-earned home in her old age ? And
she never to see me after she had bought me ?
For you know, Phil, she would never leave the
South while any of her children or grandchildren
remained in slavery. What a good mother ! Tell

her to buy *you*, Phil. You have always been a comfort to her; and I have always been making her trouble."

Philip furnished his brother with some clothes, and gave him what money he had. Benjamin pressed his hand, and said, with moistened eyes, " I part from all my kindred." And so it proved. We never heard from him afterwards.

When Uncle Philip came home, the first words he said, on entering the house, were : " O, mother, Ben is free! I have seen him in New York." For a moment, she seemed bewildered. He laid his hand gently on her shoulder, and repeated what he had said. She raised her hands devoutly, and exclaimed, " God be praised! Let us thank Him." She dropped on her knees, and poured forth her heart in prayer. When she grew calmer, she begged Philip to sit down and repeat every word her son had said. He told her all, except that Benjamin had nearly died on the way, and was looking very pale and thin.

Still the brave old woman toiled on to accomplish the rescue of her remaining children. After a while, she succeeded in buying Philip, for whom she paid eight hundred dollars, and came home with the precious document that secured his freedom. The happy mother and son sat by her hearth-stone that night, telling how proud they were of each other, and how they would prove to the world that they could take care of themselves, as they had long taken care of others. We all concluded by saying, " He that is *willing* to be a slave, let him be a slave."

My grandmother had still one daughter remaining in slavery. She belonged to the same master that I did ; and a hard time she had of it. She was a good soul, this old Aunt Nancy. She did all she could to supply the place of my lost mother to us orphans. She was the *factotum* in our master's household. She was housekeeper, waiting-maid, and everything else ; nothing went on well without her, by day or by night. She wore herself out in their service. Grandmother toiled on, hoping to purchase release for her. But one evening word was brought that she had been suddenly attacked with paralysis, and grandmother hastened to her bedside. Mother and daughter had always been devotedly attached to each other ; and now they looked lovingly and earnestly into each other's eyes, longing to speak of secrets that weighed on the hearts of both. She lived but two days, and on the last day she was speechless. It was sad to witness the grief of her bereaved mother. She had always been strong to bear, and religious faith still supported her ; but her dark life had become still darker, and age and trouble were leaving deep traces on her withered face. The poor old back was fitted to its burden. It bent under it, but did not break.

Uncle Philip asked permission to bury his

sister at his own expense; and slaveholders are always ready to grant *such* favors to slaves and their relatives. The arrangements were very plain, but perfectly respectable. It was talked of by the slaves as a mighty grand funeral. If Northern travellers had been passing through the place, perhaps they would have described it as a beautiful tribute to the humble dead, a touching proof of the attachment between slaveholders and their slaves; and very likely the mistress would have confirmed this impression, with her handkerchief at her eyes. *We* could have told them how the poor old mother had toiled, year after year, to buy her son Philip's right to his own earnings; and how that same Philip had paid the expenses of the funeral, which they regarded as doing so much credit to the master.

There were some redeeming features in our hard destiny. Very pleasant are my recollections of the good old lady who paid fifty dollars for the purpose of making my grandmother free, when she stood on the auction-block. She loved this old lady, whom we all called Miss Fanny. She often took tea at grandmother's house. On such occasions, the table was spread with a snow-white cloth, and the china cups and silver spoons were taken from the old-fashioned buffet. There were hot muffins, tea-rusks, and delicious sweetmeats. My grandmother always had a supply of such articles, because she furnished the ladies of the town with such things for their parties. She kept two cows for that purpose, and the fresh cream was Miss Fanny's delight. She invariably repeated that it was the very best in town. The old ladies had cosey times together. They would work and chat, and sometimes, while talking over old times, their spectacles would get dim with tears, and would have to be taken off and wiped. When Miss Fanny bade us " Good by," her bag was always filled with grandmother's best cakes, and she was urged to come again soon.

[Here follows a long account of persecutions endured by the granddaughter, who tells this story. She finally made her escape, after encountering great dangers and hardships. The faithful old grandmother concealed her for a long time at great risk to them both, during which time she tried in vain to buy free papers for her. At last there came a chance to escape in a vessel Northward bound. She goes on to say : —]

All arrangements were made for me to go on board at dusk. Grandmother came to me with a small bag of money, which she wanted me to take. I begged her to keep at least part of it ; but she insisted, while her tears fell fast, that I should take the whole. " You may be sick among strangers," said she ; " and they would send you to the poor-house to die." Ah, that good grandmother ! Though I had the blessed prospect of freedom before me, I felt dreadfully sad at leaving forever that old homestead, that had received and sheltered me in so many sorrows. Grandmother took me by the hand, and said, " My child, let us pray." We knelt down together, with my arm clasped round the faithful, loving old friend I was about to leave forever. On no other occasion has it been my lot to listen to so fervent a supplication for mercy and protection. It thrilled through my heart and inspired me with trust in God. I staggered into the street, faint in body, though strong of purpose. I did not look back upon the dear old place, though I felt that I should never see it again.

[The granddaughter found friends at the North, and, being uncommonly quick in her perceptions, she soon did much to supply the deficiencies of early education. While leading a worthy, industrious life in New York, she twice very narrowly escaped becoming a victim to the infamous Fugitive Slave Law. A noble-hearted lady purchased her freedom, and thereby rescued her from further danger. She thus closes the story of her venerable ancestor : —]

My grandmother lived to rejoice in the knowledge of my freedom ; but not long afterward a letter came to me with a black seal. It was from a friend at the South, who informed me that she had gone " where the wicked cease from troubling, and where the weary are at rest." Among the gloomy recollections of my life in bondage come tender memories of that good grandmother, like a few

fleecy clouds floating over a dark and troubled
sea.

H. J.

NOTE. — The above account is no fiction. The
author, who was thirty years in slavery, wrote it
in an interesting book entitled "Linda." She is
an esteemed friend of mine; and I introduce this
portion of her story here to illustrate the power
of character over circumstances. She has intense
sympathy for those who are still suffering in the
bondage from which she escaped. She is now
devoting all her energies to the poor refugees in
our camps, comforting the afflicted, nursing the
sick, and teaching the children. On the 1st of
January, 1863, she wrote me a letter, which began
as follows: "I have lived to hear the Proclama-
tion of Freedom for my suffering people. All my
wrongs are forgiven. I am more than repaid for
all I have endured. Glory to God in the highest!"

L. M. C.

WE hear men often enough speak of seeing God
in the stars and the flowers, but they will never be
truly religious, till they learn to behold Him in
each other also, where He is most easily, yet most
rarely discovered.

J. R. LOWELL.

16

AULD LANG SYNE.

By ROBERT BURNS.

SHOULD auld acquaintance be forgot,
  And never brought to min'?
Should auld acquaintance be forgot,
  And days o' lang syne?

CHORUS.

  For auld lang syne, my dear,
    For auld lang syne;
  We 'll tak' a cup o' kindness yet,
    For auld lang syne.

We twa hae ran about the braes,
  And pu'd the gowans * fine;
But we 've wandered mony a weary foot,
  Sin' auld lang syne.

We twa hae paidl't i' the burn,†
  Frae morning sun till dine;

* Wild daisies.　　　　　　　† Brook.

But seas between us braid hae roared
  Sin' auld lang syne.

CHORUS.

For auld lang syne, my dear,
  For auld lang syne ;
We 'll tak' a cup o' kindness yet,
  For auld lang syne.

OLD FOLKS AT HOME.

THEY love the places where they wandered
    When they were young ;
They love the books they 've often pondered,
  They love the tunes they 've sung.

The easy-chair, so soft and dozy,
    Is their delight ;
The ample slippers, warm and cozy,
  And the dear old bed at night.

CHORUS.

Near their hearth-stones, warm and cheery,
    Where, by night or day,
They 're free to rest when they are weary,
  There the old folks love to stay.

L. M. C.

OLD UNCLE TOMMY.

FROM THE CHRISTIAN REGISTER.

" Let him, where and when he will, sit down
Beneath the trees, or by the grassy bank
Of highway-side, and with the little birds'
Share his chance-gathered meal ; and finally,
As in the eye of Nature he has lived,
So in the eye of Nature let him die."

WORDSWORTH.

THE morning after the storm was calm and beautiful ; just one of those days so dear to every lover of Nature ; for every true worshipper of our all-bountiful Mother is a poet at heart, though his lips may often fail to utter the rich experience of his soul. The air was full of fragrance and the songs of birds. Here and there a gentle breeze would shower down the drops of moisture from the trees, forming a mimic rain ; every bush and shrub, and each separate blade of grass, glittered in the morning sunlight, as if hung with brightest jewels. The stillness was in harmony with the day of rest, and only the most peaceful thoughts were suggested by this glorious calm, returning after the tempest.

The late proprietor of the Leigh Manor had presented a small, though very perfect, chime of bells to Leighton Church; they had never been successfully played until now, when the ringers, having become more skilful, they for the first time pealed a regular chant; and right merrily did the sound go forth over the quiet plain.

> To God the mighty Lord,
>   Your joyful songs repeat;
> To Him your praise accord,
>   As good as Ho is great.

" Ah," said an old man, leaning on his staff, and gazing at the bells, " how I wish the Masther could a' heard ye! Well, p'r'aps he *does* hear the bonny bells a-praising God. God bless thee, dear Masther, and have thee forever in his holy keeping!" and raising his hat reverently from his head, the old man stood with the white hair streaming back upon his shoulders, leaving unshaded his upturned countenance, where were visible the traces of many a conflict and of many a hard-earned victory; the *traces* only, for time and living faith had smoothed the deeper marks. As in Nature this morning you saw there *had been* storm and fierce strife; but now all was at peace. The clear blue eye of the aged man shone with a brighter light than youth alone can give. It was the undying

light of immortality; for, old and poor and ignorant as he was, to worldly eyes, his soul had attained a noble stature; and as he stood there with
uncovered head, in the June sunshine, there was a
majesty about him which no mere earthly rank
can impart. You saw before you a child of the
Great Father; you *felt* that he communed in spirit
with his God, as with a dear and loving parent;
that the Most High was very nigh unto him. And
yet this man dwelt amongst the paupers of a country almshouse, and men called him insane! But,
he was " harmless," they said; so he was allowed
to come and go about the neighborhood, as he
pleased, and no one feared him.

The little children, as they passed to Sunday
School this morning, stepped more lightly, lest
they should disturb him; for he was a favorite
with the " little people," as he called them.

When beyond his hearing, they whispered to
one another, " I don't believe Uncle Tommy is
crazy, do you? I never want to plague him; he's
so kind."

" He is n't a mite like laughing Davy," said
another; " for Davy is real mischievous sometimes, and Uncle Tommy is n't a bit; what do
you s'pose folks call him crazy for?"

" I 'm sure I don't know," whispered a third,
" for he knows *ever so much*. I guess it 's 'cause
he *seems* as he does now; and nobody else ever
does, do they? That 's what folks laugh at."

"Well, it's too bad," exclaimed a rosy little girl of nine or ten summers. "I mean to go speak to him. That'll wake him up. He's always so good to us, I *hate* to have folks look queer at him, and make fun of his ways."

"Why, Nelly, he don't care for the laughing."

"No matter; I do," stoutly maintained the child; and going up to the old man, she softly pulled his clean, patched sleeve, and said, "Uncle Tommy, if you please, do look here!"

He did not seem to hear her for a little while; then passing his hand across his forehead, as if rousing himself, he turned, with a pleasant, cheering manner, to the children, who had gathered around him: "Ah! little Nelly, is it you? and all my little people? why you're out early this good morning. May the blessing of Our Father shine through your young hearts, making beautiful your lives, as the sunshine makes beautiful your fresh young faces!"

"Uncle Tommy," said John Anton, "what makes you love the sun so like everything?"

Old Tommy smiled at the boy's eagerness; but looking upward, he answered: "I love it as the first, brightest gift of Our Father. I see in it the purest emblem of Him whose dwelling *is* the light." After a moment's silence, he extended his hands over the children's heads, saying fervently, "Pour thy light into their souls, O Father, that, the eyes of the mind being opened, they may see Thee in

all thy works ! " Then taking Nelly by the
hand, he asked, if they were not too soon for
school.

" Yes," answered she ; " for we came to hear
the bells chime. It's so pleasant, Uncle Tommy,
perhaps you will tell us something. Just a little
while, till the teachers come."

" O yes, do now, Uncle Tommy, tell us some
of the nice stories you know," chimed in the
whole group.

" I 'll be still as a mouse, if you will," coaxed
a lively child, whose ceaseless motion usually disturbed all quiet talk.

Uncle Tommy patted her curly head, and good-
naturedly consented to gratify them, " if they
would try and be good as the flowers in the
meadow yonder."

" Yes, yes, we will," shouted they.

" Now lean on me, and I 'll help you, Uncle
Tommy," said Nelly, who usually assumed the
charge of him when she found an opportunity.
So, with one hand resting upon her shoulder, and
the other supported by his staff, the old man, who
looked older now, as his hat shaded his face, moved
feebly forward, surrounded by the happy children.
They walked a few steps beyond the corner of the
church, and soon came to a projection in one of
the buttresses, that was often used by the people
as a seat in summer ; hither they carefully led
Uncle Tommy, who could still enjoy his beloved

sunshine, whilst he rested his weary limbs. It was a sight worthy of an artist's pencil; the ancient stone church, the venerable man, the young children, the lofty trees, the birds, the shadows, the sunlight, and the graves.

"Sha'n't I take off your hat," asked John, "so you can feel warm?" and away went the hat, to the mutual satisfaction of Uncle Tommy and the children; for they loved him, and liked to see his white hair in the bright sunbeams, — "looking exactly like the 'Mary's threads' on the dewy grass, so silvery and shiny," Nelly used to say.

"What are you going to tell us?" urged the impatient little Janette, softly.

He looked all around before speaking; up at the distant blue sky flooded with light; abroad upon the fields clothed in richest verdure; at the gently rustling elms; the oaks, the yews, and hemlocks in the quiet churchyard; the eager living group at his feet; all were seen in that one comprehensive glance. "It is my birthday, little people," said he, at length, smilingly nodding to them.

"Why Uncle Tommy," cried the astonished children, in their simplicity, "do you have birthdays, like us? We thought you was too old!"

"Yes, yes," said he, shaking his head, "I'm very old, but I remember my birthdays still. It's ninety years, this blessed day, since I came here a wee bit of a baby; and what a blessed Father has led me the long weary way!"

" Shall you like to die, Uncle Tommy? **Do** you want to die ? " asked Nelly.

" I *want*, dear child, to live just as long as our Father pleases. I don't feel impatient to go nor to stay ; 'cause that a'n't right, Nelly. I want to do exactly as God wills ; but I sha'n't feel sorry to go when the time comes ; all I *wish* about it is, that the sun may shine like *now* when I go home, and that I may *know* it."

Another little boy here joined the group. He was the youngest son of the Rector. He had only returned home the previous day to pass the summer vacation, after a six months' absence. There was a little shyness at first between the children, which soon disappeared before the kindly influence of the old man, in whose eyes all human beings were recognized as the children of God. With him there were no rich and no poor.

" Welcome home again, little Herman ! " was his greeting, accompanied by a smile so genial, it went straight to the boy's heart.

" Thank you, Uncle Tommy," said he, shaking hands, cordially. " I am right glad to be here, I can assure you ; and very glad to see you in your old corner, looking so well. But what were you saying about ' going home,' when I interrupted you by coming up? Pray go on."

Before he could answer, Janette said, " It 's Uncle Tommy's birthday, this is ! "

" Indeed ! and how old is he ? " asked Herman, looking at the old man for a reply.

" Ninety years, thank God," was the cheerful answer.

" O what a long, long time to live! " slowly fell from Herman's lips. He was a delicate boy, and thoughtful beyond his years, as is often the case with invalid children ; and now he rested his pale, intelligent face upon his hand, with his eyes fixed on Uncle Tommy, and thought what a long, long time was ninety years! Then he looked upon the graves, and wondered whether any of those whose bodies were lying there knew what an old, old man was still seeing the sun shine so long after they were gone. There were little graves and large ones; Uncle Tommy knew almost all of them, and still he lived on *all alone;* and *they* had some of them left families. He wondered on and on; his reverie was short, but crowded with perplexing thoughts.

Uncle Tommy put an end to it, by saying, in answer to Herman's words, " The time is *only* long, when I don't mind our Father's will. When I obey, as the sun, and the wind, and all about us in Nature does, then I 'm as happy as a cretur can be ; and time seems just right. But what I was a saying about going home was this ; I a'n't in a hurry to go, 'cause I'm here so long ; nor am I wanting to stay ; only just as God pleases. But when the time *does* come, I 'll be glad to go home, after my school time here is over. P'r'aps just as you feel now, Herman ; and I hope when Uncle

Tommy has gone, with the sunshine, out there,
you little people will learn to love the fair works
of God our Father, just as *he* does now. And
don't forget when you're a going to be unkind or
naughty, that you little ones, and *all* the little
children, and *all* the grown people, are the fairest,
noblest of God's works. And if you think of
Uncle Tommy, when you see the sun shine, and
the pretty flowers and birds, and remember how
he loved them, think of him when you are a going
to strike one another, or do any naughty thing,
and remember how often he has told you about
the dear Jesus, who took little children in his arms
and blessed them, and told all the people, great and
small, to love God best, and then to love one
another as they loved themselves. Now if you
try to think of this, I don't believe you'll be
naughty very often; and the fewer times you're
naughty, the happier you'll be when you look
round on this dear beautiful world."

"But, Uncle Tommy," said Nelly, "we forget
about being good sometimes, when we get cross,
and everybody scolds at us 'cause we are so
naughty; and that makes us act worse, ever so
much; don't it, Ann?" appealing to a girl about
her own age.

"Yes," rejoined Ann, "nobody ever says anything about being good, in the way you do,
Uncle Tommy; except in Sunday School, and
in Church; and somehow it don't seem just the

same as when *you* talk. Oh, Uncle Tommy, I believe we should always be good children, if you could only be along with us all the time."

" So do I!" "And I!" was heard from the little circle.

" Dear me!" cried Nelly, impatiently, "how I do wish we had a great big world, all our own, with nobody ugly to plague us; only just for Uncle Tommy and us to live in. *Then* we'd be good as could be. Don't you wish so, dear Uncle Tommy?"

" No, dear children, I wish for no better, or bigger world to live in, than this. Our Father put us here, and put it in our own power to be happy ; that means, to be good ; and if we don't make out to do what He wants us to do here, I don't believe we should find it half as easy in a world such as folks dream about. It's a wrong notion, to my thinking, to s'pose we could behave better in some other place than in the one where our lot's cast in life, or at some other time than the present time going over our heads. Remember this, dear little people, when you grow up, and don't wish for anything it is n't God's will you should have. Try all you can to mind the Lord, who loves you so well ; and if trouble and sorrow come to you, as they do to every human cretur, and you can be sure it's not your own doing, then patiently trust in our Father, and remember what the dear bells say : —

‘For God doth prove
    Our constant friend ;
His boundless love
    Will never end.’

You ’re little and young, and full of health now,
so you don’t know what I mean, as you will
by and by, when you grow older; but you can
remember, if you can’t quite take it in, that I tell
you, after trying it for a good many years, I *know*
our happiness depends a deal more on ourselves
than on other people ; and it ’s only when we ’re
lazy, and don’t want to stir ourselves, that we
think other people have an easier time than we
do. B’lieve me, dear children, everybody has
the means of being happy or unhappy in their
hearts ; and these they must take wherever they
go ; and these make their home and their world.”

The bell for school began to ring, and the children sprang to their feet instantly, saying, “ Good
by, Uncle Tommy ! It ’s school-time now ! ”
“ Good by, little ones,” said he. “ You·go to one
school, and I ’ll go to another, among the *dumb*
children of our Lord ! ”

Nelly and Ann lingered after the others a
moment. “ Uncle Tommy,” said Ann, “ we *will*
try to do as you want us to, and remember what
you say.”

He laid his hands upon their heads, and, looking
up to Heaven, said, “ May the Spirit of the dear
Lord be with ye, and guide your tender feet in

the narrow way of life! Bless them, Father, with thy loving presence through their unending life!"

There was a moment's pause; then Ann said earnestly, "I love dearly to have you bless me, Uncle Tommy"; and with a "Good by," off she ran to school.

Nelly stopped a moment. She had nestled close to the old man's side without speaking, and now, throwing her arms around his neck with a real overflowing of her young heart, she kissed his cheek, and then darted off to join her companions in school. Uncle Tommy was surprised, for Nelly did not often express her affection by caresses, as most children do, but by kind deeds.

The action, slight though it was, touched a long silent chord in the old man's memory. The curtain veiling the past seemed withdrawn, and again he was a child. There was the path from the village across the church-yard, just as it was when first his mother had led him to church, a tiny thing clinging to her skirts. He was the youngest of seven, and the pet; O so long ago! He saw again before him his young brothers and sisters, full of healthful glee; then other forms of long-parted ones joined the procession of years; his sisters' and brothers' children; his own cherished wife and much-loved boys and girls: all gone, long, long years ago; and he alone, of all that numerous company, remained. "Thou, Father, hast ever been on my right hand and on

my left; very safely hast thou led me on through
joy and sorrow unto this shining day; blessed be
thy holy name!"

So prayed the old man his last earthly thanks-
giving. When the people were dispersing to
their homes after service, one, seeing him sitting
there in the sheltered nook, came to say "Good
morning"; and receiving no answer, he touched
his hand. It was cold. There he sat in the
glorious sunshine, his old brown hat by his side,
wreathed with fresh grass and flowers, as was
his custom; but the freed spirit had gone to the
Father he so lovingly worshipped.

They made his grave in the sunniest part of
the church-yard, where an opening in the trees
afforded a lovely view of the village and the
meadows, with the gentle flowing river, along
whose peaceful banks the old man had loved to
wander, gathering flowers and leaves and grasses,
and throwing crumbs to the birds, who knew him
too well to fly from him. Here they laid him,
at the last, and, instead of monument or head-
stone, the children brought sweet flowering shrubs,
and wild brier from the lanes or fields, to plant
around his quiet grave.

"Uncle Tommy is not *there*," said the children. "He has gone home. This is only his
poor *body*, here in the ground!" Thus did the
influence of his bright, ever-young spirit remain
with the "little people" long after Uncle Tommy
had ceased to talk with them.

SITTING IN THE SUN.

WHEN Hope deceives, and friends betray,
    And kinsmen shun me with a flout;
When hair grows.white, and eyes grow dim,
    And life's slow sand is nigh run out,
I'll ask no boon of any one,
But sing old songs, and sit i' the sun.

When memory is my only joy,
    And all my thoughts shall backward turn;
When eyes shall cease to glow with love,
    And heart with generous fire to burn,
I'll ask no boon of any one,
But sing old songs, and sit i' the sun.

When sounds grow low to deafening ears,
    And suns shine not as once they did;
When parting is no more a grief,
    And I do whatsoe'er they bid,
I'll ask no boon of any one,
But sing old songs, and sit i' the sun.

Then underneath a spreading elm,
  That guards some little cottage door,
I 'll dance a grandchild on my knee,
  And count my past days o'er and o'er;
I 'll ask no boon of any one,
But sing old songs and sit i' the sun.

                               ANONYMOUS.

――――――――

How far from here to heaven?
  Not very far, my friend;
A single hearty step
  Will all thy journey end.

Hold there! where runnest thou?
  Know heaven is *in* thee!
Seek'st thou for God elsewhere?
  His face thou 'lt never see.

Go out, God will go in;
  Die thou, and let Him live;
Be not, and He will be;
  Wait, and He 'll all things give.

I don't believe in death.
  If hour by hour I die,
'T is hour by hour to gain
  A better life thereby.

         ANGELUS SILESIUS, A. D. 1620.

AUNT·KINDLY.

By THEODORE PARKER.

ISS KINDLY is aunt to everybody,
and has been, ·for so long a time,
that none remember to the contrary.
The little children love her ; and she
helped their grandmothers to bridal ornaments
threescore years ago. Nay, this boy's grandfather
found that the way to college lay through her
pocket. Generations not her own rise up and call
her blessed. To this man's father her patient toil
gave the first start in life. When that great fortune was a seed, it was she who carried it in her
hand. That wide river of reputation ran out of
the cup which her bounty filled. Now she is old,
very old. The little children, who cling about
her, with open mouth and great round eyes, wonder that anybody should ever be so old ; or ask
themselves whether Aunt Kindly ever had a
mother to kiss her mouth. To·them she is coeval
with the sun, and, like that, an institution of the

country. At Christmas, they think she is the wife of St. Nicholas himself, such an advent is there of blessings from her hand.

Her hands are thin, her voice is feeble, her back is bent, and she walks with a staff, which is the best limb of the three. She wears a cap of antique pattern, yet of her own nice make. She has great round spectacles, and holds her book away off the other side of the candle when she reads. For more than sixty years she has been a special providence to the family. How she used to go forth, the very charity of God, to heal and soothe and bless! How industrious are her hands! How thoughtful and witty that fertile mind! Her heart has gathered power to love in all the eighty-six years of her toilsome life. When the birth-angel came to a related house, she was there to be the mother's mother; ay, mother also to the new-born baby's soul. And when the wings of death flapped in the street and shook a neighbor's door, she smoothed the pillow for the fainting head; she soothed and cheered the spirit of the waiting man, opening the curtains of heaven, that he might look through and see the welcoming face of the dear Infinite Mother; nay, she put the wings of her own strong, experienced piety under him, and sought to bear him up.

Now, these things are passed by. No, they are not passed by; for they are in the memory of the dear God, and every good deed she has done is treasured in her own heart. The bulb shuts up the summer in its breast, which in winter will come out a fragrant hyacinth. Stratum after stratum, her good works are laid up, imperishable, in the geology of her character.

It is near noon, now; and she is alone. She has been thoughtful all day, talking inwardly to herself. The family notice it, but say nothing. In her chamber, she takes a little casket from her private drawer; and from thence a book, gilt-edged and clasped; but the clasp is worn, the gilding is old, the binding faded by long use. Her hands tremble as she opens it. First she reads her own name, on the fly-leaf; only her Christian name, "Agnes," and the date. Sixty-eight years ago, this day, that name was written there, in a clear, youthful, clerkly hand, with a little tremble in it, as if the heart beat over quick. It is very well worn, that dear old Bible. It opens of its own accord, at the fourteenth chapter of St. John. There is a little folded paper there; it touches the first verse and the twenty-seventh. She *sees* neither; she reads both out of her *soul*. "Let not your heart be troubled; ye believe in God, believe also in me." "Peace I leave with you. My peace I give unto you. Not as the world giveth, give I unto you." She opens the paper. There is a little brown dust in it, the remnant of a flower. She takes the precious relic in her hand, made cold by emotion. She drops a tear on it, and the dust is transfigured before her eyes: it is a red rose of the spring, not quite half blown, dewy fresh. She is old no longer. She is not Aunt Kindly now; she is sweet Agnes, as the maiden of eighteen was, eight and sixty years ago, one day in May, when all nature was woosome and winning, and every flower-bell rung in the marriage of the year. Her lover had just put that red rose of the spring into her hand, and the good God put another on her cheek, not quite half-blown, dewy fresh. The young man's arm is around her; her brown curls fall on his shoulder; she feels his breath on her face, his cheek on hers; their lips join, and like two morning dew-drops in that rose, their two loves rush into one.

But the youth must wander away to a far land. She bids him take her Bible. They will think of each other as they look at the North Star. He saw the North Star hang over the turrets of many a foreign town. His soul went to God; — there is as straight a road thither from India as from any other spot. His Bible came back to her; the Divine love in it, without the human lover; the leaf turned down at the blessed words of St. John, first and twenty-seventh verse of the fourteenth chapter. She put the rose there to mark the spot; what marks the thought holds now the symbol of their youthful love. To-day, her soul is with him; her maiden soul with his angel-soul; and one day the two, like two dew-drops, will rush into one immortal wedlock, and the old age of earth shall become eternal youth in the kingdom of heaven.

CROSSING OVER.

FROM THE GERMAN OF UHLAND.

MANY a year is in its grave,
    Since I crossed this restless wave;
And the evening, fair as ever,
Shines on ruin, rock, and river.

Then, in this same boat, beside,
Sat two comrades old and tried;
One with all a father's truth,
One with all the fire of youth.

One on earth in silence wrought,
And his grave in silence sought;
But the younger, brighter form
Passed in battle and in storm.

So, whenc'er I turn my eye
Back upon the days gone by,
Saddening thoughts of friends come o'er me;
Friends who closed their course before me.

Yet, what binds us, friend to friend,
But that soul with soul can blend?
Soul-like were those hours of yore —
Let us walk in soul once more!

Take, O boatman, thrice thy fee!
Take! I give it willingly;
For, invisibly to thee,
Spirits twain have crossed with me.

———

THEY are all gone into a world of light,
    And I alone sit lingering here!
Their very memory is fair and bright,
    And my sad thoughts doth clear.

DEAR, beauteous Death! the jewel of the just!
    Shining nowhere but in the dark!
What mysteries do lie beyond thy dust,
    Could man outlook that mark!

HE that hath found some fledged bird's nest may know,
    At first sight, if the bird be flown;
But what fair field or grove he sings in *now*,
    That is to him unknown.

And yet, as angels, in some brighter dreams,
    Call to the soul when man doth sleep,
So some strange thoughts transcend our wonted themes,
    And into glory peep.
                              HENRY VAUGHAN.

A LOVE AFFAIR AT CRANFORD.

By MRS. GASKELL.

 THOUGHT, after Miss Jenkyns's death, that probably my connection with Cranford would cease. I was pleasantly surprised, therefore, by receiving a letter from Miss Pole proposing that I should go and stay with her. In a couple of days after my acceptance came a note from Miss Matey Jenkyns, in which, in a rather circuitous and very humble manner, she told me how much pleasure I should confer if I could spend a week or two with her, either before or after I had been at Miss Pole's ; " for," she said, " since my dear sister's death, I am well aware I have no attractions to offer : it is only to the kindness of my friends that I can owe their company."

Of course I promised to go to dear Miss Matey as soon as I had ended my visit to Miss Pole. The day after my arrival at Cranford, I went to see her, much wondering what the house would be like without Miss Jenkyns, and rather dreading the changed aspect of things. Miss Matey began to cry as soon as she saw me. She was evidently nervous from having anticipated my call. I comforted her as well as I could ; and I found the best consolation I could give was the honest praise that came from my heart as I spoke of the deceased. Miss Matey slowly shook her head over each virtue, as it was named and attributed to her sister ; at last she could not restrain the tears which had long been silently flowing, but hid her face behind her handkerchief, and sobbed aloud.

" Dear Miss Matey ! " said I, taking her hand ; for indeed I did not know in what way to tell her how sorry I was for her, left deserted in the world.

She put down her handkerchief and said : " My dear, I 'd rather you did not call me Matey. *She* did not like it. But I did many a thing she did not like, I 'm afraid ; and now she 's gone ! If you please, my love, will you call me Matilda ? "

I promised faithfully, and began to practise the new name with Miss Pole that very day ; and, by degrees, Miss Matilda's feeling on the subject was known through Cranford, and the appellation of Matey was dropped by all, except a very old woman, who had been nurse in the rector's family, and had persevered, through many long years, in calling the Miss Jenkynses " the girls " : *she* said " Matey " to the day of her death.

. . . . .

It seems that Miss Pole had a cousin, once or twice removed, who had offered to Miss Matey long ago. Now, this cousin lived four or five miles from Cranford, on his own estate; but his property was not large enough to entitle him to rank higher than a yeoman; or, rather, with something of the " pride which apes humility," he had refused to push himself on, as so many of his class had done, into the rank of the squires. He would not allow himself to be called Thomas Holbrook, Esq. He even sent back letters with this address, telling the postmistress at Cranford that his name was Mr. Thomas Holbrook, yeoman. He rejected all domestic innovations. He would have the house door stand open in summer, and shut in winter, without knocker or bell to summon a servant. The closed fist, or the knob of the stick, did this office for him, if he found the door locked. He despised every refinement which had not its root deep down in humanity. If people were not ill, he saw no necessity for moderating his voice. He spoke the dialect of the country in perfection, and constantly used it in conversation; although Miss Pole (who gave me these particulars) added, that he read aloud more beautifully, and with more feeling, than any one she had ever heard, except the late rector.

" And how came Miss Matilda not to marry him ? " asked I.

" Oh, I don't know. She was willing enough,
I think ; but you know Cousin Thomas would not
have been enough of a gentleman for the rector
and Mrs. and Miss Jenkyns." ·

" Well, but *they* were not to marry him," said
I, impatiently.

" No, but they did not like Miss Matey to marry
below her rank. You know she was the rector's
daughter, and somehow they are related to Sir
Peter Arley ; Miss Jenkyns thought a deal of
that."

" Poor Miss Matey ! " said I.

" Nay, now, I don't know anything more than
that he offered and was refused. Miss Matey
might not like him ; and Miss Jenkyns might
never have said a word: it is only a guess of
mine."

" Has she never seen him since ? " I inquired.

" No, I think not. You see Woodley (Cousin
Thomas's house) lies half-way between Cranford
and Misselton ; and I know he made Misselton his
market-town very soon after he had offered to Miss
Matey ; and I don't think he has been into Cranford above once or twice since. Once, when I
was walking with Miss Matey in High Street, she
suddenly darted from me and went up Shire Lane.
A few minutes after, I was startled by meeting
Cousin Thomas."

" How old is he ? " I asked, after a pause of
castle-building.

" He must be about seventy, I think, my dear," said Miss Pole, blowing up my castle, as if by gun-powder, into small fragments.

Very soon after, I had the opportunity of seeing Mr. Holbrook; seeing, too, his first encounter with his former love, after thirty or forty years' separation. I was helping to decide whether any of the new assortment of colored silks, which they had just received at the shop, would help to match a gray and black mousseline-de-laine that wanted a new breadth, when a tall, thin, Don Quixote-looking old man came into the shop for some woollen gloves. I had never seen the person be-fore, and I watched him rather attentively, while Miss Matey listened to the shopman. The stran-ger was rather striking. He wore a blue coat, with brass buttons, drab breeches, and gaiters, and drummed with his fingers on the counter, until he was attended to. When he answered the shop-boy's question, " What can I have the pleasure of showing you to-day, sir ? " I saw Miss Matilda start, and then suddenly sit down ; and instantly I guessed who it was. She had made some in-quiry which had to be carried round to the other shop.

" Miss Jenkyns wants the black sarcenet, two-and-twopence the yard." Mr. Holbrook caught the name, and was across the shop in two strides.

" Matey, — Miss Matilda, — Miss Jenkyns ! Bless my soul ! I should not have known you.

How are you? how are you?" He kept shaking her hand, in a way which proved the warmth of his friendship; but he repeated so often, as if to himself, "I should not have known you!" that any sentimental romance I might be inclined to build was quite done away with by his manner.

However, he kept talking to us all the time we were in the shop; and then waving the shopman, with the unpurchased gloves, on one side, with "Another time, sir! another time!" he walked home with us. I am happy to say Miss Matilda also left the shop in an equally bewildered state; not having purchased either green or red silk. Mr. Holbrook was evidently full with honest, loud-spoken joy at meeting his old love again. He touched on the changes that had taken place; he even spoke of Miss Jenkyns as "Your poor sister! Well, well! we have all our faults"; and bade us good by with many a hope that he should soon see Miss Matey again. She went straight to her room, and never came back till our early tea-time, when I thought she looked as if she had been crying.

A few days after, a note came from Mr. Holbrook, asking us, — impartially asking both of us, — in a formal, old-fashioned style, to spend a day at his house, — a long, June day, — for it was June now. He named that he had also invited his cousin, Miss Pole; so that we might join in a fly, which could be put up at his house.

I expected Miss Matey to jump at this invitation; but, no! Miss Pole and I had the greatest difficulty in persuading her to go. She thought it was improper; and was even half annoyed when we utterly ignored the idea of any impropriety in her going with two other ladies to see her old lover. Then came a more serious difficulty. She did not think Deborah would have liked her to go. This took us half a day's good hard talking to get over; but, at the first sentence of relenting, I seized the opportunity, and wrote and despatched an acceptance in her name, — fixing day and hour, that all might be decided and done with.

The next morning she asked me if I would go down to the shop with her; and there, after much hesitation, we chose out three caps to be sent home and tried on, that the most becoming might be selected to take with us on Thursday.

She was in a state of silent agitation all the way to Woodley. She had evidently never been there before, and although she little dreamt I knew anything of her early story, I could perceive she was in a tremor at the thought of seeing the place which might have been her home, and round which it is probable that many of her innocent, girlish imaginations had clustered. It was a long drive there, through paved, jolting lanes. Miss Matilda sat bolt upright, and looked wistfully out of the windows, as we drew near the end of our journey. The aspect of the country was quiet

and pastoral. Woodley stood among fields, and
there was an old-fashioned garden, where roses
and currant-bushes touched each other, and where
the feathery asparagus formed a pretty back-
ground to the pinks and gilly-flowers. There
was no drive up to the door. We got out at a
little gate, and walked up a straight, box-edged
path.

"My cousin might make a drive, I think," said
Miss Pole, who was afraid of ear-ache, and had
only her cap on.

"I think it is very pretty," said Miss Matey,
with a soft plaintiveness in her voice, and almost
in a whisper, for just then Mr. Holbrook appeared at the door, rubbing his hands in the very
effervescence of hospitality. He looked more like
my idea of Don Quixote than ever, and yet the
likeness was only external. His respectable housekeeper stood modestly at the door to bid us welcome ; and, while she led the elder ladies up-stairs
to a bed-room, I begged to look about the garden.
My request evidently pleased the old gentleman,
who took me all round the place, and showed me
his six-and-twenty cows, named after the different
letters of the alphabet. As we went along, he
surprised me occasionally by repeating apt and
beautiful quotations from the poets, ranging easily
from Shakespeare and George Herbert, to those
of our own day. He did this as naturally as if
he were thinking aloud; as if their true and beau-

tiful words were the best expression he could find for what he was thinking or feeling. To be sure he called Byron " my lord Byrron," and pronounced the name of Goethe strictly in accordance with the English sound of the letters. Altogether, I never met with a man, before or since, who had spent so long a life in a secluded and not impressive country, with ever-increasing delight in the daily and yearly change of season and beauty.

When he and I went in, we found that dinner was nearly ready in the kitchen; for so I suppose the room ought to be called, as there were oak dressers and cupboards all round, all over by the side of the fireplace, and only a small Turkey carpet in the middle of the flag-floor. The room might have been easily made into a handsome, dark-oak dining-parlor, by removing the oven, and a few other appurtenances of a kitchen, which were evidently never used; the real cooking-place being at some distance. The room in which we were expected to sit was a stiffly furnished, ugly apartment; but that in which we did sit was what Mr. Holbrook called the counting-house, where he paid his laborers their weekly wages, at a great desk near the door. The rest of the pretty sitting-room — looking into the orchard, and all covered over with dancing tree-shadows — was filled with books. They lay on the ground, they covered the walls, they strewed the table. He

17 *

was evidently half ashamed and half proud of his
extravagance in this respect.   They were of all
kinds ; poetry, and wild, weird tales prevailing.
He evidently chose his books in accordance with
his own tastes, not because such and such were
classical, or established favorites.

"Ah!" he said, "we farmers ought not to
have much time for reading; yet somehow one
can't help it."

"What a pretty room!" said Miss Matey, *sotto
voce.*

"What a pleasant place!" said I, aloud, almost simultaneously.

"Nay! if you like it," replied he; "but can
you sit on these great black leather three-cornered
chairs?   I like it better than the best parlor; but
I thought ladies would take that for the smarter
place."

It was the smarter place; but, like most smart
things, not at all pretty, or pleasant, or home-
like; so, while we were at dinner, the servant-girl
dusted and scrubbed the counting-house chairs,
and we sat there all the rest of the day.

We had pudding before meat, and I thought
Mr. Holbrook was going to make some apology
for his old-fashioned ways; for he began, "I
don't know whether you like new-fangled ways."

"O, not at all!" said Miss Matey.

"No more do I," said he.   "My housekeeper
will have things in her new fashion; or else 'I

tell her, that when I was a young man, we used
to keep strictly to my father's rule, 'No broth,
no ball; no ball, no beef'; and always began
dinner with broth. Then we had suet puddings,
boiled in the broth with the beef; and then the
meat itself. If we did not sup our broth, we
had no ball, which we liked a deal better; and
the beef came last of all; and only those had it
who had done justice to the broth and the ball.
Now, folks begin with sweet things, and turn their
dinners topsy-turvy."

When the ducks and green peas came, we
looked at each other in dismay. We had only
two-pronged, black-handled forks. It is true, the
steel was as bright as silver; but, what were we
to do? Miss Matey picked up her peas, one by
one, on the point of the prongs. Miss Pole sighed
over her delicate young peas, as she left them on
one side of her plate untasted; for they *would*
drop between her prongs. I looked at my host:
the peas were going wholesale into his capacious
mouth, shovelled up by his large round-ended
knife. I saw, I imitated, I survived! My friends,
in spite of my precedent, could not muster up
courage enough to do an ungenteel thing; and,
if Mr. Holbrook had not been so heartily hungry,
he would probably have seen that the good peas
went away almost untouched.

After dinner, a clay pipe was brought in, and
a spittoon; and, asking us to retire to another

room, where he would soon join us, if we disliked
tobacco-smoke, he presented his pipe to Miss
Matey, and requested her to fill the bowl. This
was a compliment to a lady in his youth; but it
was rather inappropriate to propose it as an honor
to Miss Matey, who had been trained by her sister
to hold smoking of every kind in utter abhor-
rence. But if it was a shock to her refinement,
it was also a gratification to her feelings, to be
thus selected; so she daintly stuffed the strong
tobacco into the pipe; and then we withdrew.

"It is very pleasant dining with a bachelor,"
said Miss Matey, softly, as we settled ourselves
in the counting-house; "I only hope it is not
improper; so many pleasant things are!"

"What a number of books he has!" said Miss
Pole, looking round the room. "And how dusty
they are!"

"I think it must be like one of the great Dr.
Johnson's rooms," said Miss Matey. "What a
superior man your cousin must be!"

"Yes!" said Miss Pole; "he's a great reader;
but I am afraid he has got into very uncouth
habits with living alone."

"Oh! uncouth is too hard a word. I should
call him eccentric: very clever people always
are!" replied Miss Matey.

When Mr. Holbrook returned, he proposed a
walk in the fields; but the two elder ladies were
afraid of damp and dirt, and had only very

unbecoming calashes to put on over their caps ;
so they declined, and I was again his companion
in a turn which he said he was obliged to take,
to see after his niece. He strode along, either
wholly forgetting my existence, or soothed into
silence by his pipe ; and yet it was not silence
exactly. He walked before me, with a stooping
gait, his hands clasped behind him, and as some
tree, or cloud, or glimpse at distant upland pastures, struck him, he quoted poetry to himself ;
saying it out loud, in a grand, sonorous voice, with
just the emphasis that true feeling and appreciation give. We came upon an old cedar-tree,
which stood at one end of the house ;

> ‘More black than ash-buds in the front of March,
> A cedar spread his dark-green layers of shade.’

Capital term, ‘ layers ! ’ Wonderful man ! ”

I did not know whether he was speaking to
me or not ; but I put in an assenting “ Wonderful,” although I knew nothing about it ; just because I was tired of being forgotten, and of being
consequently silent.

He turned sharp round. “ Ay ! you may say
‘ wonderful.’ Why, when I saw the review of
his poems in ‘ Blackwood,’ I set off within an
hour, and walked seven miles to Misselton (for
the horses were not in the way), and ordered
them. Now, what color are ash-buds in March ? ”

Is the man going mad ? thought I. He is very
like Don Quixote.

" What color are they, I say ? " repeated he, vehemently.

" I am sure I don't know sir," said I, with the meekness of ignorance.

" I knew you did n't. No more did I, an old fool that I am ! till this young man comes and tells me. Black as ash-buds in March. And I 've lived all my life in the country ; more shame for me not to know. Black ; they are jet-black, madam." And he went off again, swinging along to the music of some rhyme he had got hold of.

When we came home, nothing would serve him but that he must read us the poems he had been speaking of ; and Miss Pole encouraged him in his proposal, I thought, because she wished me to hear his beautiful reading, of which she had boasted ; but she afterwards said it was because she had got to a difficult part of crochet, and wanted to count her stitches without having to talk. Whatever he had proposed would have been right to Miss Matey, although she did fall sound asleep within five minutes after he began a long poem, called " Locksley Hall," and had a comfortable nap, un-observed, till he ended, when the cessation of his voice wakened her up, and she said, feeling that something was expected, and that Miss Pole was counting, " What a pretty book ! "

" Pretty, madam ? It 's beautiful ! Pretty, in-deed ! "

" O yes, I meant beautiful ! " said she, fluttered at his disapproval of her word. " It is so like that beautiful poem of Dr. Johnson's my sister used to read ! — I forget the name of it ; what was it, my dear ? " turning to me.

" Which do you mean, ma'am ? What was it about ? "

" I don't remember what it was about, and I've quite forgotten what the name of it was ; but it was written by Dr. Johnson, and was very beautiful, and very like what Mr. Holbrook has just been reading."

" I don't remember it," said he, reflectively ; " but I don't know Dr. Johnson's poems well. I must read them." ·

As we were getting into the fly to return, I heard Mr. Holbrook say he should call on the ladies soon, and inquire how they got home ; and this evidently pleased and fluttered Miss Matey at the time he said it ; but after we had lost sight of the old house among the trees, her sentiments towards the master of it were gradually absorbed into a distressing wonder as to whether Martha had broken her word, and seized on the opportunity of her mistress's absence to have a " follow- er." Martha looked good and steady and com- posed enough, as she came to help us out ; she was always careful of Miss Matey, and to-night she made use of this unlucky speech : " Eh, dear ma'am, to think of your going out in an

evening in such a thin shawl! It is no better
than muslin. At your age, ma'am, you should be
careful."

" My age!" said Miss Matey, almost speaking
crossly, for her, for she was usually gentle; " my
age! Why, how old do you think I am, that you
talk about my age ? "

" Well, ma'am, I should say you were not far
short of sixty; but folks' looks is often against
them, and I'm sure I meant no harm."

" Martha, I'm not yet fifty-two! " said Miss
Matey, with grave . emphasis; for probably the
remembrance of her youth had come very vividly
before her this day, and she was annoyed at finding that golden time so far away in the past.

But she never spoke of any former and more
intimate acquaintance with Mr. Holbrook. She
had probably met with so little sympathy in her
early love, that she had shut it up close in her
heart; and it was only by a sort of watching, which
I could hardly avoid since Miss Pole's confidence,
that I saw how faithful her poor heart had been in
its sorrows and its silence.

She gave me some good reason for wearing her
best cap every day, and sat near the window, in
spite of her rheumatism, in order to see, without
being seen, down into the street.

He came. He put his open palms upon his
knees, which were far apart, as he sat with his
head bent down, whistling, after we had replied to

his inquiries about our safe return. Suddenly he jumped up.

" Well, madam, have you any commands for Paris ? I 'm going there in a week or two."

" To Paris ! " we both exclaimed.

" Yes, ma'am. I 've never been there, and always had a wish to go ; and I think if I don't go soon I may'n't go at all. So as soon as the hay is got in I shall go, before harvest-time."

We were so much astonished that we had no commissions.

Just as he was going out of the room, he turned back, with his favorite exclamation, " Bless my soul, madam ! but I nearly forgot half my errand. Here are the poems for you, you admired so much the other evening at my house." He tugged away at a parcel in his coat pocket. " Good by, miss ! " said he ; " good by, Matey ! take care of yourself." And he was gone. But he had given her a book, and he had called her Matey, just as he used to do thirty years ago.

" I wish he would not go to Paris," said Miss Matilda, anxiously. " I don't believe frogs will agree with him. He used to have to be very careful what he ate, which was curious in so strong-looking a young man."

Soon after this I took my leave, giving many an injunction to Martha to look after her mistress, and to let me know if she thought that Miss Matilda was not so well ; in which case I would volun-

2

teer a visit to my old friend, without noticing Martha's intelligence to her.

Accordingly, I received a line or two from Martha every now and then; and about November I had a note to say her mistress was " very low and sadly off her food "; and the account made me so uneasy, that, although Martha did not decidedly summon me, I packed up my things and went.

I received a warm welcome, in spite of the little flurry produced by my impromptu visit, for I had only been able to give a day's notice. Miss Matilda looked miserably ill, and I prepared to comfort and cosset her.

I went down to have a private talk with Martha.

" How long has your mistress been so poorly ? " I asked, as I stood by the kitchen fire.

" Well, I think it 's better than a fortnight; it is, I know. It was one Tuesday, after Miss Pole had been here, that she went into this moping way. I thought she was tired, and it would go off with a night's rest; but no! she has gone on and on ever since, till I thought it my duty to write to you, ma'am."

" You did quite right, Martha. It is a comfort to think she has so faithful a servant about her. And I hope you find your place comfortable ? "

" Well, ma'am, missus is very kind, and there 's plenty to eat and drink, and no more work but what I can do easily ; but —" Martha hesitated.

" But what, Martha ? "

" Why, it seems so hard of missus not to let me have any followers. There's such lots of young fellows in the town, and many a one has as much as offered to keep company with me, and I may never be in such a likely place again, and it's like wasting an opportunity. Many a girl as I know would have 'em unbeknowst to missus ; but I 've given my word, and I 'll stick to it ; or else this is just the house for missus never to be the wiser if they did come. It's such a capable kitchen, — there's such good dark corners in it, — I 'd be bound to hide any one. I counted up last Sunday night, — for I 'll not deny I was crying because I had to shut the door in Jem Hearn's face ; and he 's a steady young man, fit for any girl ; only I had given missus my word." Martha was all but crying again ; and I had little comfort to give her, for I knew, from old experience, the horror with which both the Miss Jenkynses looked upon " followers " ; and in Miss Matey's present nervous state this dread was not like to be lessened.

I went to see Miss Pole the next day, and took her completely by surprise, for she had not been to see Miss Matilda for two days.

" And now I must go back with you, my dear," said she ; " for I promised to let her know how Thomas Holbrook went on ; and I 'm sorry to say his housekeeper has sent me word to-day that he has n't long to live. Poor Thomas ! That journey to Paris was quite too much for him. His housekeeper says he has hardly ever been round his fields since, but just sits with his hands on his knees in the counting-house, not reading, or anything, but only saying, what a wonderful city Paris was! Paris has much to answer for, if it's killed my cousin Thomas, for a better man never lived."

" Does Miss Matilda know of his illness?" asked I, a new light as to the cause of her indisposition dawning upon me.

" Dear! to be sure, yes! Has she not told you? I let her know a fortnight ago, or more, when first I heard of it. How odd, she should n't have told you!"

Not at all, I thought; but I did not say anything. I felt almost guilty of having spied too curiously into that tender heart; and I was not going to speak of its secrets, — hidden, Miss Matey believed, from all the world. I ushered Miss Pole into Miss Matilda's drawing-room; and then left them alone. But I was not surprised when Martha came to my bed-room door, to ask me to go down to dinner alone, for that missus had one of her bad headaches. She came into the drawing-room at tea-time; but it was evidently an effort for her. As if to make up for some reproachful feeling against her late sister, Miss Jenkyns, which had been troubling her all the afternoon, and for which she now felt penitent, she kept telling me how good and how clever Deborah was in her youth;

how she used to settle what gowns they were to
wear at all the parties; (faint, ghostly ideas of
dim parties far away in the distance, when Miss
Matey and Miss Pole were young!) and how
Deborah and her mother had started the benefit
society for the poor, and taught girls cooking and
plain sewing; and how Deborah had danced with
a lord; and how she used to visit at Sir Peter
Arley's, and try to remodel the quiet rectory
establishment on the plans of Arley Hall, where
they kept thirty servants; and how she had nursed
Miss Matey through a long, long illness, of which
I had never heard before, but which I now dated,
in my own mind, as following the dismissal of the
suit of Mr. Holbrook. So we talked softly and
quietly of old times, through the long November
evening.

The next day, Miss Pole brought us word that
Mr. Holbrook was dead. Miss Matey heard the
news in silence. In fact, from the account on the
previous day, it was only what we had to expect.
Miss Pole kept calling upon us for some expressions of regret, by asking if it was not sad that he
was gone, and saying, —

" To think of that pleasant day last June, when
he seemed so well! And he might have lived this
dozen years, if he had not gone to that wicked
Paris, where they are always having Revolu-
tions."

She paused for some demonstration on our part.

I saw Miss Matey could not speak, she was trembling so nervously, so I said what I really felt; and after a call of some duration, — all the time of which I have no doubt Miss Pole thought Miss Matey received the news very calmly, — our visitor took her leave.   But the effort at self-control Miss Matey had made to conceal her feelings, — a concealment she practised even with me; for she has never alluded to Mr. Holbrook again, although the book he gave her lies with her Bible on the little table by her bedside.   She did not think I heard her when she asked the little milliner of Cranford to make her caps something like the Hon. Mrs. Jamieson's ; or that I noticed the reply, —

" But she wears widows' caps, ma'am ? "

" O, I only meant something in that style ; not widows', of course, but rather like Mrs. Jamieson's."

This effort at concealment was the beginning of the tremulous motion of head and hands, which I have seen ever since in Miss Matey.

The evening of the day on which we heard of Mr. Holbrook's death, Miss Matilda was very silent and thoughtful ; after prayers, she called Martha back, and then she stood uncertain what to say.

" Martha ! " she said at last ; " you are young," — and then she made so long a pause, that Martha, to remind her of her half-finished sentence, dropped a courtesy, and said : " Yes, please, ma'am ; two-and-twenty last third October, please, ma'am."

" And perhaps, Martha, you may some time meet with a young man you like, and who likes you. I did say you were not to have followers ; but if you meet with such a young man, and tell me, and I find he is respectable, I have no objection to his coming to see you once a week. God forbid ! " said she, in a low voice, " that I should grieve any young hearts."

She spoke as if she were providing for some distant contingency, and was rather startled when Martha made her ready, eager answer : " Please, ma'am, there's Jem Hearn, and he's a joiner, making three-and-sixpence a day, and six foot one in his stocking-feet, please, ma'am ; and if you'll ask about him to-morrow morning, every one will give him a character for steadiness ; and he'll be glad enough to come to-morrow night, I'll be bound."

Though Miss Matey was startled, she submitted to Fate and Love.

⸻

God is our Father. Heaven is his high throne, and this earth is his footstool ; and while we sit around and meditate, or pray, one by one, as we fall asleep, He lifts us into his bosom, and our awaking is inside the gates of an everlasting world. — MOUNTFORD.

TO MY WIFE.

ON THE ANNIVERSARY OF OUR WEDDING.

NOW, Time and I, near fifty years,
    Have managed kindly to agree;
Pleased with the friendship he appears,
    And means that all the world shall see.

For, with soft touch about my eyes,
    The frosty, kindly, jealous friend
His drawing-pencil deftly plies,
    And mars the face he thinks to mend.

Nor am I called *alone* to wear
    Old Time, "His mark," in deepening trace;
That "twain are one," this limner sere
    Will print in lines on either face.

'T is not, perhaps, a gallant thing
    On such a morning to be told,
But Time doth yearly witness bring,
    That — Bless you ! *we* are growing old.

Together we have lived and loved,
   Together passed through smiles and tears,
And life's all-varying lessons proved
   Through many constant married years.

And there is joy Time cannot reach,
   A youth o'er which no power he hath,
If we cling closer, each to each,
   And each to God, in hope and faith.
ANONYMOUS.

———————

In the summer evenings, when the wind blew low,
And the skies were radiant with the sunset glow,
Thou and I were happy, long, long years ago!
Love, the young and hopeful, hovered o'er us twain,
Filled us with sad pleasure and delicious pain,
In the summer evenings, wandering in the lane.

In the winter evenings, when the wild winds roar,
Blustering in the chimney, piping at the door,
Thou and I are happy, as in days of yore.
Love still hovers o'er us, robed in white attire,
Drawing heavenly music from an earthly lyre,
In the winter evenings, sitting by the fire.
ANONYMOUS.

THE EVERGREEN OF OUR FEELINGS.

EXTRACTS FROM THE GERMAN OF J. P. RICHTER.

I OPPOSE, as I would every useless fear in men, the lamentation that our feelings grow old with the lapse of years. It is the narrow heart alone which does not grow; the wide one becomes larger. Years shrivel the one, but they expand the other. Man often mistakes concerning the glowing depths of his feelings; forgetting that they may be present in all their energy, though in a state of repose. In the wear and tear of daily life, amid the care of providing support, perchance under misdemeanors, in comparing one child with another, or in daily absences, thou mayest not be conscious of the fervent affection smouldering under the ashes of every-day life, which would at once blaze forth into a flame, if thy child were suffering innocently, or condemned to die. Thy love was already there, prior to the suffering of thy child and thyself. It is the same in wedlock and friendship. In the familiarity of daily presence, the heart beats and glows silently; but in the hours of meeting and parting, the beautiful radiance of a long-nurtured flame reveals itself. It is on such occasions that man always most pleases me. I am then reminded of the glaciers, which beam forth in rosy-red transparency only at the rising and setting of the sun, while throughout the day they look gray and dark.

A golden mine of affection, of which the smallest glimmer is scarcely visible, lies buried in the breast until some magic word reveals it, and then man discovers his ancient treasure. To me, it is a delightful thought that, during the familiarity of constant proximity, the heart gathers up in silence the nutriment of love, as the diamond, even beneath water, imbibes the light it emits. Time, which deadens hatred, secretly strengthens love; and in the hour of threatened separation its growth is manifested at once in radiant brightness.

Another reason why man fancies himself chilled by old age, is that he can then feel interested only in higher objects than those which once excited him. The lover of nature, the preacher, the poet, the actor, or the musician, may, in declining years, find themselves slightly affected by what delighted them in youth; but this need produce no fear that time will mar their sensi-

bility to nature, art, and love. Thou, as well as
I, may indeed weep less frequently than formerly,
at the theatre or at concerts; but give us a truly
excellent piece, and we cannot suppress the emotion it excites. Youth is like unbleached wax,
which melts under feeble sun-beams, while that
which has been whitened is scarcely warmed by
them. The mature or aged man avoids those
tears which youth invites; because in him they
flow too hot, and dry too slowly.

Select a man of my age, and of my heart, with
my life-long want of highland scenery, and con-
duct him to the valley of the Rhine! Bring him
to that long, attractive, sea-like river, flowing
between vine-clad hills on either side, as between
two regions of enchantment, reflecting only scenes
of pleasure, creating islands for the sake of clasp-
ing them in its arms; let also a reflection of the
setting sun glow upon its waters; and surely
youth would again be mirrored in the old man,
and that still ocean of infinity, which in the true
and highest heaven permits us to look down.

Memory, wit, fancy, acuteness, cannot grow
young again in old age; but the *heart* can. In
order to be convinced of this, we need only
remember how the hearts of poets have glowed in
the autumn and winter seasons of life. He who
in old age can do without love, never in his youth
possessed the right sort, over which years have no
power. During winter, it is the withered branch-

es, not the living germs, that become encrusted with ice. The loving heart will indeed often bashfully conceal a portion of its warmth behind children and grandchildren; so that last love is perhaps as coy as the first. But if an aged eye, full of soul, is upraised, gleaming with memories of its spring-time, is there anything in that to excite ridicule? Even if it were silently moistened, partly through gladness, and partly through a feeling of the past, would it not be excusable? Might not an aged hand presume to press a young hand, merely to signify thereby, I, too, was once in Arcadia, and within me Arcadia still remains? In the better sort of men love is an interior sentiment, born in the soul; why should it not continue with the soul to the end? It is a part of the attraction of tender and elevated love that its consecrated hours leave in the heart a gentle, continuous, distinct influence; just as, sometimes, upon a heavenly spring-evening, fragrance, exhaled from warm blossoms in the surrounding country penetrates every street of a city that has no gardens.

I would exhort men to spare every true affection, and not to ridicule the overflowings of a happy heart with more license than they would the effusions of a sorrowing one. For the youth of the soul is everlasting, and eternity is youth.

OUR SECRET DRAWER.

THERE is a secret drawer in every heart,
   · Wherein we lay our treasures, one by one;
Each dear remembrance of the buried past,
   Each cherished relic of the time that 's gone.

The old delights of childhood, long ago;
   The things we loved because we knew them best;
The first discovered primrose in our path;
   The cuckoo's earliest note; the robin's nest;

The merry haymakings around our home;
   Our rambles in the summer woods and lanes;
The story told beside the winter fire,
   While the wind moaned across the window panes;

The golden dreams we dreamt in after years,
   Those magic visions of our young romance;
The sunny nooks, the fountains and the flowers,
   Gilding the fairy landscape of our trance;

'The link which bound us, later still, to one
    Who fills a corner in our life to-day,
Without whose love we dare not dream how dark
    The rest would seem, if it were gone away;

The song that thrilled our souls with very joy;
    The gentle word that unexpected came;
The gift we prized because the thought was kind;
    The thousand, thousand things that have no name;

All these, in some far hidden corner lie,
    Within the mystery of that secret drawer,
Whose magic springs though stranger hands may touch,
    Yet none may gaze upon its guarded store.

ANONYMOUS.

" How seldom, friend, a great, good man inherits
Honor, or wealth, with all his worth and pains."
" For shame, dear friend, renounce this canting strain.
What wouldst thou that the great, good man obtain?
Place, title, salary, — a gilded chain?
Or throne on corpses which his sword has slain?
Goodness and greatness are not *means*, but *ends*.
Hath he not always treasures, always friends,
The great, good man?   Three treasures, love, and light,
And calm thoughts, regular as infant's breath;
And three true friends, more sure than day and night, —
Himself, his Maker, and the angel Death."

COLERIDGE.

THE GOLDEN WEDDING.

The German custom of observing a festival called the Silver Wedding, on the twenty-fifth anniversary of marriage, and a Golden Wedding on the fiftieth anniversary, have now become familiar to us by their frequent observance in this country. The following description of such an anniversary in Sweden is from the graceful pen of Fredrika Bremer, in her work entitled "The Neighbors."

HERE was a patriarch and wife, and only to see that ancient, venerable couple made the heart rejoice. Tranquillity was upon their brows, cheerful wisdom on their lips, and in their glance one read love and peace. For above half a century this ancient couple have inhabited the same house and the same rooms. There they were married, and there they are soon to celebrate their golden nuptials. The rooms are unchanged, the furniture the same it has been for fifty years; but everything is clean, comfortable, and friendly, as in a one-year-old dwelling, though much more simple than the houses of our time. I know not what spirit of peace and grace it is which breathes upon me in this house! Ah! in this house fifty years have passed as a beautiful day. Here a virtuous couple have lived, loved, and worked together. Many a pure joy has blossomed here; and when sorrow came, it was not bitter, for the fear of God and mutual love illuminated the dark clouds. Hence has emanated many a noble deed, and many a beneficent influence. Happy children grew up. They gathered strength from the example of their parents, went out into the world, built for themselves houses, and were good and fortunate. Often do they return to the parental home, to bless and to be blessed.

A long life of integrity, industry, and beneficence has impressed itself on the father's expansive forehead, and on his frank, benevolent deportment. His figure is yet firm, and his gait steady. The lofty crown is bald, but the venerable head is surrounded by silver-white locks, like a garland. No one in the city sees this head without bowing in friendly and reverential greeting. The whole country, as well as the city, loves him as their benefactor, and venerates him as their patriarch. He has created his own fortune, and sacrificed much for the public good; and notwithstanding much adversity and loss, he has never let his spirit sink. In mind and conversation he is still cheerful, full of jest and sprightliness. But for several years his sight has failed him greatly; and at times

18 *   AA

the gout troubles his temper. But an angel moves round the couch to which suffering confines him; his feet are moved and enwrapped by soft white hands; the sick-chamber and the countenance of the old man grow bright before his orphan grand-child, Serena.

In the aged countenance and bowed form of the mother you see an old woman. But show her something beautiful, speak to her of something worthy of love, and her mien, her smile, beams from the eternal youth which dwells immortal in her sensitive spirit. Then you involuntarily ex-claim, "What beautiful age!" If you sit near her, and look into her mild, pious eyes, you feel as if you could open your whole soul, and believe in every word she speaks, as in the Gospel. She has lived through much and experienced much; yet she still says she will live in order to learn. Truly we must all learn from *her*. Her tone and man-ner betoken true politeness, and much knowledge of life. She alone has educated her children, and she still thinks and acts both for children and chil-dren's children.

Will you see in one little circumstance a minia-ture picture of the whole? Every evening the old man himself roasts two apples; every evening, when they are done, he gives one of them to his "handsome old wife," as he calls her. Thus for fifty years have they divided everything with each other.

．　　　．　　　．　　　．　　　．

And now the day for their Golden Wedding has arrived. The whole city and country take an interest in it. It is as if all the people in the place were related to the old Dahls. The young people come from east and west, — Dahls here, Dahls there, brave men and handsome children. A swarm of cousins encounter one another at every step. Brotherships and friendships are concluded.

If you wish to learn the true value of marriage, — if you wish to see what this union may be for two human hearts, and for life, — then observe, not the wedded ones in their honeymoon, nor by the cradle of their first child ; not at a time when novelty and hope yet throw a morning glory over the young and new-born world of home; but survey them, rather, in the more remote years of manhood, when they have proved the world and each other ; when they have conquered many an error, and many a temptation, in order to become only the more united to each other ; when labors and cares are theirs ; when, under the burden of the day, as well as in hours of repose, they support one another, and find that they are sufficient for each other. Or survey them still farther in life. See them arrived at that period when the world, with all its changes and agitations, rolls far away from them ; when every object around becomes more dim to them ; when their house is still ; when they are solitary, yet they stand there hand in hand, and each reads in the other's eyes only love ; when they, with the same memories and the same hopes, stand on the boundaries of another life, into which they are prepared to enter, of all desires retaining only the one that they may die on the same day. Yes, then behold them ! And, on that account, turn now to the patriarchs, and to their Golden Wedding.

There is, indeed, something worth celebrating, thought I, when I awoke in the morning. The sun seemed to be of the same opinion, for it shone brightly on the snow-covered roof of the aged pair. I wrapped myself in my cloak, and went forth to carry my congratulations to the old people, and to see if I could be helpful to Serena. The aged couple sat in the anteroom, clad in festal attire, each in their own easy-chair. A large bouquet of fresh flowers and a hymn-book were on the table. The sun shone in through snow-white curtains. It was peaceful and cheerful in the room. The patriarch appeared, in the sunny light, as if surrounded by a glory. I offered my congratulations with emotion, and was embraced by them, as by a father and mother. " A lovely day, Madame Werner," said the old gentleman, as he looked toward the window. " Yes, beautiful indeed," I answered. " It is the feast of love and truth on the earth." The two old people smiled, and clasped each other's hands.

There was great commotion in the hall, caused by the arrival of troops of children and grand-

children, who all, in holiday garb, and with joyous looks, poured in to bring their wishes of happiness to the venerable parents. It was charming
to see these groups of lovely children cling round
the old people, like young saplings round aged
stems. It was charming to see the little rosy
mouths turned up to kiss, the little arms stretching to embrace them, and to hear the clamor of
loving words and exulting voices.

I found Serena in the kitchen, surrounded by
people, and dealing out viands; for to-day the
Dahls made a great distribution of food and
money to the poor. Serena accompanied the gifts
with friendly looks and words, and won blessings
for her grandparents.

.   .   .   .   .

At eight in the evening, the wedding guests
began to assemble. In the street where they
lived the houses were illuminated in honor of the
patriarchs, and lamps burned at the corners. A
great number of people, with glad countenances,
wandered up and down the street, in the still,
mild winter evening. The house of the Dahls
was thrown into the shade by the brilliancy of
those in the neighborhood; but there was light
within.

Serena met me at the door of the saloon. She
wore a white garland in her light-brown hair.
How charming she was in her white dress, with
her kindly blue eyes, her pure brow, and the

heavenly smile on her lips! She was so friendly, so amiable, to everybody! Friends and relatives arrived; the rooms became filled. They drank tea, ate ices, and so on; and then there fell at once a great silence. The two old people seated themselves in two easy-chairs, which stood near each other in the middle of the saloon, on a richly embroidered mat. Their children and their children's children gathered in a half-circle round them. A clergyman of noble presence stepped forward, and pronounced an oration on the beauty and holiness of marriage. He concluded with a reference to the life of the venerable pair, which was in itself a better sermon on the excellence of marriage, for the human heart, and for life, than was his speech, though what he said was true and touching. There was not a dry eye in the whole company. All were in a solemn, affectionate mood.

Meantime, preparations for the festival were completed in the second story, to which the guests ascended. Here *tableaux* were presented, whose beauty and grace exceeded everything I had anticipated. The last one consisted of a well-arranged group of all the descendants of the Dahls, during the exhibition of which a chorus was sung. The whole exhibition gave great and general pleasure. When the chorus ceased, and the curtain fell, the doors of the dance-saloon flew open; a dazzling light streamed thence, and lively music set all the hearts and feet of the young people in lively motion.

We sat talking pleasantly together, till supper was served, in various little tables, in three rooms. Lagman Hok raised his glass, and begged permission to drink a toast. All were attentive. Then, fixing a mild, confident gaze on the patriarchs, he said, in a low voice: "Flowers and Harps were woven into the mat on which our honored friends this evening heard the words of blessing pronounced over them. They are the symbols of Happiness and Harmony; and these are the Penates of this house. That they surround you in this festive hour, venerable friends, we cannot regard as an accident. I seemed to hear them say, ' During your union you have so welcomed and cherished us, that we are at home here, and can never forsake you. Your age shall be like your youth!'"

THE wisest man may be wiser to-day than he was yesterday, and to-morrow than he is to-day.

COLTON.

THE WORN WEDDING RING.

By W. C. BENNETT.

YOUR wedding ring wears thin, dear wife. Ah,
  summers not a few,
Since I put it on your finger first, have passed o'er me
  and you.
And, love, what changes we have seen! what cares and
  pleasures too!
Since you became my own dear wife, when this old
  ring was new.

O blessings on that happy day, the happiest of my life,
When, thanks to God, your low, sweet "Yes" made you
  my loving wife!
Your heart will say the same, I know; that day's as
  dear to you,
The day that made me yours, dear wife, when this old
  ring was new.

How well do I remember now your young, sweet face
  that day!
How fair you were, how dear you were, my tongue
  could hardly say;

Nor how I doated on you.   Ah, how proud I was of you!
But did I love you more than now, when this old ring
    was new?

No! No! no fairer were you then, than at this hour, to
    me ;
And dear as life to me this day, how could you dearer
    be?
As sweet your face might be that day as now it is, 't is
    true ;
But did I know your *heart* as well, when this old ring
    was new?

O partner of my gladness, wife, what care, what grief,
    is there
For me you would not bravely face? with me you
    would not share?
O, what a weary want had every day, if wanting *you!*
Wanting the love that God made mine when this old
    ring was new!

Years bring fresh links to bind us, wife, — small voices
    that are here,
Small faces round our fire that make their mother's yet
    more dear,
Small, loving hearts, your care each day makes yet
    more like to you,
More like the loving heart made mine when this old
    ring was new.

And, blessed be God, all He has given are with us yet;
    around
Our table every little life lent to us still is found ;

Though cares we 've known, with hopeful hearts the
    worst we 've struggled through ;
Blessed be His name for all His love since this old ring
    was new.

The past is dear ; its sweetness still our memories treas-
    ure yet ;
The griefs we 've borne, together borne, we would not
    now forget.
Whatever, wife, the future brings, heart unto heart still
    true,
We 'll share, as we have shared all else, since this old
    ring was new.

And if God spare us, 'mongst our sons and daughters to
    grow old,
We know His goodness will not let your heart or mine
    grow cold.
Your aged eyes will see in mine all they 've still shown
    to you ;
And mine in yours all they have seen since this old
    ring was new.

And O, when death shall come at last to bid me to my
    rest,
May I die looking in those eyes, and resting on that
    breast !
O, may my parting gaze be blessed with the dear sight
    of you !
Of those fond eyes, — fond as they were when this old
    ring was new.

CHAMBERS'S JOURNAL.

HINTS ABOUT HEALTH.

By L. MARIA CHILD.

HERE are general rules of health, that cannot be too often repeated and urged, concerning which physicians of all schools are nearly unanimous. All who are acquainted with the physical laws of our being, agree that too much food is eaten. As far back as the twelfth century, the School of Salerno, the first Medical School established in Europe, published Maxims for Health, among which were the following: "Let these three things be your physicians; cheerfulness, moderate repose, and diet." "Eat little supper, and you will sleep quietly." A few years ago, the celebrated French physician, Dumoulin, in his last illness, said to friends who were lamenting the loss of his medical services, "I shall leave behind me three physicians much greater than I am: water, exercise, and diet."

The Rev. Sydney Smith says: "The longer I

live, the more I am convinced that half the unhappiness in the world proceeds from little stop-
pages ; from a duct choked up, from food pressing in the wrong place, from a vexed duodenum,
or an agitated pylorus.   The deception, as practised upon human creatures, is curious and entertaining.   My friend sups late ; he eats some strong
soup, then a lobster, then some tart, and he di-
lutes these excellent varieties with wine.   The
next day I call upon him.   He is going to sell
his house in London, and to retire into the country.   He is alarmed for his eldest daughter's health.
His expenses are hourly increasing, and nothing
but a timely retreat can save him from ruin.   All
this is the lobster.   Old friendships are sometimes destroyed by toasted cheese, and hard salted
meat has led to suicide.   I have come to the
conclusion that mankind consume twice too much
food.   According to my computation, I have eaten
and drunk, between my tenth and seventieth
year, forty-four horse-wagon loads more than was
good for me."

The example of Ludovicus Cornaro is a very
striking proof of the advantages of abstinence.
Modern physicians agree with him, that it is particularly wise for people, as they grow older, to
diminish the quantity of *solid* food.   Little should
be eaten, especially by those who do not exercise
greatly ; and that little should be light and nu-
tritious.   It is also important that food and sleep
should be taken at regular intervals.

Early rising, and frequent, though not excessive exercise, are extremely conducive to good health and good spirits. There is now living in South Kingston, R. I., an old man, named Ebenezer Adams, who is past ninety, and has never called upon a physician, or taken a single prescription, in his whole life. He has mowed every season for the last seventy-five years. The past summer he has raised with his own hands one hundred and thirty bushels of potatoes, and harvested them himself; conveying them about three quarters of a mile, in a wheelbarrow, to his house. He has raised and harvested forty bushels of corn himself. He has mowed and put up, without the help of man or beast, six tons of hay. He hauled it on hay-poles of his own manufacture, and put it in the barn himself. He carries his corn two miles and a half, two bushels at a time, in a wheelbarrow, to the mill, himself. Rainy weather, and in winter, he is at work at his trade as a cooper. His uninterrupted health is doubtless mainly owing to constant exercise in the open air.

The Rev. John Wesley, speaking of his remarkable freedom from fatigue amid the incessant labors of his old age, says: "I owe it to the goodness of God. But one natural cause undoubtedly is my continual exercise, and change of air. How the latter contributes to health, I know not; but it undoubtedly does."

The Duke of Wellington, who retained his mental and physical faculties, in a remarkable degree, to an advanced age, lived with so much simplicity, that a celebrated cook left his service on the plea that he had no opportunity to display his skill. He was in the habit of applying vigorous friction to all his body daily. He slept on his narrow, iron camp bedstead, and walked briskly, or rode on horseback, while other gentlemen were sleeping. He made no use of tobacco in any form. For many years he refrained from the use of wine, saying he found no advantage from it, and relinquished it for the sake of his health.

The Hon. Josiah Quincy is a memorable example of vigorous old age. He has always been an early riser, and very active in his habits, both intellectual and physical. For many years, he has practised gymnastics fifteen minutes every morning, before dressing; throwing his limbs about with an agility which few young men could surpass. Believing the healthy state of the skin to be of great importance, he daily applies friction to his whole body, by means of horse-hair gloves. He is temperate in his diet, and rarely tastes of wine. He is careful not to let his mind rust for want of use. He is always adding to his stock of knowledge, and he takes a lively interest in public affairs. He is now past ninety; yet few have spoken so wisely and boldly as he has concerning the national emergencies which have been occurring during the last ten years. He profits by a hint he received from the venerable John Adams, in answer to the question how he had managed to preserve the vigor of his mind to such an advanced age. " Simply by exercising it," replied Mr. Adams. " Old minds are like old horses ; you must exercise them if you wish to keep them in working order."

A few years since, the Rev. Daniel Waldo addressed the graduates at Yale College, on Commencement Day. In the course of his remarks, he said : " I am now an old man. I have seen nearly a century. Do you want to know how to grow old slowly and happily ? Let me tell you. Always eat slowly ; masticate well. Go to your food, to your rest, to your occupations, smiling. Keep a good nature and a soft temper everywhere. Never give way to anger. A violent tempest of passion tears down the constitution more than a typhus fever."

Leigh Hunt says : " Do not imagine that mind alone is concerned in your bad spirits. The body has a great deal to do with these matters. The mind may undoubtedly affect the body ; but the body also affects the mind. There is a reaction between them ; and by lessening it on either side you diminish the pain of both. If you are melancholy, and know not why, be assured it must arise entirely from some physical weakness, and do your best to strengthen yourself. The blood of a melancholy man is thick and slow. The blood of a lively man is clear and quick. Endeavor, therefore, to put your blood in motion. Exercise is the best way to do it."

The homely old maxim, —

> " After breakfast, work a while ;
> After dinner, sit and smile ;
> After supper, walk a mile," —

contains a good deal of practical wisdom. Manual labor in the forenoon ; cheerful conversation, or music, after dinner ; a light supper, at five or six o'clock, and a pleasant walk afterward, will preserve health, and do much to restore it, if undermined. A walk at any period of the day does the body twice as much good if connected with some object that interests the mind or heart. To walk out languidly into infinite space, merely to aid digestion, as rich epicures are wont to do, takes half the virtue out of exercise.

An aged clergyman, who had never known a day's illness, was asked how he accounted for it. He replied, " Dry feet and early rising have been my only precautions." In " Hall's Journal of Health " I find the following advice, of which I know the value by experience : " If you are well, let yourself alone. This is our favorite motto. But to you whose feet are inclined to be cold, we suggest that as soon as you get up in the morning, put your feet at once in a basin of cold water, so as to come half-way to the ankles ; keep them in half a minute in winter, or two minutes in summer, rubbing them both vigorously ; wipe dry, and hold

to the fire, if convenient, in cold weather, until
every part of the foot feels as dry as your hand,
then put on your socks or stockings.   On going to
bed at night, draw off your stockings, and hold the
foot to the fire for ten or fifteen minutes, until perfectly dry, and get right into bed.   This is a most
pleasant operation, and fully repays for the trouble
of it.   No one can sleep well or refreshingly with
cold feet.   Never step from your bed with the
naked feet on an uncarpeted floor.   I have known
it to be the exciting cause of months of illness.
Wear woollen, cotton, or silk stockings, whichever
keep your feet most comfortable ; do not let the
experience of another be your guide, for different
persons require different articles ; what is good for
a person whose feet are naturally damp, cannot be
good for one whose feet are always dry."

In Italy, and all the other grape-growing countries of Europe, people have the habit of drinking
wine with breakfast.   Cornaro followed the general custom, and he recommends a moderate use
of wine as essential to old people.   But at that remote period there was less knowledge of the physical laws than there now is.   He confesses that
he always found old wine very deleterious to him,
and that for many years he never tasted any but
new wine.   Sir Walter Raleigh, who was born
only ninety years later than Cornaro, gives the
following sensible advice : " Except thou desire to
hasten thy end, take this for a general rule : that

thou never add any artifical heat to thy body by wine or spice, until thou find that time hath decayed thy natural heat ; and the sooner thou dost begin to help Nature, the sooner she will forsake thee, and leave thee to trust altogether to art."

The late Dr. Warren, in his excellent little book on the " Preservation of Health," bears the following testimony : " Habitual temperance in regard to the quantity of food, regular exercise, and abstinence from all stimulants except for medicinal purposes, would greatly diminish or obviate the evils of age. It is idle to say that men can and do live sometimes even to great age under the practice of various excesses, particularly under the use of stimulants. The natural and sufficient stimulus of the stomach is healthy food. Any stimulus more active produces an unnatural excitement, which will ultimately tell in the great account of bad habits. The old adage, ' Wine is the milk of age,' is not supported by exact observation of facts. For more than twenty years I have had occasion to notice a great number of instances of the sudden disuse of wine without mischievous results. On the contrary, the disuse has generally been followed by an improvement of appetite, freedom from habitual headache, and a tranquil state of body and mind. Those who have been educated to the use of wine do, indeed, find some inconvenience from the substitution of a free use of water. If, however, they begin by taking the pure fluid in moderate quantities only, no such inconvenience occurs. The preceding remarks may be applied to beer, cider, and other fermented liquors. After the age of sixty, I myself gave up the habit of drinking wine ; and, so far from experiencing any inconvenience, I have found my health better without it than with it."

Dr. Warren's exhortations against the use of tobacco are very forcible. He says : " The habit of smoking• impairs the natural taste and relish for food, lessens the appetite, and weakens the powers of the stomach. Tobacco, being drawn in with the vital breath, conveys its poisonous influence into every part of the lungs. The blood, having imbibed the narcotic principle, circulates it through the whole system. Eruptions on the skin, weakness of the stomach, heart, and lungs, dizziness, headache, confusion of thought, and a low febrile action must be the consequence. Where there is any tendency to diseases of the lungs, the debility of these organs consequent on the smoking of tobacco must favor the deposit of tuberculous matter, and thus sow the seeds of consumption.

" Snuff received into the nostrils enters the cavities opening from them, and makes a snuff-box of the olfactory apparatus. The voice is consequently impaired, sometimes to a remarkable degree. I knew a gentleman of the legal profession who, from the use of snuff occasionally, lost the power of speaking audibly in court. Moreover, portions of this powder are conveyed into the lungs and stomach, and exert on those organs their deleterious effects.

" The worst form in which tobacco is employed is in chewing. This vegetable is one of the most powerful of narcotics. A very small portion of it — say a couple of drachms, and perhaps even less — received into the stomach might prove fatal. When it is taken into the mouth in smaller portions, and there retained some time, an absorption of part of it into the system takes place, which has a most debilitating effect. If we wished to reduce our physical powers in a slow yet certain way, we could not adopt a more convenient process. The more limited and local effects are indigestion, fixed pains about the region of the stomach, debility of the back, affections of the brain, producing vertigo, and also affections of the mouth, generating cancer."

Too much cannot be said in favor of frequently washing the whole person in cold water, or, if not entirely cold in winter, at least as nearly so as it can be without producing a chill. . It operates both as a purifier and a tonic. The health in all respects greatly depends upon keeping the pores of the skin open. Attacks of rheumatism might often be warded off by this habit. The washing should be in a warm room, and followed immediately by a smart rubbing with a coarse towel.

When wounds, bruises, or cracks in the skin

become inflamed and feverish, there is no application better than a linen rag, doubled six or eight times, wet with cold water, and bound on with a thick, dry, cotton bandage, which completely covers it. Inveterate sores will be healed by a repetition of this application. The same is true of sore throat; but the wet cloth should be carefully and completely covered with dry woollen, so as to exclude the air. When removed, it should be done soon after one rises in the morning; the throat should then be plentifully sponged with cold water, and wiped thoroughly dry. There is danger of taking cold after the application of hot or warm water; but it is not so with the use of cold water.

It is a great preservation to the eyesight to plunge the face into cold water every morning, and wink the eyes in it while one counts thirty or forty. In order to do this, one must draw in the breath when about to plunge the head into the water, and hold the breath while it remains there. It seems difficult to do this at first, but it soon becomes easy. It is well to repeat the operation six or eight times every morning. In cold weather, put in warm water enough to prevent a painful chill.

Before retiring to rest, great care should be taken to remove every particle of food from between the teeth with a tooth-pick of willow, or ivory, and cleanse the mouth very thoroughly by the use of the brush, and rinsing. It is more important at night than in the morning; because during sleep an active process of fermentation goes on, which produces decay. It is an excellent plan to hold a piece of charcoal in the mouth frequently. It arrests incipient toothache and decay, and tends to preserve the teeth by its antiseptic properties. If chewed, it should not be swallowed, except occasionally, and in small quantities; and it should never be rubbed on the teeth, as it injures the enamel.

Old people are generally reluctant to admit that the present generation is wiser than the past; but in one respect all must allow that there is obvious improvement. Far less medicine is taken than formerly; and more attention is paid to diet. Still, people by no means pay sufficient attention to the good old maxim, "An ounce of prevention is worth a pound of cure." Nature gives us kindly warnings, which we thoughtlessly neglect. When the head aches and the skin is hot, we often continue to eat hearty food, merely because we like the taste of it; and the result of this imprudence is a fever, which might have been easily and cheaply prevented by living two or three days on bread and water, or simple gruels.

Fruits are among the best as well as the pleasantest of remedies. Fresh currants agree with nearly all dyspeptics, and are excellent for people of feverish tendencies; cranberries also. The abundant use of apples is extremely conducive to health. The free use of grapes is said to cure liver-complaints, and to be in other respects salutary for the system. Linnæus tells us that he was cured of severe rheumatism by eating strawberries, and that he afterward habitually resorted to them when he had an attack of that painful disease. Captain Cook has also recorded, that when he touched at an island where strawberries were in great profusion, the crew devoured them eagerly, and were cured of a scorbutic complaint, which had afflicted them greatly. Lemonade and oranges are recommended for rheumatism; vegetable acids in general being salutary for that disease.

Mother Nature is much kinder to us than
we are to ourselves. She loves to lead
us gently, and the violent reactions
from which we suffer we bring
upon ourselves by violat-
ing the laws she is con-
stantly striving to
teach us.

"How shall I manage to be healthy?" said a wealthy invalid to the famous Dr. Abernethy. "Live on sixpence a day, and earn it," was his laconic reply.

THE INVALID'S PRAYER.

By REV. SAMUEL JOHNSON.

O THOU, whose wise, paternal love
   Hath cast my active vigor down,
Thy choice I thankfully approve :
  And, prostrate at Thy gracious throne,
I offer up my life's remains ;
I choose the state my God ordains.

Cast as a broken vessel by,
   Thy will I can no longer do ;
But while a daily death I die,
   Thy power I can in weakness show ;
My patience shall thy glory raise,
My steadfast trust proclaim thy praise.

———————————

TRIALS make our faith sublime,
   Trials give new life to prayer,
Lift us to a holier clime,
   Make us strong to do and bear.
COWPER.

THE OLD PASTOR AND HIS SON.

FROM THE GERMAN OF JEAN PAUL RICHTER.

N the little village of Heim, Gottreich Hartmann resided with his old father, who was a curate.' The old man had wellnigh outlived all those whom he had loved, but he was made happy by his son. Gottreich' discharged for him his duties in the parish, not so much in aid of his parent's untiring vigor, as to satisfy his own energy, and to give his father the exquisite gratification of being edified by his child and companion.

In Gottreich there thrilled a spirit of true poetry ; and his father also had, in his youth, a poet's ardor, of like intensity, but it had not been favored by the times. Son and father seemed to live in one another ; and on the site of filial and paternal love there arose the structure of a rare and peculiar friendship. Gottreich not only cheered his father by the new birth of his own lost poet-youth, but by the still more beautiful

19 *

similarity of their faith. The father found again his old Christian heart sending forth new shoots in the bosom of Gottreich, and moreover the best justification of the convictions of his life and of his love.

If it be pain for us to love and to contradict at the same time, to refuse with the head what the heart grants, it is all the sweeter to us to find ourselves and our faith transplanted into a younger being. Life is then as a beautiful night, in which, as one star goes down, another rises in its place. Gottreich possessed a paradise, in which he labored as his father's gardener. He was at once the wife, the brother, the friend of his parent; the all that is to be loved by man. Every Sunday brought him a new pleasure, — that of preaching a sermon before his father. If the eyes of the old man became moistened, or if he suddenly folded his hands in an attitude of prayer, that Sunday became the holiest of festivals. Many a festival has there been in that quiet little parsonage, the joyfulness of which no one understood and no one perceived. The love and approbation of an energetic old man, like Hartmann, whose spiritual limbs had by no means stiffened on the chilly ridge of years, could not but exercise a powerful influence on a young man like Gottreich, who, more tenderly and delicately formed both in body and mind, was wont to shoot forth in loftier and more rapid flame.

To these two happy men was added a happy woman also. Justa, an orphan, sole mistress of her property, had sold the house which had been her father's in the city, and had removed into the upper part of a good peasant's cottage, to live entirely in the country. Justa did nothing by halves; she often did things more than completely, as most would think at least, in all that touched her generosity. She had not long resided in the village of Heim, and seen the meek Gottreich, and listened to some of his spring-tide sermons, ere she discovered that he had won her heart, filled as it was with the love of virtue. She nevertheless refused to give him her hand until the conclusion of the great peace, after which they were to be married. She was ever more fond of doing what is difficult than what is easy. I wish it were here the place to tell of the May-time life they led, which seemed to blossom in the low parsonage-house, near the church-door, under Justa's hand; how she came from her own cottage, in the morning, to order matters in the little dwelling for the day; how the evenings were passed in the garden, ornamented with a few pretty flower-beds, and commanding a view of many a well-watered meadow, and distant hill, and stars without number; how these three hearts played into one another, no one of which, in this most pure and intimate intercourse, knew or felt anything which was not of the fairest; and how cheerfulness and good intention marked the passage of their lives. Every bench was a church seat, all was peaceful and holy, and the firmament above was an infinite church-dome.

In many a village and in many a house is hidden a true Eden, which has neither been named nor marked down; for happiness is fond of covering over and concealing her tenderest flowers. Gottreich reposed in such tenderness of love and bliss, of poetry and religion, of spring-time, of the past and of the future, that, in the depths of his heart, he feared to speak out his happiness, save in prayer. In prayer, thought he, man may say all his happiness and his misery. His father was very happy also. There came over him a warm old age; no winter night, but a summer evening without chill or darkness; albeit the sun of his life was sunk pretty deep below the mound of earth under which his wife was lain down to sleep.

In these sweetest May-hours of youth, when heaven and earth and his own heart were beating together in triune harmony, Gottreich gave ardent words to his ardent thoughts, and kept them written down, under the title of " Reminiscences of the best Hours of Life, for the Hour of Death." He meant to cheer himself, in his last hours, with these views of his happy life; and to look back, through them, from the glow of his evening to the bright morning of his youth.

Thus lived these three beings, ever rejoicing more deeply in one another, and in their genial happiness, when the chariots of war began to roll over the land.* Gottreich became another man. The active powers of his nature, which had heretofore been the quiet audience of his poetical and oratorical powers, now arose. It seemed as if the spirit of energy, which hitherto had wasted itself .on empty air, like the flames of a bituminous soil, were now seeking an object to lay hold of. He did not venture to propose separating from his father, but he alternately refreshed and tormented himself inwardly with the idea of sharing the labors and combats of his countrymen., He confided his wishes to Justa only; but she did not give him encouragement, because she feared the old man's solitude would be too great for him to bear. But at last the old man himself became inspirited for the war, by Gottreich and his betrothed; and he said to his son that he had better go; that he knew he had long desired it, and had only been silent through love for him. He hoped, with God's aid, to be able to discharge his pastoral duties for a year, and thus he also would be doing something to serve his country.

Gottreich departed, trusting to the autumnal strength of his father's life. He enlisted as a common soldier, and preached also wherever he was

---

* The war.of 1813, against Napoleon, to secure the independence of Germany.

able. The entrance on a new career awakens
new energies and powers, which rapidly unfold
into life and vigor. Although fortune spared him
the wounds which he would willingly have brought
back with him into the peaceful future of his life,
in memory of the focus of his youth, as it were,
yet it was happiness enough to take part in the
battles, and, like an old republican, to fight together with a whole nation, for the common cause. .

At length, in the beautiful month of May, the
festivals of victory and peace began in more than
one nation ; and Gottreich was unwilling to pass
those days of rejoicing so far from the friends who
were dearest to him. He longed for their company, that his joy might be doubled ; so he took
the road to Heim. Thousands at that time journeyed over the liberated land, from a happy past
to a happy future. But there were few who saw,
like Gottreich, so pure a firmament over the mountains of his native valleys, in which not a star was
missing, but every one of them was bright and
twinkling. Justa had, from time to time, sent
him the little annals of the parsonage. She had
written how she longed for his return, and how his
father rejoiced ; how well the old man stood the
labors of his office ; and how she had still better
secrets in store for him. To these belonged, perhaps, her promise, which he had not forgotten, to
give him her hand after the great peace.

With such prospects before him, Gottreich ever

enjoyed in thought that holy evening when he
should see the sun go down at Heim, — when he
should arrive unexpectedly, to relieve the old man
from all his cares, and begin to prepare the tranquil festivities of the village. As he was thinking
of that day's meeting, when he should clasp those
fond hearts to his own, and as the mountains above
his father's village were seen more and more clearly in relief against the blue sky, the Reminiscences
of the best hours of life, which he had written for
the hour of death, echoed and re-echoed in his
soul ; and, as he went along, he dwelt particularly
upon one among them, which commemorated the
joy of meeting again here below.

A shower was coming up behind him, of which
he seemed to be the happy messenger ; for the
parched ground, the drooping flowers, and the
ears of corn had long been thirsting for water
from the warm clouds. A parishioner of Heim,
who was laboring in the fields, saluted him as he
passed, and expressed joy that Gottreich and the
rain had both come at last. Soon he caught sight
of the low church-steeple, peeping above the clustered trees ; and he entered upon that tract in the
valley where the parsonage lay, all reddened by
the evening sun. At every window he hoped to
see his betrothed one, thinking perchance she
might be looking out on the sunset before the
storm came on. As he drew nearer, he hoped to
see the lattice open, and Whitsuntide-brooms in

the chief apartment; but he saw nothing of all this.

At last, he quietly entered the parsonage-house, and slowly opened the well-known door. The room was empty, but he heard a noise overhead. When he entered the chamber, it was filled with a glow from the west, and Justa was kneeling by the bed of his father, who was sitting half upright, and looking, with a stiff, haggard countenance, toward the setting sun before him. One exclamation, and a clasp of her lover to her breast, was all his reception. His father stretched out his withered hand slowly, and said, with difficulty, "Thou art come at the right time"; but without adding whether he spoke of the preachings, or alluded to their approaching separation. Justa hastily related how the old man had overworked himself, till body and spirit had given way together, so that he no longer took a share in anything, though he longed to be with the sharers; and how he lay prostrate, with broken wings, looking upward, like a helpless child. The old man had grown so hard of hearing, that she could say all this in his presence.

Gottreich would fain have infused into that old and once strong heart the fire of victory which was reflected in his own bosom; but he heard neither wish nor question of it. The old man continued to gaze steadily upon the setting sun, and at last it was hidden by the storm-clouds. The landscape grew dark, the winds stood pent, and the earth was oppressed. ' Suddenly there came a gush of rain and a crash of thunder. The lightning flashed around the old man. He looked up, altered and astonished. "Hist!" he said; "I hear the rain once more. Speak quickly, children, for I shall soon depart!" Both his children clung to him, but he was too weak to embrace them.

And now warm, refreshing fountains from the clouds bathed all the sick earth, from the dripping trees to the blades of grass. The sky glistened mildly, as with tears of joy, and the thunder went rumbling away behind the distant mountains. The sick man pointed upward, and said: "Seest thou the majesty of God? My son, now, in my last hour, strengthen my weary soul with something holy, — something in the spirit of love, and not of penance; for if our hearts condemn us not, then have we confidence toward God. Say something to me rich in love of God and of his works."

The eyes of the son overflowed, to think that he should read at the death-bed of his father those Reminiscences which he had prepared for his own. He said this to him, but the old man answered, "Hasten, my son!" And, with faltering voice, Gottreich began to read : —

"Remember, in thy dark hour, those times when thou hast prayed to God in ecstasy, and when thou hast thought on him, the Infinite One; the greatest thought of finite man."

c c

Here the old man clasped his hands, and prayed low.

" Hast thou not known and felt the existence of that Being, whose infinity consists not only in his power, his wisdom, and his eternity, but also in his love, and in his justice? Canst thou forget the time when the blue sky, by day and by night, opened on thee, as if the mildness of God was looking down on thee? Hast thou not felt the love of the Infinite, when he veiled himself in his image, the loving hearts of men ; as the sun, which reflects its light not on the moon only, but on the morning and evening star also, and on every little twinkler, even the farthest from our earth ?

" Canst thou forget, in the dark hour, that there have been mighty men among us, and that thou art following after them? Raise thyself, like the spirits who stood upon their mountains, having the storms of life only about them, never above them ! Call back to thee the kingly race of sages and poets, who have inspirited and enlightened nation after nation !."

" Speak to me of our Redeemer," said the father.

" Remember Jesus Christ, in the dark hour. Remember him, who also passed through this life. Remember that soft moon of the Infinite Sun, given to enlighten the night of the world. Let life be hallowed to thee, and death also ; for he

shared both of them with thee. May his calm
and lofty form look down on thee in the last darkness, and show thee his Father."

A low roll of thunder was heard from clouds
which the storm had left. Gottreich continued to
read : —

" Remember, in the last hour, how the heart of
man can love. Canst thou forget the love wherewith one heart repays a thousand hearts, and the
soul during a whole life is nourished and vivified
from another soul? Even as the oak of a hundred years clings fast to the same spot, with its
roots, and derives new strength, and sends forth
new buds during its hundred springs?"

" Dost thou mean me?" said the father.

" I mean my mother also," replied the son.

The father, thinking on his wife, murmured very
gently, " To meet again. To meet again." And
Justa wept while she heard how her lover would
console himself in his last hours with the reminis-
cence of the days of *her* love.

Gottreich continued to read : " Remember, in
the last hour, that pure being with whom thy life
was beautiful and great; with whom thou hast
wept tears of joy; with whom thou hast prayed
to God, and in whom God appeared unto thee; in
whom thou didst find the first and last heart of
love; — and then close thine eyes in peace!"

Suddenly, the clouds were cleft into two huge
black mountains; and the sun looked forth from

between them, as it were, out of a valley between
buttresses of rock, gazing upon the earth with
its joy-glistening eye.

"See!" said the dying man. "What a glow!"

"It is the evening sun, father."

"This day we shall see one another again,"
murmured the old man. He was thinking of his
wife, long since dead.

The son was too deeply moved to speak to
his father of the blessedness of meeting again in
this world, which he had enjoyed by anticipation
during his journey. Who could have courage
to speak of the joys of an earthly meeting to one
whose mind was absorbed in the contemplation
of a meeting in heaven?

Gottreich, suddenly startled, asked, "Father,
what ails thee?"

"I do think thereon; and death is beautiful,
and the parting in Christ," murmured the old
man. He tried to take the hand of Gottreich,
which he had not strength to press. He repeated,
more and more distinctly and emphatically, "O
thou blessed God!" until all the other luminaries
of life were extinguished, and in his soul there
stood but the one sun, God!

At length he roused himself, and, stretching forth
his arm, said earnestly, "There! there are three
fair rainbows over the evening sun! I must go
after the sun, and pass through them with him."
He sank backward, and was gone.

At that moment the sun went down, and a broad rainbow glimmered in the east.

" He is gone," said Gottreich, in a voice choked with grief. " But he has gone from us unto his God, in the midst of great, pious, and unmingled joy. Then weep no more, Justa."

His youth was innocent ; his riper age
Marked with some act of goodness every day ;
And, watched by eyes that loved him, calm and sage,
Faded his late declining years away.
Cheerful he gave his being up, and went
To share the holy rest that waits a life well spent.

That life was happy. Every day he gave
Thanks for the fair existence that was his :
For a sick fancy made him not her slave,
To mock him with her phantom miseries.
No chronic tortures racked his aged limbs,
For luxury and sloth had nourished none for him.

Why weep ye, then, for him, who. having won
The bound of man's appointed years, at last,
Life's blessings all enjoyed, life's labors done.
Serenely to his final rest has passed, —
While the soft memory of his virtues yet
Lingers, like twilight hues when the bright sun is set?

W. C. BRYANT.

REST AT EVENING.

By ADELAIDE A. PROCTER.

WHEN the weariness of life is ended,
    And the task of our long day is done,
And the props, on which our hearts depended,
    All have failed, or broken, one by one;
Evening and our sorrow's shadow blended,
    Telling us that peace has now begun.

How far back will seem the sun's first dawning,
    And those early mists so cold and gray!
Half forgotten even the toil of morning,
    And the heat and burden of the day.
Flowers that we were tending, and weeds scorning,
    All alike, withered and cast away.

Vain will seem the impatient heart, that waited
    Toils that gathered but too quickly round;
And the childish joy, so soon elated
    At the path we thought none else had found;
And the foolish ardor, soon abated
    By the storm which cast us to the ground.

Vain those pauses on the road, each seeming
    As our final home and resting-place ;
And the leaving them, while tears were streaming
    Of eternal sorrow down our face ;
And the hands we held, fond folly dreaming
    That no future could their touch efface.

All will then be faded : Night will borrow
    Stars of light to crown our perfect rest ;
And the dim vague memory of faint sorrow
    Just remain to show us all was best ;
Then melt into a divine to-morrow :
    O, how poor a day to be so blest !

Cambridge : Stereotyped and Printed by Welch, Bigelow, & Co.